Walter Besant

The Ivory Gate

Walter Besant

The Ivory Gate

ISBN/EAN: 9783337044862

Printed in Europe, USA, Canada, Australia, Japan

Cover: Foto ©Andreas Hilbeck / pixelio.de

More available books at **www.hansebooks.com**

THE IVORY GATE

A Novel

BY

WALTER BESANT

AUTHOR OF "ALL SORTS AND CONDITIONS OF MEN"
"CHILDREN OF GIBEON" ETC.

NEW YORK

HARPER & BROTHERS, FRANKLIN SQUARE

1892

CONTENTS

CONTENTS

THE IVORY GATE

PROLOGUE

WHO IS EDMUND GRAY?

Mr. Edward Dering, in a rare interval of work, occupied himself with looking into his bank-book. Those humble persons whom the City, estimating the moral and spiritual worth of a man by his income, calls "small" frequently and anxiously examine their bank-books, add up the columns, and check the entries. Mr. Dering, who was not a small man, but a big man, or rather, from the City point of view, a biggish man, very seldom looked at his bank-book—first, because, like other solicitors in large practice, he had clerks and accountants to do that kind of work for him; next, because, like many solicitors, while he managed the affairs of other people with unceasing watchfulness, he was apt to neglect his own affairs. Happily, when one has an income of some thousands, private affairs from time to time force themselves upon their owner in the most agreeable manner possible. They obtrude themselves upon him. They insist upon being noticed. They compel him to look after them respectfully: to remove them from the dulness of the bank, and to make them comfortable in investments.

Mr. Dering opened the book, therefore, having for the moment nothing else to do, looked at the balance, was satisfied with its appearance, and began working backwards, that is to say upwards, to read the entries. Presently he came to one at which he stopped, holding his forefinger on the name.

1

It was on the right-hand side, the side which to small men is so terrifying, because it always does its best to annihilate the cash balance, and seems bent upon transforming addition into multiplication, so amazing are the results. The name which Mr. Dering read was Edmund Gray. The amount placed in the same line opposite to that name was £720. Therefore, he had drawn a check to the order of Edmund Gray for the sum of £720.

Now, a man may be in very great practice indeed; but if, like. Mr. Dering, he knows the details of every case that is brought into the house he would certainly remember drawing a check for £720, and the reason why it was drawn, and the person for whom it was drawn, especially if the check was only three weeks old. Seven hundred and twenty pounds! It is a sum in return for which many and very substantial services must be rendered.

"Edmund Gray!" he murmured. "Strange! I cannot remember the name of Edmund Gray. Who is Edmund Gray? Why did I give him seven hundred and twenty pounds?"

The strange fact that he should forget so large a sum amused him at first. Beside him lay a book which was his private diary. He opened it, and looked back for three months. He could find no mention anywhere of Edmund Gray. To repeat: he knew all the details of every case that came into the house; he signed all the checks; his memory was as tenacious and as searching as the east wind in April; yet this matter of Edmund Gray and his check for £720 he could not recall to his mind by any effort.

There is a certain stage in brain fatigue when one cannot remember names; it is the sure and certain symptom of overwork; the wise man recognizes the symptom as a merciful warning, and obeys it. Mr. Dering knew this symptom. "I must take a holiday," he said. "At sixty-seven one cannot afford to neglect the least loss of memory. Edmund Gray! To forget Edmund Gray —and seven hundred and twenty pounds! I must run down to the sea-side for a fortnight's rest."

He shut up the bank-book, and tried to go back to his work. But this name came back to him. "Edmund Gray," he murmured—"Edmund Gray. Who on earth is this Edmund Gray? Why did he get a check for seven hundred and twenty pounds?"

The thing ceased to amuse him; it began to irritate him; in two minutes it began to torture him; he leaned back in his chair; he drummed with his fingers on the table; he took up the book and looked at the entry again. He got up and walked about the room—a long lean figure in a tight frock-coat. To walk about the room and to swing your arms often stimulates the memory. In this case, however, no good effect followed. The *nommé* Edmund Gray remained a name and nothing more—the shadow of a name. Mr. Dering rapped the table with his paper-knife, as if to conjure up that shadow. Futile superstition! No shadow appeared. But how could the shadow of a name—an unknown name—carry off seven hundred and twenty golden sovereigns?

"I feel as if I am going mad," he murmured. "Seven hundred and twenty pounds paid by myself in a single lump, only three weeks ago, and I remember nothing about it! I have no client named Edmund Gray. The money must therefore have been paid by me for some client to this unknown person. Yet it was paid by my check, and I don't remember it. Strange! I never forgot such a thing before."

There was an office-bell on the table. He touched it. A clerk —an elderly clerk, an ancient clerk—obeyed the call. He was the clerk who sat in the room outside Mr. Dering's office; the clerk who wrote the checks for the chief to sign, brought back the letters when they had been copied, directed the letters for the post, received visitors, and passed in cards; in fact, the private secretary, stage-manager—we all want a stage-manager in every profession—or confidential clerk. As befits a man of responsibility he was dressed all in black, his office-coat being as shiny as a mirror on the arms and on the shoulders; by long habit it hung in certain folds or curves which never unbent; his face was quite shaven and shorn; all that was left of his white hair was cut short; his eyes were keen and even foxy; his lips were thin; his general expression was one of watchfulness: when he watched his master it was with the attention of a servant; when he watched anybody else it was as one who watches a rogue, and would outwit him, if he could, at his own roguery. In certain commercial walks of the lower kind where honor and morality consist in the success of attempts to cheat each other, this kind of expression is not uncommon. Whether his expression was good or bad, he was an excellent clerk: he was always at his post at nine in the morning; he never left the office before seven, and, because Mr. Dering was a whale for work, he sometimes stayed without a grumble until eight or even nine. Man and boy, Checkley had been in the office of Dering & Son for fifty-five years, entering as an errand boy at twelve.

"Checkley," said his master, "look at this bank-book. Credit side. Fourth entry. Have you got it?"

"Edmund Gray—seven hundred and twenty pounds," the clerk read.

"Yes. What is that check for? Who is Edmund Gray?"

The clerk looked surprised. "I don't know," he said.

"Why did I pay that money?"

The clerk shook his head.

"Did you look at the book when you laid it on the table?"

The clerk nodded.

"Well—what did you think of it?"

"I didn't think of it at all. It wasn't one of the checks you told me to draw about that time ago. If I had thought I should have supposed it was your private business."

"I was not aware, Checkley, that I have any private affairs that you do not know."

"Well—but you might have."

"True. I might have. Just so. As I haven't, who—I ask you again—who is this Edmund Gray?"

"I don't know."

"Have you ever heard of any Edmund Gray?"

"Never to my knowledge."

"This is the first time you have heard that name?" the lawyer persisted.

"The very first time."

"Consider. Is there any Edmund Gray in connection with any of my clients?"

"Not to my knowledge."

"Not to your knowledge. Has any Edmund Gray ever been employed about the office?"

"No—certainly not."

"We have recently been painted and papered and whitewashed and new-carpeted, at great expense and inconvenience. Did Edmund Gray conduct any of those operations?"

"No."

"Has the name of Edmund Gray ever been mentioned in any letters that have come here?"

It was notorious in the office that Checkley read all the letters that came, and that he never forgot the contents of any. If you named any letter he would at once tell you what was written in it, even if it were twenty years old.

"I have never even heard the name of Edmund Gray, in any letter or in any connection whatever," the clerk replied, firmly.

"I put all these questions, Checkley, because I was pretty certain myself from the beginning; but I wanted to make myself quite certain. I thought it might be a trick of failing memory. Now, look at the name carefully." The clerk screwed up his eyes tightly in order to get a good grip of the name. "You see I have given him a check for seven hundred and twenty pounds, only three weeks ago. I am not the kind of man to give away seven hundred and twenty pounds for nothing. Yet I have actually forgotten the whole business."

Certainly he did not look the kind of man to forget such a simple thing as the giving-away of £720. Quite the contrary. His grave face, his iron-gray hair, his firm lips, his keen, steady eyes, apart from the methodical regularity with which his papers were arranged before him, all proclaimed that he was very far from being that kind of man. Very much the reverse, indeed.

"You don't mean to say, sir," Checkley began, with a change in his face from watchfulness to terror—"you can't mean—"

"I mean this, Checkley. I know of no Edmund Gray, and unless the bank has made a mistake there has been committed a —what do they call it in the law-courts?"

The clerk held the bank-book in his hand, staring at his master with open eyes. "What?" he repeated. "What do they call it? Good Lord! They call it forgery—and for seven hundred and twenty pounds! And on you, of all people in the world! And in this office! In our office!—our office! What a dreadful thing, to be sure! Oh! what a dreadful thing to happen! In our office—here!" The clerk seemed unable to express his astonishment.

"First of all, get me the cancelled checks."

The checks always came back in the pocket of the bank-book. Checkley was accustomed to take them out, and to file them in their proper place.

Again, Mr. Dering neither drew his checks nor wrote his letters with his own hand. He only signed them. One clerk wrote the letters, another drew the checks by his instruction and dictation.

Checkley went back to his own room, and returned with a bundle of cancelled drafts. He then looked in the safe—a great fireproof safe—that stood open in one corner of the room, and took out the current check-book.

"Here it is," he said. "Check drawn by you yourself, in your own handwriting and properly signed—payable to order, not crossed, and duly endorsed. Now you understand why I know nothing about it. Edmund Gray, Esquire, or order. Seven hundred and twenty pounds. Signed Dering & Son. Your own handwriting and your own signature."

"Let me look." Mr. Dering took the paper and examined it. His eyes hardened as he looked. "You call this my handwriting, Checkley?"

"I—I—I did think it was," the clerk stammered. "Let me look again. And I think so still," he added, more firmly.

"Then you're a fool. Look again. When did I ever sign like that?"

Mr. Dering's handwriting was one of those which are impossible to be read by any except his own clerks, and then only when they know what to expect. Thus, when he drew up instructions in lawyer language, he expressed the important words by an initial, a medial, or a final consonant, and made scratches for all the words between. His clerks, however, understood him very well. If he had written a love-letter or a farce, or a *ballade* or a story, no one—neither clerks nor friends nor compositors—would have understood anything but a word here and a word there. For his signature, however, that was different. It was the signature of the firm; it was a signature a hundred and twenty years old; it was an eighteenth-century signature: bold, large, and clear, every letter fully formed; with dots and flourishes, the last letter concluding with a fantasia of penmanship belonging to a time when men knew how to write, belonging to the decorative time of penmanship.

"Two of the dots are out of place," said Checkley, "and the flourish isn't quite what it should be. But the check itself looks like your hand," he added, stoutly. "I ought to have seen that there was something wrong about the signature, though it isn't much. I own to that. But the writing is like yours, and I would swear to it still."

"It isn't my handwriting at all, then. Where is the counterfoil?"

Checkley turned over the counterfoils. "What is the date?" he asked. "March the 4th? I can't find it. Here are checks for the 3d and for the 6th, but none at all for the 4th."

"Let me look." Strange! There was no counterfoil. And the numbers did not agree with that on the check.

"You haven't got another check-book, have you?"

"No; I certainly have not."

Mr. Dering sat with the check in his hand, looking at it. Then he compared it with a blank check. "Why," he said, "this check is drawn from an old book—two years old—one of the books before the bank amalgamated and changed its title and the form of the checks—not much of a change, it is true—but—how could we be such fools, Checkley, as not to see the difference?"

"Then somebody or other must have got hold of an old check-book. Shameful! To have check-books lying about for every common rogue to go and steal!"

Mr. Dering reflected. Then he looked up, and said: "Look again in the safe. In the left-hand compartment over the drawer I think you will find an old check-book. It belonged to a separate account—a trust. That has been closed. The book should be there. Ah! There it is. I wonder now," the lawyer went on, "how I came to remember that book? It is more than two years since I last used it or even thought of it. Another trick of memory. We forget nothing, in fact, nothing at all. Give it to me. Strange, that I should remember so slight a thing. Now —here are the checks, you see—color the same—lettering the same—size the same—the only difference being the style and title of the company. The fellow must have got hold of an old book left about, as you say, carelessly. Ah!"—his color changed —"here's the very counterfoil we wanted! Look! the number corresponds. The check was actually taken from this very book! a book in my own safe! in this very office! Checkley, what does this mean?"

Checkley took the book from his master with a trembling hand, and read feebly the writing of the counterfoil, "March 4th, 1883. Edmund Gray, seven hundred and twenty pounds."

"Lord knows what it means," he said. "I never came across such a thing in my life before."

"Most extraordinary! It is two years since I have given a thought to the existence of that book. Yet I remembered it the moment when it became useful. Well, Checkley, what have you got to say? Can't you speak?"

"Nothing—nothing. O Lord, what should I have to say? If you didn't draw that check with your own hand—"

"I did not draw that check with my own hand."

"Then—then it must have been drawn by somebody else's hand."

"Exactly."

"Perhaps you dictated it."

"Don't be a fool, Checkley. Keep your wits together, though this is a new kind of case for you. Criminal law is not exactly in your line. Do you think I should dictate my own handwriting as well as my own words?"

"No. But I could swear—I could indeed—that it is your writing."

"Let us have no more questions and answers. It is a forgery. It is a forgery. It is not a common forgery. It has been committed in my own office. Who can have done it? Let me think." He placed the check and the old check-book before him. "This book has been in my safe for two years. I had forgotten its very existence. The safe is only used for my private papers. I open it every morning myself at ten o'clock. I shut it when I go upstairs to lunch. I open it again when I return. I close it when I go away. I have not departed from that custom for thirty years. I could no more sit in this room with the safe shut—I could no more go away with the safe open—than I could walk the streets in my shirt-sleeves. Therefore, not only has the forgery been committed by some one who has had access to my safe, but by some one who has stolen the check in my very presence and before my eyes. This consideration should narrow the field." He looked at the check again. "It is dated March the 4th. The date may mean nothing. But it was presented on the 5th. Who came to my room on the 4th or the days preceding? Go and find out."

Checkley retired, and brought back his journal.

"You saw on the 4th—" He read the list of callers.

"That doesn't help," said Mr. Dering.

"On the 1st, 2d, 3d, and 4th you had Mr. Arundel working with you here every day from ten till twelve."

"Mr. Arundel? Yes, I remember. Anybody else?"

"Nobody else."

"You forget yourself, Checkley," Mr. Dering said. "You were, as usual, in and out at different times."

"O Lord! sir—I hope you don't think—" the old clerk stammered, turning pale.

"I think nothing. I want to find out. Go to the bank. See the manager. Let him tell you if he can find out by whom the check was cashed. If in notes—it must have been in notes—let those notes be instantly stopped. It is not crossed, so that we must not expect anything so simple as the Clearing House. Go at once, and find out exactly what happened."

This happened at about half-past ten. The bank was no more than five-minutes' walk. Yet it was twelve o'clock when the clerk returned.

"Well, what have you found out?" asked the master.

"I have found out a great deal," Checkley began, eagerly. "First, I saw the manager, and I saw the pay-clerk. The check was handed in by a commissionaire. Everybody trusts a commissionaire. The pay-clerk knows your signature, and thought it was all right. I showed the check to the manager. He knows your handwriting, and he says he would swear that the check was drawn by you yourself. So I am not such a fool as you think."

"Go on."

"The commissionaire told the pay-clerk that he was ordered to take it all in ten-pound notes. He took them, put them in his pouch, and walked away. He was a one-armed man, and took a long time over the job, and didn't seem a bit in a hurry."

"About the notes?"

"The manager will stop them at once. But he says that if the thing was done by an old hand there must be confederates in it, and there will be trouble. However, the notes are stopped. That's done. Then I went on to the commissionaires' barracks in the Strand. The sergeant very soon found the man, and I had a talk with him. He was employed by an old gentleman, he says, staying at the Cecil Hotel, Strand. The old gentleman sent him to the bank with instructions to get the money in ten-pound

1*

notes; and very particular he was with him about not losing any of them on the way. He didn't seem a bit in a hurry either. Took the notes from the man and laid them in a pocket-book. It was in the coffee-room, and half a dozen other gentlemen were there at the same time. But this gentleman seemed alone."

"Humph! A pretty cool business, upon my word! No hurry about it. Plenty of time. That was because they knew that the old check-book would not be found and examined."

"Why did they write the check on the counterfoil? Why did they put the check-book back again—after they had taken it out?"

"I don't know. The workings of a forger's brain are not within the compass of my experiences. Go on, Checkley!"

"The commissionaire says that he is certain he would know the gentleman again."

"Very good indeed, if we can only find the gentleman."

"I then went on to the Cecil Hotel, and saw the head waiter of the coffee-room. He remembered the commissionaire being sent for; he saw the bundle of bank-notes brought back from the bank, and he remembers the old gentleman very well. Says he should certainly know him again."

"Did he describe him?"

"There didn't seem anything particular to describe. He was of average height, so to speak, dressed in gray trousers and a black frock-coat, and was gray-haired. Much as if I was to describe you."

"Oh! The notes are stopped. Yet in three weeks there has been ample time to get them all changed. Every note may have been changed into gold in three weeks. An elderly gentleman, gray hair, average height; that tells us nothing. Checkley, the thing has been done by some one who had, or still has, access to my safe. Perhaps, in some way or other, keys have been procured. In that case—" He stepped over to the safe, and opened a drawer. "See, Checkley; this drawer is untouched—it is full of jewelry and things which belonged to my mother. Nothing touched. Here is a bag of spade guineas—again nothing taken. What do you say to that? If the forger had possessed keys he would, first of all, clear out the things which he could turn into money without any difficulty and very little risk. Nothing taken except that check, and the check-book replaced. What do you say to that? Eh?"

"I don't know what to say. I'm struck stupid. I never heard of such a thing before."

"Nor I. Why, it must have been done in this room, while the safe was open, while I was actually present. That is the only solution possible. Again, who has been in this room?"

"All the callers—I read their names to you—your clients."

"They all sit in that chair. They never leave that chair so long as they are with me." He indicated the chair which stood at the corner of the lawyer's great table at his left hand. Now the safe was in the far corner, on the other side of the room. "They could not possibly— Checkley, the only two who could possibly have access to that safe in office-hours are yourself and Mr. Arundel."

"Good heavens! sir—you can't believe—you can't actually think—"

"I believe nothing. I told you so before. I think nothing. I want the facts."

The room was long rather than square, lit by two large windows, overlooking the gardens of New Square, Lincoln's Inn. The lawyer sat with his back to the fire, protected by a cane-screen, before a large table. On his left hand, at the corner of the table, stood the clients' chair; on his right hand, between the two windows, was a small table with a couple of drawers in it. And in the corner, to the left of any one writing at the small table, and on the right hand of the lawyer, was the open safe already mentioned. There were two doors, one communicating with the clerk's room, the other opening directly on the stairs. The latter was locked on the inside.

"Call Mr. Arundel," said the chief.

While Checkley was gone he walked to the window, and observed that any one sitting at the table could, by merely reaching out, take anything from the safe and put it back again unobserved, if he himself happened to be occupied or looking another way. His grave face became dark. He returned to his own chair, and sat thinking, while his face grew darker and his eyes harder, until Mr. Arundel appeared.

Athelstan Arundel was at this time a recently admitted member of the respectable but too-numerous family of solicitors. He was between two and three and twenty years of age, a tall and handsome young fellow, of a good manly type. He was an exarticled clerk of the house, and had just been appointed a managing clerk until something could be found for him. The Arundels were a City family of some importance; perhaps something in a City firm might presently be achieved by the united influence of family and money. Meantime, here he was, at work, earning a salary and gaining experience. Checkley, for his part—who was as jealous of his master as only an old servant or a young mistress has the right to be—had imagined symptoms or indications of a growing preference or favor towards this young gentleman on the part of Mr. Dering. Certainly, he had Mr. Arundel in his own office a good deal, and gave him work of a most confidential character. Besides, Mr. Dering was executor and trustee for young Arundel's mother, and he had been an old friend and school-fellow of his father, and had known the young man and his two sisters from infancy.

"Mr. Arundel," the lawyer began. At his own house he addressed his ward by his Christian name; in the office, as managing clerk, he prefixed the courtesy title. "An extremely disagreeable thing has happened here—nothing short of a forgery. Don't interrupt me, if you please"—for the young man looked as if he was about to practise his interjections—"it is a most surprising thing, I admit. You needn't say so, however—that wastes time. A forgery. On the 5th of this month, three weeks ago, a check, apparently in my handwriting, and with my signature so skilfully executed as to deceive even Checkley and the manager of the bank, was presented at my bank and duly cashed. The amount is large—seven hundred and twenty pounds—and the sum was paid across the counter in ten-pound notes, which are now stopped—if there are any left." He kept his eyes fixed on the young man, whose face betrayed no other emotion than that of natural surprise. "We shall doubtless trace these notes, and through them, of course, the forger. We have already ascertained who presented the check. You follow?"

"Certainly. There has been a forgery. The forged check has been cashed. The notes are stopped. Have you any clue to the forgery?—any suspicions?"

"As yet, none. We are only beginning to collect the facts." The lawyer spoke in the coldest and most austere manner. "I am laying them, one by one, before you."

Young Arundel bowed.

"Observe, then, that the forged check belongs to a check-book which has been lying, forgotten by me, in this safe for two years. Here is the book. Turn to the last counterfoil. Here is the check, the forged check, which corresponds. You see?"

"Perfectly. The book has been in the safe for two years. It has been taken out by some one—presumably the forger; the check has been forged, the counterfoil filled up, and the book replaced. Why was all this trouble taken? If the man had got the check, why did he fill up the counterfoil? Why did he return the book? I beg your pardon."

"Your questions are pertinent. I come to the next point. The safe is never opened but by myself. It is open so long as I am in the room, and at no other time."

"Certainly. I know that."

"Very well. The man who took out the check-book, forged the check, and replaced the book must have done it in my very presence."

"Oh! could not some one—somehow—have got a key?"

"I thought of that. It is possible. But the drawers are full of valuables, jewelry, curios—all kinds of things which could easily be turned into money. And they were not touched. Now, had the safe been opened by a key, these things would certainly have vanished."

"So it would seem."

"These are the main facts, Mr. Arundel. Oh! one more. We have found the messenger who cashed the check. Perhaps there are one or two other points of more or less importance. There is only one more point I wish to bring before you. Of course I make no charge—I insinuate none. But this must be remembered — there are only two persons who have had access to this safe in such a manner as to make it possible for them to take anything out of it—Checkley—"

"No—no—no!" cried the old man.

"And you yourself. At the time of the robbery you were working at that table, with the safe open and within reach of your left hand. This is a fact, mind—one of the facts of the case—not a charge."

"What?" cried the young man, his cheek aflame, "you mean—"

"I mean nothing—nothing at all. I want you and Checkley—who alone have used this room, not counting callers who sat in that chair—to know the facts."

"The facts—yes—of course—the facts. Well"—he spoke rapidly and a little incoherently—"it is true that I worked here —but—oh! it is absurd. I know nothing of any check-book lying in your safe. I was working at this table"—he went to the table—"sitting in this chair. How could I get up and search about in a safe for an unknown and unsuspected check-book before your very eyes?"

"I do not know. It seems impossible. I only desire you to consider, with me, the facts."

Had Mr. Dering spoken just a little less coldly, with just a little less dryness in his manner, what followed would perhaps have been different.

"Yes—the facts," repeated the young man. "Well, let us get at the facts. The chief fact is that whoever took that check and filled it up must have known of the existence of that check-book more than two years old."

"It would seem so."

"Who could know about that old check-book? Only one who had been about your office more than two years, or one who had had opportunities of examining the safe. Now, you sat there—I sat here"—he seated himself, only turning the chair round. "How is it possible for a man sitting here to take anything out of that safe without your seeing him? How is it possible for him, without your knowledge, to examine slowly and carefully the contents of the safe?"

"Everything is possible," said Mr. Dering, still coldly. "Let us not argue on possibilities. We have certain facts before us. By the help of these I shall hope to find out others."

"At five o'clock every day I put the work in the drawer of this table, and come away." He opened the drawer, as if to illustrate this unimportant fact. He saw in it two or three pieces of paper with writing on them. He took them out. "Good heavens!" he cried. "They are imitations of your handwriting."

Checkley crossed the room swiftly, snatched them from him, and laid them before his master. "Imitations of your handwriting," he said. "Imitations—exercises in forgery—practice makes perfect—found in the drawer. Now!"

Mr. Dering looked at the papers, and laid them beside the forged check. "An additional fact," he said. "These are certainly imitations. The probable conclusion is that they were made by the same hand that forged this check."

"Found in the drawer," said Checkley, "used by Mr. Arundel, never by me. Ah! The only two, are we? These imitations will prove that I'm not in it."

"The fact that these imitations are found in the drawer," said Mr. Dering, "is a fact which may or may not be important."

"What?" cried the young man, flaring up—"you think that *I* made those imitations?"

"I do not permit myself—yet—to make any conclusions at all. Everything, however, is possible."

Then this foolish young man lost his temper and his head.

"You have known me all my life," he cried. "You have known me and all my people. Yet at the first moment you are ready to believe that I have committed a most abominable forgery! You—my father's oldest friend—my mother's trustee—my own guardian! You!"

"Pardon me. There are certain facts in this case. I have laid them before you. I have shown—"

"To suspect me!" Arundel repeated; "and all the time another man—that man, your clerk—who knows everything ever done in this office is in and about the place all day long."

"The imitations," said Checkley quietly, "were found in his own drawer—by himself."

"Who put them there? Who made them? You—villain and scoundrel!"

"Stop, stop," said Mr. Dering coldly. "We go too fast. Let us first prove our facts. We will then proceed to conclusions."

"Well, sir, you clearly believe that I forged your name and robbed you of all this money. I have not got ten pounds in the world; but that is not, I suppose, a fact which bears on the case. You think I have seven hundred pounds somewhere. Very good. Think so, if you please. Meanwhile, I am not going to stay in the service of a man who is capable of thinking such a thing. I leave your service—at once. Get some one else to serve you—somebody who likes being charged with forgery and theft." He flung himself out of the room, and banged the door behind him.

"He has run away," said Checkley. "Actually run away at the very outset! What do you think now?"

"I do not think. We shall, I dare say, find out the truth in due course. Meantime, these documents will remain in my keeping."

"Only I hope, sir," the clerk began, "that after what you've just seen and heard—after such insolence and running away and all—"

"Don't be an ass, Checkley. So far as appearances go no one could get at the safe except you and Arundel. So far as the ascertained facts go there is nothing to connect either of you with the thing. He is a foolish young man; and if he is innocent, which we must, I suppose, believe"—but his look did not convey the idea of robust faith—"he will come back when he has cooled down."

"The imitations of your handwriting in his drawer—"

"The man who forged the check," said Mr. Dering, "whoever he was, could easily have written those imitations. I shall see that hot-headed boy's mother, and bring him to reason. Now, Checkley, we will resume work. And not a word of this business, if you please, outside. You have yourself to think of as well, remember. You, as well as that boy, have access to the safe. Enough—enough."

Athelstan Arundel walked home all the way, foaming and raging. No omnibus, cab, or conveyance ever built could contain a young man in such a rage. His mother lived at Pembridge Square, which is four good measured miles from Lincoln's Inn. He walked the whole way, walking through crowds, and under the noses of dray-horses, carriage-horses, and cart-horses, without taking the least notice of them. When he reached home, he dashed into the drawing-room, where he found his two sisters—Hilda and Elsie—one of them a girl of eighteen, the other of thirteen. With flaming cheeks and fiery eyes he delivered himself of his story; he hurled it at their heads; he called upon them to share his indignation, and to join with him in scorn and contempt of the man—their supposed best friend, trustee, guardian, adviser; their father's best friend—who had done this thing —who had accused him, on the bare evidence of two or three circumstantial facts, of such a crime!

There is something magnetic in all great emotions; one proof of their reality is that they are magnetic. It is only an actor who can endow an assumed emotion with magnetism. Elsie, the younger girl, fell into a corresponding sympathy of wrath; she was equal to the occasion; passion for passion, she joined him and fed the flame. But—for all persons are not magnetic—the elder sister remained cold. From time to time she wanted to know exactly what Mr. Dering had said; this her brother was too angry to remember; she was pained and puzzled; she neither soothed him nor sympathized with him.

Then the mother returned, and the whole story was told again, Elsie assisting. Now, Mrs. Arundel was a woman of great sense; a practical woman; a woman of keen judgment. She prided herself upon the possession of these qualities, which are not supposed to be especially feminine. She heard the story with disturbed face and knitted brow.

"Surely," she said, "what you tell me, Athelstan, is beyond belief. Mr. Dering, of all men, to accuse you—*you*—of such a thing! It is impossible."

"I wish it were impossible. He accuses me of forging that check for seven hundred and twenty pounds. He says that while I was working in his office for him, a fortnight ago, I took a certain check-book out of the safe, forged his writing on a check, and returned the check-book. This is what he says. Do you call that accusing, or don't you?"

"Certainly. If he says that. But how can he—Mr. Dering, the most exact and careful of men? I will drive to Lincoln's Inn at once, and find out. My dear boy, pray calm yourself. There is—there must be—some terrible mistake."

She went immediately, and she had a long interview with the solicitor.

Mr. Dering was evidently much disturbed by what had happened. He did not receive her as he usually received his clients, sitting in his arm-chair. He pushed back the chair and stood up, leaning a hand on the back of it, a tall, thin, erect figure, gray-haired, austere of face. There was little to reassure the mother in that face. The very trouble of it made her heart sink.

"I certainly have not accused Athelstan," he said. "It is, however, quite true that there has been a robbery here, and that of a large sum of money—no less than seven hundred and twenty pounds."

"But what has that to do with my boy?"

"We have made a few preliminary inquiries. I will do for you, Mrs. Arundel, what I did for your son, and you shall yourself understand what connection those inquiries have with him."

He proceeded coldly and without comment to set forth the

case so far as he had got at the facts. As he went on the mother's heart became as heavy as lead. Before he finished she was certain. There is, you see, a way of presenting a case without comment which is more efficacious than any amount of talk; and Mrs. Arundel plainly perceived—which was indeed the case—that the lawyer had by this time little doubt in his own mind that her son had done this thing.

"I thought it right," he continued, "to lay before him these facts at the outset. 'If he is innocent,' I thought, 'he will be the better able to prove his innocence, and perhaps to find the guilty person. If he is guilty, he may be led to confession or restitution.' The facts about the check-book and the safe are very clear. I am certain that the safe has not been opened by any other key. The only persons who have had access to it are Checkley and your son Athelstan. As for Checkley—he wouldn't do it; he could not possibly do it; the thing is quite beyond him."

Mrs. Arundel groaned. "This is terrible," she said.

"Meantime, the notes are numbered; they may be traced; they are stopped; we shall certainly find the criminal by means of those notes."

"Mr. Dering"—Mrs. Arundel rose and laid her hand on his—"you are our very old friend. Tell me—if this wretched boy goes away—if he gives back the money that remains—if I find the rest—will there be—any further—investigation?"

"To compound a felony is a crime. It is, however, one of those crimes which men sometimes commit without repentance or shame. My dear lady, if he will confess and restore—we shall see."

Mrs. Arundel drove home again. She came away fully persuaded in her own mind that her son—her only son—and none other, must be that guilty person. She knew Mr. Dering's room well—she had sat there hundreds of times; she knew the safe; she knew old Checkley. She perceived the enormous improbability of this ancient clerk's doing such a thing. She knew, again, what temptations assail a young man in London; she saw what her trustee thought of it; and she jumped to the conclusion that her son—and none other—was the guilty person. She even saw how he must have done it—she saw the quick look while Mr. Dering's back was turned; the snatching of the check-book; the quick replacing it. Her very keenness of judgment helped her to the conviction. Women less clever would have been slower to believe. Shameful, miserable termination of all her hopes for her boy's career! But that she could think of afterwards. For the moment the only thing was to get the boy away—to induce him to confess—and to get him away.

He was calmer when she got home, but he was still talking about the thing—he would wait till the right man was discovered; then he would have old Dering on his knees. The thing would be set right in a few days. He had no fear of any delay. He was quite certain that it was Checkley—that old villain. Oh! he couldn't do it by himself, of course—nobody could believe that of him. He had accomplices—confederates—behind him. Checkley's part of the job was to steal the check-book, and give it to his confederates, and share the swag.

"Well, mother?" he asked.

His mother sat down. She looked pale and wretched.

"Mother!" cried Hilda, the elder sister. "Quick! What has happened? What does Mr. Dering say?"

"He accuses nobody," she replied, in a hard, dry voice. "But—"

"But what?" asked Hilda.

"He told me everything—everything—and—and— Oh!" She burst into sobs and crying, though she despised women who cry. "It is terrible—it is terrible—it is incredible. Yet what can I think? What can any one think? Leave us, Hilda. Leave us, Elsie." The two girls went out unwillingly. "Oh, my son! —how can I believe it? And yet—on the one hand a boy of two-and-twenty, exposed to all the temptations of town; on the other an old clerk of fifty years' service and integrity. And when the facts are laid before you both—calmly and coldly— you fly into a rage and run away, while Checkley calmly remains to await the inquiry."

Mrs. Arundel had been accustomed all her life to consider Mr. Dering as the wisest of men. She felt instinctively that he regarded her son with suspicion. She heard all the facts; she jumped to the conclusion that he was a prodigal and a profligate; that he had fallen into evil ways, and spent money in riotous living. She concluded that he had committed this crime in order to get more money for skittles and oranges.

"Athelstan"—she laid her hand upon his arm, but did not

dare to lift her eyes and behold that guilty face—"Athelstan, confess—make reparation so far as you can—confess—oh! my son—my son! You will be caught and tried and found guilty, and—oh! I cannot say it—through the notes which you have changed. They are all known and stopped."

The boy's wrath was now changed to madness.

"You!" he cried—"you? My own mother? *You* believe it —no? Oh! we are all going mad together. What? Then I am turned out of this house, as I am turned out of my place. I go, then—I go; and "—here he swore a mighty oath, as strong as anybody out of Spain can make them—"I will never—never— never come home again till you come yourself to beg forgiveness. *You*—my own mother!"

Outside, in the hall, his sisters stood, waiting and trembling.

"Athelstan," cried the elder, Hilda, a girl of eighteen or nineteen, "what, in the name of Heaven, have you done?"

"Go ask my mother. She will tell you. She knows, it seems, better than I know myself. I am driven away by my own mother. She says that I am guilty of—of—of forgery."

"If she says so, Athelstan," his sister replied coldly, "she must have her reasons. She would not drive you out of the house for nothing. Don't glare like that. Prove your innocence."

"What? You, too? Oh! I am driven away by my sisters as well—"

"No, Athelstan—no," cried Elsie, catching his hand. "Not both your sisters."

"My poor child!"—he stooped and kissed her—"they will make you believe what they believe. Good heavens! They make haste to believe it; they are glad to believe it."

"No—no! Don't go, Athelstan." Elsie threw her arms about him. "Stay, and show that they are wrong. Oh! you are innocent. I will never—never—*never* believe it."

He kissed her again, and tore himself away. The street-door slammed behind him; they heard his footsteps as he strode away. He had gone.

Then Elsie fell into loud weeping and wailing. But Hilda went to comfort her mother.

"Mother," she said, "did he really—really and truly do it?"

" What else can I believe? Either he did it or that old clerk. Where is he?"

" He is gone. He says he will come back when his innocence is proved. Mother, if he is innocent, why does he run away? It's foolish to say that it is because we believe it. I've said nothing except that you couldn't believe it without reasons. Innocent young men don't run away when they are charged with robbery. They stay and fight it out. Athelstan should have stayed."

Later on, when they were both a little recovered, Hilda tried to consider the subject more calmly. She had not her mother's cleverness, but she was not without parts. The following remarks—made by a girl of eighteen—prove so much.

" Mother," she said, " perhaps it is better, so long as this suspicion rests upon him, that he should be away. We shall certainly know where he is—he will want money, and will write for it. If it should prove that somebody else did the thing we can easily bring him back as a martyr—for my own part I should be so glad that I would willingly beg his pardon on my knees—and of course we could easily get him replaced in the office. If it is proved that he did do it—and that, you think, they will be certain to find out—Mr. Dering, for your sake, will be ready to hush it up. Perhaps we may get the notes back—he can't have used them all ; in any case, it will be a great comfort to feel that he is out of the way. A brother tried in open court—convicted—sentenced—oh !" She shuddered. " We should never get over it ; never, never ! It would be a most dreadful thing for Elsie and me. As for his going away, if people ask why he is gone, and where, we must invent something—we can easily make up a story—hint that he has been wild ; there is no disgrace, happily, about a young man being wild—that is the only thing that reconciles one to the horrid selfishness of wild young men ; and if, by going away in a pretended rage, Athelstan has really enabled us to escape a horrid scandal—why, mother, in that case we may confess that the blow has been by Providence most mercifully softened for us—most mercifully. We ought to consider that, mother."

" Yes, dear, yes. But he is gone. Athelstan is gone. And his future seems ruined. There is no hope for him. I can see no hope whatever. My dear, he was so promising. I thought that all the family influence would be his—we haven't got a single City solicitor in the whole family. I thought that he was so clever and so ambitious, and so eager to get on and make money and be a credit to the family. Solicitors do sometimes—especially City solicitors—become so very, very rich; and now it is all gone and done—and nothing left to hope but the miserable wish that there should be no scandal."

"It is, indeed, dreadful. But still—consider—no scandal. Mother, I think we should find out, if we can, something about his private life—how he has been living. He has been out a good deal of evenings lately. If there is any—any person on whom he has been tempted to spend money—if he has been gambling, or betting, or any of the things that I read of "—this young lady, thanks to the beneficent assistance of certain works of fiction, was tolerably acquainted with the ways of young men and their temptations—" it would be a satisfaction to know it at least."

The ladies of a family where there is a " wild " young man do not generally find it easy to get at the facts of his wildness; they remain locked up in the bosoms of his companions. No details could be learned about any wildness—quite the contrary. He seemed, so far as could be learned, to have led a very quiet and regular life. "But then," said the philosopher of eighteen, quoting from a novel, " men shelter each other. They are all bad together."

But—no scandal.

Everybody knows that kind of brother or sister by whom all family events are considered with a view to the scandal likely to be caused and the personal injury resulting to himself or herself; or the envy that will follow and the personal advantage accruing from that event. That her brother was perhaps a shameful criminal might be considered by Hilda Arundel later on; at first, she was only capable of perceiving that this horrid fact, unless it could be hidden away and kept secret, might very materially injure herself.

Almost naturally, she folded her hands sweetly and laid her comely head a little on one side—it is an attitude of resignation which may be observed in certain pictures of saints and holy women. Hilda knew many little attitudes. Also, quite naturally, she glanced at a mirror on the wall, and observed that her pose was one of sorrow borne with Christian resignation.

We must blame neither Hilda nor her mother. The case, as put by Mr. Dering, in the form of plain fact without any comment, did seem very black, indeed, against Athelstan. In every family the first feeling in such a case—it is the instinct of self-preservation—is to hush up the thing if possible—to avoid a scandal.

Such a scandal as the prosecution of a brother for forgery—with a verdict of guilty—is a most truly horrible, deplorable, fatal thing. It takes the respectability out of a family perhaps at a critical moment, when the family is just assuming the robes of respectability; it ruins the chances of the girls; it blights the prospects of the boys; it drives away friends; it is a black spot which all the soaps ever advertised could never wash off. Therefore, while the mother hoped, first of all, that the boy would escape the clutch of the law, Hilda was, first of all, grateful that there would be no scandal. Mr. Dering would not talk about it. The thing would not interfere with her own prospects. It was sad, it was miserable; but yet—no scandal. With what a deep, deep sigh of satisfaction did the young lady repeat that there would probably be no scandal!

As for Elsie, that child went about for many days with tearful eyes, red cheeks, and a swollen nose. She was rebellious and sharp with her mother, and to her sister she refused to speak. The days went on. They became weeks, months, years—otherwise they would not have been days. Nothing at all was heard of Athelstan. He sent no letters to any one; he did not even write for money; they knew not where he was or what he was doing. He disappeared. It was understood that there had been wildness.

Now—which was very remarkable—though the forger had had a clear run of three weeks, it could not be discovered that any of the notes had been presented. Perhaps they were sent abroad; yet foreign and colonial banks would know the numbers of stopped notes. And towards the discovery of the forger no further step had been taken. The commissionaire who took the check had been, as you have seen, easily found; he said he should know the old gentleman who gave him the forged draft to cash. He said, being again interrogated, that Checkley was not in the least like that old gentleman. What could be thought, then? Athelstan must have "made-up" as an old man—he was fond of private theatricals; he could make-up very well; of course he had made-up. And then, this point being settled, they left off talking about the business.

Other things happened—important things—which made the memory of the prodigal son to wax dim. First of all came Hilda's case. She was a graceful young person, with features of great regularity; her expression was cold, her eyes were hard, and her lips were a little thin, but these things at nineteen are hardly perceived. She was that sort of girl who seems created for the express purpose, first, of wearing and beautifying costly raiment, and next, of sitting in a splendid vehicle. The finer the dress, the more beautiful she looked. The grander the carriage, the more queenly she seemed. In rags her coldness would be arctic, her hardness would be granitic; in silk and velvet she became a goddess. It was therefore most fitting that she should marry a rich man. Now, to be rich in these days one must be old. It is the price that one has to pay for wealth. Sometimes one pays the price, and does not get what one has paid for. That seems hardly fair. There was a certain rich man—Mr. Dering's younger brother, Sir Samuel Dering, knight—one of the most substantial City men, a man who had a house in Kensington Palace Gardens, a yacht, a country place in Sussex, and piles of papers in a safe, meaning investments. He was a widower without encumbrance; he was fifty-seven years of age, not yet decayed; he wanted a wife to be the mistress of his house and to look well at his dinner-parties. Of course, when one does want a wife, at any age, one wants her young. Hilda Arundel, his brother's ward, looked as if she would discharge the duties required of the position admirably. He suggested the arrangement to his brother, who spoke about it.

There was a good deal of talking about it. Mrs. Arundel showed that she knew the value of her daughter, but there was no doubt about the conclusion of the matter. There was a grand wedding, at which all the richer Arundels were present and none of the poor relations. Mr. Dering, the young lady's guardian, gave her away; Hilda became Lady Dering, and has been perfectly happy ever since. Elsie remained with her mother. Her brother was never spoken of between them. But she remembered him, and she was firm in her conviction that his innocence would be, some day, established.

After a few years, nothing at all having been heard of the notes,

Mr. Dering made application to the Bank of England, and received from it the sum of seven hundred and twenty pounds in new, crisp notes in the place of those of which he had been robbed, so that the actual loss at four per cent. compound interest amounted to no more than £155 19s. 9¾d., which is more than one likes to lose, yet is not actually embarrassing to a man whose income is about six thousand a year. He ceased to think about the business altogether, except as a disagreeable episode of his office.

Thus Athelstan Arundel became completely forgotten. His old friends—the young men with whom he had played and sported—only remembered him from time to time as a fellow who had come to some unknown grief, and had gone away. There is always some young fellow in every set of young fellows who gets into some scrape, and so leaves the circle, and is no more seen or heard of. We go on just the same without him; very seldom that such a man is remembered long. It is the way of the world; we cannot stop to lament over the fallen; we must push on; others fall; close up the ranks; push on; Time drives; the memory of the fallen swiftly waxes dim.

Four years or so after the mysterious business of Edmund Gray, Mr. Dering received a letter with an American stamp, marked "Private and Confidential." He laid this aside until he had got through the business letters, then he opened it. He turned first to the signature. "Ha!" he said, "'Athelstan Arundel.' At last. Now we shall see—we shall see."

He expected a full confession of the crime. "We should never expect," says the sage, "what we desire, because we never obtain what we expect." It would have made Mr. Dering more comfortable in his mind had the letter contained a confession. Of course Athelstan had done it. Nobody else could have done it. Yet when he thought about the business at all there always arose in his mind an uneasy feeling that perhaps the boy had been treated unwisely. It might have been more prudent to have kept the facts from him, although they pointed so strongly in his direction, until proof positive was obtained. It might, again, have been better had the facts been put before him with a few words of confidence, even though that confidence did not exist. Time only strengthened Mr. Dering's suspicions against the young man. The thing *must* have been done by Checkley or by him.

2

Now, Checkley was not able, if he had wished, to imitate any handwriting. No! It was done by Athelstan. Why he did it, what he got by it, seeing that those notes had never been presented, no one could explain. Bu the did it—he did it. That was certain.

Mr. Dering, therefore, began to read the letter with interest. Its commencement was without any opening words of respect or friendliness. And it was not by any means the letter of a wicked man turning away from his wickedness. Not a word of repentance from beginning to end.

"'Four years ago,'" Mr. Dering read, "'you drove me from your place and changed my whole life, by a suspicion—amounting to a charge—of the gravest kind. You assumed, without explanation or examination, that because certain facts seemed to point in a certain direction, I had been guilty of an enormous crime, that I had robbed my father's oldest friend, my mother's trustee, my own guardian, my employer, of a great sum of money. You never asked yourself if this suspicion was justified by any conduct of mine—you jumped at it.'"

"Quite wrong. Wilfully wrong," said Mr. Dering. "I laid the facts before him—nothing but the facts. I brought no charge."

"'I dare say that by this time the criminal has been long since detected. Had I remained I would have brought the thing home to him. For of course it could be none other than your clerk. I have thought over the case thousands of times. The man who forged the check must have been one of two—either your clerk—the man Checkley—or myself. It did not take you long, I apprehend, to learn the truth. You would discover it through the presentation of the notes.'" "This is a very crafty letter," said Mr. Dering—"when he never presented any of the notes. Very crafty." He resumed the letter—"'Enough said about that. I dare say, however, that I shall some day or other—before you are dead, I hope—return, in order to receive some expression of sorrow from you if you can feel shame.'" "Certainly not," said Mr. Dering, with decision. "'Meantime, there is a service which I must ask of you for the sake of my people. There is no one else whom I can ask. It is the reason of my writing this letter.

"'I came away with ten pounds—all I had in the world—in my

pocket. Not seven hundred and twenty pounds, as you imagined or suspected. Ten pounds. With that slender capital I got across the Atlantic. I have now made twelve thousand pounds. I made it in a very short time by extraordinary good luck.'" Mr. Dering laid down the letter, and considered. Twelve thousand pounds might be made—perhaps—by great good luck—with a start of seven hundred and twenty, but hardly with ten, pounds. A silver reef—or more likely a gambling-table or other crime. It will be observed that his opinion of the young man was now very bad indeed; otherwise, he would have reflected that as none of those notes had been presented, none of them had been used. Even if an English ten-pound note is converted into American dollars, the note comes home after a few years. "'Extraordinary good luck.'" He read the words again, and shook his head. "'Now, I want you to take charge of this money; to say nothing at all about it; to keep the matter a profound secret; to invest it, or put it in some place of safety where confidential clerks with a taste for forgery cannot get at it; and to give it, on her twenty-first birthday, to my sister Elsie. Do not tell her or anybody from whom the money comes. Do not tell anybody that you have heard from me. When I came away she was the only one of all my friends and people who declared that she believed in me. I now strip myself of my whole possessions in order to show this mark of my love and gratitude towards her. In sending you this money I go back to the ten pounds with which I started.'"

Mr. Dering laid the letter down. The words, somehow, seemed to ring true. Could the boy—after all?— He shook his head, and went on, "'You will give Elsie this money on her twenty-first birthday, to be settled on her for herself. — ATHELSTAN ARUNDEL.'"

The letter was dated, but no address was given. The post-mark was Idaho, which, as we all know, is in the far West.

He looked into the envelope. There fell out a paper, which was a draft on a well-known London firm, payable to his order, for twelve thousand and fifty pounds.

"This is very unbusiness-like," said Mr. Dering. "He puts all this money in my hands, and vanishes. These are the ways he learns, in America, I suppose. Puts the money blindly in my hands, without giving me the means of communicating with him.

Then he vanishes. How could he prove that it was a trust?
Well, if I could only think—but I cannot, the circumstantial
evidence is too strong—that the boy was innocent, I should be
very sorry for him. As for Elsie—she must be seventeen now,
about seventeen—she will get this windfall in four years or so.
It will be a wonderful lift for her. Perhaps it may make all the
difference in her future! If I could only think that the boy
was innocent—a clever lad, too, which makes it more probable.
But I can't—no, I can't. Either Checkley or that boy—and
Checkley couldn't do it. He couldn't if he were to try. What
did the boy do it for? And what did he do with those notes?"

CHAPTER I

UP THE RIVER

"CAN you not be content, George?" asked the girl sitting in
the stern. "I think that I want nothing more than this. If we
could only go on always, and always, and always, just like this."
She had taken off her right-hand glove, and she was dropping her
fingers into the cool waters of the river as the boat slowly drifted
down stream. "Always like this," she repeated softly—"with
you close to me, so that I could touch you if I wanted to — so
that I could feel safe, you know; the sun behind us, warm and
splendid; such a sweet and fragrant air about us; trees and gardens and fields and lanes on either side; and both of us always
young, George, and — and nice to look at, and all the world before us."

She, for one, was not only young and nice to look upon, but
fair—very fair—to look upon. Even young persons of her own
sex, critics and specialists in the art and science of beauty —
rivals as well—had to confess that Elsie was rather pretty. I believe that few such critics ever go further. She was, to begin
with, of sufficient stature in a time when dumpy women are not
considered, and when height is a first necessity of comeliness ; she
paid, next, such obedience to the laws of figure as becomes the
age of twenty, and is, with stature, rigorously demanded at this

end of the century. Her chief points, perhaps, lay in her eyes, which were of a darker shade of blue than is common. They were soft, yet not languid; they were full of light; they were large, and yet they could be quick. Her face was subject to sudden changes that made it like a spring-time sky of shower, rainbow, sunshine, and surprise. Her hair was of a very common brown, neither dark nor light. She was attired, this evening, in a simple gray frock of nun's cloth with a bunch of white roses on her left shoulder.

When one says that her companion was a young man, nearly all is said, because the young men of the present day are surprisingly alike. Thousands of young men can be found like George Austin. They are all excellent fellows, of much higher principles, in some things, than their fathers before them; not remarkably intellectual, to judge by their school record, yet with intelligence and application enough to get through their examinations moderately—for the most part they do pass them with moderate success; they are not ambitious of obtaining any of the great prizes —which, indeed, they know to be out of their reach—but they always set before themselves and keep always well in sight the ideal suburban villa and the wife; they always work steadily, if not feverishly, with the view of securing these two blessings; they always hope to secure an income that will enable them to maintain that wife—with a possible following of babies—in silk attire (for Sundays)—in ease as to household allowance, and in such freedom of general expenditure as may enable her to stand up among her neighbors in church without a blush.

The world is quite full of such men; they form the rank and file, the legionaries; their opinion on the subject of labor is purely Scriptural—namely, that it is a curse ; they do not particularly love any kind of work; they would prefer, if they had the choice, to do nothing at all ; when they get their summer holiday they do nothing all day long, with zeal; they give no more thought to their work than is sufficient for the bread-winning; whether they are professional men or trading men their view of professional work is solely that it brings in the money. If such a young man becomes a clerk he never tries to learn any more after he has left school; he accepts the position—a clerk and a servant he is, a clerk and a servant he will remain. If he is engaged in trade he gives just so much attention to his business as will keep his connection together—that and no more; others may soar; others may become universal providers; for his part he is contented with his shop and his Sunday feast. If he becomes a professional man he learns no more of his science than is wanted every day. The lawyer passes his examination and puts away his law-books—he knows enough for professional purposes; the doctor reads no more; he knows enough for the ordinary needs of the G. P.; the school-master lays aside his books, scholarship and science interest him no longer—he has learned enough to teach his boys; the curate makes no further research into the history and foundations of his Church—he has learned enough. In a word, the average young man is without ambition; he is inclined to be lazy; he loves the present far more than the future — indeed, all his elders unite in letting him know that his own is quite the most enviable time of life; he likes to enjoy whatever he can afford, so that he very often eats up all his wages; he does not read too much; he does not think too much; he does not vex his soul too much with the problems of life—greater problems or lesser problems, he accepts the teaching of his newspaper, and agrees with the words and the wisdom of yesterday's leading article; he accepts religion, politics, morals, social systems, con- stitutions, things present, past, and future, as if—which is per- fectly true—he had nothing to do with them, and could not help it whatever was to happen. He never wants to alter anything; he believes that all British institutions are built on the solid rock and fashioned out of the hardest granite—any exceptions to this rule, he thinks, have come straight down from heaven.

Observe, if you please, that this kind of young man confers the greatest possible benefits upon the country. He ought to be made a baronet at least if honors meant anything. His apparent sluggishness keeps us from the constant changes which trouble some nations; his apparent lack of ambition makes it easy for the restless spirits to rise; were the country full of aspiring young men we should be forever having civil wars, revolutions, social upsydowns, new experiments, new religions, new govern- ments, new divisions of property, every year. Again, it is this young man who, by his steady attention to business—his readiness to work as much as is wanted but no more, his disregard of theories and speculations, his tenacity, his honesty, his loyalty, his courage, and his stout heart—has built up the British name so that there has never been any name like unto it, nor ever will be again, for these solid and substantial virtues.

Being, then, just a young man of the time, George Austin was naturally like most young men in dress, in appearance, in language, and in manners. And had it not been for the strange experience which he was to undergo, he would have remained to this day just like other young men. He was better looking than most, having a good figure, a well-shaped head, and regular features, with eyes rather fuller of possibilities than falls to the lot of most young men. In short, a good-looking fellow, showing a capability for something or other in his firm mouth, ample cheek, strong chin, and resolute carriage. He would have made a fine soldier, but perhaps an unsuccessful general for want of that quality which in poets is called genius. In the same way he would in a lower walk keep a business together, but would fail to achieve a great fortune for lack of the same quality. As for his age, he was seven-and-twenty.

"Always like this," the girl went on — "always floating down the stream under a summer sky; always sweet looks and love and youth. It seems as if we could never be unhappy, never be worried, never want anything, on such an evening as this." She turned, and looked up the stream on which lay the glory of the sinking sun — she sighed. "It is good to come out on such an evening only to have a brief dream of what might be. When will the world give up their foolish quarrels, and join together to make the lives of all happy?"

They had been talking, among other things, of Socialism, all out of yesterday's leading article.

"When there is enough of good things to go round; when we invent a way to make all men ready to do their share as well as to devour it; when we find out how to make everybody contented with his share."

Elsie shook her head, which was filled with vague ideas — the ideas of a restless and a doubting time. Then she went back to her original proposition. "Always like this, George—and never to get tired of it. Time to stand still—nothing to change; never to get tired of it; never to want anything else. That is heaven, I suppose."

"We are on earth, Elsie," said her lover, "and on earth everything changes. If we were to go on drifting down the stream we should get into trouble over the weir. To capsize would be a pretty interruption to your heaven, wouldn't it? And the sun will soon be setting, and the river will get misty, and the banks will grow ugly. But the chief thing is that we shall both grow old. And there is such a lot that we have got to do before we grow old."

"Everything has to be done," said Elsie. "I suppose we have done nothing yet."

"We have got to get married, for the first thing, before we grow old."

"Couldn't you love an old woman, George?"

"Not so well, Elsie," her lover replied, truthfully. "At least, I think not. And oh! Elsie, whenever I do think of the future my heart goes down into my boots, for the prospect grows darker and darker."

Elsie sighed. She knew already, too well, what was in his mind. Plenty of girls, in these days, know the familiar tale.

"Darker every day," he repeated. "They keep on crowding into the profession by multitudes, as if there was room for any number. They don't understand that, what with the decay of the landed interest and of the country towns, and the cutting down of the costs, and the work that goes to accountants, there isn't half the business to do that there was. There don't seem any partnerships to be had for love or money, because the few people who have got a good thing have got no more than enough for themselves. It is no use for the young fellows to start by themselves; so they have got to take whatever they can get, and they are glad to get even a hundred a year to begin with—and I am seven-and-twenty, Elsie, and I'm drawing two hundred pounds a year."

"Patience, George; something will turn up. You will find a partnership somewhere."

"My child, you might as well tell Robinson Crusoe that a boiled leg of mutton, with caper-sauce, is going to turn up on his desert island. We must not hope for the impossible. I ought to be grateful, I suppose, considering what other men are doing. I am planted in a good, solid house. It won't run away, so long as the old man lives."

"And after that?"

"Well, Mr. Dering is seventy-five. But he will not die yet,

not for a long time to come. He is made of granite; he is never ill; he never takes a holiday; he works harder than any of his people, and he keeps longer hours. To be sure, if he were to die without taking a partner—well, in that case, there would be an end of everything, I suppose. Elsie, here's the position." She knew it already, too well — but it pleased them both to parade the facts as if they were something quite novel. "Let us face it " — they were always facing it: " I am managing clerk to Dering & Son ; I get two hundred pounds a year; I have no prospect of anything better; I am bound all my life to be a servant. Elsie, it is not a brilliant prospect. I found out at school that it was best not to be too ambitious. But a servant all my life — I confess that did not enter into my head. If I knew any other trade I would cut the whole business. If there was any mortal thing in the whole world by which I could keep myself I would try it. But there's nothing. I have but one trade. I can't write novels or leading articles; I can't play on any instrument; I can't paint or act or sing or anything—I am only a solicitor— that's all. Only a solicitor who can't get on—a clerk, Elsie. No wonder her ladyship turns up her nose—a clerk." He leaned his chin upon his hands and laughed the conventional laugh of the young man down on his luck.

"Poor George !" she sighed. In such a case there are only two words of consolation. One may say, " Poor George !" or one may say, " Patience!" There is nothing else to say. Elsie first tried one method and then the other, as a doctor tries first one remedy and then another when Nature sulks and refuses to get well.

" And," he went on, piling up the misery, " I am in love with the sweetest girl in the whole world, and she is in love with me !"

" Poor George !" she repeated, with a smile. "That is, indeed, a dreadful misfortune."

" I am wasting your youth, Elsie, as well as my own."

" If it is wasted for your sake, George, it is well spent. Some day, perhaps—"

" No—no—not some day—immediately—at once." The young man changed color, and his eyes sparkled. It was not the first time that he had advanced this revolutionary proposal. " Let prudence go to the—"

2**

"Not there, George—oh! not there. To the winds, perhaps, or to that famous city of Palestine. But not there. Why, we might never get her back again—poor Prudence! And we shall be sure to want her all our lives—very badly. We will, if you please, ask her to go for a short voyage for the benefit of her health. We will give her six months' leave of absence, but we shall want her services again after her holiday, if you think we can do without her for so long."

"For a whole twelvemonth, Elsie. Let us brave everything, get married at once, live in a garret, and have a splendid time— for a whole twelvemonth—on my two hundred pounds."

"And am I to give up my painting?"

"Well, dear, you know you have not yet had a commission from anybody."

"How can you say so, George? I have painted you—and my sister—and my mother—and your sisters. I am sure that no studio, even of an R. A., could make a braver show of work. Well, I will give it up—until Prudence returns. Is it to be a garret? —a real garret, with sloping walls, where you can only stand upright in the middle?"

"We call it a garret. It will take the form, I suppose, of a tiny house in a cheap quarter. It will have six rooms, a garden in front and a garden behind. The rent will be thirty pounds. For a whole twelvemonth it will be a real slice of Eden, Elsie, and you shall be Eve."

Elsie laughed. "It will be great fun. We will make the Eden last longer than a twelvemonth. I dare say I shall like it. Of course I shall have to do everything for myself. To clean the doorsteps will be equivalent to taking exercise in the fresh air; to sweep the floors will be a kind of afternoon dance or a game of lawn-tennis; to wash up the cups and saucers will be only a change of amusement. There is one thing, George—one thing" —she became very serious—"I suppose you never—did you ever witness the scouring of a frying-pan? I don't think I *could* do that. And did you ever see beefsteaks before they are cooked? They suggest the animal in the most terrible way. I don't really think I could handle those bleeding lumps."

"You sha'n't touch a frying-pan, and we will have nothing roasted or fried. We will live on cold Australian beef, eaten out of its native tin; the potatoes shall be boiled in their skins.

And perhaps—I don't know—with two hundred pounds a year we could afford a servant—a very little one—just a girl warranted not to eat too much."

"What shall we do when our clothes are worn out?"

"The little maid shall make some more for you, I suppose. We certainly shall not be able to buy new things—not nice things, that is—and you must have nice things, mustn't you?"

"I do like things to be nice," she replied, smoothing her dainty skirts with her dainty hand. "George, where shall we find this house—formerly Eve's own country villa before she—resigned her tenancy, you know?"

"There are places in London where whole streets are filled with families living on a hundred and fifty pounds a year. Checkley —the chief's private clerk—lives in such a place; he told me so himself. He says there is nobody in his parish who has got a bigger income than himself; he's a little king among them because he gets four hundred pounds a year, besides what he has saved—which is enormous piles. Elsie, my dear, we must give up our present surroundings, and take up with gentility in its cheapest form."

"Can we not go on living among our own friends?"

George shook his head wisely. "Impossible. Friendship means equality of income. You can't live with people unless you do as they do. People of the same means naturally live together. Next door to Lady Dering is another rich madam, not a clerk's wife. For my own part, I shall sell my dress clothes for what they will fetch—you can exchange your evening things for morning things. That won't matter much. Who cares where we live, or how we live, so that we live together? What do you say, Elsie, dear?"

"The garret I don't mind—nor the doorsteps—and since you see your way out of the difficulty of the frying-pan—"

"You will be of age next week, when you can please yourself."

"Hilda gives me no peace or rest. She says there can be no happiness without money. She has persuaded my mother that I am going to certain starvation. She promises the most splendid establishment if I will only be guided by her."

"And marry a man fifty years older than yourself, with one foot already well in—"

"She says she has always been perfectly happy. Well, George, you know all that. Next Wednesday, which is my birthday, I am to have a grand talk with my guardian. My mother hopes that he will bring me to my senses. Hilda says that she trusts entirely to Mr. Dering's good sense. I shall arm myself with all my obstinacy. Perhaps, George—who knows?—I may persuade him to advance your salary."

"No, Elsie. Not even you would persuade Mr. Dering to give a managing clerk more than two hundred pounds a year. But don't forget any piece of that armor, child. The breastplate—there was a poor damsel once who forgot that, and was caught by an appeal to her heart; nor the helmet—another poor damsel was once caught by an appeal to her reason after forgetting the helmet. The shield, of course, you will not forget; and for weapons, my dear, take your sweet eyes and your lovely face and your winning voice, and I swear that you will subdue even Mr. Dering himself—that hardened old parchment."

This was the kind of talk which these lovers held together whenever they met. George was poor—the son of a clergyman, whose power of advancing him ceased when he had paid the fees for admission. He was only a clerk, and he saw no chance of being anything else but a clerk. Elsie could bring nothing to the family nest, unless her mother made her an allowance. Of this there could be no hope. The engagement was considered deplorable; marriage, under the circumstances, simple madness. And Hilda had done so well for herself, and could do so much for a sister so pretty, so bright as Elsie! Oh! she was throwing away all her chances. Did one ever hear of anything so lamentable? No regard for the family; no ambition; no sense of what a girl owes to herself; no recognition or gratitude for the gift of good looks—as if beauty were given for the mere purpose of pleasing a penniless lover! And to go and throw herself away upon a twopenny lawyer's clerk!

"George," she said, seriously, "I have thought it all out. If you really mean it—if you really can face poverty—mind, it is harder—much—for a man than for a woman—"

"I can face everything—with you, Elsie," replied the lover. Would he have been a lover worth having if he had not made that answer? And, indeed, he meant it, as every lover should.

"Then—George—what in the whole world is there for me unless I can make my dear boy happy? I will marry you as soon as you please—rich or poor, for better or worse—whatever they may say at home. Will that do for you, George?"

Since man is so constituted that his happiness wholly depends upon the devotion of a woman, I believe that no dear boy ever had a better chance of happiness than George Austin—only a managing clerk—with his Elsie. And so this history begins where many end, with an engagement.

CHAPTER II

IN THE OFFICE

"I'll take in your ladyship's name. There is no one with him at this moment. Oh, yes, my lady," Checkley smiled superior. "We are always busy. We have been busy in this office for fifty years and more. But I am sure he'll see you. Take a chair, my lady. Allow me."

Checkley, the old clerk, had other and younger clerks with him; but he kept in his own hands the duty or the privilege of going to the private room of the chief. He was sixty-seven when last we saw him. Therefore, he was now seventy-five—a little more bent in the shoulders, a little more feeble, otherwise unaltered. In age we either shrivel or we swell. Those live the longest who shrivel; and those who shrivel presently reach a point when they cease to shrink any more till they reach the ninetieth year. Checkley was bowed and bent and lean; his face was lined multitudinously; his cheeks were shrunken, but not more so than eight years before. He wrote down the name of the caller—Lady Dering—on a square piece of paper, and opened the door with an affectation of extreme care not to disturb the chief's nerves by a sharp turn of the handle, stepped in as if it were most important that no one should be able to peep into the room, and closed the door softly behind him. Immediately he reappeared, and held the door wide open, inviting the lady to step in. She was young, of good stature and figure, extremely handsome in face—of what is called the classical type, and very richly dressed. Her carriage might have been seen, on looking out of the window, waiting in the square.

"Lady Dering, sir," said Checkley.   Then he swiftly vanished, closing the door softly behind him.

"I am glad to see you, Hilda."   The old lawyer rose, tall and commanding, and bowed, offering his hand with a stately and old-fashioned courtesy which made ladies condone his unmarried condition.   "Why have you called this morning?   You are not come on any business, I trust.   Business with ladies who have wealthy husbands generally means trouble of some kind.   You are not, for instance, in debt with your dress-maker?"

"No—no.   Sir Samuel does not allow of any difficulties or awkwardness of that kind.   It is not about myself that I am here, but about my sister Elsie."

"Yes?   What about her?   Sit down, and let me hear."

"Well, you know, Elsie has always been a trouble to us on account of her headstrong and wilful ways.   She will not look on things from a reasonable point of view.   You know that my mother is not rich, as I have learned to consider rich, though, of course, she has enough for a simple life and a man-servant and a one-horse brougham.   Do you know," she added pensively, "I have often found it difficult not to repine at a Providence which removes a father when he was beginning so well, and actually on the high-road to a great fortune."

"It is certainly difficult to understand the wisdom of these disappointments and disasters.   We must accept, Hilda, what we cannot escape or explain."

"Yes—and my mother had nothing but a poor thousand a year!—though I am sure that she has greatly bettered her circumstances by her transactions in the City.   Well—I have done all I can, by precept and by example, to turn my sister's mind into the right direction.   Mr. Dering"—by long habit Hilda still called her guardian, now her brother-in-law, by his surname—"you would hardly believe the folly that Elsie talks about money."

"Perhaps because she has none.   Those who have no property do not understand it.   Young people do not know what it means or what it commands.   And whether they have it or not young people do not know what the acquisition of property means—the industry, the watchfulness, the carefulness, the self-denial.   So Elsie talks folly about money—well, well"—he smiled indulgently—"we shall see."

"It is not only that she talks, but she acts. Mr. Dering, we are in despair about her. You know the Rodings?"

"Roding Brothers? Everybody knows Roding Brothers."

"Algy Roding, the eldest son of the senior partner—enormously rich—is gone—quite gone—foolish about Elsie. He has been at me a dozen times about her. He has called at the house to see her. He cares nothing at all about her having no money. She refuses even to hear his name mentioned. Between ourselves, he has not been, I believe, a very steady young man; but, of course, he would settle down; we could entirely trust to a wife's influence in that respect; the past could easily be forgotten —in fact, Elsie need never know it; and the position would be splendid. Even mine would not compare with it."

"Why does she object to the man?"

"Says he is an ugly little snob. There is a becoming spirit for a girl to receive so rich a lover! But that is not all. She might have him if she chose, snob or not, but she prefers one of your clerks—actually, Mr. Dering, one of your clerks."

"I have learned something of this from your mother. She is engaged, I am told, to young Austin, one of my managing clerks."

"Whose income is two hundred pounds a year. Oh! think of it! She refuses a man with ten thousand a year at the very least, and wants to marry a man with two hundred."

"I suppose they do not propose to marry on this—this pittance—this two hundred a year?"

"They are engaged; she refuses to break it off; he has no money to buy a partnership; he must, therefore, continue a clerk on two hundred."

"Managing clerks get more, sometimes; but, to be sure, the position is not good, and the income must always be small."

"My mother will not allow the man in the house. Elsie goes out to meet him; oh! it is most irregular. I should be ashamed for Sir Samuel to know it. She actually goes out of the house every evening, and they walk about the square garden or in the Park till dark. It is exactly like a housemaid going out to meet her young man."

"It does seem an unusual course, but I am no judge of what is becoming to a young lady."

"Well—she needn't go on like a housemaid," said her sister. "Of course the position of things at home is strained, and I don't know what may happen at any moment. Elsie says that she shall be twenty-one next week, and that she means to act on her own judgment. She even talks of setting up a studio somewhere, and painting portraits for money. That is a pleasant thing for me to contemplate—my own sister earning her own living by painting!"

"How do you think I can interfere in the matter? Lovers' quarrels or lovers' difficulties are not made or settled in this room."

"Mr. Dering, there is no one in the world of whom she is afraid except yourself. There is no one of whose opinion she thinks so much. Will you see her? Will you talk with her? Will you admonish her?"

"Why, Hilda, it so happens that I have already invited her to call upon me on her birthday, when she ceases to be my ward. I will talk to her if you please. Perhaps you may be satisfied with the result of my conversation."

"I shall—I am sure I shall."

"Let me understand. You desire that your sister shall marry a man who, if he is not already rich, should be at least on the high-road to wealth. You cannot force her to accept even the richest young man in London unless she likes him, can you?"

"No, certainly not. And we can hardly expect her to marry, as I did myself, a man whose wealth is already established. Unless she would take Algy Roding."

"Very good. But he must have a certain income, so as to insure the means of an establishment conducted at a certain level?"

"Yes. She need not live in Palace Gardens, but she ought to be able to live—say in Pembridge Square."

"Quite so. I suppose with an income of fifteen hundred or so to begin with? If I make her understand that, you will be satisfied?"

"Perfectly. My dear Mr. Dering, I really believe you have got the very young man up your sleeve. But how will you persuade her to give up the present intruder?"

"I promise nothing, Hilda—I promise nothing. I will do my best, however."

Hilda rose, and swept back her dress.

"I feel an immense sense of relief," she said. "The dear

child's happiness is all I desire. Perhaps if you were to dismiss the young man immediately, with ignominy, and were to refuse him a written character on the ground of trying to win the affections of a girl infinitely above him in station, it might produce a good effect on Elsie—showing what you think of it—as well as an excellent lesson for himself and his friends. There is no romance about a cast-off clerk. Will you think of this, Mr. Dering? The mere threat of such a thing might make him ready to give her up; and it might make her inclined, for his own sake, to send him about his business."

"I will think of it, Hilda. By the way, will you and my brother dine with me on Monday, unless you are engaged? We can talk over this little affair then at leisure."

"With pleasure. We are only engaged for the evening. Now I won't keep you any longer. Good-by."

She walked away, smiling graciously on the clerks in the outer office, and descended the stairs to the carriage, which waited below.

Mr. Dering returned to his papers. He was not changed in the eight years since the stormy interview with this young lady's brother—his small whiskers were a little whiter; his iron-gray hair was unchanged; his lips were as firm and his nostrils as sharp, his eyes as keen as then.

The room looked out pleasantly upon the garden of New Square, where the sunshine lay warm upon the trees with their early summer leaves. Sunshine or rain, all the year round, the solicitor sat in his high-backed chair before his great table. He sat there this morning, working steadily until he had got through what he was about. Then he looked at his watch. It was past two o'clock. He touched a bell on the table, and his old clerk came in.

Though he was the same age as his master, Checkley looked a great deal older. He was bald, save for a small white patch over each ear. He was bent, and his hands trembled. His expression was sharp, foxy, and suspicious. He stood in the unmistakable attitude of a servant, hands hanging in readiness, head a little bent.

"The clerks are all gone, I suppose?" said Mr. Dering.

"All gone. All they think about when they come in the morning is how soon they will get away. As for any pride in their work, they haven't got it."

"Let them go. Checkley, I have wanted to speak to you for some time."

"Anything the matter?" The old clerk spoke with the familiarity of long service, which permits the expression of opinions.

"The time has come, Checkley, when we must make a change."

"A change? Why, I do my work as well as ever I did—better than any of the younger men. A change?"

"The change will not affect you."

"It must be for you, then. Surely you're never going to retire!"

"No—I mean to hold on as long as I can. That will only be for a year or two at most. I am seventy-five, Checkley."

"What of that? So am I. You don't find me grumbling about my work, do you? Besides, you eat hearty. Your health is good."

"Yes, my health is good. But I am troubled of late, Checkley—I am troubled about my memory."

"So is many a younger man," returned the clerk stoutly.

"Sometimes I cannot remember in the morning what I was doing the evening before."

"That's nothing—nothing at all."

"Yesterday I looked at my watch, and found that I had been unconscious for three hours."

"You were asleep. I came in, and saw you sound asleep." It was not true, but the clerk's intentions were good.

"To go asleep in the morning argues a certain decay of strength. Yet I believe that I get through the work as well as ever. The clients do not drop off, Checkley? There is no sign of mistrust—eh? No suspicion of failing powers?"

"They think more of you than ever."

"I believe they do, Checkley."

"Everybody says you are the top of the profession."

"I believe I am, Checkley—I believe I am. Certainly, I am the oldest. Nevertheless, seventy-five is a great age to be continuing work. Things can't last much longer."

"Some men go on to eighty, and even ninety."

"A few—a few only," the lawyer sighed. "One may hope, but must not build upon the chance of such merciful prolongation. The older I grow, Checkley, the more I enjoy life, especially the only thing that has ever made life happy for me—this work. I cling to it "—he spread his hands over the papers—" I cling to it. I cannot bear to think of leaving it."

"That—and your savings," echoed the clerk.

"It seems as if I should be content to go on for a hundred years more at the work of which I am never tired. And I must leave it before long—in a year—two years—who knows? Life is miserably short—one has no time for half the things one would like to do. Well "—he heaved a deep sigh—" let us work while we can. However, it is better to climb down than to be pulled down or shot down. I am going to make preparations, Checkley, for the end."

"What preparations? You're not going to send for the minister, are you?"

"No. Not that kind of preparation. Nor for the doctor either. Nor for a lawyer to make my will. All those things are duly attended to. I have resolved, Checkley, upon taking a partner."

" *You* take a partner? *You?* At your time of life?"

"I am going to take a partner. And you are the first person who has been told of my intention. Keep it a secret for the moment."

"Take a partner? Divide your beautiful income by two?"

"Yes, Checkley. I am going to give a share in that beautiful income to a young man."

"What can a partner do for you that I can't do? Don't I know the whole of the office work? Is there any partner in the world who can draw up a conveyance better than me?"

"You are very useful, Checkley, as you always have been. But you are not a partner, and you never can be."

"I know that very well. But what's the good of a partner at all?"

"If I have a partner he will have his own room, and he won't interfere with you. There's no occasion for you to be jealous."

"As for jealous—well—after more than sixty years' work in this office it would seem hard to be turned out by some new-comer. But what I say is—what is the good of a partner?"

"The chief good is that the house will be carried on. It is a hundred and twenty years old. I confess I do not like the thought of its coming to an end when I disappear. That will be to me the most important advantage to be gained by taking a partner. The next advantage will be that I can turn over to him a quantity of work. And, thirdly, he will bring young blood and new connections. My mind is quite made up, Checkley. I am going to take a partner."

"Have you found one yet?"

"I have. But I am not going to tell you who he is till the right time comes."

Checkley grumbled inaudibly.

"If I had been less busy," Mr. Dering went on, "I might have married, and had sons of my own to put into the house. But somehow, being very much occupied always, and never thinking about such things, I let the time pass by. I was never, even as a young man, greatly attracted to love or to young women. Their charms, such as they are, seem to me to depend upon nothing but a single garment."

"Take away their frocks," said Checkley, "and what are they? All alike—all alike—I've been married myself—women are expensive frauds."

"Well—things being as they are, Checkley, I am going to take a partner."

"You'll do as you like," said his servant. "Mark my words, however—you've got ten years more of work in you yet, and all through these ten years you'll regret having a partner. Out of every hundred pounds his share will have to come. Think of that!"

"It is eight years, I remember," Mr. Dering went on, "since first I thought of taking a partner. Eight years—and for much the same reason as now. I found my memory going. There were gaps in it—days, or bits of days—which I could not recollect. I was greatly terrified. The man whom I first thought of for partner was that young Arundel, now—"

"Who forged your name. Lucky you didn't have him."

"Who ran away in a rage because certain circumstances seemed to connect him with the crime."

"Seemed? Did connect him."

"Then the symptoms disappeared. Now they have returned, as I told you. I have always regretted the loss of young Arundel. He was clever and a quick worker."

"He was a forger," said the clerk stoutly. "Is there anything more I can do for you?"

"Nothing; thank you."

"Then I'll go. On Saturday afternoon I collect my little rents. Not much in your way of thinking—a good deal to me. I hope you'll like your partner when you do get him. I hope I sha'n't live to see him the master here and you knuckling under. I hope I sha'n't see him driving away the clients."

"I hope you will not see any of these distressing consequences, Checkley. Good-day."

The old clerk went away, shutting the outer door after him. Then the lawyer was the sole occupant of the rooms. He was also the sole occupant of the whole house, and perhaps of the whole square. It was three o'clock.

He sat leaning back in his chair, looking through the open window upon the trees in the square garden. Presently there fell upon his face a curious change. It was as if the whole of the intelligence was taken out of it; his eyes gazed steadily into space, with no expression whatever in them; his lips slightly parted; his head fell back; the soul and spirit of the man had gone out of him, leaving a machine which breathed.

The watch in his pocket ticked audibly—there was no other sound in the room; the old man sat quite motionless.

Four o'clock struck from the clock tower in the high court of justice, from St. Clement's Church, from Westminster, from half a dozen clocks which could be heard in the quiet of the Saturday afternoon. But Mr. Dering heard nothing.

Still he sat in his place with idle hands, and a face like a mask for lack of thought.

The clocks struck five.

He neither moved nor spoke.

The clocks struck six—seven—eight.

The shades of evening began to gather in the corners of the room as the sun sank lower towards his setting. At twilight in the summer there is never anybody to fear—man, woman, or cat —in the chambers, and at that hour the mice come out. They do not eat parchment or foolscap or red tape, but they eat the luncheon crumbs. Mr. Checkley, for instance, always brought his dinner in a paper parcel in his coat-tail pocket, and ate it when so disposed, sprinkling crumbs lavishly — the only lavishment of which he was ever guilty — on the floor. Junior clerks brought buns and biscuits, or even apples, which they devoured furtively.

Mr. Dering himself took his luncheon in his own room, leaving crumbs. There was plenty for a small colony of mice. They came out, therefore, as usual; they stopped at sight of a man, an unwonted man, in a chair. But he moved not; he was asleep; he was dead; they ran without fear all about the rooms.

It was past nine, when the chambers were as dark as at this season of the year they ever are, that Mr. Dering returned to consciousness.

He sat up, staring about him. The room was dark. He looked at his watch. Half-past nine. "What is this?" he asked. "Have I been asleep for seven hours? Seven hours? I was not asleep when Checkley went away. Why did I fall asleep? I feel as if I had been somewhere—doing something. What? I cannot remember. This strange sensation comes oftener. It is time that I should take a partner before something worse happens. I am old—I am old." He rose, and walked across the room erect and with firm step. "I am old and worn-out and spent. Time to give up the keys—old and spent."

CHAPTER III

THE SELECT CIRCLE

At half-past nine on this Saturday evening the parlor of the Salutation Inn, High Holborn, contained most of its customary visitors. They came every evening at eight; they sat till eleven, drinking and talking. In former days every tavern of repute kept such a room for the select circle—a club, or society, of *habitués*, who met every evening for a pipe and a cheerful glass. In this way all respectable burgesses, down to fifty years ago, spent their evenings. Strangers might enter the room, but they were made to feel that they were there on sufferance; they were received with distance and suspicion. Most of the regular visitors knew each other; when they did not, it was tavern politeness not to ask. A case is on record of four cronies, who used the Cock in Fleet Street for thirty years, no one of them knowing either the name or the trade of the other three—yet when one died the other three pined away. This good old custom is now decayed. The respectable burgess stays at home, which is much more monotonous. Yet there may still be found a parlor here and there with a society meeting every evening all the year round.

The parlor of the Salutation was a good-sized room, wainscoted and provided with a sanded floor. It was furnished with a dozen wooden chairs and three small round tables, the chairs disposed in a circle so as to prevent corners or cliques in conversation. Sacred is the fraternity, liberty, and equality of the parlor. The room was low, and in the evenings always hot with its two flaming, unprotected gas-jets; the window was never opened, except in the morning; and there was always present a rich perfume of tobacco, beer, and spirits, both that anciently generated and that of the day's creation.

Among the frequenters — who were, it must be confessed, a somewhat faded or decayed company—was, to put him first, because he was the richest, the great Mr. Robert Hellyer, of Barnard's Inn, usurer or money-lender. Nobody quite likes the profession—one knows not why. Great fortunes have been made in it; the same fortunes have been dissipated by the money-lenders' heirs. Such fortunes do not stick, somehow. Mr. Hellyer, for instance, was reputed wealthy beyond the dreams of the wildest desire. It was also said of him, under breath and in whispers and envious murmurs, that, should a man borrow a five-pound note of him that borrower would count himself lucky if he escaped with the loss of seventy-five, and might generally expect to lose the whole of his household furniture and the half of his income, for the rest of his natural life. To be sure, he sometimes had losses, as he said himself, with a groan—as when an unscrupulous client jumped off the Embankment when he had not paid more than fifty pounds on the original five; or when a wicked man sold off his furniture secretly, in contempt of the bill of sale, and got clean out of the country with his wife and children. But, on the whole, he did pretty well. It was further said, by old clients, that his heart was a simple piece of round granite, for which he had no use, and that he made money out of it by letting it out at so much an hour for a paving mallet.

Mr. Robert Hellyer was not a genial man or a cheerful or a pleasant man to look upon; he neither loved nor comprehended a jest; he never smiled; he kept his mind always employed on the conduct of his business. Every night—forgive the solitary weakness—he drank as much as he could carry. In appearance he was red-faced, thick-necked, and stout; his voice was thick even in the morning, when he was under no compulsion to thickness. It was believed by his friends that his education had been imperfect; this was because he never gave anybody reason to suppose that he had ever received any education at all. To such men as Mr. Hellyer, who every night take much strong drink, and on no occasion whatever take any exercise, sixty is the grand climacteric. He was a year ago just fifty-nine. Alas! he has not even reached his grand climacteric. Already he is gone. He was cut off by pneumonia, or apoplexy, last Christmas. Those who saw the melancholy *cortége* filing out of the narrow gates of Barnard's Inn mournfully remarked that none of his money was taken with him, and asked what happiness he could possibly find in the next world, which he would begin with nothing—nothing at all, not even credit—an absolute pauper.

Mr. Robert Hellyer sat on one side of the empty fireplace. On the opposite side, a great contrast to his coarse and vulgar face, sat an elderly man, tall, thin, dressed in a coat whose sleeves were worn to shininess. His face was dejected; his features were still fine; he was evidently a gentleman. This person was a barrister, decayed and unsuccessful; he lived in a garret in Gray's Inn. There are a good many wrecks at the bar, but few quite so forlorn as this poor old man. He still professed to practise, and picked up a guinea now and then by defending criminals. On these casual fees he managed to live. His clothes were threadbare; it was many years since he had had a great-coat; on rainy and cold days he had a thin cape which he wore over his shoulders. Heaven knows how he dined and breakfasted; every evening, except in the hot days of summer, he came to this place for light and warmth. Unless he was very poor indeed he called for a pint of old and mild, and read the day's paper. Sometimes he talked, but not often; sometimes one or other of the company would offer him a more costly drink, which he always accepted with all that was left to him of courtesy. Outside, he had no friends—they had all forgotten him or died; it is very easy for a poor man to be forgotten. He had no relations—they had all died, emigrated, or dispersed; the relations of the unsuccessful are easily lost. When he talked, he sometimes became animated, and would tell anecdotes of the bar and of the time when he was called, nearly fifty years agone, by the benchers of Gray's Inn. What had become of the hopes and ambitions with which that young man entered upon the profession, which was to lead him to the parlor of the Salutation and the company that gathered there—and to the bare and miserable garret of Gray's Inn, forgotten and alone?

Another man, also elderly, who sat next to the barrister, was a gentleman who sold an excellent business and retired, in order to betake himself more completely to toping. He drank in three taverns during the day. One was in Fleet Street, where he took his chop at three; one was near Drury Lane Theatre, where he dallied with a little whiskey from five to nine; and this was the third. He was a quiet, happy, self-respecting, dignified old man. In the evening he spoke not at all—for sufficient reasons; but he benevolently inclined his head if he was addressed.

Next to him sat a younger man, a solicitor, whose practice consisted of defending prisoners in the police courts; he had with him two friends, and he had a confident swagger which passed for ability. Next to him and his friends was a house-agent, who had been a member for an Irish borough. And there was a gentleman whose wife sang in music halls, so that this fortunate person could—and did—sit about in taverns all day long; his appearance was that of a deboshed City clerk, as he was. Not to mention other members of the company, Checkley was there, occupying a chair next to the money-lender.

Here he was called Mr. Checkley. He came every evening at nine o'clock, Sundays included. Like the money-lender, he wanted his little distractions, and took them in this way. Here, too, he was among those who respected him, not so much on account of his public and private virtues, or for his eminence in the law, as his money. It is not often that a solicitor's clerk becomes a warm man, but then it is not often that one of the calling deliberately proposes to himself early in life to save money, and lives till seventy-five steadily carrying out his object. If you are good at figures you will understand how Mr. Checkley succeeded. Between the ages of eighteen and twenty-five he had an income which averaged about seventy-five pounds; he lived upon fifty pounds a year. From twenty-five to thirty-five he made an average of one hundred and fifty pounds; he still lived upon fifty pounds a year. At thirty-five he was induced by prudential con-

3

siderations to marry; the lady, considerably his senior, had a thousand pounds. She was even more miserly than himself; and in a year or so after marriage she fell into a decline, owing to insufficient nourishment, and presently expired. On the whole, he calculated that he was the better man for the marriage by a thousand pounds. From thirty-five to forty-five his income rose to two hundred pounds; it then for twenty-five years stood at three hundred pounds a year; at the age of seventy Mr. Dering gave him four hundred pounds. Therefore, to sum up, he had put by out of his pay the sum of eleven thousand six hundred and seventy-five pounds—and this without counting the compound interest, always mounting up from his investments, which were all of a careful kind, such as he understood—tenement houses, of which he had a good number; shares in building societies; money lent on bills of sale or on mortgage. At home—Mr. Checkley lived on the ground floor of one of his own houses—he grew more miserly as he grew older. The standard of luxury is not high when fifty pounds a year covers all; but of late he had been trying to keep below even that humble amount. He conducted his affairs in the evening, between his office hours and nine, at his own house or among the people where his property lay. It was in the district visited by few, lying east of Gray's Inn Road; his own house was in a certain small square, a good half of the houses in which belonged to him.

At nine o'clock he arrived at the tavern. Here his drinks cost him nothing. A custom had grown up in the course of years for the money-lender to consult him on the many difficult points which arise in the practice of his profession. He was one of those who like to have one foot over the wall erected by the law, but not both. In other words he was always trying to find out how far the law would allow him to go, and where it called upon him to stop. With this view he schemed perpetually to make his clients sign bonds under the delusion that they meant a hundredth part of what they really did mean. And as, like all ignorant men, he had the most profound belief in the power and the knowledge and the chicanery of lawyers, he was pleased to obtain Checkley's advice in return for Checkley's drinks.

It was a full gathering. The old clerk arrived late; he was gratified at hearing the ex-M.P. whispering to his neighbors that the new arrival was worth his twenty thousand pounds if a penny.

He swelled with honorable pride. Yes. Twenty thousand pounds! And more—more. Who would have thought, when he began as an office-boy, that he could ever achieve so much?

The money-lender, bursting with a new case, real or supposed, took his pipe out of his mouth, and communicated it in a hoarse whisper.

"Suppose—" it began.

"Then," Checkley replied when the case was finished, "you would lay yourself open to a criminal prosecution. Don't you go so much as to think of it. There was a case twenty-five years ago exactly like it. The remarks of the judge were most severe, and the sentence was heavy."

"Ah!" The usurer's red face grew redder. "Then it can't be thought of. Pity, too. There's a houseful of furniture and a shopful of stuff. And a young man as it would do good to him just to start fair again. Pity. Put a name to it, Mr. Checkley."

"Rum—hot—with lemon," replied the sage. "You get more taste in your mouth, more upliftin' for your heart as they say, more strengthenin' for the stomach, better value all round for your money out of rum than any other drink that I know."

At this point, and before the waiter could execute the order, voices and steps were heard outside the room—the voices of two men. That of one loud, eager, noisy. That of the other quiet, measured, and calm.

Checkley sat upright suddenly, and listened.

"That is young Cambridge," said the old barrister. "I thought he would be here—Saturday night and all." He smiled, as if expectant of something, and drank off the rest of his beer at a draught.

"Most distinguished Cambridge man," whispered the ex-M.P. to his neighbors. "Wanst a Fellow of Cambridge College. Great scholar. Ornament to any circle. Dhrinks like an oyster. Son of a bishop, too—son of an Irish bishop—talks Greek like English. He'll come in directly. He's taking something outside. He's always half dhrunk to begin, and quite dhrunk to finish. But he only talks the better—being Oirish. Most remarkable man."

The voice of this distinguished person Checkley knew. But the other voice—that he knew as well. And he could not remember whose voice it was. Very well, indeed, he remembered the sound of it. Some men never forget a face; some men never forget a shape or figure; some men never forget a voice; some men never forget a handwriting. A voice is the simplest thing, after all, to remember, and the most unchanging. From eighteen till eighty a man's voice changes not, save that in volume it decreases during the last decade; the distinguishing quality of the voice remains the same to the end.

"Have a drink, my dear fellow." That was the voice of the pride of Cambridge.

"Thanks. I don't want a drink."

Whose voice was it? Checkley sat up, eager for the door to be opened and that doubt to be resolved.

It was opened. The two men came in, first the Cambridge man, leading the way. He was a good-looking, smooth-faced man of thirty-two or so, with bright blue eyes—too bright—a fine face, full of delicacy and mobility, a high, narrow forehead, and quick, sensitive lips; a man who was obviously in want of some one to take him in hand and control him; one of those men who have no will of their own, and fall naturally before any temptation which assails them. The chief temptation which assailed Freddy Carstone—it seems to stamp the man that his friends all called him Freddy; a Freddy is amiable, weak, beloved, and given to err, slip, fall, and give way—was the temptation to drink. He was really, as the ex-M.P. told his neighbors, a very fine scholar; he had been a fellow of his college, but never received any appointment or office of lecturer there, on account of this weakness of his, which was notorious. When his fellowship expired he came to London, lived in Gray's Inn, and took pupils. He had the reputation of being an excellent coach if he could be caught sober. He was generally sober in the morning, often a little elevated in the afternoon, and always cheerfully—not stupidly—drunk at night.

"You must have a drink," Freddy repeated. "Not want a drink? Hang it! old man, it isn't what you want, it's what you like. If I only took what I wanted I should be—what should I be? Fellow and tutor of the college—very likely master—most probably archdeacon — certainly bishop. Wasn't my father a bishop? Now, if you take what you like, as well as what you want — what happens? You go easily and comfortably downhill—down—down—down—like me. Tobogganing isn't easier; the switchback railway isn't more pleasant. Always take what you like."

"No—no, Freddy; thanks."

"What? You've got ambitions still? You want to be climbing? Man alive! it's too late. You've stayed away from your friends too long. You can't get up. Better join us at the Salutation Club. Come in with me. I'll introduce you. They'll be glad to have you. Intellectual conversation carried on nightly. Romantic scenery from the back window. Finest parlor in London. Come in, and sample the Scotch. Not want a drink? Who ever saw a man who didn't want a drink?"

The other man followed reluctantly, and at sight of him Cheekley jumped in his chair. Then he snatched the paper from the hands of the ancient barrister and buried his head in it. The action was most remarkable and unmistakable. He hid himself behind the paper. For the man whom the Cambridge scholar was dragging into the room was none other than Athelstan Arundel—the very man of whom Mr. Dering had been speaking that very afternoon; the very man whose loss he had been regretting; the man accused by himself of forgery. So great was his terror at the sight of this man that he was fain to hide behind the paper.

Yes, the same man; well dressed, apparently, and prosperous—in a velvet jacket and a white waistcoat, with a big brown beard—still carrying himself with that old insolent pride, as if he had never forged anything; looking not a day older, in spite of the eight years that had elapsed. What was he doing here?

"Come in, man," said Freddy, again. "You shall have one drink at least, and as many more as you like. Robert, two Scotch and soda. We haven't met for eight long years. Let us sit down and confess our sins for eight years. Where have you been?"

"For the most part—abroad."

"You don't look it. He who goes abroad to make his fortune always comes home in rags, with a pistol in his coat-tail and a bowie-knife in his belt—at least we are taught so. You wear velvet and fine linen. You haven't been abroad. I don't believe you've been farther than Camberwell. In fact, Camberwell has been your headquarters. You've been living in Camberwell—on

Camberwell Green, which is a slice of Eden, with—perhaps—didn't pretty Polly Perkins live on Camberwell Green?—for eight long years."

"Let me call upon you in your lodgings, where we can talk."

"I haven't got any lodgings. I am in chambers—I live all by myself in Gray's Inn. Come and see me. I am always at home in the mornings—to pupils only—and generally at home in the afternoon to pupils and topers and lushingtons. Here's your whiskey. Sit down. Let me introduce you to the company. This is a highly intellectual society—not what you would expect of a Holborn parlor. It is a club which meets here every evening—a first-class club. Subscription, nothing. Entrance fee, nothing. Order what you like. Don't pretend not to know your brother-members. Gentlemen, this is my old friend, Mr. Athelstan Arundel, who has been abroad—on Camberwell Green, for the sake of Polly Perkins—for eight years, and has now returned."

The ex-M.P. nudged his neighbors to call their attention to something good. The rest received the introduction and the remarks which followed in silence.

"Arundel, the gentleman by the fireplace—he with the pipe—is our Shylock, sometimes called the Lord Shylock." The money-lender looked up with a dull and unintelligent eye; I believe the allusion was entirely above his comprehension. "Beside him is Mr. Vulpes—he with his head buried in the paper—you'll see him presently. Mr. Vulpes is advanced in years, but well preserved, and knows every letter of the law; he is, indeed, an ornament of the lower branch. Vulpes will let you a house—he has many most charming residences—or will advance you money on mortgage. He knows the law of landlord and tenant, and the law regarding bills of sale. I recommend Vulpes to your friendly consideration. Here is Senex Bibulus Benevolens." The old gentleman kindly inclined his head, being too far gone for speech. "Here is a most learned counsel, who ought, had merit prevailed, to have been by this time lord chancellor, chief justice, judge, or master of the rolls—or queen's counsel at least. So far he is still a junior, but we hope for his speedy advancement. Sir, I entreat the honor of offering you a goblet of more generous drink. Robert, Irish whiskey and a lemon for this gentleman. There"—he pointed to the ex-M.P., who again nudged his neighbors and grinned—" is our legislator and statesman, the pride of his constituents, the darling of Ballynacuddery till they turned him out. There "—he pointed to the deboshed clerk—" is a member of a great modern profession, a gentleman with whom it is indeed a pride to sit down. He is Monsieur le Mari— *Monsieur le Mari complaisant et content.*"

" I don't know what you mean," said the gentleman indicated. " If you want to talk Greek, talk it outside."

" I cannot stay," said Athelstan, looking about the room with scant respect. " I will call upon you at your chambers."

" Do — do, my dear fellow." Athelstan shook hands, and walked away. " Now, there's a man, gentlemen, who might have done anything—anything he might have done. Rowed stroke to his boat. Threw up everything eight years ago, and went away—nobody knew why. Sad to see so much promise wasted. Sad—sad. He hasn't even touched his drink. Then I must—myself." And he did.

Observe that there is no such lamentation over the failure of a promising young man as from one who has also failed. For, by a merciful arrangement, the failure seldom suspects himself of having failed.

" Now, Mr. Checkley," said the barrister, " he's gone away, and you needn't hide yourself any longer—and you can let me have my paper again."

Mr. Checkley spoke no more that evening. He drank up his rum-and-water, and he went away mightily perturbed. That Athelstan Arundel had come back portended that something would happen. And, like King Cole's prophet, he could not foretell the nature of the event.

CHAPTER IV

A REBELLIOUS CHILD

ELSIE left her lover at the door. Most accepted suitors accompany their sweethearts into the very bosom of the family—the *gynæceum*—the parlor, as it used to be called. Not so George

Austin. Since the engagement—the deplorable engagement—it was understood that he was not to presume upon entering the house. Romeo might as well have sent in his card to Juliet's mamma. In fact, that lady could not possibly have regarded the pretensions of Romeo more unfavorably than Mrs. Arundel did those of George Austin. This not on account of any family inequality, for his people were no more decidedly of the middle class than her own. That is to say, they numbered as many members who were presentable, and quite as many who were not. Our great middle class is pretty well alike in this respect. In every household there are things which may be paraded and things *lucenda*—members successful, members unsuccessful, members disgraceful. All the world knows all the things which must be concealed; we all know that all the world knows them; but still we pretend that there are no such things, and so we maintain the family dignity. Nor could the widow object to George on account of his religious opinions, in which he dutifully followed his forefathers; or of his abilities, manners, morals, culture, accomplishments, or outward appearance, in all of which he was everything that could be expected of a young man who had his own fortune to make. A rich young man has no need of manners, morals, abilities, or accomplishments—a thing too often forgotten by satirists when they depict the children of Sir Midas Gorgias and his tribe. The lady's objection was simply and most naturally that the young man had nothing, and would probably never have anything; that he was a managing clerk, without money to buy a partnership, in a highly congested profession. To aggravate this objection, he stood in the way of two most desirable suitors who were supposed to be ready should Elsie give them any encouragement. They were a rich old man, whose morals could no longer be questioned; and a rich young man, whose morals would doubtless improve with marriage—if, that is, they wanted improvement, for on this delicate subject ladies find it difficult to get reliable information. And, again, the exalted position of the elder sister should have been an example and a beacon. Which of you, mesdames, would look on with patience to such a sacrifice—a young and lovely daughter thrown away, with all her charms and all her chances, upon a man with two hundred pounds a year and no chance of anything much better? Think of it—two hundred pounds a year—for a gentlewoman!

There are some families—many families—with whom the worship of wealth is hereditary. The Arundels have been City people, married with other City people—in trade—for two hundred years and more ; they are all members of City companies; there have been lord mayors and sheriffs among them ; some of them —for they are now a clan—are rich ; some are very rich ; one or two are very, very rich ; those who fail and go bankrupt quickly drop out of sight. All their traditions are of money-getting ; they estimate success and worth and respect by the amount a man leaves behind—it is the good old tradition ; they talk of money ; they are not vulgar, or loud, or noisy, or disagreeable in any way, but they openly and without disguise worship the great god Plutus, and believe that he, and none other, is the God of the Christians. They have as much culture as other people, at least to outward show ; they furnish their houses as artistically as other people ; they buy pictures and books ; but ideas do not touch them ; if they read new ideas they are not affected by them, however skilfully they may be put ; they go to church and hear the parable about Dives, and they wonder how Dives could have been so hard-hearted. Then they go home, and talk about money.

Elsie's father, a younger son of the richest branch of this family, started with a comfortable little fortune and a junior partnership. He was getting on very well indeed ; he had begun to show the stuff of which he was made—a good, stout, tenacious kind of stuff, likely to last and to hold out ; he was beginning to increase his fortune ; he looked forward to a successful career ; and he hoped to leave behind him, after many, many years, perhaps three quarters of a million. He was only thirty-five years of age, yet he was struck down and had to go. His widow received little more than her husband's original fortune ; it was small compared with what she might fairly expect when she married, but it was large enough for her to live with her three children in Pembridge Square. What happened to the son, you know. He went away in a royal rage, and had never been heard of since. The elder daughter, Hilda, when about two-and-twenty, as you also know, had the good fortune to attract the admiration of a widower of very considerable wealth, the brother of her guardian. He was thirty-five years older than herself, but he was rich—nay, very rich indeed. Jute, I believe, on an extensive scale, was the

3*

cause of his great fortune.   He was knighted on a certain great occasion when warden of his company, so that he offered his bride a title and precedence, as well as a great income, a mansion in Palace Gardens, a handsome settlement, carriages and horses, and everything else that the feminine heart can desire.

The widow, soon after her husband died, found the time extremely dull without the daily excitement of the City talk to which she had been accustomed.   There was no one with whom she could discuss the money market.   Now, all her life she had been accustomed to talk of shares, and stocks, and investments, and fluctuations, and operations, and buying in and selling out.   She began, therefore, to watch the market on her own account.   Then she began to operate; then she gave her whole time and all her thoughts to the business of studying, watching, reading, and forecasting.   Of course, then, she lost her money, and fell into difficulties?   Nothing of the kind—she made money.   There is always plenty of virtuous indignation ready for those foolish persons who dabble in stocks.   They are gamblers; they always lose in the long run—we all know that, the copy-books tell us so. If two persons play heads-and-tails for sovereigns, do they both lose in the long run ?   If so, who wins?   Where does the money go ?   Even a gambler need not always lose in the long run, as all gamblers know.   *La Veuve* Arundel was not in any sense a gambler.   Nor was she a dabbler.   She was a serious and calculating operator.   She took up one branch of the great money market, and confined her attentions to that branch, which she studied with so much care and assiduity that she became a professional; that is to say, she threw into the study all her energies, all her thoughts, and all her intellect.   When a young man does this on the Stock Exchange he may expect to win.   Mrs. Arundel was not an ordinary young man—she was a sharp and clever woman; by hard work she had learned all that can be learned, and had acquired some of that prescience which comes of knowledge—the prophet of the future is, after all, he who knows and can discuss the forces and the facts of the present; the Sibyl at the present day would be a journalist.   She was clear-headed, quick to see, and ready to act; she was of a quick temper as well as a quick perception; and she was resolute.   Such qualities in most women make them absolute sovereigns in the household. Mrs. Arundel was not an absolute sovereign—partly because she thought little of her household, and partly because her children were distinguished by much the same qualities, and their subjection would have proved difficult if not impossible.

This was the last house in London where one might have expected to find a girl who was ready to despise wealth and to find her happiness in a condition of poverty. Elsie was completely out of harmony with all her own people. There is a good deal of opinion going about in favor of the simple life; many girls have become Socialists in so far as they think the amassing of wealth neither desirable nor worthy of respect; many would rather marry a man of limited means who has a profession than a rich man who has a business; many girls hold that art is a much finer thing than wealth. Elsie learned these pernicious sentiments at school; they attracted her at first because they were so fresh; she found all the best literature full of these sentiments; she developed in due course a certain natural ability for art; she attended an art school; she set up an easel; she painted in pastel; she called her room a studio. She gave her friends the greatest uneasiness by her opinions; she ended, as you have seen, by becoming engaged to a young man with nothing. How could such a girl be born of such parents?

When she got home on Saturday evening she found her mother playing a game of double *vingt-et-un* with a certain cousin, one Sydney Arundel. The game is very good for the rapid interchange of coins; you should make it a time game, to end in half an hour—one hour—two hours, and at the end you will find that you have had a very pretty little gamble. Mrs. Arundel liked nothing better than a game of cards—provided the stakes were high enough to give it excitement. To play cards for love is indeed insipid—it is like a dinner of cold boiled mutton or like sandwiches of veal. The lady would play anything—piquet, écarté, double dummy—and her daughter Elsie hated the sight of cards. As for the cousin, he was on the Stock Exchange; he came often to dinner, and to talk business after dinner; he was a kind of musical box or barrel organ in conversation, because he could only play one tune. His business as well as his pleasure was in the money market.

"So you have come home, Elsie?" said Mrs. Arundel, coldly.

"Yes, I have come home." Elsie seated herself at the window, and waited.

"Now, Sydney"—her mother took up the cards—"my deal; will you take any more?"

She was a good-looking woman still, though past fifty—her abundant hair had gone pleasantly gray, her features were fine, her brown eyes were quick and bright; her lips were firm, and her chin straight. She was tall and of good figure; she was clad in black silk, with a large gold chain about her neck and good lace upon her shoulders. She wore many rings and a bracelet. She liked, in fact, the appearance of wealth as well as the possession of it; she therefore always appeared in costly raiment; her house was furnished with a costly solidity; everything, even the bindings of her books, was good to look at; her one man-servant looked like the responsible butler of a millionaire, and her one-horse carriage looked as if it belonged to a dozen.

The game went on. Presently the clock struck ten. "Time," said the lady. "We must stop. Now then. Let us see—I make it seventy-three shillings. Thank you. Three pounds thirteen—an evening not altogether wasted. And now, Sydney, light your cigar—you know I like it. You shall have your whiskey-and-soda, and we will talk business. There are half a dozen things that I want to consult you about. Heavens! why cannot I be admitted to the Exchange? A few women among you—clever women, like myself, Sydney—would wake you up."

They talked business for an hour, the lady making notes in a little book, asking questions and making suggestions. At last the cousin got up—it was eleven o'clock—and went away. Then her mother turned to Elsie.

"It is a great pity," she said, "that you take no interest in these things."

"I dislike them very much, as you know," said Elsie.

"Yes—you dislike them because they are of real importance. Well—never mind. You have been out with the young man, I suppose?"

"Yes—we have been on the river together."

"I supposed it was something of the kind. So the house-maid keeps company with the pot-boy without consulting her own people?"

"It is nothing unusual for me to spend an evening with George. Why not? You will not suffer me to bring him here."

"No," said her mother, with firmness. "That young man shall

never, under any circumstances, enter this house with my knowledge! For the rest," she added, "do as you please."

This was the kind of amiable conversation that had been going on day after day since Elsie's engagement—protestations of ceasing to interfere, and continual interference.

There are many ways of considering the subject of injudicious and unequal marriages. You may ridicule; you may cajole; you may argue; you may scold; you may coax; you may represent the naked truth as it is, or you may clothe its limbs with lies— the lies are of woven stuff, strong, and home-made. When you have an obdurate, obstinate, contumacious, headstrong, wilful, self-contained maiden to deal with, you will waste your breath whatever you do. The mother treated Elsie with scorn, and scorn alone. It was her only weapon. Her elder sister tried other weapons—she laughed at the makeshifts of poverty; she cajoled with soft flattery and golden promises; she argued with logic pitiless; she scolded like a fishwife; she coaxed with tears and kisses; she painted the loveliness of men who are rich, and the power of women who are beautiful. And all in vain. Nothing moved this obdurate, obstinate, contumacious, headstrong, wilful Elsie. She would stick to her promise; she would wed her lover even if she had to entertain poverty as well all her life.

"Are you so infatuated," the mother went on, "that you cannot see that he cares nothing for your happiness? He thinks about nobody but himself. If he thought of you he would see that he was too poor to make you happy, and he would break it off. As it is, all he wants is to marry you."

"That is, indeed, all. He has never disguised the fact."

"He offers you the half of a bare crust."

"By halving the crust we shall double it."

"Oh! I have no patience. But there is an end. You know my opinion, and you disregard it. I cannot lock you up, or beat you, for your foolishness. I almost wish I could. I will neither reason with you any more nor try to dissuade you. Go your own way."

"If you would only understand. We are going to live very simply. We shall put all unhappiness outside the luxuries of life. And we shall get on, if we never get rich. I wish I could make you understand our point of view. It makes me very unhappy that you will take such a distorted view."

"I am glad that you can still feel unhappiness at such a cause as my displeasure."

"Well, mother, to-night we have come to a final decision."

"Am I to learn it?"

"Yes—I wish to tell you at once. We have been engaged for two years. The engagement has brought me nothing but wretchedness at home. But I should be still more wretched—I should be wretched all my life—if I were to break it off. I shall be of age in a day or two, and free to act on my own judgment."

"You are acting on your own judgment already."

"I have promised George that I will marry him when he pleases—that is, about the middle of August, when he gets his holiday."

"Oh! The misery of poverty will begin so soon? I am sorry to hear it. As I said before, I have nothing to say against it—no persuasion or dissuasion; you will do as you please."

"George has his profession, and he has a good name already. He will get on. Meantime, a little plain living will hurt neither of us. Can't you think that we may begin in a humble way and yet get on? Money—money—money. Oh! Must we think of nothing else?"

"What is there to think of but money? Look round you, silly child! What gives me this house—this furniture—everything? Money. What feeds you and clothes you? Money. What gives position, consideration, power, dignity? Money. Rank without money is contemptible. Life without money is miserable, wretched, intolerable. Who would care to live when the smallest luxury—the least comfort—has to be denied for want of money. Even the art of which you talk so much only becomes respectable when it commands money. You cannot keep off disease without money; you cannot educate your children without money; it will be your worst punishment in the future that your children will sink and become servants. Child!" she cried passionately, "we must be masters or servants—nay, lords or slaves. You leave the rank of lord and marry the rank of slave. It is money that makes the difference—money—money —money—that you pretend to despise. It is money that has done everything for you. Your grandfather made it—your father made it—I am making it. Go on in your madness and your folly. In the end, when it is too late, you will long for money, pray for money, be ready to do anything for money—for your husband and your children."

"We shall have, I hope, enough. We shall work for enough —no more."

"Well, child," her mother returned quietly, "I said that I would say nothing. I have been carried away. Let there be no more said. Do as you please. You know my mind—your sister's mind—your cousins'—"

"I do not wish to be guided by my cousins."

"Very well. You will stay here until your wedding-day. When you marry, you will leave this house—and me and your sister and all your people. Do not expect any help from me. Do not look forward to any inheritance from me. My money is all my own, to do with as I please. If you wish to be poor, you shall be poor. Hilda tells me that you are to see your guardian on Monday. Perhaps he may bring you to your senses. As for me, I shall say no more."

With these final words the lady left the room and went to bed. How many times had she declared that she would say no more?

The next day being Sunday, the bells began to ring in the morning, and the two ladies sallied forth to attend divine service as usual. They walked side by side in silence. That sweet and gracious nymph, the Lady Charity, was not with them in their pew. The elder lady, externally cold, was full of resentment and bitterness; the younger was more than usually troubled by the outbreak of the evening before. Yet she was no nearer surrender. The sermon, by a curious coincidence, turned upon the perishable nature of earthly treasures, and the vanity of the objects desired by that unreasoning person whom they used to call the worldling. The name has perished, but the creature still exists, and is found in countless herds in every great town. The parsons are always trying to shoot him down, but they never succeed. There was just a fiery passage or two directed against the species. Elsie hoped that the words would go home. Not at all. They fell upon her mother's heart like seed upon the rock. She heard them, but heeded them not. The worldling, you see, never understands that he is a worldling. Nor does Dives believe himself to be anything more than Lazarus, such is his modesty.

The service over, they went home in silence. They took their early dinner in silence, waited on by the solemn man-servant.

After dinner, Elsie sought the solitude of her studio. And here —nobody looking on—she obeyed the first law of her sex, and had a good cry. Even the most resolute of maidens cannot carry through a great scheme against great opposition without the consolation of a cry.

On the table lay a note from Mr. Dering:

"My DEAR WARD,—I am reminded that you come of age on Monday. I am also reminded by Hilda that you propose to take a very important step against the wish of your mother. Will you come and see me at ten o'clock to talk this over? Your affectionate guardian."

Not much hope to be got out of that letter. A dry note from a dry man. Very little doubt as to the line which he would take. Yet, not an unkind letter. She put it back in her desk, and sighed. Another long discussion. No, she would not discuss— she would listen, and then state her intention. She would listen again, and once more state her intention.

On the easel stood an almost finished portrait in pastel, executed from a photograph. It was the portrait of her guardian. She had caught—it was not difficult with a face so marked—the set expression, the closed lips, the keen eyes, and the habitual look of caution and watchfulness which become the characteristics of a solicitor in good practice. So far it was a good likeness. But it was an austere face. Elsie, with a few touches of her thumb and the chalk which formed her material, softened the lines of the mouth, communicated to the eyes a more genial light, and to the face an expression of benevolence which certainly had never before been seen upon it.

"There!" she said. "If you would only look like that to-morrow, instead of like your photograph, I should have no fear at all of what you would say. I would flatter you, and coax you, and cajole you, till you had doubled George's salary and promised to get round my mother. You dear old man! You kind old man! You sweet old man! I could kiss you for your kindness."

CHAPTER V

SOMETHING HAPPENS

So far a truly enjoyable Sunday. To sit in church beside her angry mother, both going through the forms of repentance, charity, and forgiveness; and to dine together, going through the ordinary forms of kindliness while one, at least, was devoured with wrath—waste of good roast lamb and gooseberry tart!

Elsie spent the afternoon in her studio, where she sat undisturbed. People called, but her mother received them. Now that the last resolution had been taken; now that she had promised her lover to brave everything and to live the simplest possible life for love's sweet sake, she felt that sinking which falls upon the most courageous when the boats are burned. Thus Love makes loving hearts to suffer.

The evening, however, made amends. For then, like the housemaid, who mounted the area stair as Elsie went down the front door-steps, she went forth to meet her lover, and in his company forgot all her fears. They went to church together. There they sat side by side, this church not having adopted the barbarous custom of separating the sexes—a custom which belongs to the time when women were monkishly considered unclean creatures, and the cause, to most men, of everlasting suffering, which they themselves would most justly share. This couple sat hand in hand; the service was full of praise and hope and trust; the psalms were exultant, triumphant, jubilant; the sermon was a ten minutes' ejaculation of joy and thanks; there was a procession with banners, to cheer up the hearts of the faithful—what is faith without a procession? Comfort stole back to Elsie's troubled heart; she felt less like an outcast; she came out of the church with renewed confidence.

It was still daylight. They walked round and round the nearest square. Jane, the house-maid, and her young man were doing the same thing. They talked with confidence and joy of the future before them.   Presently the rain began to fall, and Elsie's spirits fell too.

"George," she said, "are we selfish—each of us?   Is it right for me to drag and keep you down?"

"You will not.   You will raise me and keep me up.   Never doubt that, Elsie.   I am the selfish one, because I make you sacrifice so much."

"Oh no—no!   It is no sacrifice for me.   You must make me brave, George, because I am told every day by Hilda and my mother the most terrible things.   I have been miserable all day long.   I suppose it is the battle I had with my mother yesterday."

"Your mother will be all right again as soon as the thing is done.   And Hilda will come round too.   She will want to show you her new carriage and her newest dress.   Nobody admires and envies the rich relation so much as the poor relation.   That is the reason why the poor relation is so much courted and petted in every rich family.   We shall be the poor relations, you know, Elsie."

"I suppose so.   We must accept the part and play it properly." She spoke gayly, but with an effort.

"She will give you some of her old dresses.   And she will ask us to some of her crushes—but we won't go.   Oh! Hilda will come round.   As for your mother"—he repressed what he was about to say—"as for your mother, Elsie, there is no obstinacy so desperate that it cannot be softened by something or other.   The constant dropping, you know.   Give her time.   If she refuses to change—why—then "—again he changed the words in time—"dear child! we must make our own happiness for ourselves without our own folk to help us."

"Yes, we will.   At the same time, George, though I am so valiant in talk, I confess that I feel as low as a school-boy who is going to be punished."

"My dear Elsie," said George, with a little exasperation, "if they will not come round, let them stay flat, or square, or sulky, or anything.   I can hardly be expected to feel very anxious for a change of temper in people who have said so many hard things of me.   To-morrow, dear, you shall get through your talk with Mr. Dering.   He's as hard as nails; but he's a just man, and he is sensible.   In the evening I will call for you at nine, and you shall tell me what he said.   In six weeks we can be married.   I will see about the banns. We will find a lodging somewhere, pack up our things, get married, and move in. We can't afford a honeymoon, I am afraid. That shall come afterwards, when the ship comes home."

"Yes. When I am with you I fear nothing. It is when you are gone—when I sit by myself in my own room, and know that in the next room my mother is brooding over her wrath and keeping it warm—that I feel so guilty. To-night it is not that I feel guilty at all—it is quite the contrary; but I feel as if something were going to happen."

"Something *is* going to happen, dear. I am going to put a wedding-ring round this pretty finger."

"When one says 'something,' in the language of superstition one means something bad, something dreadful, something that shall stand between us and force us apart, something unexpected."

"My child," said her lover, "all the powers of all the devils shall not force us apart"—a daring and comprehensive boast.

She laughed a little, lightened by words so brave. "Here we are, dear," she said, as they arrived at the house. "I think the rain means to come down in earnest. You had better make haste home. To-morrow evening, at nine, I will expect you."

She ran lightly up the steps, and rang the bell; the door was opened; she turned her head, laughed, waved her hand to her lover, and ran in.

There was standing on the curb beneath the street-lamp a man apparently engaged in lighting a cigar. When the girl turned the light of the lamp fell full upon her face. The man stared at her, forgetting his cigar light, which fell burning from his hand into the gutter. When the door shut upon her he stared at George, who, for his part, his mistress having vanished, stared at the door.

All this staring occupied a period of at least half a minute. Then George turned, and walked away; the man struck another light, lit his cigar, and strode away too, but in the same direction. Presently he caught up with George, and laid a hand upon his shoulder.

"Here, you sir," he said gruffly; "I want a word with you before we go any further."

George turned upon him savagely. Nobody likes a heavy hand

laid upon his shoulder. In the old days it generally meant a writ and Whitecross Street, and other unpleasant things.

"Who the devil are you?" he asked.

"That is the question I was going—" He stopped and laughed. "No—I see now. I don't want to ask it. You are George Austin, are you not?"

"That is my name. But who are you, and what do you want with me?"

The man was a stranger to him. He was dressed in a velvet coat and a white waistcoat; he wore a soft felt hat; and, with the velvet jacket, the felt hat, and a full beard, he looked like an artist of some kind. At the end of June it is still light at half-past nine. George saw that the man was a gentleman; his features, strongly marked and clear cut, reminded him of something—but vaguely; they gave him the common feeling of having been seen or known at some remote period. The man looked about thirty, the time when the physical man is at his best; he was of good height, well set up, and robust. Something, no doubt, in the art world, or something that desired to appear as if belonging to the art world. Because, you see, the artists themselves are not so picturesque as those who would be artists if they could. The unsuccessful artist, certainly, is sometimes a most picturesque creature. So is the model. The rags and duds and threadbarity too often enter largely into the picturesque. So with the plough-boy's dinner under the hedge or the cotter's Saturday night. And the village beer-shop may make a very fine picture, but the artist himself does not partake in those simple joys.

"Well, sir, who are you?" George repeated, as the other man made no reply.

"Do you not remember me? I am waiting to give you a chance."

"No—certainly not."

"Consider. That house into which you have just taken my—a young lady—does it not connect itself with me?"

"No. Why should it?"

"Then I suppose that I am completely forgotten?"

"It is very strange. I seem to recall your voice."

"I will tell you who I am by another question. George Austin, what in thunder are you doing with my sister?"

"Your sister?" George jumped up, and stared. "Your sister?

Are you—are you Athelstan come home again? Really and truly Athelstan?"

"I am really and truly Athelstan. I have been back in England about a fortnight."

"You are Athelstan?" George looked at him curiously. When the reputed black sheep comes home again it is generally in rags, with a long story of fortune's persecutions. This man was not in the least ragged. On the contrary, he looked prosperous. What had he been doing? For although Elsie continued passionate in her belief in her brother's innocence, everybody else believed that he had run away to escape consequences, and George among the number had accepted that belief.

"Your beard alters you greatly. I should not have known you. To be sure, it is eight years since I saw you last, and I was only just beginning my articles when you—left us." He was on the point of saying, "when you ran away."

"There is a good deal to talk about. Will you come with me to my rooms? I am putting up in Half Moon Street."

Athelstan hailed a passing hansom, and they drove off.

"You have been a fortnight in London," said George, "and yet you have not been to see your own people."

"I have been eight years away, and yet I have not written a single letter to my own people?"

George asked no more questions. Arrived at the lodging, they went in and sat down. Athelstan produced soda-and-whiskey and cigars.

"Why have I not called upon my own people?"—Athelstan took up the question again—"because, when I left home I swore that I would never return until they came to beg forgiveness. That is why. Every evening I have been walking outside the house, in the hope of seeing some of them without their seeing me. For, you see, I should like to go home again; but I will not go as I went away, under a shameful cloud. That has got to be lifted first. Presently I shall know whether it is lifted. Then I shall know how to act. To-night I was rewarded by the sight of my sister Elsie, walking home with you. I knew her at once. She is taller than I thought she would become when I went away. Her face hasn't changed much, though. She always had the gift of sweet looks, which isn't quite the same thing as beauty. My sister Hilda, for instance, was always called a handsome girl, but she never had Elsie's sweet looks."

"She has the sweetest looks in the world."

"What are you doing with her, George Austin, I ask again?"

"We are engaged to be married."

"Married? Elsie married? Why—she's—well, I suppose she must be grown up by this time."

"Elsie is very nearly one-and-twenty. She will be twenty-one to-morrow."

"Elsie going to be married. It seems absurd. One-and-twenty to-morrow. Ah!" He sat up eagerly. "Tell me, is she any richer? Has she had any legacies or things?"

"No. How should she? Her *dot* is her sweet self, which is enough for any man."

"And you, Austin? I remember you were an articled clerk of eighteen or nineteen when I went away—are you rich?"

Austin blushed. "No," he said, "I am not. I am a managing clerk at your old office. I get two hundred a year, and we are going to marry on that."

Athelstan nodded. "A bold thing to do. However— Twenty-one to-morrow—we shall see."

"And I am sorry to say there is the greatest opposition—on the part of your mother and your other sister. I am not allowed in the house, and Elsie is treated as a rebel."

"Oh, well! If you see your way, my boy, get married, and have a happy life, and leave them to come round at their leisure. Elsie has a heart of gold. She can believe in a man. She is the only one of my people who stood up for me when they accused me, without a shadow of proof, of— The only one—the only one. It is impossible for me to forget that—and difficult," he added, "to forgive the other thing. Is my sister Hilda still at home?"

"No. She is married to Sir Samuel, brother of your Mr. Dering. He is a great deal older than his wife—but he is very rich."

"Oh! And my mother?"

"I believe she continues in good health. I am not allowed the privilege of calling upon her."

"And my old chief?"

"He also continues well."

"And now, since we have cleared the ground so far, let us come to business. How about that robbery?"

"What robbery?" The old business had taken place when

George was a lad just entering upon his articles. He had ceased to think of it.

"What robbery? Man alive!"—Athelstan sprang to his feet—"there is only one robbery to me in the whole history of the world since men and robberies began. What robbery? Look here, Master George Austin, when a man is charged with murder there is for that man only one murder in the whole history of the world. All the other murders, even that of Abel himself, are of no concern at all —not one bit. He isn't interested in them. They don't matter to him a red cent. That's my case. The robbery of eight years ago, which took a few hundred pounds from a rich man, changed my whole life; it drove me out into the world; it forced me for a time to live among the prodigals and the swine and the husks. It handed me over to a thousand devils, and you ask me what robbery?"

"I am very sorry. It is now a forgotten thing. Nobody remembers it any more. I doubt whether Mr. Dering himself ever thinks of it."

"Well, what was discovered, after all? Who did it?"

"Nothing at all has been discovered. No one knows to this day who did it."

"Nothing at all? I am disappointed. Hasn't old Checkley done time for it? Nothing found out?"

"Nothing. The notes were stopped in time, and were never presented. After a few years the Bank of England gave Mr. Dering notes in the place of those stolen. And that is all there is to tell."

"Nothing discovered! And the notes never presented? What good did the fellow get by it, then?"

"I don't know, but nothing was discovered."

"Nothing discovered," Athelstan repeated. "Why, I took it for granted that the truth had come out long since. I was making up my mind to call upon old Dering—I don't think I shall go now. And my sister Hilda will not be coming here to express her contrition—I am disappointed."

"You can see Elsie if you like."

"Yes—I can see her," he repeated. "George"—he returned to the old subject—"do you know the exact particulars of that robbery?"

"There was a forged check, and the bank paid it across the counter."

"The check," Athelstan explained, "was made payable to the order of a certain unknown person named Edmund Gray. It was endorsed by that name. To prove that forgery they should have got the check and examined the endorsement. That was the first thing, certainly. I wonder how they began."

"I do not know. It was while I was in my articles, and all we heard was a vague report. You ought not to have gone away. You should have stayed to fight it out."

"I was right to give up my berth after what the chief said. How could I remain, drawing his pay and doing his work, when he had calmly given me to understand that the forgery lay between two hands, and that he strongly suspected mine!"

"Did Mr. Dering really say so? Did he go so far as that?"

"So I walked out of the place. I should have stayed at home, and waited for the clearing-up of the thing, but for my own people—who—well, you know— So I went away in a rage."

"And have you come back—as you went—in a rage?"

"Well, you see, that is the kind of fire that keeps alight of its own accord."

"I believe that some sort of a search was made for this Edmund Gray, but I do not know how long it lasted or who was employed."

"Detectives are no good. Perhaps the chief didn't care to press the business. Perhaps he learned enough to be satisfied that Checkley was the man. Perhaps he was unwilling to lose an old servant. Perhaps the villain confessed the thing. It all comes back to me fresh and clear, though for eight long years I have not talked with a soul about it."

"Tell me," said George, a little out of sympathy with this dead-and-buried forgery—"tell me where you have been, what you have done, and what you are doing now?"

"Presently—presently," he replied, with impatience. "I am sure now that I was wrong. I should not have left the country. I should have taken a lodging openly, and waited and looked on. Yes, that would have been better. Then I should have seen that old villain, Checkley, in the dock. Perhaps it is not yet too late. Still—eight years. Who can expect a commissionaire to remember a single message after eight years?"

"Well—and now tell me," George said again, "what you have been doing."

"The black sheep always turns up, doesn't he? You learn at home that he has got a berth in the Rocky Mountains; but he jacks it up, and goes to Melbourne where he falls on his feet; but gets tired, and moves on to New Zealand and so home again. It's the regular round."

"You are apparently the black sheep whose wool is dyed white. There are threads of gold in it. You look prosperous."

"A few years ago I was actually in the possession of money. Then I became poor again. After a good many adventures I became a journalist. The profession is in America the refuge of the educated unsuccessful and the hope of the uneducated unsuccessful. I am doing as well as journalists in America generally do. I am over here as the representative of a Frisco paper, and I expect to stay for some time—so long as I can be of service to my people. That's all."

"Well—it might be a great deal worse. And won't you come to Pembridge Square with me?"

"When the cloud is lifted—not before. And—George—not a word about me. Don't tell—yet—even Elsie."

CHAPTER VI

SOMETHING MORE HAPPENS

Checkley held the door of the office wide open, and invited Elsie to enter. The aspect of the room, solid of furniture, severe in its fittings, with its vast table covered with papers, struck her with a kind of terror. At the table sat her guardian, austere of countenance.

All the way along she had been imagining a dialogue. He would begin with certain words. She would reply, firmly but respectfully, with certain other words. He would go on. She would again reply. And so on. Everybody knows the consolations of imagination in framing dialogues at times of trouble. They never come off. The beginning is never what is expected, and the sequel, therefore, has to be changed on the spot. The conditions of the interview had not been realized by Elsie. Also

4

the beginning was not what she expected. For her guardian, instead of frowning with a brow of corrugated iron and holding up a finger of warning, received her more pleasantly than she had imagined it possible for him, bade her sit down, and leaned back, looking at her kindly.

"And so," he said, "you are twenty-one—twenty-one—to-day. I am no longer your guardian. You are twenty-one. Everything that is past seems to have happened yesterday. So that it is needless to say that you were a baby only yesterday."

"Yes, I am really twenty-one."

"I congratulate you. To be twenty-one is, I believe, for a young lady at least, a pleasant time of life. For my own part I have almost forgotten the memory of youth. Perhaps I never had the time to be young. Certainly I have never understood why some men regret their youth so passionately. As for your sex, Elsie, I know very little of it except in the way of business. In that way, which does not admit of romance, I must say that I have sometimes found ladies importunate, tenacious, exacting, persistent, and even revengeful."

"Oh!" said Elsie, with a little winning smile of conciliation. This was only a beginning—a prelude—before the unpleasantness.

"That, Elsie, is my unfortunate experience of women—always in the way of business, which, of course, may bring out the worst qualities. In society, of which I have little experience, they are doubtless charming—charming." He repeated the word, as if he had found an adjective of whose meaning he was not quite clear. "An old bachelor is not expected, at the age of seventy-five, to know much about such a subject. The point before us is that you have this day arrived at the mature age of twenty-one. That is the first thing, and I congratulate you—the first thing."

"I wonder," thought Elsie timidly, "when he will begin upon the next thing—the real thing."

There lay upon the table before him a paper with notes upon it. He took it up, looked at it, and laid it down again. Then he turned to Elsie, and smiled—he actually smiled—he unmistakably smiled. "At twenty-one," he said, "some young ladies who are heiresses come into their property—"

"Those who are heiresses. Unhappily, I am not."

"Come into their property — their property. It must be a beautiful thing for a girl to come into property, unexpectedly, at twenty-one. For a man, a temptation to do nothing and to make no more money. Bad! Bad! But for a girl already engaged, a girl who wants money, a girl who is engaged—eh?—to a penniless young solicitor—"

Elsie turned crimson. This was the thing she expected.

"Under such circumstances, I say, such a stroke of fortune would be providential and wonderful, would it not?"

She blushed, and turned pale, and blushed again. She also felt a strong disposition to cry, but repressed that disposition.

"In your case, for instance, such a windfall would be most welcome. Your case is rather a singular case. You do not belong to a family which has generally disregarded money—quite the reverse; you should inherit the love of money—yet you propose to throw away what I believe are very good prospects, and—"

"My only prospect is to marry George Austin."

"So you think. I have heard from your mother, and I have seen your sister Hilda. They object very strongly to the engagement."

"I know, of course, what they would say."

"Therefore I need not repeat it," replied Mr. Dering dryly. "I learn, then, that you are not only engaged to this young gentleman, but that you are also proposing to marry upon the small income which he now possesses."

"Yes — we are prepared to begin the world upon that income."

"Your mother asked me what chance he has in his profession. In this office he can never rise to a considerable salary as managing clerk. If he had money he might buy a partnership. But he has none, and his friends have none. And the profession is congested. He may remain all his life in a position not much better than he now occupies. The prospect, Elsie, is not brilliant."

"No—we are fully aware of that. And yet—"

"Allow me, my dear child. You are yourself—we will say for the moment—without any means of your own."

"I have nothing."

"Or any expectations, except from your mother, who is not yet sixty."

"I could not count upon my mother's death. Besides, she says that, if I persist, she will not leave me anything at all."

"So much I understand from herself. Her present intention is to remove your name from her will in case you go on with this proposed marriage."

"My mother will do what she pleases with her property," said Elsie. "If she thinks that I will give way to a threat of this kind she does not know me."

"Do not let us speak of threats. I am laying before you facts. Here they are plainly. Young Austin has a very small income; he has very little prospect of getting a substantial income; you, so far as you know, have nothing; and also, so far as you know, you have no prospect of anything. These are the facts, are they not?"

"Yes, I suppose those are the facts. We shall be quite poor —very likely quite poor always." The tears rose to her eyes, but this was not a place for crying.

"I want you to understand these facts very clearly," Mr. Dering insisted. "Believe me, I do not wish to give you pain."

"All this," said Elsie, with the beginnings of the family obstinacy in her eyes, "I clearly understand. I have had them put before me too often."

"I also learn from your sister, Lady Dering, that if you abandon this marriage she is ready to do anything for you that she can. Her house, her carriage, her servants—you can command them all, if you please. This you know. Have you considered the meaning of what you propose? Can you consider it calmly?"

"I believe we have."

"On the one side poverty—not what is called a small income —many people live very well on what is called a small income —but grinding, hard poverty, which exacts real privations and burdens you with unexpected loads. My dear young lady, you have been brought up to a certain amount of plenty and ease, if not to luxury. Do you think you can get along without plenty and ease?"

"If George can, I can."

"Can you become a servant—cook, house-maid, lady's-maid— as well as a wife—a nurse as well as a mother?"

"If George is made happier by my becoming anything—anything—it will only make me happier. Mr. Dering, I am sure you wish me well—you are my father's old friend, you have always advised my mother in her troubles, my brother was articled to you—but—" She paused, remembering that he had not been her brother's best friend.

"I mean the best possible for you. Meantime, you are quite fixed in your own mind; you are set upon this thing—that is clear. There is one other way of looking at it. You yourself seem chiefly desirous, I think, to make the man you love happy. So much the better for him. Are you quite satisfied that the other party to the agreement—your lover—will remain happy while he sees you slaving for him, while he feels his own helplessness, and while he gets no relief from the grinding poverty of his household; while—lastly—he sees his sons taking their place on a lower level, and his daughters taking a place below the rank of gentlewomen?"

"I reply by another question. You have had George in your office as articled clerk and managing clerk for eight years. Is he, or is he not, steadfast, clear-headed, one who knows his own mind, and one who can be trusted in all things?"

"Perhaps," said Mr. Dering, inclining his head. "How does that advance him?"

"Then, if you trust him, why should not I trust him? I trust George altogether—altogether. If he does not get on it will be through no fault of his. We shall bear our burdens bravely, believe me, Mr. Dering. You will not hear him—or me—complain. Besides, I am full of hope. Oh! it can never be in this country that a man who is a good workman should not be able to get on. Then, I can paint a little—not very well, perhaps; but I have thought—you will not laugh at me—that I might paint portraits, and get a little money that way."

"It is quite possible that he may succeed, and that you may increase the family income. Everything is possible. But, remember, you are building on possibilities, and I on facts. Plans very beautiful and easy at the outset often prove most difficult in the carrying-out. My experience of marriages is learned by fifty years of work—not imaginative, but practical. I have learned that without adequate means no marriage can be happy. That is to say, I have never come across any case of wedded poverty where the husband or the wife, or both, did not regret the day when they faced poverty together instead of separately. That, I say, is my experience of such marriages. It is so easy to say that hand-in-hand evils may be met and endured which would be intolerable if one was alone. It isn't only hand-in-hand, Elsie. The hands are wanted for the baby, and the evils will fall on the children yet unborn."

Elsie hung her head. Then she replied, timidly, "I have thought even of that. It only means that we go lower down in the social scale."

"Only? Yet that is everything. People who are well up the ladder too often deride those who are fighting and struggling to get up higher. It is great folly or great ignorance to laugh. Social position, in such a country as ours, means independence, self-respect, dignity, all kinds of valuable things. You will throw these all away—yet your grandfathers won them for you by hard work. You are yourself a gentlewoman—why? Because they made their way up in the world, and placed their sons also in the way to climb. That is how families are made—by three generations at least of steady work uphill."

Elsie shook her head sadly. "We can only hope," she murmured.

"One more word, and I will say no more. Remember that, love or no love, resignation or not, patience or not, physical comfort is the beginning and the foundation of all happiness. If you and your husband can satisfy the demands of physical comfort you may be happy—or at least resigned. If not— Well, Elsie, that is all. I should not have said so much had I not promised your mother and your sister. I am touched, I confess, by your courage and your resolution."

"We mean never to regret, never to look back, and always to work and hope," said Elsie. "You will remain our friend, Mr. Dering ?"

"Surely, surely. And now—"

"Now "—Elsie rose—"I will not keep you any longer. You have said what you wished to say very kindly, and I thank you."

"No. Sit down again ; I haven't done with you yet, child. Sit down again. No more about that young villain—George Austin." He spoke so good-humoredly that Elsie complied, wondering, but no longer afraid. "Nothing more about your engagement. Now, listen carefully, because this is most important. Three or four years ago a person wrote to me. That person informed me that he—for convenience we will call the person a man—wished to place a certain sum of money in my hands in trust for you."

"For me? Do you mean—in trust? What is trust?"

"He gave me this sum of money to be given to you on your twenty-first birthday."

"Oh!" Elsie sat up with open eyes. "A sum of money?—and to me?"

"With a condition or two. The first condition was, that the interest should be invested as it came in; the next, that I was on no account—mind, on no account at all—to tell you or any one of the existence of the gift or the name of the donor. You are now twenty-one. I have been careful not to afford you the least suspicion of this happy windfall until the time should arrive. Neither your mother, nor your sister, nor your lover, knows or suspects anything about it."

"Oh!" Elsie said once more. An interjection may be defined as a prolonged monosyllable, generally a vowel, uttered when no words can do justice to the subject.

"And here, my dear young lady"—Elsie cried "Oh!" once more, because—the most curious thing in the world—Mr. Dering's grave face suddenly relaxed, and the lines assumed the very benevolence which she had, the day before, imparted to his portrait and wished to see upon his face—"here, my dear young lady"—he laid his hand upon a paper—"is the list of the investments which I have made of that money. You have, in fact, money in corporation bonds—Newcastle, Nottingham, Wolverhampton. You have water shares—you have gas shares—all good investments, yielding at the price of purchase an average of nearly three and two-thirds per cent."

"Investments? Why—how much money was it, then? I was thinking, when you spoke of a sum of money, of ten pounds, perhaps."

"No, Elsie, not ten pounds. The money placed in my hands for your use was over twelve thousand pounds. With accumulations, there is now a little under thirteen thousand."

"Oh!" cried Elsie, for the third time and for the same reason. No words could express her astonishment.

"Yes; it will produce about four hundred and eighty pounds a year. Perhaps, as some of the stock has gone up, it might be sold out and placed to better advantage. We may get it up to five hundred pounds."

"Do you mean, Mr. Dering, that I have actually got five hundred pounds a year—all my own?"

"That is certainly my meaning. You have nearly five hundred pounds a year all your own—entirely your own, without any conditions whatever—your own."

"Oh!" She sat in silence, her hands locked. Then the tears came into her eyes. "Oh, George!" she murmured, "you will not be so very poor after all."

"That is all I have to say to you at present, Elsie," said Mr. Dering. "Now you may run away and leave me. Come to dinner this evening. Your mother and your sister are coming. I shall ask Austin as well. We may, perhaps, remove some of those objections. Dinner at seven sharp, Elsie. And now you can leave me."

"I said last night," said Elsie, clasping her hands with feminine superstition, "that something was going to happen, but I thought it was something horrid. Oh! Mr. Dering, if you only knew how happy you have made me! I don't know what to say. I feel stunned. Five hundred pounds a year! Oh! it is wonderful! What shall I say? What shall I say?"

"You will say nothing. Go away now. Come to dinner this evening. Go away, my young heiress. Go, and make plans how to live on your enlarged income. It will not prove too much."

Elsie rose. Then she turned again. "Oh! I had actually forgotten. Won't you tell the man—or the woman—who gave you that money for me that I thank him from my very heart? It isn't that I think so much about money; but, oh! the dreadful trouble that there has been at home because George has none—and this will do something to reconcile my mother. Don't you think it will make all the difference?"

"I hope that before the evening you will find that all opposition has been removed," said her guardian cautiously.

She walked away in a dream. She found herself in Lincoln's Inn Fields; she walked all round that great square, also in a dream. The spectre of poverty had vanished. She was rich;

she was rich—she had five hundred pounds a year. Between them they would have seven hundred pounds a year. It seemed enormous. Seven hundred pounds a year! Seven—seven—seven hundred pounds a year!

She got out into the street called Holborn, and she took the modest omnibus, this heiress of untold wealth. How much was it? Thirteen millions? or thirteen thousand? One seemed as much as the other. Twelve thousand, with accumulations; with accumulations — ations — ations. The wheels of the vehicle groaned out these musical words all the way. It was in the morning, when the Bayswater omnibus is full of girls going home to lunch after shopping or looking at the shops. Elsie looked at these girls as they sat along the narrow benches. "My dears," she longed to say, but did not, "I hope you have every one got a brave lover, and that you have all got twelve thousand pounds apiece—with accumulations—twelve thousand pounds—with accumulations—ations—ations—realizing four hundred and eighty pounds a year, and perhaps a little more. With accumulations—ations—ations—accumulations."

She ran into the house and up the stairs, singing. At the sound of her voice her mother, engaged in calculations of the greatest difficulty, paused, wondering. When she understood that it was the voice of her child and not an organ-grinder, she became angry. What right had the girl to run about singing? Was it insolent bravado?

Elsie opened the door of the drawing-room, and ran in. Her mother's cold face repelled her. She was going to tell the joyful news, but she stopped.

"You have seen Mr. Dering?" asked her mother.

"Yes; I have seen him."

"If he has brought you to reason—"

"Oh! He has—he has. I am entirely reasonable."

Mrs. Arundel was astonished. The girl was flushed of face and bright of eye; her breath was quick; her lips were parted. She looked entirely happy.

"My dear mother," she went on, "I am to dine with him to-night. Hilda is to dine with him to-night. You are to dine with him to-night. It is to be a family party. He will bring us all to reason—to a bagful of reasons."

"Elsie, this seems to me to be mirth misplaced."

4*

"No—no—in its right place—reasons all in a row and on three shelves, labelled and arranged and classified."

"You talk in enigmas."

"My dear mother"—yet that morning the dear mother would not speak to the dear daughter—"I talk in enigmas, and I sing in conundrums. I feel like an oracle or a Delphic old woman for dark sayings."

She ran away, slamming the door after her. Her mother heard her singing in her studio all to herself. "Can she be in her right mind?" she asked, anxiously. "To marry a pauper, to receive the admonition of her guardian—and such a guardian—and to come home singing. 'Twould be better to lock her up than let her marry."

CHAPTER VII

SOMETHING ELSE HAPPENS

Mr. Dering lay back in his chair, gazing at the door—the unromantic office-door—through which Elsie had just passed. I suppose that even the dryest of old bachelors and lawyers may be touched by the sight of a young girl made suddenly and unexpectedly happy. Perhaps the mere apparition of a lovely girl—dainty and delicate and sweet, daintily and delicately apparelled, so as to look like a goddess or a wood-nymph rather than a creature of clay—may have awakened old and long-forgotten thoughts before the instincts of youth were stifled by piles of parchment. It is the peculiar and undisputed privilege of the historian to read thoughts, but it is not always necessary to write them down.

He sat up, and sighed. "I have not told her all," he murmured. "She shall be happier still." He touched his hand-bell. "Checkley," he said, "ask Mr. Austin kindly to step this way. A day of surprise—of joyful surprise—for both."

It was, indeed, to be a day of good fortune, as you shall see.

He opened a drawer, and took out a document, rolled and tied, which he laid upon the table before him.

George obeyed the summons, not without misgiving; for Elsie, he knew, must by this time have had the dreaded interview, and the call might have some reference to his own share in the great contumacy. To incur the displeasure of his employer in connection with that event might lead to serious consequences.

Astonishing thing! Mr. Dering received him with a countenance that seemed transformed. He smiled benevolently upon him. He even laughed. He smiled when George opened the door; he laughed when, in obedience to a gesture of invitation, George took a chair. He actually laughed; not weakly or foolishly, but as a strong man laughs.

"I want ten minutes with you, George Austin"—he actually used the Christian name—"ten minutes or a quarter of an hour, or perhaps half an hour." He laughed again. "Now, then"—his face assumed its usual judicial expression, but his lips broke into unaccustomed smiles—" now then, sir, I have just seen my ward—my former ward, for she is now of age—and have heard —well, everything there was to hear."

"I have no doubt, sir, that what you heard from Elsie was the exact truth."

"I believe so. The questions which I put to her I also put to you. How do you propose to live?—on your salary? You have been engaged to my late ward without asking the permission of her guardians—that is, her mother and myself."

"That is not quite the case. We found that her mother opposed the engagement, and therefore it was not necessary to ask your permission. We agreed to let the matter rest until she should be of age. Meanwhile, we openly corresponded and saw each other."

"It is a distinction without a difference; perhaps what you would call a legal distinction. You now propose to marry. Elsie Arundel is no longer my ward; but, as a friend, I venture to ask you how you propose to live? A wife and a house cost money. Shall you keep house and wife on your salary alone? Have you any other resources?"

There are several ways of putting these awkward questions. There is especially the way of accusation, by which you charge the guilty young man of being, by his own fault, one of a very large family; of having no money and no expectations—nothing at all, unless he can make it for himself. It is the manner generally adopted by parents and guardians. Mr. Dering, however, when he put the question, smiled genially and rubbed his hands—a thing so unusual as to be terrifying in itself—as if he were uttering a joke—a thing he never had done in his life. The question, however, even when put in this, the kindest, way, is one most awkward for any young man, and especially for a young man in either branch of the law, and most especially for a young man beginning the ascent of the lower branch.

Consider, of all the professions, crowded as they are, there is none so crowded as this branch of the law. " What," asks anxious Quiverful Père, " shall I do with this boy of mine? I will spend a thousand pounds upon him, and make him a solicitor. Once he has passed, the way is clear for him." " How," asks the ambitious man of trade, " shall I advance my son? I will make him a lawyer; once passed, he will open an office and get a practice and become rich. He will be a gentleman, and his children will be born gentlemen." Very good; a most laudable custom it is in this realm of Great Britain for the young men still to be pressing upwards, though those who are already high up would fain forget the days of climbing, and sneer at those who are making their way. But, applied to this profession, climbing seems no longer practicable. This way of advance will have to be abandoned.

Consider, again. Every profession gets rich out of its own mine. There is the mine ecclesiastic, the mine medical, the mine artistic, the mine legal. The last named contains leases, covenants, agreements, wills, bonds, mortgages, actions, partnerships, transfers, conveyances, county courts, and other treasures, all to be had for the digging. But—and this is too often forgotten—there is only a limited quantity to be taken out of the mine every year, and there is not enough to go round except in very minute portions. And since, until we become Socialists at heart, we shall all of us continue to desire for our share that which is called the mess of Benjamin, and since all cannot get that mess—which Mr. Dering had enjoyed for the whole of his life—or anything like that desirable portion, most young solicitors go in great heaviness of spirit—hang their heads, corrugate their foreheads, write despairing letters to the girls they left behind them, and with grumbling gratitude take the hundred or two hundred a year which is offered for their services as managing clerks. Again, the legal mine seems of late years not to yield anything like so much as formerly. There has been a cruel shrinkage all over the country, and especially in country towns; the boom of building seems to have come to an end; the agricultural depression has dragged down with it an immense number of people who formerly flourished with the lawyers, and, by means of their savings, investments, leases, and partnerships and quarrels, made many a solicitor fat and happy. That is all gone. It used to be easy, if one had a little money, to buy a partnership. Now it is no longer possible—or, at least, no longer easy. Nobody has a business greater than he himself can manage; everybody has got a son coming in.

These considerations show why the question was difficult to answer.

Said George in reply, but with some confusion, "We are prepared to live on little; we are not in the least extravagant. Elsie will rough it. Besides, she has her art—"

"Out of which she makes at present nothing a year."

"But she will get on—and I may hope, may reasonably hope, some time to make an income larger than my present one."

"You may hope—you may hope. But the position is not hopeful. In fact, George Austin, you must marry on ten times your present income, or not at all."

"But, I assure you, sir, our ideas are truly modest, and we have made up our minds how we can live and pay our way."

"You think you have. That is to say, you have prepared a table of expenses showing how, with twopence to spare, you can live very well on two hundred pounds a year. Of course you put down nothing for the thousand-and-one little unexpected things which everybody of your education and habits pays for every day."

"We have provided as far as we can see."

"Well, it won't do. Of course I can't forbid the girl to marry you—she is of age. I can't forbid you—but I can make it impossible—impossible for you, Master Austin—impossible."

He rapped the table. The words were stern, but the voice was kindly, and he smiled again as he spoke. "You thought you would do without me, did you? Well—you shall see—you shall see."

George received this threat without words, but with a red face and with rising indignation. Still when one is a servant, one must endure the reproofs of the master.   He said nothing, therefore, but waited.

"I have considered for some time," Mr. Dering continued, "how to meet this case in a satisfactory manner.   At last I made up my mind.   And if you will read this document, young gentleman, you will find that I have made your foolish proposal to marry on love, and nothing else, quite impossible—quite impossible, sir."   He slapped the table with the paper, and tossed it over to George.

George took the paper, and began to read it.   Suddenly he jumped out of his chair.   He sprang to his feet.   "*What?*" he cried.

"Go on—go on," said Mr. Dering benevolently.

"Partnership?   Partnership?"   George gasped.   "What does it mean?"

"It is, as you say, a deed of partnership between myself and yourself.   The conditions of the partnership are duly set forth— I hope you will see your way to accepting them.   A deed of partnership.   I do not know within a few hundreds what your share may be, but I believe you may reckon on at least two thousand for the first year, and more—much more—before long."

"More than a thousand?"

"You have not read the deed through.   Call yourself a lawyer?   Sit down, and read it word for word."

George obeyed, reading it as if it were a paper submitted to him for consideration, a paper belonging to some one else.

"Well?   You have read it?"

"Yes, I have read it through."

"Observe that the partnership may be dissolved by death, bankruptcy, or mutual consent.   I receive two thirds of the proceeds for life.   That—alas!—will not be for long.   Well, young man, do you accept this offer?"

"Accept?   Oh!   Accept?   What can I do?   What can I say— but accept?"   He walked to the window, and looked out.   I suppose he was admiring the trees in the square, which were certainly very beautiful in early July.   Then he returned, his eyes humid.

"Aha!"   Mr. Dering chuckled, "I told you that I would make it impossible for you to marry on two hundred pounds a year.   I waited till Elsie's birthday.   Well?   You will now be able to revise that little estimate of living on two hundred a year. Eh?"

"Mr. Dering," said George, with breaking voice, "I cannot believe it. I cannot understand it. I have not deserved it."

"Shake hands, my partner."

The two men shook hands.

"Now sit down, and let us talk a bit," said Mr. Dering. "I am old. I am past seventy. I have tried to persuade myself that I am still as fit for work as ever. But I have had warnings. I now perceive that they must be taken as warnings. Sometimes it is a little confusion of memory—I am not able to account for little things—I forget what I did yesterday afternoon. I suppose all old men get these reminders of coming decay. It means that I must reduce work and responsibility. I might give up business altogether, and retire—I have money enough and to spare; but this is the third generation of a successful house, and I could not bear to close the doors, and to think that the firm would altogether vanish. So I thought I would take a partner, and I began to look about me. Well—in brief, I came to the conclusion that I should find no young man better qualified than yourself for ability, and for power of work, and for all the qualities necessary for the successful conduct of such a house as this. Especially, I considered the essential of good manners. I was early taught by my father that the greatest aid to success is good breeding. I trust that, in this respect, I have done justice to the teaching of one who was the most courtly of his time. You belong to an age of less ceremony and less respect to rank. But we are not always in a barrack or in a club. We are not all comrades or equals. There are those below to consider as well as those above. There are women; there are old men. You, my partner, have shown me that you can give to each the consideration, the deference, the recognition, that he deserves. True breeding is the recognition of the individual. You are careful of the small things which smooth the asperities of business. In no profession, not even that of medicine, is a good manner more useful than in ours, and this you possess. It also pleases me," he added, after a pause, "to think that, in making you my partner, I am also promoting the happiness of a young lady I have known all her life."

George murmured something. He looked more like a guilty

school-boy than a man just raised to a position most enviable. His cheeks were flushed, and his hands trembled. Mr. Dering touched his bell.

"Checkley," he said, when that faithful retainer appeared, "I have already told you of my intention to take a partner. This is my new partner."

Checkley changed color. His old eyes—or was George wrong? —flashed with a light of malignity as he raised them. It made him feel uncomfortable—but only for a moment.

"My partner, Checkley," repeated Mr. Dering.

"Oh!" His voice was dry and grating. "Since we couldn't go on as before— Well, I hope you won't repent it."

"You shall witness the signing of the deed, Checkley. Call in a clerk. So—there we have it, drawn, signed, and witnessed. Once more, my partner, shake hands."

Elsie retired to her own room after the snub administered to her rising spirits. She soon began to sing again, being much too happy to be affected by anything so small. She went on with her portrait, preserving some, but not all, of the softness and benevolence which she had put into it, and thereby producing what is allowed to be an excellent portrait but somewhat flattering. She herself knows very well that it is not flattering at all, but even lower than the truth—only the other people have never seen the lawyer in an expansive moment.

Now while she was thus engaged, her mind going back every other minute to her newly acquired inheritance, a cab drove up to the house, the door flew open, and her lover—her George—flew into her arms.

"You here—George! Actually in the house? Oh! but you know—"

"I know—I know. But I could not possibly wait till this evening. My dear child, the most wonderful—the most wonderful thing—the most extraordinary thing—in the whole world has happened—a thing we could never hope and never ask—"

"Mr. Dering has told you, then?"

"What? Do you know?"

"Mr. Dering told me this morning. Oh, George! isn't it wonderful?"

"Wonderful? It is like the last chapter of a novel!" This he said speaking as a fool, because the only last chapter in life is that in which Azrael crosses the threshold.

"Oh, George!—I have been walking in the air—I have been flying—I have been singing and dancing. I feel as if I had never before known what it was to be happy. Mr. Dering said something about having it settled—mind—it's all yours, George—yours as well as mine."

"Yes," said George, a little puzzled, "I suppose in the eyes of the law it is mine, but then it is yours as well. All that is mine is yours."

"Oh! Mr. Dering said it was mine in the eyes of the law. What does it matter, George, what the stupid old law says?"

"Nothing, my dear—nothing at all."

"It will be worth five hundred pounds a year very nearly. That, with your two hundred pounds a year, will make us actually comfortable after all our anxieties."

"Five hundred a year? It will be worth four times that, I hope."

"Four times? Oh, no!—that is impossible. But Mr. Dering told me that he could hardly get so much as four per cent., and I have made a sum and worked it out. Rule for simple interest —multiply the principal by the rate per cent., and again by the time, and divide by a hundred. It is quite simple. And what makes the sum simpler, you need only take one year."

"What principal, Elsie? by what interest? You are running your little head against rules of arithmetic. Here there is no principal and no interest. It is a case of proceeds, and then division."

"We will call it proceeds if you like, George, but he called it interest. Anyhow, it comes to five hundred a year, very nearly ; and with your two hundred—"

"I don't know what you mean by your five hundred a year. As for my two hundred, unless I am very much mistaken, that will very soon be two thousand."

"Your two hundred will become—? George, we are talking across each other."

"Yes. What money of yours do you mean?"

"I mean the twelve thousand pounds that Mr. Dering holds for me—with accumulations—accumulations"—she began to sing the rhyme of the omnibus-wheels—"accumulations—ations—ations."

"Twelve thousand pounds? Is this Fairyland? Twelve thousand? I reel—I faint—I sink—I melt away. Take my hands—both my hands, Elsie; kiss me kindly—it's better than brandy—kindly kiss me. Twelve thousand pounds! with accumulations—"

"—ations—ations—ations," she sang. "Never before, George, have I understood the loveliness and the power of money. They were given to Mr. Dering by an anonymous person to be held for me—secretly. No one knows—not even, yet, my mother."

"Oh! It is altogether too much—too much; once there was a poor but loving couple, and Fortune turned her wheel, and—You don't know — you most unsuspecting ignorant thing — you can't guess— Oh! Elsie, I am a partner—Mr. Dering's partner."

They caught hands again—then they let go—then they sat down and gazed upon each other.

"Elsie," said George.

"George," said Elsie.

"We can now marry like everybody else—but much better. We shall have furniture now."

"All the furniture we shall want, and a house where we please. No contriving now—no pinching."

"No self-denying for each other, my dear."

"That's a pity, isn't it? But, George, don't repine. The advantages may counterbalance the drawbacks. I think I see the cottage where we *were* going to live. It is in Islington, or near it—Barnsbury, perhaps. There is a little garden in front and one at the back. There is always washing hung out to dry—I don't like the smell of suds. For dinner one has cold Australian tinned meat for economy, not for choice. The rooms are very small, and the furniture is shabby, because it was cheap and bad to begin with. And when you come home—oh, George!"—she stuck her forefinger in her chalk and drew two or three lines on his face—"you look like that, so discontented, so grumpy, so gloomy. Oh! my dear, the advantages—they do so greatly outbalance the drawbacks; and George—you will love your wife all the more—I am sure you will—because she can always dress properly, and look nice, and give you a dinner that will help to rest you from the work of the day."

Once more this foolish couple fell into each other's arms, and kissed again with tears and smiles and laughter.

"Who," asked Mrs. Arundel, ringing the bell upstairs—"who is with Miss Elsie below?"

On hearing that it was Mr. George Austin, whose presence in the house was forbidden, Mrs. Arundel rose solemnly and awfully, and walked down the stairs. She had a clear duty before her. When she threw open the door the lovers were hand in hand, dancing round the room, laughing—but the tears were running down Elsie's cheeks.

"Elsie," said her mother, standing at the open door, "perhaps you can explain this."

"Permit me to explain," said George.

"This gentleman, Elsie, has been forbidden the house."

"One moment—" he began.

"Go, sir." She pointed majestically to the window.

"Oh!" cried Elsie. "Tell her, George—tell her; I cannot." She fell to laughing and crying together, but still held her lover by the hand.

"I will have no communication whatever with one who robs me of a daughter," said this Roman matron. "Will you, once more, leave the house, sir?"

"Mother, you *must* hear him."

"Nothing," said Mrs. Arundel, "will ever induce me to speak to him—nothing."

"Mother, don't be silly!" Elsie cried. "You don't know what has happened. You *must* not say such things. You will only be sorry for them afterwards."

"Never—never. One may forgive such a man, but one can never speak to him; never—whatever happens—never." The lady looked almost heroic as she waved her right hand in the direction of the man.

"I will go," said George, "but not till you have heard me. I am rich—Elsie is rich—we shall not marry into poverty. The whole situation is entirely changed."

"Changed," Elsie repeated, taking George's arm.

"My dear George," said Mrs. Arundel, when she had heard the

whole story, and by cross-examination persuaded herself that it was true, " you know on what a just basis my objections were founded.   Otherwise, I should have been delighted at the outset. Kiss me, Elsie.   You have my full consent, children.   These remarkable events are providential.   On Mr. Dering's death or retirement you will step into an enormous practice.   Follow his example—take no partner till old age compels you ; keep all the profits for yourself—all.   My dear George, you should be a very happy man.   Not so rich, perhaps, as my son-in-law, Sir Samuel, but above the ordinary run of common happiness.   As for the past—   We will now go down to lunch.   There is the bell. These emotions are fatiguing."

CHAPTER VIII

IN HONOR OF THE EVENT

MAY one dwell upon so simple a thing as a small family dinner-party ?   It is generally undramatic and uneventful ; it is not generally marked even by a new dish or a bottle of rare wine. Yet there lingers in the mind of every man the recollection of pleasant dinners.   I should like to write a " Book of Dinners," not a book for the *gourmet*, but a book of memories.   It might be a most delightful volume.   There would be in it the school-boys' dinner.   I remember a certain dinner at eighteen-pence a head, at Richmond, before we had the row in the boat, when we quarrelled, and broke the oars over each other's heads, and very nearly capsized ; a certain undergraduates' dinner, in which four men— three of whom are now ghosts—joined ; the Ramblers' dinner—of lamb-chops and bottled ale, and mirth and merriment ; the two-by-two dinner in the private room—a dainty dinner of sweet lamb, sweet bread, sweet pease, sweet looks, sweet Moselle, and sweet words.   Is it really true that one never—never—gets young again ? Some people do, I am sure, but they are under promise to say nothing about it.   I shall—and then that dinner may perhaps— one cannot say—one never knows—and I suppose, if one was young again, that they would be found just as pretty as they ever were.   There is the official dinner, stately and cold ; the City dinner, which generally comes to a man when his digestion is no longer what it was; the family dinner, in which the intellect plays so small a part, because no one wastes his fine things on his brothers and sisters; the dinner at which one has to make a speech. Indeed, this "Book of Dinners" promises to be a most charming volume. I should attempt it, however, with trembling, because, to do it really well, one should be, first of all, a scholar, if only to appreciate things said and spoken, and in order to connect the illustrious past with food and drink. Next, he ought to be still young; he certainly must have a proper feeling for wine, and must certainly understand when and why one should be grateful to good Master Cook; he should be a past or present master in the art of love and a squire of dames; he should be good at conversation; he must, in the old language, be a worshipper of Bacchus, Venus, Phœbus Apollo, the Muses nine, and the Graces three. He must be no poor weakling, unable to enjoy the good creatures of flesh, fowl, fish, and wine; no boor; and no log, insensible to loveliness.

Dinner, which should be a science, has long been treated as one of the fine arts. Now every fine art, as we all know, has its fashions and its caprices. Those who are old enough to remember the dinners of twenty, thirty, or forty years ago can remember many of their fashions and caprices. In the thirties, for instance, everything was carved upon the table. It required a strong man to give a dinner-party. Fortunately, a dinner then consisted of few dishes. They drank sherry with dinner, and port afterwards. The champagne, if there was any, was sweet. The guests were bidden for half-past six; they sat down to dinner before seven. At eight the ladies went upstairs; at half-past ten the men joined them. Their faces were flushed, their shoulders were inclined to lurch, and their speech was the least bit thick. Wonderful to relate, brandy-and-water used to be served to these topers in the drawing-room itself.

Mr. Dering had altered little in his dinner customs. They mostly belonged to the sixties, with a survival of some belonging to the thirties. Things were carved upon the sideboard— this was in deference to modern custom; champagne formed an integral part of the meal, but the dinner itself was solid; the cloth after dinner was removed, leaving the dark, polished mahogany, after the old fashion; the furniture of the room was also in the old style—the chairs were heavy and solid; the walls were hung with a dark crimson paper of velvety texture; the curtains and the carpets were red; there were pictures of game and fruit; the sideboard was as solid as the table.

Checkley, the clerk, who was invited, as a faithful servant of the house, to the celebration of the new partnership, was the first to arrive. Dressed in a hired suit, he looked like an undertaker's assistant; the gloom upon his face heightened the resemblance. Why the partnership caused this appearance of gloom I know not. Certainly he could never expect to be made a partner himself. It was perhaps a species of jealousy which filled his soul. He would no longer know so much of the business.

George came with the mother-in-law elect and the *fiancée*. Forgiveness, peace, amnesty, and charity sat all together upon the brow of the elder lady. She was magnificent in a dark crimson velvet, and she had a good deal of gold about her arms and neck. Jewish ladies are said to show, by the magnificence of their attire, the prosperity of the business. Why not? It is a form of enjoying success. There are many forms. One man buys books—let him buy books; another collects pictures. Why not? One woman wears crimson velvet. Why not? In this way she enjoys her wealth and proclaims it. Again, why not? It seems to the philosopher a fond and a vain thing to deck the person at all times, and especially fond when the person is middle-aged and no longer beautiful. We are not all philosophers. There are many middle-aged men who are extremely happy to put on their uniforms and their medals and their glittering helmets. Mrs. Arundel wore her velvet as if she enjoyed the color of it, the richness of it, the light and shade that lay in its folds, and the soft feel of it. She wore it, too, as an outward sign that this was a great occasion. Her daughter, Lady Dering, came also arrayed in a queenly dress of amber silk, with an aigrette of feathers in her hair. To be sure, she was going on somewhere after the dinner. Elsie, for her part, came in a creamy white almost like a bride, but she looked much happier than most brides. Hilda's husband, Sir Samuel, who was some fourteen years younger than his brother, was in appearance a typical man of wealth. The rich man can no longer, as in the days of good old Sir Thomas Gresham, illustrate his riches by costly furs, embroidered doublets, and heavy chains. He has to wear broadcloth and black. Yet there is an air, a carriage, which belongs to the rich man. In appearance Sir Samuel was tall, like his brother, but not thin like him; he was corpulent; his face was red; he was bald; and he wore large whiskers, dyed black. The late dissensions were completely forgotten. Hilda embraced her sister fondly. "My dear," she whispered, "we have heard all. Everything—everything is changed by these fortunate events. They do you the greatest credit. George"—she took his hand and held it tenderly—"I cannot tell you how happy this news has made us all. You will be rich in the course of years. Sir Samuel was only saying, as we came along—"

"I was saying, young gentleman," the knight interrupted, "that the most beautiful thing about money is the way it develops character. We do not ask for many virtues—only honesty and diligence—from the poor. When a man acquires wealth we look for his better qualities."

"Yes, indeed," Hilda murmured, "his better qualities begin to show. Elsie, dear, that is a very pretty frock—I don't think I have seen it before. How do you like my dress?"

George accepted this sudden turn in opinion with smiles. He laughed at it afterwards. For the moment it made him feel almost as if he was being rewarded for some virtuous action.

Dinner was announced at seven—such were the old-fashioned manners of this old gentleman. He led in Mrs. Arundel, and placed Elsie on his left. At first the dinner promised to be a silent feast. The two lovers were not disposed to talk much—they had not yet recovered from the overwhelming and astonishing events of the day. Sir Samuel never talked at the beginning of dinner; besides, there was turtle soup and red mullet and whitebait—it is sinful to divert your attention from these good creatures. His wife never talked at dinner or at any other time more than she could help. Your statuesque beauty seldom does. Talking much involves smiling and even laughing, which distorts the face. A woman must encourage men to talk; this she can do without saying much herself.

Presently Mr. Dering roused himself, and began to talk, with a visible effort, first to Mrs. Arundel of things casual; then to Elsie; and then to his brother, but always with an effort, as if he were thinking of other things. And a constraint fell upon the party.

When the cloth was removed, and the wine and fruit were placed upon the dark and lustrous board, he filled a glass and made a kind little speech.

"My partner," he said, "I drink to you. May your connection with the house be prosperous! It is a very great good-fortune for me to have found such a partner. Elsie, I join you with my partner. I wish you both every happiness."

He drained the bumper, and sent round the decanters.

Then he began to talk, and his discourse was most strange. "Had it been," said his brother afterwards, "the idle fancies of some crack-brained writing fellow, I could have understood it; but from him—from a steady old solicitor—a man who has never countenanced any kind of nonsense— To be sure he said it was only an illusion. I hope it isn't a softening. Who ever heard of such a man as that having dreams and illusions?"

Certainly no one had ever before heard Mr. Dering talk in this new manner. As a rule he was silent and grave, even at the head of his own table. He spoke little, and then gravely. To-night his talk as well as his face was changed. Who would have thought that Mr. Dering should confess to illusions, and should relate dreams, and should be visited by such dreams? Remember that the speaker was seventy-five years of age, and that he had never before been known so much as to speak of benevolence. Then you will understand something of the bewilderment which fell upon the whole company.

He began by raising his head, and smiling with a strange and new benignity—but Elsie thought of her portrait. "We are all one family here," he said, "and I may talk. I want to tell you of a very remarkable thing that has recently happened to me. It has been growing, I now perceive, for some years. But it now holds me strongly, and it is one reason why I am anxious to have the affairs of the house in the hands of a younger man. For it may be a sign of the end. At seventy-five anything uncommon may be a sign."

"You look well, Mr. Dering, and as strong as most men of sixty," said Mrs. Arundel.

"Perhaps. I feel well and strong. The fact is that I am troubled—or pleased—or possessed—by an illusion."

"You with an illusion?" said his brother.

"I myself. An illusion possesses me. It whispers me from

time to time that my life is wholly spent in promoting the happiness of other people."

"Well," said his brother, "since you are a first-class solicitor, and manage the affairs of many people very much to their advantage, you certainly do promote their happiness."

"Yes, yes—I suppose so. My illusion further is that it is done outside my business—without any bill afterwards"—Checkley looked up with eyes wide open. "I am made to believe that I am working and living for the good of others. A curious illusion, is it not?"

The City man shook his head. "That any man can possibly live for the good of others is, I take it, always and under all circumstances an illusion. In the present state of society—and a very admirable state it is"—he rolled his bald head as he spoke, and his voice had a rich roll in it—"a man's first duty—his second duty—his third duty—his hundredth duty—is to himself. In the City it is his business to amass wealth—to roll it up—roll it up"—he expressed the words with feeling—"to invest it profitably—to watch it, and to nurse it as it fructifies—fructifies. Afterwards, when he is rich enough, if ever a man can be rich enough, he may exercise as much charity as he pleases—as he pleases. Charity seems to please some people as a glass of fine wine"—he illustrated the comparison—"pleases the palate—pleases the palate."

The lawyer listened politely, and inclined his head.

"There is at least some method in my illusion," he went on. "You mentioned it. The solicitor is always occupied with the conduct of other people's affairs. That must be admitted. He is always engaged in considering how best to guide his fellowman through the labyrinthine world. He receives his fellow-man at his entrance into the world, as a ward; he receives him grown up, as a client; he advises him all his life at every step and in every emergency. If the client goes into partnership, or marries, or buys a house or builds one, or gets into trouble, the solicitor assists and advises him. When the client grows old, the solicitor makes his will. When the client dies, the solicitor becomes his executor and his trustee, and administers his estate for him. It is thus a life, as I said, entirely spent for other people. I know not of any other, unless it be of medicine, that so much can be said. And think what terrors, what anxieties, what disappoint-

5

ments, the solicitor witnesses and alleviates! Think of the family scandals he hushes up and keeps secret! Good heavens! if a solicitor in large practice were to tell what he knows, think of the terrible disclosures! He knows everything. He knows more than a Roman Catholic priest, because his penitents not only reveal their own sins, but also those of their wives and sons and friends and partners. And anxiety, I may tell you, makes a man better at confessing than penitence. Sometimes we bring actions at law, and issue writs, and so forth. Well now, this part of our business, which is disagreeable to us, is actually the most beneficent of any. Because, by means of the cases brought before the High Court of Justice, we remind the world that it must be law-abiding as well as law-worthy. The law, in order to win respect, must first win fear. Force comes before order. The memory of force must be kept up. The presence of force must be felt. For instance, I have a libel case just begun. It is rather a bad libel. My libeller will suffer; he will bleed; but he will bleed for the public good, because thousands who are only anxious to libel and slander, to calumniate and defame their neighbors, will be deterred. Oh! it will be a most beneficent case—far-reaching—striking terror into the hearts of ill-doers. Well—this, my friends, is my illusion. It is, I suppose, one of the many illusions with which we cheat old age and rob it of its terrors. To anybody else I am a hard-fisted lawyer, exacting his pound of flesh from the unfortunate debtor, and making myself rich at the expense of the creditor."

"Nonsense about how a man gets rich," said the man of business. "He can only get rich if he is capable. Quite right. Let the weak go under. Let the careless and the lazy starve."

"At the same time," said Elsie softly, "it is not all illusion. There are others besides the careless and the lazy—"

"Sometimes," the old lawyer went on, "this illusion of mine—oh! I know it is only illusion—takes the form of a dream, so vivid that it comes back to me afterwards as a reality. In this dream, which is always the same, I seem to have been engaged in some great scheme of practical benevolence."

"Practical— What? You engaged in practical benevolence?" the City man asked, in profound astonishment. The illusion was astonishing enough; but to have his brother talk of practical benevolence was amazing indeed.

"Practical benevolence," repeated Mr. Dering. His voice

dropped. His eyes looked out into space; he seemed as one who narrates a story. "It is a curiously persistent dream. It comes at irregular intervals; it pleases me while it lasts. Oh! in the evening, after dinner—while one takes a nap in the easy-chair, perhaps—it is, as I said, quite vivid. The action of this dream always takes place in the same room—a large room, plainly furnished, and looking out upon an open space—I should know it if I saw it; and it fills me with pleasure—in my dream—just to feel that I am—there is no other word for it—diffusing happiness. How I manage this diffusion I can never remember; but there it is—good, solid happiness, such as, in waking moments, one feels to be impossible."

"Diffusing happiness—you!" said his brother.

"A very beautiful dream," said Elsie. But no one dared to look in each other's face.

"This strange dream of mine," continued Mr. Dering, "does not form part of that little illusion, though it seems connected with it. And, as I said, mostly it comes in the evening. The other day, however, I had it in the afternoon—went to sleep in my office, I suppose. Did you find me asleep, Checkley? It was on Friday."

"No. On Friday afternoon you went out."

"Ah! When I came back, then—I had forgotten that I went out. Did I go out? Strange! Never mind. This continuous dream opens up a world of new ideas and things which are, I perceive, when I am awake, quite unreal and illusory. Yet they please. I see myself, as I said, diffusing happiness with open hands. The world which is thus made happier consists entirely of poor people. I move among them unseen; I listen to them; I see what they do, and I hear what they say. Mind—all this is as real and true to me as if it actually happened. And it fills me with admiration of the blessed state of poverty. In my dream I pity the rich with all my heart. To get rich, I think—in this dream—they must have practised so many deceptions—"

"Brother! brother!" Sir Samuel held up both hands.

"In my dream—only in my dream. Those who inherit riches are burdened with the weight of their wealth, which will not suffer them to enter into the arena; will not allow them to develop and to exercise their talents; and afflicts them with the mental and bodily diseases that belong to indolence. The poor, on the other hand, who live from day to day, sometimes out of work for weeks together, practise easily the simple virtues of brotherly love, charity, and mutual helpfulness. They have learned to combine for the good of all, rather than to fight, one against another, for selfish gain. It is the only world where all are borrowing and lending, giving and helping."

"Brother, this dream of yours is like a Socialist tract."

"It may be. Yet you see how strongly it takes hold of me—that, while I see the absurdity of the whole thing, it is not unpleasing to recall the recollection of it. Well—I do not know what set me talking about this dream."

The smiles left his face; he became grave again; he ceased to talk; for the rest of the evening he was once more the old solicitor, weighed down with the affairs of other people.

"Checkley"—it was on the door-step, and Sir Samuel waited while his wife said a few fond things to her sister—"what the devil came over my brother to-night?"

"I don't know indeed, Sir Samuel. I never heard him talk like that before. Doin' good to 'em?—servin' a writ upon 'em is more our line. I think he must be upset somewhere in his inside, and it's gone to his head."

"Practical benevolence? Living for other people? Have you heard him complain of anything?"

"No, Sir Samuel. He never complains. Eats hearty; walks upright and strong; works like he always has worked. Doin' good! And the blessedness of being pore! Seems most wonderful. Blessedness of being pore! Well, Sir Samuel, I've enjoyed that blessedness myself, and I know what it's like. Any or'nary preachin' chap might talk that nonsense; but for your eminent brother, Sir Samuel, such a lawyer as him—to be talking such stuff—if I may humbly so speak of my learned master's words—it is, Sir Samuel, it really is!"

"He said it was a dream, remember. But I agree with you, Checkley. It is amazing."

"Humph! The *blessedness* of being pore! And over such a glass of port, too! I thought I should ha' rolled off my chair—I did, indeed. Here's your good lady, Sir Samuel."

"Elsie," said Mrs. Arundel in the carriage, "I think it was high time that Mr. Dering should take a partner. *He* to dream of practical benevolence ? *He* to be diffusing happiness with open hands ? Oh! most lamentable—I call it. However, the deeds are signed, and we are all right. In case of anything happening, it is a comfort to think that George's position would be only improved."

CHAPTER IX

AT THE GATES OF PARADISE

MANY women have advanced the doctrine that the happiest time of life is that of their engagement. Of course no man can possibly understand this theory; but from a woman's point of view it can be defended because it is, for some girls, the most delightful thing in the world to be wooed; and until the church service is actually said, and the ring is on the finger, the bride is queen and mistress; afterwards—not always. But the happiness of it depends upon its being a courtship without obstacles. Now in the case of the young couple whose fortunes we are following there was plenty of love, with excellent wooing; but the engagement had been opposed by the whole tribe of Arundels, so that every time she met her lover it was in open rebellion against her mother. To go home from a walk with him only to find the silence of resentment at home is not pleasant. Again, we have seen how they were looking forward to a life of poverty—even of privation. Dame Penury, with her pinching ways and shrewish tongue, was going to be their constant lodger. Then the young man could not choose but ask himself whether he was not a selfish beast to take a girl out of plenty into privation. And the girl could not choose but ask herself whether she was not selfish in laying this great burden upon the back of her lover. No one can be indifferent to such a prospect; no one can contemplate with pleasure the cheese-parings, the savings, the management, of such a life; no one can like having to make a penny do the work of sixpence; no one can rejoice as one steps down, down, down the social ladder; no one can anticipate with satisfaction the loss of gentlehood for the daughters, and the loss of an adequate education for the sons.

"You will make me happy," said the lover, "at the cost of everything that makes life happy for yourself."

"If I make you happy," said the girl, "I ask for nothing more. But oh! I am laying a heavy burden upon you. Can you bear it? Will you never blame me if the burden is greater than you can bear?"

And now all the trouble vanished like a cloud from the morning sky—vanished so completely that there was not a trace of it left anywhere. The accusing figure of her mother was changed into a smiling face of pleased and satisfied maternity; reproaches were turned into words of endearment, angry looks to presents and caresses. And as for her sister, you might have thought that all this good fortune was actually achieved and conquered by Elsie—otherwise, how could one justify the praise and flattery that Hilda now lavished upon her? She gave a great dinner as a kind of official reception of the bridegroom into the family; she also gave a dance, at which she herself was the most beautiful woman—she stood in a conspicuous place all the evening, magnificently dressed, statuesque, wonderful! and Elsie was the prettiest girl at the party; but between the most beautiful woman and the prettiest girl was a difference! There is nothing like good fortune to bring out a girl's good qualities; Elsie had always had friends; now she might have numbered them by hundreds. Good fortune breeds friends as the sunshine creates the flowers. She was congratulated, caressed, and flattered enough to turn her head. Now, girls are so constituted that they love admiration, which is a kind of affection, even when it takes the form of flattery; and their heads may be easily turned; but they are as easily turned back again. And the house—the widow's house—which for so many years had been so dull and quiet a place, was transformed into a place of entertainment. It only wanted colored lamps to make it another Vauxhall; it was crowded every night with the younger friends of bride and bridegroom. George had many friends. He was gregarious by nature; he was a rowing man on the athletic side; he had a healthy love and a light hand for things like billiards, shooting, and fishing; they are tastes which assist in the creation of friendships.

These friends—young fellows of like mind—came to the house in multitudes to rally round the man about to desert their ranks. Young men are forgiving. George would row no more among them; he would be lost to the billiard-table, and to the club itself; yet they forgave him, and accepted his invitation, and went to see the bride. They found her with the friends of her own age. Heavens! how the daring of one man in taking away a maiden from the band encourages others! There are six love-stories, at least, all rising out of these evenings, and all of surpassing interest, had one the time to write them. They are both grave and gay; there are tears in every one; the course of true love in no case ran smooth except in the story of the Two Stupids. Love's enemies can never effect aught against a stupid, and so these Two Stupids became engaged without opposition, and were married with acclamations; but they are too stupid—perhaps—to know their own happiness.

All this went on for three weeks. It was arranged that the happy pair should be married in the middle of August; they had resolved to spend their honeymoon in France, staying a few days in Paris, and then going on to see the towns and the country along the Loire, with the old city of Tours for their centre. They proposed to live entirely upon fruit and wine and kisses. No place in the world like Touraine for those who are so young, and so much in love, and so perfectly satisfied with so simple a diet. Even for those who take a cutlet with the fruit and the wine, there is no place equal to Touraine. Meantime, against the home-coming, a desirable flat was secured—not one of your little economical flats, all drawing-room, with two or three rabbit-hutches for bedrooms, but a large and highly decorated flat, with all the newest appliances, large rooms, and a lift and plenty of space for the dinner-parties and receptions which Elsie would have to give. The servants were engaged. The furniture was ordered, all in the advanced taste of the day—carpets, curtains, pictures, over-mantels, cabinets, screens. Elsie went every day to her new home, and found something omitted, and sat down in it to wonder what it would be like—this new life she was entering upon. Oh! it was a busy time. Then there was her trousseau—everybody knows the amount of thought and care required for a trousseau; this was approaching completion—everybody knows the happiness, peculiar and unlike any other kind of happiness, with which a girl contemplates a heap of "things" all her own. I suppose that it is only at her wedding that she can enjoy this happiness, for afterwards the "things" are not her own, but the things of the family. The bride's dress, another thing of supreme importance, had been tried on, though as yet it was very, very far from being finished. The bridesmaids, two of George's sisters, had also already tried on their dresses. They came every day—two very sweet girls, who have both to do with those six love-stories which will never, I fear, be told—to talk over the events and to see the presents. These came in daily, and were laid out in a room by themselves, looking very splendid; their splendor proved the wealth and the position of the pair, because rich presents are only given to rich people.

In a word, everybody was heartily, loyally sympathetic, as if to make up for the previous harshness and coldness. For three weeks this happiness lasted! It was on Monday, June 29th, that the golden shower descended upon them; it was on Monday, July 20th, that the rain of gold ceased, and another kind of cloud came up which speedily changed into a driving storm of rain and sleet, and hail and ice and snow.

Look at them on Sunday. Before the storm there is generally a brief time of sunshine, warm and fine; after the storm, the calm that follows is a time of dismay, speechless and tearless. Sunday was the day before the storm; it was a day of sunshine without and within. The lovers spent the whole day together, hand in hand. They went to church together, they sat side by side, they warbled off the same hymn-book. The service proved, as the preacher used to say, a season of refreshment, for never doth religion so uplift the soul as when it is entirely happy; the voices of the choir chanting the psalms filled them with joy, and would have done so even if they had been penitential minors and the lamentation of a sinner. Their hearts rose higher and higher as the preacher exhorted, and would have flown upwards just as much whether he had brandished the terrors of the law or held out the gracious promise of the Gospel. For, you see, at such a time as this, whatever was said or done only led this faithful pair farther and deeper into the shady glades and fragrant lawns and flowery dells of Love's Paradise.

Every church, at every service, and especially in the evening, contains many such lovers. You may know them by certain infallible signs. They sit very close together; they sing off the same book; their faces betray by the rigidity of their attitude, which is that of pretended attention, the far-away expression of their eyes, and the absence of any external sign of emotion or sympathy with the preacher, that their hands, beneath some folds of the feminine gabardine, are closely clasped. It has sometimes pleased the philosopher, and relieved the tedium of a dull sermon, to look round the congregation, and to pick out the lovers—here a pair and there a pair. Even in the church, you see, Love is conqueror and king.

These lovers, therefore, went to church in a frame of mind truly heavenly; nobody in the whole congregation felt more deeply pious; every response was an act of praise; every prayer an act of gratitude; every hymn a personal thank-offering. Beneath those calm faces was flying and rushing a whirlwind and confusion of hopes, memories, plans, projects, and gratitudes. He who looks back upon the days immediately before his wedding-day—most men no more remember their own emotions than a child remembers yesterday's ear-ache—will wonder how he lived through that time of change, when all that he prayed for was granted, but on the condition of a turning upside down of all his habits, customs, and petted ways.

All round them sat the people, no doubt with minds wholly attuned to the service of prayer and praise. Well, the sheep in a flock to outward seeming are all alike, yet every animal has his own desires and small ambitions for himself. So, I suppose, with the congregation. As every man shuts the street-door behind him, and trudges along the way to church—the *Via Sacra*—with wife and children, he carries in his waistcoat pocket, close to his heart, a little packet of business cares to think upon during the sermon. And if all the thoughts of all the people could be collected after the sermon, instead of the offertory, they would make a salutary oblation indeed.

"George," said Elsie, as they came out, "let us go into the Gardens, and sit under a tree, and talk. Let us get away from everybody for half an hour."

Kensington Gardens were filled with the customary throng of those who, like themselves, had been to church. The carping philosopher says unkind things about church, and gardens, and fashion. As if church would ever keep like from congregating with like! There were shoals of beautiful girls, dressed as well as they knew or could afford; dozens of young fellows, and with them the no-longer-quite-so-young, the no-longer-young, the no-

5*

longer-young-at-all, the middle-aged, the elderly, and the old, not to speak of the children. Elsie looked up and down the walk. "We are never so much alone as in a crowd," she said, with the air that some girls assume of saying an original thing—which no woman ever did say yet, unless by accident.

They joined the stream; presently George led the girl out of the road and across the grass to a place where two or three chairs were set under the trees. They sat down. Then occurred the miracle wrought in these gardens every day and all day long. Out of the ground sprang a man—for such he seemed, though doubtless a spirit-messenger—who demanded twopence. This paid, he vanished straightway. After the ceremony they talked.

"George," said the girl, "every day now, wherever I am, even at church, I feel as if I should like to jump up and to sing and dance. This morning I should have liked a service all to ourselves—you to read, and I to sing; you to pray, and I to praise. I kept wondering if there was any girl in the place so happy as myself—or so unhappy as I was three short weeks ago."

"Elsie," said George—a simple thing to say, but it had a thousand meanings.

"We have not deserved it; indeed, indeed, we have not. Why are we singled out for such joy? We already had the greatest thing of all—we had love. That is happiness enough for some women. We only wanted a little more money, and now we have all this great fortune."

"It is wonderful, Elsie."

She laid her hand on his, and spoke, in her sweet, low voice, gazing upwards. "George! I am so happy that I want everybody else to be happy as well. The angels, I am sure, must lose some of their joy in wishing that all were with them. I pity all those poor girls who have no lovers; all those poor married people who are lying in poverty; all those poor creatures who are trying for what they cannot get; all those who are weeping outside the gates of Heaven. George, it is a beautiful world, and it should be such a happy world; there should be nothing but joy all through life. There is such an abundance of happiness possible in it. Sadness is only a passing cloud; anxiety is only a touch of east wind; evil and pain are only fleeting shadows."

She sighed, and clasped her hands, and the tears rose to her eyes.

"We shall grow old together, George," she went on, murmuring rather than speaking—I omit her lover's interruptions and interjections. "You will always love me, long after my beauty —you know you *will* call it beauty, George—is past and gone; even when I am a poor old crone, doubled up in my arm-chair; you will always love me. My life will be full—full—full of love. Perhaps—" Here her face flushed, and she stopped. "We shall have no trouble about money; we shall go on always learning more and more, growing wiser and wiser and wiser. You will be a wise and a good man, thinking and working all your life for other people, just as Mr. Dering imagined—three weeks ago. Everybody will love and respect you. Then you will grow gray-headed, you poor, dear boy! and all the world will say how wise and strong you are; and I shall be prouder of my old husband than even I was of my young lover. The life that others have dreamed we shall live. Every day shall come laden with its own joy, so that we would not, if we could help it, suffer it to go away." She struck a deeper note, and her voice trembled and sank and her eyes filled with tears. "Life shall be all happiness, as God intended for us. Even death will be little sorrow, for the separation will be so short." Once more she laid her hand on his.

Even to the most frivolous the prospect of the wedded life awakens grave and solemn thoughts; for those who have eyes to see and ears to hear and brains to understand, there is no prospect so charged with chances and possibilities, where even life itself may become a death in life.

When George left her in the evening he drove to see Athelstan.

"So," he said, "you have been courting all day, I suppose. You ought to have had enough of it. Sit down, and have something—a pipe—a cigar. Well—you are going to be very jolly, I suppose. Elsie's little fortune will help a bit, won't it?"

"I should think so, indeed."

"Yes—I've been very glad ever since you told me that the child had had this stroke of luck. I wonder who gave her the money? To be sure there is plenty of money knocking about among the Arundels. Most of us have had a sort of instinct for making money. Put us down anywhere among a lot of men in a city, and we begin to transfer the contents of their pockets to our own."

"Meanwhile, give up this old resentment. Come back to your own people. Come to our wedding."

"I cannot possibly, unless you will tell me who forged that check. How could I go back to people who still believe me guilty? When you are married, I will go and see Elsie, which I can do with a light heart. You have not told any one about my return?"

"Certainly not. No one suspects, and no one talks or thinks about you."

Athelstan laughed a little. "That is a doubtful piece of information. Am I to rejoice or to weep because I am completely forgotten and out of mind? It is rather humiliating, isn't it?"

"You are not forgotten at all. That is a different thing. Only they do not speak of you."

"Well, George, never mind that now. I am glad you came to-night, because I have some news for you. I have found the commissionnaire who took the check to the bank—actually found the man."

"No! After all these years?"

"I wrote out the particulars of the case—briefly. Yesterday I took the paper to the commissionnaires' barrack in the Strand, and offered a reward for the recovery of the man who had cashed the check. That same evening the man presented himself, and claimed the reward. He remembered the thing very well—for this reason: the gentleman who employed him first sent him with a bag to a parcel-delivery office; he did not look at the address. The gentleman was staying at the Cecil Hotel. Now, the commissionnaire was a one-armed man. Because he had only one arm, the gentleman—who was a pleasant-spoken gentleman—gave him ten shillings for his trouble, which was nine shillings more than his proper pay. The gentleman sent him to the bank with this check to cash, and he returned with seven hundred and twenty pounds in ten-pound notes. Then it was that the gentleman— who seems to have been a free-handed gentleman—gave him ten shillings. The man says that he would know that gentleman anywhere. He was old, and had gray hair. He says that he should know him wherever he saw him. What do you think of that?"

"Well—it is something, if you could find that old man."

"Why, of course it was Checkley—gray-haired Checkley.

We'll catch that old fox yet. Beware of Checkley. He's a fox. He's a worm. He's a creeping centipede. When the old man goes you must make Checkley pack."

CHAPTER X

A MYSTERIOUS DISCOVERY

On Monday morning the unexpected happened. It came with more than common malignity. In fact, nothing more threatening to the persons chiefly concerned in the calamity could have happened, though at first they were happily spared the comprehension of its full significance.

There is a wide-spread superstition—so wide that it must be true—that at those rare moments when one feels foolishly happy, at peace with all the world, at peace with one's own conscience, all injuries forgiven, the future stretched out before like a sunlit peaceful lake, some disaster, great or small, is certainly imminent. "Don't feel too happy," says Experience Universal. "The gods resent the happiness of man. Affect a little anxiety. Assume a certain sadness. Restrain that dancing leg. If you must shake it, do so as if by accident, or as if in terror—for choice, shake it over an open grave in the church-yard. Stop singing that song of joy; try the lamentation of a sinner instead. So will the gods be deceived. Above all, never allow yourself to believe that the devil is dead. He is not even asleep. By carefully observing these precautions, a great many misfortunes may be averted. If, for instance, George had gone home soberly on Sunday night, instead of carrying on like a school-boy in play-time, obviously happy, and so inviting calamity, perhaps he would never have been connected—as he afterwards became—with this disaster.

You have heard that Mr. Dering was a man of method. Every morning he arrived at his office at a quarter before ten; he hung up his coat and hat in a recess behind the door; he then opened his safe with his own hand. Checkley had already laid out the table with a clean blotting-pad, pens, and letter-paper; he had also placed the letters of the day upon the pad. The reading of the letters began the day's work. The lawyer read them, made notes upon them, rang for his shorthand clerk, and dictated answers. These despatched, he turned to the standing business. This morning, with the usual routine, he was plodding through the letters of the day, taking up one after the other and reading half mechanically. Presently he opened one, and looked at the heading. "Ellis & Northcote," he said. "What do they want?" Then he suddenly stopped short, and started. Then he began the letter again, and again he stopped short. It was from his brokers in the City, and it recommended a certain advantageous investment. That was not in itself very extraordinary. But it contained the following remarkable passage: "You have made such great transfers and so many sales during the last few months that you have probably more profitable uses for money in your own business. But if you should have a few thousands available at the present moment it is a most favorable opportunity—"

"Great transfers and many sales?" asked Mr. Dering, bewildered. "What transfers? What sales does he mean?"

He turned over the pages of his diary. He could find no transactions of the kind at all. Then he reflected again. "I can remember no transfers," he murmured. "Is this another trick of memory?"

Finally he touched the bell upon his table.

"Checkley," said Mr. Dering, on the appearance of the ancient clerk, "I have got a letter that I don't understand at all. I told you that my memory was going. Now you see. Here is a letter about transfers and sales of stock. What transfers? I don't understand one word of it. My memory is not only going—it is gone."

"Memory going? Nonsense!" the old man shook his head. "No, no; your memory is all right. Mine is as clear as a bell —so's yours. You eat hearty—so do I. You sleep well—so do I. We're both as hale and hearty as ever."

"No, no; my memory is not what it was. I've told you so a dozen times. I lose myself sometimes. Yesterday, when the clock struck twelve, I thought it was only ten. I had lost two hours. And sometimes, when I walk home, I lose recollection of the walk afterwards."

"Tut, tut! nobody of your age is such a young man as you. Why, you walk like five-and-twenty. And you eat hearty—you eat very hearty." His words were encouraging, but he looked anxiously at his master. Truly, there was no apparent decay in Mr. Dering. He sat as upright, he looked as keen, he spoke as clearly as ever.

"Well—about this letter. My friend Ellis, of Ellis & Northcote, writes to me about something or other, and speaks of my effecting great transfers and sales of stock lately. What does he mean?"

"You haven't bought or sold any stock lately that I know of."

"Well, you would have known. Have we had to make any investments for clients of late? There was the Dalton-Smith estate."

"That was eleven months ago."

"I suppose he must mean that—he can't mean anything else. Yes, that is it. Well, I've got a partner now, so that it matters less than it would have done—had my memory played me tricks with no other responsible man in the place."

"You didn't want a partner," said Checkley jealously. "You had *me*."

"He must mean that," Mr. Dering repeated. "He can't mean anything else. However— Has my bank-book been made up lately?"

"Here it is. Made up last Friday—nothing been in or out since."

Mr. Dering had not looked at his book for three or four months. He was well served; his people took care of his bank-book. Now he opened it, and began to run his finger up and down the pages.

"Checkley," he said, "what has happened to Newcastle Corporation Stock? The dividends were due some weeks ago—they are not paid yet. Is the town gone bankrupt? And—eh? Where is Wolverhampton? And—and—" He turned over the pages quickly. "Checkley, there is something wrong with the book. Not a single dividend of anything entered for the last four months. There ought to have been about six hundred pounds in that time."

"Queer mistake," said Checkley. "I'll take the book round to the bank, and have it corrected."

"A very gross and careless mistake, I call it. Tell the manager I said so. Let it be set right at once, Checkley—at once—and while you wait. And bring it back to me."

The bank was in Chancery Lane, close to the office. The old clerk went off on his errand.

"A very careless mistake," the lawyer repeated; "any clerk of mine who committed such a mistake should be dismissed at once." In fact, the certainty of full and speedy justice kept Mr. Dering's clerks always at a high level of efficiency.

He returned to the letters, apparently with no further uneasiness.

After ten minutes, Checkley taking longer than he expected, Mr. Dering became aware that his attention was wandering. "Great transfers and many sales," he repeated. "After all, he must mean the investment of that Dalton-Smith money. Yet that was only a single transaction. What can he mean? He must have made a mistake. He must be thinking of another client. It's his memory, not mine, that is confused. That's it —his memory."

The large open safe in the corner was filled with stacks of paper tied up and endorsed. These papers contained, among other things, the securities for the whole of Mr. Dering's private fortune, which was now very considerable. Even the greatest City magnate would feel for Mr. Dering the respect due to wealth if he knew the amount represented by the contents of that safe. There they were—the leases, agreements, mortgages, deeds, bonds, conveyances, shares—all the legal documents by which the wicked man is prevented from seizing and appropriating the rich man's savings. Formerly the rich man kept his money in a box with iron bands. He locked up the box, and put it in a recess in the cellar contrived in the stone wall. If he was only a bourgeois it was but a little box, and he put it in a secret place (but everybody knew the secret) at the head of his bed. If he were a peasant he tied his money up in a clout, and put it under the hearth-stone. In any case thieves broke in, and stole those riches. Now, grown wiser, he has no box of treasures at all; he lends it all in various directions and to various associations and companies. Every rich man is a money-lender; he is either Shylock the Great or Shylock the Less, according to the amount he lends. Thieves can steal nothing but paper, which is no use to them. As we grow wiser still we shall have nothing at all in any house that can be of any use to any thief, because everything in the least valuable will have its papers, without the production of which nothing of value will be bought or sold. And all the gold and silver, whether forks or mugs, will be lodged in the bank. Then everybody will become honest, and the eighth commandment will be forgotten.

Among Mr. Dering's papers were share certificates, bonds, and scrip of various kinds, amounting in all to a great many thousands. Of this money a sum of nearly thirteen thousand pounds belonged to Elsie, but was still in her guardian's name. This, of course, was the fortune which had fallen so unexpectedly into the girl's hands. The rest, amounting to about twenty-five thousand pounds, was his own money. It represented, of course, only a part—only a small part—of his very respectable fortune.

Mr. Dering, whose memory, if it were decaying, was certainly clear on some points, looked across the room at the open safe, and began to think of the papers representing their investments. He remembered perfectly all the different corporation stock. All the water, gas, railway shares; the Indian stock and the Colonial stock; the debenture companies and the trading companies. He was foolish, he thought, to be disturbed by a mere mistake of the broker; his recent lapses of memory had made him nervous; there could be nothing wrong, but that clerk at the bank ought to be dismissed for carelessness. There could be nothing wrong; for the sake of assurance he would turn out the papers, but there could be nothing wrong.

He knew very well where they were; everything in his office had its place; they were all tied up together in a bulky parcel, bestowed upon a certain shelf or compartment of the safe. He pushed back his chair, got up, and walked over to the safe.

Strange! The papers were not in their place. Again he felt the former irritation at having forgotten something. It was always returning—every day he seemed to be forgetting something. But the certificates must be in the safe. He stood irresolutely looking at the piles of papers, trying to think how they could have been displaced. While he was thus wondering and gazing Checkley came back, bank-book in hand.

"There is something wrong," he said. "No dividends at all have been paid to your account for the last three months. There is no mistake at the bank. I've seen the manager; and he's looked into it, and says there can't be any mistake about the entries."

"No dividends? What is the meaning of it, Checkley? No

dividends? Why, there's thirty-eight thousand pounds worth of stock. The certificates are kept here in the safe; only, for some reason or other, I can't find them at the moment. They must be in the safe somewhere. Just help me to find them, will you?"

He began to search among the papers—at first a little anxiously, then nervously, then feverishly.

"Where are they?" he cried, tossing over the bundles. "They must be here. They must be here. Let us turn out the whole contents of the safe. We must find them. They have never been kept in any other place. Nobody has touched them or seen them except myself."

The old clerk pulled out all the papers in the safe, and laid them in a great pile on the table. When there was nothing left in the safe, they began systematically to go through the whole. When they had finished they looked at each other blankly.

Everything was there except the certificates and scrip representing the investment of thirty-eight thousand pounds. These alone could not be found. They examined every packet; they opened every bundle of papers; they looked into every folded sheet of parchment or foolscap. The certificates were not in the safe. "Well," said the clerk at last, "they're not here, you see. Now then!"

In the midst of their perplexity happened a thing almost as surprising, and quite as unexpected, as the loss of the certificates. Among the papers was a small round parcel tied up with red tape. Checkley opened it. "Bank-notes," he said, and laid it aside. They were not at the moment looking for bank-notes, but for certificates. When he was satisfied that these were not in the safe, and had thrown, so to speak, the responsibility of finding out the cause of their absence upon his master, he took up once more this bundle. It was, as he had said, a bundle of bank-notes rolled up and tied round. He untied the knot and laid them flat, turning up the corners, and counting. "Curious," he said; "they're all ten-pound notes—all ten-pound notes; there must be more than fifty of them. And the outside one is covered with dust. What are they?"

"How should I know?" said Mr. Dering irritably. "Give them to me. Bank-notes? There are no bank-notes in my safe."

"Forgotten!" the clerk murmured. "Client's money, perhaps. But the client would have asked for it. Five or six hundred pounds. How can five hundred pounds be forgotten? Even a Rothschild would remember five hundred pounds. Forgotten!" He glanced suspiciously at his master, and shook his head, fumbling among the papers.

Mr. Dering snatched the bundle from his clerk. Truly, they were bank-notes—ten-pound bank-notes—and they had been forgotten. The clerk was right. There is no firm in the world where a bundle worth five hundred pounds could be forgotten and no inquiry made after it. Mr. Dering stared blankly at them. "Notes!" he cried—"notes! Ten-pound notes! What notes? Checkley, how did these notes come here?"

"If you don't know," the clerk replied, "nobody knows. You've got the key of the safe."

"Good heavens!" If Mr. Dering had been twenty years younger, he would have jumped. Men of seventy-five are not allowed to jump. The dignity of age does not allow of jumping. "This is most wonderful! Checkley, this is most mysterious!"

"What is it?"

"These notes—the devil is in the safe to-day, I do believe. First, the certificates are lost—that is, they can't be found; and next, these notes turn up."

"What notes are they, then?"

"They are nothing else than the bank-notes paid across the counter for that forged check of eight years ago. Oh! there is no doubt of it—none whatever. I remember the numbers—the consecutive numbers—seventy-two of them—seven hundred and twenty pounds. How did they get here? Who put them in? Checkley, I say, how did these notes get here?"

He held the notes in his hand, and asked these questions in pure bewilderment and not in the expectation of receiving any reply.

"The notes paid to that young gentleman when he forged the check," said Checkley, "must have been put back in the safe by him. There's no other way to account for it. He was afraid to present them. He heard you say they were stopped, and he put them back. I think I see him doing it. While he was flaring out he done it—I'm sure I see him doing it."

Mr. Dering received this suggestion without remark. He laid

down the notes, and stared at his clerk. The two old men stared blankly at each other. Perhaps Checkley's countenance, of the two, expressed the greater astonishment.

"How did those notes get into the safe?" the lawyer repeated. "This is even a more wonderful thing than the mislaying of the certificates. You took them out. Show me exactly where they were lying."

"They were behind these books. See! the outside note is covered with dust."

"They must have been lying there all these years. In my safe! The very notes paid across the counter to the forger's messenger! In my safe! What does this mean? I feel as if I were going mad. I say— What does all this mean, Checkley?"

The clerk made answer slowly, repeating his former suggestion,

"Since young Arundel forged the check, young Arundel got the notes. Since young Arundel got the notes, young Arundel must have put them back. No one else could. When young Arundel put them back, he done it because he was afraid of your finding out. He put them back unseen by you that day when you charged him with the crime."

"I did not charge him. I have charged no one."

"I charged him, then, and you did not contradict. I'd charge him again if he was here."

"Any man may charge anything upon any other man. There was no proof whatever, and none has ever come to light."

"You're always for proofs that will convict a man. I only said that nobody else could do the thing. As for putting the notes back again in the safe, now I come to think of it"—his face became cunning and malignant—"I do remember—yes—oh! yes—I clearly remember—I quite clearly remember—I see it as plain as if it was before me. He got sidling nearer and nearer the safe while we were talking; he got quite close—so; he chucked a bundle in when he thought I wasn't looking. I think —I almost think—I could swear to it."

"Nonsense," said the lawyer. "Your memory is too clear. Tie up the notes, Checkley, and put them back. They may help, perhaps, some time, to find out the man. Meantime, let us go back to our search. Let us find those certificates."

They had now examined every packet in the safe; they had

looked at every paper; they had opened every book and searched through all the leaves. There was no doubt left—the certificates were not there.

Checkley began to tie up the bundles again. His master sat down, trying to remember something—everything—that could account for their disappearance.

CHAPTER XI

A MYSTERIOUS DISCOVERY—(*Continued*)

THE safe disposed of, there remained a cupboard, two tables full of drawers, twenty or thirty tin boxes. Checkley examined every one of these receptacles. In vain. There was not anywhere any trace of the certificates.

"Yet," said Mr. Dering, "they must be somewhere. We have been hunting all the morning, and we have not found them. They are not in this room; yet they must be somewhere. Certificates and such things don't fly away. They are of no use to any one. People don't steal certificates. I must have done something with them."

"Did you take them home with you?"

"Why should I do that? I have no safe or strong-room at home."

"Did you send them to the bank for greater safety? To be sure, they would be no more safe there than here."

"Go, and ask. See the manager. Ask him if he holds any certificates of mine."

The clerk turned to obey.

"No." Mr. Dering stopped him. "What's the good? If he held the things there would have been dividends. Yet what can I do?" For the first time in his life the lawyer felt the emotion that he had often observed in clients at times of real disaster. He felt as if there was nothing certain—not even property; as if the law itself—actually the law—was of no use. His brain reeled, the ground was slipping under his feet, and he was falling forward through the table, and the floor, and the foundation—

forward and down—down—down. "What can I do?" he repeated. "Checkley, go. See the manager. There may be something to find out. I can't think properly. Go!"

When the clerk left him he laid his head upon his hands, and tried to put things quite clearly before himself. "Where can the certificates be?" he asked himself, repeating this question twenty times. He was quite conscious that if he had been consulted on such a point by a client he would have replied with the greatest readiness, suggesting the one really practical thing to do. For himself he could advise nothing. "Where can the certificates be? Nobody steals corporation stock and gas companies' shares. They are no good if you do steal them. They can't be sold without the authority of the owner; he has got to sign transfer-papers; if they were stolen the dividends would go on being paid to the owner just the same. Besides—" Somewhere about this point he bethought him of the bank-book. If the stock had been sold the money would appear to his credit. He snatched the book, and looked at it. No; there was no entry which could possibly represent the sale of stock. He knew what every entry meant, and when the amount was paid in; his memory was perfectly clear upon this point.

Checkley's suggestion occurred to him. Had he taken the certificates home with him? He might have done, for some reason which he had now forgotten. Yes; that was the one possible explanation. He must have done. For a moment he breathed again—only for a moment, because he immediately reflected that he could not possibly do such a thing as take those securities to a house where he never transacted any business at all. Then he returned to his former bewilderment and terror. What had become of them? Why had he taken them out of the safe? Where had he bestowed them?

And why were there no dividends paid to him on these stocks? Why? He turned white with terror when he realized that if he got no more dividends he could have no more stocks.

During a long professional career of fifty years Mr. Dering had never made a mistake—at least he thought so. If he had not always invested his money to the greatest profit, he had invested it safely. He did not get the interest that some City men expect, but he made no losses. He looked upon himself, therefore, as a man of great sagacity, whereas in such matters he was

only a man of great prudence.   Also, during this long period he
was always in the enjoyment of a considerable income.   Therefore, he had never known the least anxiety about money.   Yet all
his life he had been counselling other people in their anxieties.
It was exactly as if a specialist in some mortal disease should be
himself attacked by it.   Or it was as if the bo'sun, whose duty it
is to superintend the flogging, should be himself tied up.

Nothing came to him; no glimmer of light; not the least recollection of anything.   Then he thought, desperately, that perhaps if he were to imagine how it would be if somebody else, not
himself at all, were to come to himself, and lay the story before
him, as a solicitor, for advice.   Or how it would be if he himself
were to go to himself, as a solicitor, and put the case.

When Checkley came back he found his master leaning back
in his chair, his eyes wide open and staring at him as he opened
the door—yet they saw nothing.   Checkley stood under the gaze
of those eyes, which saw him not.   "Good Lord!" he murmured.
"Is the time come?   Is he going to die?"

His face was white.   He seemed to be listening anxiously; his
lips were parted.   "He's in a fit of some kind," thought the old
clerk.

He stood watching.   He ought, perhaps, to have called for
assistance.   He did not think of it.   He stood and watched, his
face as pale as his master's.   Was it the end?   If so—we all
think of ourselves first—what about his berth and salary?

Suddenly his master's eyes closed; he dropped his head; he
heaved a deep sigh; he moved his head, and opened his eyes.
He was restored to himself.   The fit, whatever it was, had passed.

"Checkley," he said, "I've been trying to put the thing to
myself as if some other man—a client—was putting his case to
me.   I began very well.   The other man came—that is, I myself
called upon myself.   I sat and heard my own story.   I forget,
somehow, what the story was"—he shook his head impatiently.
" Forget — forget — I always forget.   But I remember that it
wasn't the story I wanted him to tell.   It was another story altogether.   He didn't tell me what I wanted to know—that is, what
has become of the certificates?   I'm no nearer than I was.   He
made out that I was actually selling the certificates myself."

"You're wandering a bit," said Checkley, anxiously watching
him; "that's all.   You'll be all right presently.   You've bin

shook up a bit, with the certificates and the notes and all. If I were you I'd have a glass of something stiff."

"No, no; I shall come round presently. Yes—that's it. I'm a good deal upset by this business. Somehow, I don't seem able to think clearly about it. Let me see"—he sighed heavily—"I think you went somewhere—somewhere—for me, before—before the other man came."

"For Lord's sake, don't talk about the other man. There's no such person. Yes, I did go for you—I went to ask the manager of the bank whether he held any stock for you."

"The manager of the bank? True. Well, and does he hold anything?"

"Not a scrap. Never had any."

"Then Checkley"—Mr. Dering dropped his hands helplessly—"what is to be done?"

"I don't know, I'm sure," the clerk replied, with equal helplessness. "I never heard of such a thing before in all my life. Thirty-eight thousand pounds! It can't be. Nobody ever heard of such a thing before. Perhaps they are about the place somewhere. Let's have another search."

"No, no. It is useless. Why—I have had no dividends. The shares were all transferred, and nothing has been paid for them. The shares have been stolen. Checkley, I can't think. For the first time in my life I can't think. I want some one to advise me. I must put the case in somebody's hands."

"There's your young partner—a chance for him to show that he's worth his pay. Why don't you consult him, and then come back to the old plan of you and me? We're knocked a bit silly just at first, but the case'll come to us in the long run. You would have a partner—nothing would do but a partner. The boy's in his own room now, I suppose, with a crown upon his head and the clerks kneelin' around—as grand as you please. Send for *him*."

Mr. Dering nodded.

The partner, when he arrived a few minutes later, found the chief walking about the room in uncontrollable agitation. On the table lay piled the whole contents of the safe. In front of it stood the ancient clerk, trembling and shaking—head, hands, knees, and shoulders—following the movements of his master with eyes full of anxiety and terror. This strange fit, this forgetfulness, this rambling talk about another man, this new restlessness, frightened him.

"You are come at last." Mr. Dering stopped, and threw himself into his chair. "Now, my partner, hear the case, and resolve the difficulty for us if you can. Tell him, Checkley—or—stay; no, I will tell it myself. Either I have lost my reason and my memory, or I have been robbed."

George stood at the table and listened. Something of the utmost gravity had happened. Never before had he seen his chief in the least degree shaken out of his accustomed frigidity of calm. Now he was excited; his eyes were restless; he talked fast; he talked badly. He made half a dozen attempts to begin; he marshalled his facts in a slovenly and disorderly manner, quite unlike his usual clear arrangement; for fifty years he had been marshalling facts and drawing up cases, and at his own he broke down.

"I think I understand the whole," said George, when his chief paused and Checkley ceased to correct and to add. "You had certificates representing investments to the amount of thirty-eight thousand pounds; these are gone, unaccountably gone; no dividends have been paid for some months, and your broker speaks of large transfers."

"That's not all," said Checkley. "Tell him about the notes."

"Yes. The fact may have some bearing upon the case. While we were looking for the certificates, and in order, I suppose, to complicate things and to bewilder me the more, we found in the safe the very notes—give me the bundle, Checkley—there they are—that were paid over the bank counter to the man who forged my name eight years ago."

"What? The case in which Athelstan Arundel was accused?"

"The same. There they are—you hold them in your hand—the very notes! Strange! on the very day when I am threatened with another and a worse robbery! Yes—yes; the very notes!—the very notes! This is wonderful. Who put them there?"

"How can I know?"

"Well— But in any case one thing is certain—Athelstan's name is cleared at last. You will tell his mother that."

"Not at all," said Checkley. "Why shouldn't he put 'em in himself? I saw him edging up towards the safe—"

6

"Saw him edging—stuff and nonsense! His name is cleared.
This will be joyful news to his mother and sisters."

"Austin, get me back my certificates," said Mr. Dering. "Never mind those notes now. Never mind the joyful news. Never mind Athelstan's name—that can wait. The thought of him and the old forgery only bewilders my brain at this juncture. I cannot act. I cannot think. I feel as if I were blinded and stupefied. Act for me—think for me—work for me. Be my solicitor, George, as well as my partner."

"I will do my best. It is difficult at first to understand—for what has happened? You cannot find—you have mislaid—certain papers; certain dividends which were due do not appear to have been paid; and your brokers, Ellis & Northcote, have used a phrase in a letter which you do not understand. Would it not be well to get them here; or shall I go into the City and ask them exactly what they meant and what has been done?"

"If I could remember any transactions with them during the last six months. But I cannot, except a small purchase of corporation stock last month—a few hundreds! And here are the papers belonging to that."

"Which of the partners do you deal with?"

"The old man, Ellis—he's always acted for me. He has been my friend for close on fifty years."

"Well, I will send for him, and tell him to come as soon as possible, and to bring along with him all the letters and papers he has."

"Good, good," said Mr. Dering, more cheerfully. "That is practical. I ought to have thought of that at the very outset. Now we shall get along. The first thing is to arrive at the facts —then we can act. If it was another man's case I should have known what to do. But when it is your own—and to lose the certificates, and when a sum of nearly forty thousand pounds is at stake—it looks like losing the money itself—and the feeling of uncertainty—"

"All taken together, becomes rather overwhelming. Of course I should like to see the letter-book, and we must run through the letters to see if they throw any light upon the business. Perhaps the papers themselves may be found among them."

The presence of this young man, cheerful, decided, taking practical measures at once—cheered up the lawyer, and steadied his shattered nerves. But Checkley, the clerk, looked on gloomily. He replaced the papers in the safe, and stood beside it, as if to guard it; he followed the movements of the new partner with watchful, suspicious eyes; and he muttered sullenly between his teeth.

First George sent a telegram to the City for the broker. Then, while the old clerk still stood beside the safe, and Mr. Dering continued to show signs of agitation uncontrollable, sometimes walking about the room and sometimes sitting at his table, sometimes looking into the empty shelves of the safe, he began to look through the copied letters—those, that is, which had gone out of Mr. Dering's office. He searched for six months, working backwards.

"Nothing for six months," he said. "Checkley, give me the letters." He went through these. They were the letters received at the office, all filed, endorsed, and dated. There was not one during the letters of six months which he examined which had anything to do with the sales of stocks and shares.

"If," he said, "you had written to Ellis & Northcote a copy of your letter would be here in this book. If they had written to you, their letters would be among these bundles. Very well. Since no such letters are here, it is clear that no such letters were written. Therefore, no sales."

"Then," said Mr. Dering, "where are my certificates? Where are my dividends?"

"That we shall see. At present we are only getting at the facts."

Then Mr. Ellis, senior partner of Ellis & Northcote, arrived, bearing a small packet of papers. Everybody knew Mr. Ellis, of Ellis & Northcote, one of the most respectable stock-brokers in London—citizen and Loriner. He belongs eminently to the class called worthy—an old gentleman, carefully dressed, of smooth and polished appearance, pleasing manners, and great integrity. Nobody could look more truly *integer valie* than Mr. Ellis. Nor does his private practice belie his reputation and his appearance. His chin and lips looked as if they could not possibly endure the burden of beard or moustache; his sentiments, once observed at a glance, would certainly be such as one expects from a citizen of his respectability.

"Here I am, dear sir," he said cheerfully—"here I am, in immediate obedience to your summons. I hope that there is nothing wrong, though your request that I should bring with me certain papers certainly made me a little apprehensive."

"There is, I fear, a good deal wrong," said Mr. Dering. "Sit down, my old friend. Give Mr. Ellis a chair, Checkley. Austin, you will tell him what he wants to know."

"You wrote to Mr. Dering yesterday, recommending a certain investment?"

"I certainly did. A very favorable opportunity it is, and a capital thing it will prove."

"You mentioned in your letter certain transfers and sales which, according to your letter, he had recently effected?"

"Certainly."

"What sales were they?"

Mr. Ellis looked at his papers. "February last, sale of various stock, all duly enumerated here, to the value of £6500. March last, sale of various stock, also all duly enumerated, to the value of £12,000 odd. April last, sale of stock to the value of £20,000 —more or less—realizing—"

"You note the dates and amounts, Austin?" said Mr. Dering.

"Certainly. We will, however, get the dates and the amounts more exactly in a moment. Now, Mr. Ellis, of course you received instructions with the papers themselves. Were they in writing or by word of mouth?"

"In writing. By letters written by Mr. Dering himself."

"Have you got those letters with you?"

CHAPTER XII

A MYSTERIOUS DISCOVERY—(*Concluded*)

"EVERYTHING is here, and in proper order." He laid his hand upon the papers. "Here, for instance, is the first letter, dated February 14th, relating to these transactions. You will, no doubt, remember it, Mr. Dering." He took up a letter, and read it aloud:

"'MY DEAR ELLIS,—I enclose a bundle of certificates and shares. They amount to somewhere about £6500 at current price. Will you have these transferred to the name of Edmund Gray, gentleman, of 22 South Square, Gray's Inn? Mr. Edmund Gray is a client, and I will have the amount paid to my account by him. Send me, therefore, the transfer papers and the account showing the amount due to me by him, together with your commission.

"'Very sincerely yours,

"'EDWARD DERING.'

"That is the letter. The proceeding is not usual, yet not irregular. If, for instance, we had been instructed to buy stock for Mr. Dering— But, of course, you know."

"Pardon me," said George. "I am not so much accustomed to buy stock as my partner. Will you go on?"

"We should have done so, and sent our client the bill for the amount, with our commission. If we had been instructed to sell we should have paid in to Mr. Dering's bank the amount realized, less our commission. A transfer is another kind of work. Mr. Dering transferred this stock to Edmund Gray, his client. It was, therefore, for him to settle with his client the charges for the transfer and the value of the stock. We, therefore, sent a bill for these charges. It was sent by hand, and a check was received by return of the messenger."

George received the letter from him, examined it, and laid it before his partner.

Mr. Dering read the letter, held it to the light, examined it very carefully, and then tossed it to Checkley.

"If anybody knows my handwriting," he said, "it ought to be you. Whose writing is that?"

"It looks like yours. But there is a trembling in the letters. It is not so firm as the most of your work. I should call it yours, but I see by your face that it is not."

"No; it is not my writing. I did not write that letter. This is the first I have heard of the contents of that letter. Look at the signature, Checkley. Two dots are wanting after the word 'Dering,' and the flourish after the last 'n' is curtailed of half its usual dimensions. Did you ever know me to alter my signature by a single curve?"

"Never," Checkley replied. "Two dots wanting and half a flourish. Go on, sir; I've just thought of something—but go on."

"You don't mean to say that this letter is a forgery?" asked Mr. Ellis. "Why—then— Oh! it is impossible. It must, then, be the beginning of a whole series of forgeries. It's quite impossible to credit it. The letter came from this office; the postmark shows it was posted in this district; the answer was sent here. The transfers—consider—the transfers were posted to this office; they came back, duly signed and witnessed, from this office. I forwarded the certificate made out in the name of Edmund Gray to this office, and I got an acknowledgment from this office. I sent the account of the transaction, with my commission charges, to this office, and got a check for the latter, from this office. How can such a complicated business as this—only the first of these transactions—be a forgery? Why, you want a dozen confederates, at least, for such a job as this."

"I do not quite understand yet," said George, inexperienced in the transfer of stocks and shares.

"Well, I cannot sell stock without the owner's authority; he must sign a transfer. But if I receive a commission from a lawyer to transfer his stock to a client, it is not my business to ask whether he receives the money or not."

"Yes, yes. And is there nothing to show for the sale of this six thousand pounds' worth of paper?" George asked Mr. Dering.

"Nothing at all. The letters and everything are a forgery."

"And you, Mr. Ellis, received a check for your commission?"

"Certainly."

"Get me the old checks and the check-book," said Mr. Dering. The check was drawn, as the letter was written, in Mr. Dering's handwriting, but with the slight difference he had pointed out in the signature.

"You are quite sure," asked George, "that you did not sign that check?"

"I am perfectly certain that I did not."

"Then as for this Edmund Gray, of 22 South Square, Gray's Inn—what do you know about him?"

"Nothing at all—absolutely nothing."

"I know something," said Checkley. "But go on—go on."

"He may be a non-existent person, for what you know."

"Certainly. I know nothing about any Edmund Gray."

"Wait a bit," murmured Checkley.

"Well, but," Mr. Ellis went on, "this was only a beginning. In March you wrote to me again; that is to say, I received a letter purporting to be from you. In this letter—here it is—you instructed me to transfer certain stock—the papers of which you enclosed—amounting to about twelve thousand pounds—to Edmund Gray aforesaid. In the same way as before the transfer papers were sent to you for signature; in the same way as before they were signed and returned; and in the same way as before the commission was charged to you and paid by you. It was exactly the same transaction as before—only for double the sum involved in the February business."

Mr. Dering took the second letter, and looked at it with a kind of patient resignation. "I know nothing about it," he said—"nothing at all."

"There was a third and last transaction," said the broker—"this time in April. Here is the letter written by you, with instructions exactly the same as in the previous cases, but dealing with stock to the amount of nineteen thousand pounds, which we duly carried out, and for which we received your check—for commission."

"Every one of these letters—every signature of mine to transfer-papers and to checks—was a forgery," said Mr. Dering slowly. "I have no client named Edmund Gray; I know no one of the name; I never received any money from the transfers; these investments are stolen."

"Let me look at the letters again," said George. He examined them carefully, comparing them with each other. "They are so wonderfully forged that they would deceive the most careful. I should not hesitate, myself, to swear to the handwriting."

It has already been explained that Mr. Dering's handwriting was of a kind that is not uncommon with those who write a great deal. The unimportant words were conveyed by a curve, with or without a tail, while the really important words were clearly written. The signature, however, was large, distinct, and florid—the signature of the house, which had been flourishing for a hundred years and more, a signature which had never varied.

"Look at it," said George again. "Who would not swear to this writing?"

"I would for one," said Mr. Ellis, "and I have known it for forty years and more. If that is not your own writing, Dering, it is the very finest imitation ever made."

"I don't think my memory can be quite gone. Checkley, have we ever had a client named Edmund Gray?"

"No, never. But you've forgotten one thing. That forgery eight years ago—the check of seven hundred and twenty pounds —was payable to the order of Edmund Gray."

"Ah! So it was. This seems important."

"Most important," said George. "The forger could not possibly by accident choose the same name. This cannot be coincidence. Have you the forged check?"

"I have always kept it," Mr. Dering replied, "on the chance of using it to prove the crime and convict the criminal. You will find it, Checkley, in the right-hand drawer of the safe. Thank you. Here it is—'Pay to the order of Edmund Gray'; and here is his endorsement. So we have his handwriting, at any rate."

George took it. "Strange," he said. "I should, without any hesitation, swear to your handwriting here as well. And look, the signature to the check is exactly the same as that of these letters—the two dots missing after the name, and the flourish after the last 'n' curtailed."

It was so. The handwriting of the check and of the letters was the same; the signatures were slightly, but systematically, altered in exactly the same way in both letters and check.

"This again," said George, "can hardly be coincidence. It seems to me that the man who wrote that check also wrote those letters."

The endorsement was in a hand which might also be taken for Mr. Dering's own. Nothing to be got out of the endorsement.

"But about the transfer-papers?" said George. "They would have to be witnessed as well as signed?"

"They were witnessed," said the broker, "by a clerk named Lorry."

"Yes, we have such a man in our office. Checkley, send for Lorry."

Lorry was a clerk employed in Mr. Dering's outer office. Being interrogated, he said that he had no recollection of witnessing a signature for a transfer-paper. He had witnessed many signatures, but was not informed what the papers were. Asked if he remembered especially witnessing any signature in February, March, or April, he replied that he could not remember any, but that he had witnessed a great many signatures; that sometimes Mr. Dering wanted him to witness his own signature, sometimes those of clients. If he were shown his signature he might remember. Lorry, therefore, was allowed to depart to his own place.

"There can be no longer any doubt," said George, "that an attempt has been made at a robbery on a very large scale."

"An attempt only?" Mr. Dering asked. "Where are my certificates?"

"I say attempt, because you can't really steal stock. Dividends are only paid to those who lawfully possess it. This Edmund Gray we can find if he exists. I take it, however, that he does not. It is probably a name assumed by the forger. And I suppose that he has made haste to sell his stock. Whether or no, you will certainly recover your property. People may as well steal a field as steal stocks and shares."

"We can easily find out for you," said Mr. Ellis, "what has become of your paper."

"If the thieves have kept it," George went on, "all they could make would be the dividends for four months. That, however, is only because the bank-book was not examined for so long. They could not reckon upon such an unusual stroke of luck. It seems almost certain that they must get rid of the stock as quickly as they could. Suppose that they have realized the whole amount. It is an immense sum of money. It would have to be paid by check into a bank; the holder could only draw out the money gradually. He might, to be sure, go to America, and have the whole amount transferred; but that would not help him much unless he could draw it out in small sums payable to confederates. In fact, the robbery seems to me hedged about with difficulties almost impossible."

"It is the most extraordinary attempt at robbery that ever was," said Mr. Ellis. "Thirty-eight thousand pounds in shares! Well, I will find out for you if they have been sold, and to whom. Meantime, my old friend, don't you be down-hearted about it. As Mr. Austin says, you will certainly get your property back again. What? We live in a civilized country. We cannot have large sums like forty thousand pounds stolen bodily. Property isn't kept any longer in bags of gold. Bank-notes, banks, investments, all tend to make great robberies impossible. Courage; you will get back your property."

Mr. Dering shook his head doubtfully.

"There is another chance," George suggested. "One has

6*

heard of robberies effected with the view of blackmail afterwards. Suppose we were to get a letter offering the whole to be returned for a certain sum."

"No, no. It is now four months since the thing was done. They have sold out the stock, and disappeared—gone to America, as you suggested. Why, the things may have been sold a dozen times over in the interval. That is the danger. Suppose they *have* been sold a dozen times over. Consider. Here is a share in the Great Western. I transfer it from A to B. Very good. The share now belongs to B, and stands in his name, whether honestly come by or not. B sends it to another broker, who sells it to C. He, again, to D. Every transaction is right and in form except the first. You can trace the share from owner to owner. B has vanished. A says to C, 'You bought that share of a thief.' C says, 'Very sorry. How was I to know? D has got it now.' D says that it is his, and he will stick to it. We go to law about the share. What is going to happen? Upon my word, I don't know. Well—but this is only conjecture. Let me first find out what has become of the shares. Of course, there is a record; I have only to refer. I will let you know by to-morrow morning if I can."

When Mr. Ellis was gone, George began to sum up, for the clearing of his own mind, the ascertained facts of the case, so far as they had got.

"First," he said, "the letters to Ellis & Northcote were written on our headed paper. Clearly, therefore, the writer must have had access to the office. Next, he knew and could copy your handwriting. Third, he was able to intercept the delivery of letters, and to prevent your getting any he wished to stop, because the correspondence was conducted openly through the post. That seems to be a very important point. Fourth, the letters were all, apparently, in your handwriting, very skilfully imitated, instead of being dictated and then signed. Fifth, he must at least have known of the last forgery, or how did he arrive at the name of Edmund Gray? And was it out of devilry and mockery because that forgery escaped detection, that he used the name again? Sixth, he must have had access to the safe where the check-book (as well as the certificates) was kept. Seventh, he must have known the office pretty well, or how did he find out the name of your brokers? Eighth, the handwriting appeared to be exactly the same as that of the former forgery."

"It is the same as last time," said Checkley. "That forgery was done in the office if ever a thing was done here. Same with this—same with this. Well, time will show. Same with this." He glared from under his great eyebrows at the young partner, as if he suspected that the young gentleman could throw some light upon that mystery if he wished.

"We have given time long enough to discover the author of the last business," said Mr. Dering, "but he has not chosen to do so as yet. The loss of property," he groaned—"the loss of close on forty thousand pounds."

"I don't believe it is lost," said George. "It can't be lost. It is a bit of a railway—part of a reservoir—a corner of the gas-works; you can't lose these things—unless, indeed, the difficulty suggested by Mr. Ellis occurs."

Here Mr. Dering pushed back his chair, and began again to walk about the room in restless agitation. He was no longer the grave and serious lawyer; he became one of his own clients, lamenting, as they had so often lamented in that room, the greatness of his misfortune. He uttered the usual commonplaces of men in distress—there is a dreadful sameness about the lamentation of ill luck. We all know them—the hardness of the thing; the injustice of it; the impossibility of warding it off; his own sagacity in taking every precaution; the dreadfulness of being singled out of a whole generation for exceptional misfortune. Mr. Dering himself—the grave, calm, reserved old lawyer, who seemed made of granite—broke down under the blow, and became an ordinary human creature. In the lower walks they weep. Checkley would have wept. Mr. Dering became eloquent, wrathful, sarcastic. No retired general who has ruined himself by gambling in stocks could so bemoan his luck. George listened, saying nothing. It was an experience. No man so strong but has his weak point. No man is completely armored against the arrows of fate.

Presently he grew a little more calm, and sat down. "Forgive me, George," he said gently—"forgive this outbreak. There is more in the business than you know of. I feel as if I know something about it, but can't bring it out. I am growing so forgetful—I forget whole days—I am filled with the feeling that I ought to know about it. As for the loss, what I have said is true. You do not yet feel as I do about property—you are too young. You have not got any property yet. Wait a few years—then you will be able to agree with me that there is nothing in the world so hard as to lose your property—the property that you have made—by your own exertions—for yourself."

"Now you talk like yourself," said Checkley. "That's sense. Nothing so dreadful as to lose property. It's enough to kill people. It has killed many people."

"Property means everything. You understand that the more the older you get."

"You do," said Checkley. "There's nothing in the world worth considering except property."

"It means, remember, all the virtues—prudence, courage, quick sight, self-restraint, tenacity, all the fighting qualities. We do well to honor rich men. I hoped to receive honor myself as a rich man. When you have put together a few thousands—by the exercise of these finer qualities, so that the thought of this gives you dignity—"

"Ah!" cried Checkley, straightening himself.

"To feel that they are gone—gone—gone— It is cruel. George, you don't understand it. You are young; as yet you have no money. Checkley, you have saved—"

"A trifle, a trifle." But he covered his mouth with his hand to conceal the smile of satisfaction.

"You are reputed rich."

"No—no—no. Not rich. My chances have been few. I have not let them go. But rich? No, no."

"How would you regard the loss — the robbery of your property, Checkley?"

The old clerk shook his head. He had no words adequate to the question.

"Apart from the loss," Mr. Dering went on, "there is the sense of insecurity. I felt it once before, when the other forgery took place. There seems no safety anywhere. Papers that I keep in my private safe, to which no one has a key but myself, which I never leave open if I leave the room even to go into another room, are taken. Check-books which I keep there are taken out, and checks stolen. Finally, things are put in—the bundle of notes, for instance. I say that I feel a sense of helplessness, as if everything might be taken from me, and I should be powerless to resist."

"Let us first get back the certificates," said George, "and we will find out and defeat this gang, if it is a gang, of confederates. Yes — it is as you say — the ground itself seems sinking beneath one's feet, when one's own investments are sold for nothing by a letter so like your own writing that it would deceive anybody."

"Done in the office," Checkley murmured — "in the office. Same as last time. Well — we shall find him — we shall find him." He began to bundle the papers back into the safe, murmuring, "Same as last time — done in the office — we shall find him — we shall find him. We found him before, and we'll find him now."

<hr>

CHAPTER XIII

THE FIRST FIND

"Yes," said George, thoughtfully, "a day or two ought to unravel this matter. We must first, however, before going to the police, find out as much as we can ourselves. Let me take up the case by myself for a bit."

"No, no," Checkley grumbled. "Police first. Catch the man first."

"Put aside everything," said the chief — "everything, George. Forget everything until you have found out the mystery of the conspiracy."

"It looks to me like a long firm," George went on — "a long firm with a sham name and a respectable address. Of course there is no such person, really, as Edmund Gray."

"It is not only the loss — perhaps, let us hope" — Mr. Dering sighed — "only a temporary loss; if a real loss, then a most terrible blow — not only that, but it is the sense of insecurity. No one ever found out about that check — and here are the notes in the safe all the time."

"He put 'em in," said Checkley.

"This is the second time — and the same name still — Edmund Gray. It fills me with uneasiness. I am terrified, George. I know not what may be the next blow — what may be taken from me — my mortgages, my houses, my land, everything. Go. I can do the work of the office—all the work —by myself. But this work I cannot do. I am not able to think about it. These thoughts overpower me and cloud my reason."

" Well," said George, " I will do what I can. I don't suppose there is any Edmund Gray at all, but one must try to find out. There can be no harm in paying a visit to Gray's Inn. If the thing had been done yesterday it would be necessary to strike at once, with a warrant for the arrest of the said Edmund Gray. As it is four months since the last robbery, there can be small harm in the delay of a day or two. I will go and inquire a little."

Nothing easier than to inquire. There was the man's address; everybody knows Gray's Inn; everybody knows South Square. The place is only ten minutes' walk from Lincoln's Inn. George took his hat, walked over, and proceeded straight to No. 22, expecting to find no such name on the door-posts. On the contrary, there it was, " 2d Floor, Mr. Edmund Gray," among the other occupants of the staircase. He mounted the stairs. On the second-floor right was the name over the door, Mr. Edmund Gray. But the outer door was closed. That is a sign that the tenant of the chambers is either not at home or not visible. On the first floor were the offices of a firm of solicitors. He sent in his card. The name of Dering & Son commands the respectful attention of every solicitor in London. One of the partners received him. The firm of Dering & Son was anxious to see Mr. Edmund Gray, who had the chambers overhead. At what hours was Mr. Edmund Gray generally in his rooms? Nobody knew— not either of the partners, not any of the clerks. He might have been met going up and down the stairs, but nobody knew him by sight or anything about him. This, at first sight, seemed suspicious; afterwards George reflected that men may live for years on the same staircase, and never know anything about each other. Men who live in Gray's Inn do not visit each other; there is little neighborly spirit among men in chambers, but rather an unspoken distrust.

" But," said the partner, " I can tell you who is his landlord. He does not take the rooms of the inn direct, but, as we do, from one who has several sets on a long lease and sublets the rooms. They may know something about the man at the steward's office across the square. If not, the landlord will certainly know."

George asked if Edmund Gray was newly arrived. No. It appeared that he had been in the inn for a long time. "But then," his informant added, "he may have been here a hundred years for all we know; we never think of our neighbors in chambers. Opposite is a man whose name has been over the door as long as I can remember anything. I don't know who he is or what is his business. I don't even know him by sight. So with Mr. Edmund Gray. If I were to meet him on the stairs I should not be any the wiser. You see I am only here in the daytime. Now, the other man on the second floor I do know something about, because he is a coach and was a fellow of my college. And the man in the garrets I hear about occasionally, because he is an old barrister who sometimes defends a prisoner."

At the steward's office George put the same question. "I am a solicitor," he said. "Here is my card. I am most anxious to see Mr. Edmund Gray, of No. 22. Could you save me time by letting me know at what hour he is in his chambers?"

They could tell him nothing. Mr. Gray was not a tenant of the inn. Very likely he was a residential tenant who came home in the evenings after business.

Everything learned is a step gained. Whether Edmund Gray was a man or a long firm, the name had been on the door for many years. But—many years?—could a confederacy of swindlers go on for many years, especially if they undertook such mighty schemes for plunder as this business?

Next he went to the address of the landlord. He was a house agent in Bloomsbury, and apparently a person of respectability.

"If you could tell me," George began, with the same question, "at what hours I could find your tenant in his chambers, or if you could give me his business address, we should be very greatly obliged. We want to find him at once—to-day, if possible—on very important business.

"Well, I am sorry, very sorry—but, in fact, I don't know anything about my tenant's hours, nor can I give you his place of business. I believe he has no business."

"Oh! But you took him as a tenant. You must have had some references."

"Certainly. And upon that I can satisfy you very shortly." He opened a great book, and turned over the pages. "Here it is—'No. 22 South Square, Gray's Inn, second floor, north side—to Edmund Gray, gentleman. Rent, forty pounds a year. Date of taking the rooms, February, 1882, at the half-quarter. Reference, Messrs. Dering & Son, Solicitors, New Square, Lincoln's Inn.'"

"Why—you mean that he referred to us—to Messrs. Dering & Son—in the year 1882?"

"That is so. Would you like to see the letter which we received on application? Wait a moment." He rang the bell, and a clerk appeared, to whom he gave instructions. "I am bound to say," the landlord went on, "that a more satisfactory tenant than Mr. Gray does not exist. He pays his rent regularly by post-office order every quarter on the day before quarter-day."

"Oh! I wonder—" But he stopped, because to begin wondering is always futile, especially at so early a stage. When there are already accumulated facts to go upon, and not till then, wondering becomes the putting together of the puzzle.

"Well, here is the letter. 'Gentlemen'"—the house-agent read the letter received on application to the reference—"'In reply to your letter of the 13th, we beg to inform you that Mr. Edmund Gray is a client of ours, a gentleman of independent means, and that he is quite able to pay any reasonable rent for residence or chambers. Your obedient servants, DERING & SON.' I suppose," he added, "that a man doesn't want a better reference than your own?"

"No; certainly not." George looked at the letter. It presented, as to handwriting, exactly the same points of likeness and of difference as all the other letters in this strange case—the body of the letter apparently written in the hand of Mr. Dering; that is, so as to deceive everybody; the signature with one or two small omissions. "Certainly not," he repeated. "With such a reference, of course, you did not hesitate. Did you ever see Mr. Gray?"

"Certainly. I have seen him often. First, when he was getting his rooms furnished, and afterwards on various occasions."

"What kind of a man is he, to look at?"

"Elderly. Not exactly the kind of man you'd expect to have chambers. Mostly they're young ones who like the freedom. An elderly gentleman; pleasant in his manners; smiling and affable; gray-haired."

"Oh!" Then there was a real Edmund Gray, of ten years'

standing in the inn, who lived, or had chambers, at the number stated in the forged letters.

"I suppose," said the house agent, "that my respectable tenant has not done anything bad?"

"N-no—not to my knowledge. His name occurs in rather a disagreeable case. Would you be so very kind as to let him know, in case you should meet him—but of course we shall write to him —that we are most anxious to see him?"

This the landlord readily promised. "There is another person," he said, who can tell you a great deal more than anybody else. That is his laundress. I don't know who looks after him, but you can find out at the inn. The policeman will know. Go, and ask him."

In the game of battledore and shuttlecock the latter has no chance except to take the thing coolly, without temper. George was the shuttlecock. He was hit back into Gray's Inn—this time into the arms of the policeman.

"Well, sir," said the guardian of the peace, "I do not know anything about the gentleman myself. If he was one of the noisy ones I should know him. But he isn't, and therefore I have never heard of him. But if he lives at No. 22 I can tell you who does his rooms—and it's old Mrs. Cripps, and she lives in Leather Lane."

This street, which is now, comparatively speaking, purged and cleansed, is not yet quite the ideal spot for one who would have pure air and cleanliness combined with godliness of conversation. However, individual liberty is nowhere more absolutely free and uncontrolled than in Leather Lane.

Mrs. Cripps lived on the top floor, nearest to heaven, of which she ought to be thinking, because she was now old and near her end. She was so old that she was quite past her work, and only kept on Mr. Gray's rooms because he never slept there, and they gave her no trouble except to go to them in the morning with a duster and to drop asleep for an hour or so. What her one gentleman gave her, moreover, was all she had to live upon.

Though the morning was warm, she was sitting over the fire watching a small pan, in which she was stewing a savory mess, consisting of an ornamental block with onions, carrots, and turnips. Perhaps she was thinking—the poor old soul!—of the days gone by—gone by for fifty years—when she was young, and wore a feather in her hat.　Old ladies of her class do not think much about vanished beauty, but they think a good deal about vanished feathers and vanished hats; they remember the old free carriage in the streets with the young friends, and the careless laugh, and the ready jest.　It is the ancient gentlewoman who remembers the vanished beauty, and thinks of what she was fifty years ago.

Mrs. Cripps heard a step on the narrow stair leading to her room—a manly step.　It mounted higher and more slowly, because the stairs were dark as well as narrow.　Then the visitor's hat knocked against the door.　He opened it, and stood there looking in.　A gentleman!　Not a district visitor or a sister trying to persuade her to early church, nor yet the clergyman—a young gentleman.

"You are Mrs. Cripps?" he asked.　"The policeman at Gray's Inn directed me here.　You are laundress, I believe, to Mr. Edmund Gray, of No. 22?"

"Suppose I am, sir?" she replied suspiciously.　A laundress is like the hall porter of a club—you must not ask her about any of her gentlemen.

"I have called to see Mr. Edmund Gray on very important business.　I found his door shut.　Will you kindly tell me at what hours he is generally in his chambers?"

She shook her head, but she held out her hand.

The young gentleman placed half a sovereign in her palm. Her fingers closed over the coin.　She clutched it, and she hid it away in some secret fold of her ragged dress.　There is no woman so ragged, so dropping to pieces with shreds and streamers and tatters, but she can find a safe hiding-place, somewhere in her rags, for a coin or for anything else that is small and precious.

"I never tell tales about my gentlemen," she said, "especially when they are young and handsome like you.　A pore laundress has eyes and ears and hands, but she hasn't got a tongue.　If she had there might be terrible, terrible trouble.　Oh dear! yes. But Mr. Gray isn't a young gentleman—he's old, and it isn't the same thing."

"Then," said George, "how and when can I find him?"

"I was coming to that.　You can't find him.　Sometimes he comes, and sometimes he doesn't come."

"Oh!　He doesn't live in the rooms, then?"

"No. He doesn't live in the rooms. He uses the rooms sometimes."

"What does he use them for?"

"How should I know? All the gentlemen do things with pens and paper. How should I know what they do? They make their money with their pens and paper. I dun know how they do it. I suppose Mr. Gray is making his money like the rest of them."

"Oh! he goes to the chambers, and writes?"

"Sometimes it's weeks and weeks and months and months before he comes at all. But always my money regular and beforehand sent in an envelope and a postal-order."

"Well, what is his private address? I suppose he lives in the country?"

"I don't know where he lives. I know nothing about him. I go there every morning, and I do the room. That's all I know."

There was no more information to be obtained. Sometimes he came to the inn; sometimes he stayed away for weeks and weeks and for months and months.

"I might ha' told you more, young gentleman," murmured the old woman, "and I might ha' told you less. P'r'aps you'll come again."

He went back to Lincoln's Inn, and set down his facts.

First, there was a forgery in the year 1883, in which the name of Edmund Gray was used. Next, in the series of forgeries just discovered, not only was the name of Edmund Gray used throughout, but the handwriting of the letters and checks was exactly the same as that of the first check, with the same peculiarities in the signature. This could hardly be a coincidence. The same man must have written the whole.

Then, who was Edmund Gray?

He was a real personage — a living man, not a firm — one known to the landlord of the chambers and to the laundress, if to nobody else. He did not live in the chambers, but he used them for some business purposes; he sometimes called there, and wrote. What did he write? Where was he, and what was he doing when he was not at the chambers? He might be one —leader or follower—of some secret gang. One has read of such gangs, especially in French novels, where the leaders are noble dukes of the first rank, and princesses—young, lovely—of the highest fashion. Why should there not be such a gang in London? Clever conspirators could go a very long way before they were even suspected. In this civilization of checks and registered shares and official transfers, property is so much defended that it is difficult to break through the armor. But there must be weak places in that armor. It must be possible for the wit of man to devise some plan by means of which property can be attacked successfully. Had he struck such a conspiracy?

Thus. A man calling himself Edmund Gray gets a lease of chambers by means of a forged letter in answer to a reference. It is convenient for certain conspirators, hereinafter called the company, to have an address, though it may never be used. The conspiracy begins by forging a check to his order for seven hundred and twenty pounds. That was at the outset, when the conspirators were young. It was found dangerous, and the notes were therefore replaced in the safe. Note that the company, through one or other of its members, has access to that safe. This might, perhaps, be by means of a key—in the evening, after office hours; or by some one who was about the place all day.

Very good. The continued connection of some member of the firm with Dering & Son is proved by the subsequent proceedings. After eight years, the company having matured their machinery, and perhaps worked out with success other enterprises, return to their first quarry, where they have the advantage of access to the letters, and can look over their disposition. They are thus enabled to conduct their successive *coups*, each bigger than the one before. And for four months the thing remains undiscovered. Having the certificates in their hands, what was to prevent them from selling the whole and dividing the proceeds? Nothing. Yet, in such a case they would disappear, and here was Edmund Gray still fearlessly at large. Why had he not got clear away long before?

Again. All the correspondence concerning Edmund Gray was carried on between the office and the brokers. There were no letters from Edmund Gray at all. Suppose it should be found impossible to connect Edmund Gray with the transactions carried on in his name. Suppose the real Edmund Gray were to deny any knowledge at all of the transactions. Suppose he were to

say that ten years before he had brought a letter of introduction
to Mr. Dering, and knew nothing more about him. Well, but
the certificates themselves—what about them? Their possession
would have to be accounted for. So he turned the matter over
and over and arrived at nothing, not even the next step to take.

He went back to the chief, and reported what he had discovered—the existence of an Edmund Gray, the letter of recommendation to the landlord. "Another forgery," groaned Mr.
Dering.

"It is done in the office," said George. "It is all done in the
office—letters, checks, everything."

"The office," Checkley repeated. "No doubt about it."

"Give up everything else, George," said Mr. Dering eagerly—
"everything else. Find out—find out. Employ detectives. Spend
money as much as you please. I am on a volcano—I know not
what may be taken from me next. Only find out, my partner,
my dear partner—find out."

When George was gone, Checkley went after him and opened
the door mysteriously, to assure himself that no one was listening.

"What are you going on like that for, Checkley?" asked his
master irritably. "Is it another forgery? It rains forgeries."

"No, no. Look here. Don't trouble too much about it.
Don't try to think how it was done. Don't talk about the other
man. Look here. You've sent that young gentleman to find out
this business. Well, mark my words—he won't. He won't, I
say. He'll make a splash, but he won't find anything. Who found
out the last job?"

"You said you did. But nothing was proved."

"I found that out. Plenty of proof there was. Look here "
—his small eyes twinkled under his shaggy eyebrows—"I'll find
out this job as well, see if I don't. Why "—he rubbed his hands
—"ho! ho! I *have found out*. Don't ask me—don't put a single question. But I've got 'em—oh! I've got 'em, I've got 'em
for you—as they say—on toast."

CHAPTER XIV

AFTER such a prodigious event as the discovery of these unparalleled forgeries, anything might happen without being regarded. People's minds are open at such times to see, hear, and accept everything. After the earthquake ghosts walk, solid things fly away of their own accord, good men commit murder, rich men go empty away, and nobody is in the least surprised.

See what happened, the very next day, at the office in New Square. When George arrived in the morning he found that the senior partner had not yet appeared. He was late. For the first time for fifty years and more he was late. He went to his place, and the empty chair gave an air of bereavement to the room. Checkley was laying out the table; that is, he had done so a quarter of an hour before, but he could not leave off doing it; he was loath to leave the table before the master came; he took up the blotting-pad and laid it down again; he arranged the pens; he lingered over the job.

"Not come yet?" George cried, astonished. "Do you think that yesterday's shock has been too much for him?"

"I believe it's killed him," said the old clerk—"killed him. That's what it has done"—and he went on muttering and mumbling. "Don't," he cried, when George took up the letters. "P'r'aps he isn't dead yet—you haven't stepped into his shoes just yet. Let them letters alone."

"Not dead yet. I hope not." George began to open the letters, regardless of the surly and disrespectful words. One may forgive a good deal to fidelity. "He will go on for many years after we have got the money back for him."

"After some of us"—Checkley corrected him—"have got his money back for him." He turned to go back to his own office, then turned again, and came back to the table. He laid both hands upon it, leaned forward, shaking his head, and said, with trembling voice, "Did you never think, Mr. Austin, of the black ingratitood of the thing? Him that done it, you know—him that eat his bread and took his money." When Checkley was greatly moved his grammar went back to the early days before he was confidential clerk.

"I dare say it was ungrateful. I have been thinking, hitherto, of stronger adjectives."

"Well, we've agreed—all of us—haven't we?—that it was done in this office? Some one in the office done it with the help of some one out; some one who knows his ways"—he pointed to the empty chair—"some one who'd known all his ways for a long time, ten years at least."

"Things certainly seem to point that way—and they point to you," he would have added, but refrained.

The old man shook his head again, and went on, "They've eaten his bread and done his work; and—and—don't you call it, Mr. Austin—I ask you plain—don't you call it black ingratitood?"

"I am sure it is. I have no doubt whatever about the ingratitude. But, you see, Checkley, that vice is not one which the courts recognize. It is not one denounced in the Decalogue. There is a good deal to consider, in fact, before we get to the ingratitude. It is probably a criminal conspiracy; it is a felony; it is a thing to be punished by a long term of penal servitude. When we have worried through all this and got our conspirators under lock and key, we will proceed to consider their ingratitude. There is also the bad form of it, and the absence of proper feeling of it, and the want of consideration of the trouble they give. Patience! We shall have to consider the business from your point of view presently."

"I wouldn't scoff and snigger at it, Mr. Austin, if I were you. Scoffin' and sniggerin' might bring bad luck. Because, you know, there's others besides yourself determined to bring this thing to a right issue."

George put down his papers, and looked at this importunate person. What did he mean? The old man shrunk and shrivelled and grew small. He trembled all over. But he remained standing with his hands on the table, leaning forward. "Eight years ago," he went on, "when that other business happened—when Mr. Arundel cut his lucky—"

"I will have nothing said against Mr. Arundel. Go to your own room."

"One word—I will speak it. If *he's* dead, I shall not stay long here. But I shall stay so long as he's alive, though you are his partner. Only one word, sir. If Mr. Arundel hadn't—run away—he'd 'a' been a partner instead of you."

"Well?"

"Well, sir—s'pose he'd been found out *after* he was made a partner, instead of before?"

George pointed to the door. The old man seemed off his head—was it with terror? Checkley obeyed. But at the door he turned his head, and grinned. Quite a theatrical grin. It expressed malignity and the pleasure of anticipation. What was the matter with the old man? Surely, terror. Who, in the office, except himself, had the control of the letters? Who drew that quarterly check? Surely, terror.

It was not until half-past eleven that Mr. Dering arrived at the office. He usually passed through the clerks' office outside his own; this morning he entered by his own private door, which opened on the stairs. No one had the key except himself. He generally proceeded in an orderly and methodical manner to hang up his hat and coat, take off his gloves, place his umbrella in the stand, throw open the safe, sit down in his chair, adjusted at a certain distance of three inches or so, put on his glasses, and then, without either haste or dawdling, to begin the work of the day. It is very certain that to approach work always in exactly the same way saves the nerves. The unmethodical workman gets to his office at a varying hour, travels by different routes—now on an omnibus, now on foot; does nothing to-day in the same way that he did it yesterday. He breaks up early. At sixty he talks of retiring; at seventy he is past his work.

This morning Mr. Dering did nothing in its proper order. First, he was nearly two hours late. Next, he came in by his private door. George rose to greet him, but stopped because—a most wonderful thing—his partner made as if he did not observe his presence. His eyes went through George in creepy and ghostly fashion. The junior partner stood still, silent, in bewilderment. Saw one ever the like, that a man should at noontide walk in his sleep? His appearance, too, was strange—his hat, pushed a little back, gave a touch of recklessness—actually recklessness—to the austere old lawyer; his eyes glowed pleasantly; and on his face—that grave and sober face—there was a pleased and satisfied smile; he looked happy, interested, benevolent, but not—no—not Mr. Edward Dering. Again, his coat, always tightly buttoned, was now hanging loose; outside, it had been swinging in the breeze to the wonder of Lincoln's Inn; and he wore no gloves, a thing most remarkable. He looked about the room, nodded his head, and shut the door behind him.

"He's somnambulating," George murmured, "or else I am invisible. I must have eaten fern-seed without knowing it."

Mr. Dering, still smiling pleasantly, walked across the room to the safe, and unlocked it. He had in his hand a brown-paper parcel tied with red tape—this he deposited in the safe, locked it up, and dropped the keys in his pocket. The window beside the safe was open. He sat down, looking out into the square.

At this moment Checkley opened the door softly, after his wont, to bring in more letters. He stopped short, seeing his master thus seated, head in hand, at the window. He recognized the symptoms of yesterday—the rapt look, the open eyes that saw nothing. He crept on tiptoe across the room. "Hush!" he whispered. "Don't move. Don't speak. He went like this yesterday. Don't make the least noise. He'll come round presently."

"What is it?"

"Kind of fit, it is. Trouble done it. Yah! Ingratitood." He would have hissed the word, but it has no sibilant. You can't hiss without the materials. "Yesterday's trouble. That's what's done it."

They stood watching in silence for about ten minutes. The office was like the court of the sleeping princess. Then Checkley sneezed. Mr. Dering probably mistook the sneeze for a kiss, for he closed his eyes for a moment, opened them again, and arose once more himself, grave and austere.

He nodded cheerfully, took off his hat, hung it on its peg, buttoned his coat, and threw open the safe. Evidently he remembered nothing of what had just passed.

"You are early, George," he said. "You are before me, which is unusual. However, the early bird—we know."

"Before you for once. Are you quite well this morning? None the worse for yesterday's trouble?"

7

"He's always well," said Checkley, with cheerfulness assumed. "Nobody ever sees him ill—*he* get ill?   Not him.   Eats as hearty as five-and-twenty, and walks as upright."

"I am perfectly well, to the best of my knowledge.   Yesterday's business upset me for the time, and it kept me awake most of the night.   It is certainly a very great trouble.   You have no news, I suppose, that brought you here earlier than usual?"

"Nothing new since yesterday."

"And you feel pretty confident?"

"I feel like a sleuth-hound.   I understand the pleasures of the chase.   I long to be on the scent again.   As for Edmund Gray, he is as good as in prison already."

"Good!   I was for the moment shaken out of myself.   I was bewildered.   I was unable to look at the facts of the case calmly. For the first time in my life I wanted advice.   Well, I now understand what a great thing it is that our profession exists for the assistance of men in trouble.   How would the world get along at all without solicitors?"

He took his usual place at the table, and turned over his letters. "This morning," he went on, "I feel more assured.   My mind is clear again.   I can talk about the case.   Now then, let us see —Edmund Gray is no shadow, but a man.   He has made me recommend him to his landlord.   He is a clever man and a bold man.   Don't be in a hurry about putting your hands upon him. Complete your case before you strike.   But make no delay."

"There shall be none.   And you shall hear everything from day to day, or from hour to hour."

Left alone, Mr. Dering returned to his papers and his work.

At half-past one Checkley looked in.   "Not going to take lunch this morning?"

"Lunch?   I have only just—"   Mr. Dering looked at his watch.   "Bless me!   Most extraordinary!   This morning has slipped away.   I thought I had only just sat down.   It seems not more than half an hour since Mr. Austin left me.   Why, I should have forgotten all about it, and let the time go by—nothing worse for a man of my years than irregular feeding."

"It's lucky you've got me," said his clerk.   "Half a dozen partners wouldn't look after your meal-times.   Ah!" as his master went upstairs to the room where he always had his luncheon laid out, "he's clean forgotten.   Some of these days, walking about wrapped up in his thoughts, he'll be run over. Clean forgotten it, he has. Sits down in a dream; walks about in a dream; some of these days he'll do something in a dream. Then there'll be trouble." He closed the door, and returned to his own desk, where he was alone, the juniors having gone out to dinner. His own dinner was in his coat-pocket. It consisted of a saveloy cut in thin slices and laid in bread with butter and mustard—a tasty meal. He slowly devoured the whole to the last crumb. Then, Mr. Dering having by this time finished his lunch and descended again, Checkley went upstairs and finished the pint of claret, of which his master had taken one glass. "It's sour stuff," he said. "It don't behave as wine in a man's inside ought to behave. It don't make him a bit joyfuller. But it's pleasant, too. Why they can't drink port wine—which is real wine—when they can afford it, I don't know."

It was past three in the afternoon when George returned, not quite so confident in his bearing, yet full of news.

"If you are quite ready to listen," he said, "I've got a good deal to tell. First of all, I thought I would have another shot at Gray's Inn. I went to the chambers. The outer door was open, which looked as if the man was at home. I knocked at the inner door, which was opened by the laundress, the old woman whom I saw yesterday. 'Well, sir,' she said, 'you are unlucky. The master has been here this very morning, and he hasn't been long gone. You've only missed him by half an hour or so.' I asked her if he would return that day, but she knew nothing. Then I asked her if she would let me write, and leave a note for him. To this she consented, rather unwillingly. I went in, therefore, and wrote my note at Mr. Gray's table. I asked him to call here on important business, and I marked the note 'Urgent.' I think there can be no harm in that. Then I looked about the room. It is one of those old wainscoted rooms, furnished simply, but everything solid and good—a long table, nearly as large as this one of yours; solid chairs; a solid sofa. Three or four pictures on the wall, and a bookcase full of books. No signs of occupation; no letters; no flowers. Everything covered with dust, although the old woman was there. I could have wished to examine the papers on the table, but the presence of the old woman forbade that dishonorable act. I did, however, look at the books. And I made a most curious discovery. Mr. Edmund Gray is a

Socialist. All his books are on Socialism; they are in French, German, and English—all books of Socialism. And the pictures on the wall are portraits of distinguished Socialists. Isn't that wonderful? Did one ever hear before of Socialism and forgery going together?"

"Not too fast. We haven't yet connected Edmund Gray with the forgery. At present we only know that his name was used."

"Wait a bit. I am coming to that. After leaving the chambers I went into the City, and saw Mr. Ellis. First of all, none of the stock has been sold."

"Oh! they have had four months, and they have not disposed of it? They must have met with unforeseen difficulties. Let me see."

Mr. Dering was now thoroughly alert. The weakness of the morning had completely passed away. "What difficulties? Upon my word! I cannot understand that there could have been any. They have got the papers from a respectable solicitor through a respectable broker. No, no. Their course was perfectly plain. But rogues often break down through their inability to see the strength of their own case."

"Next, Mr. Ellis has ascertained that some of the dividends are received by your bank. I therefore called on the manager. Now, be prepared for another surprise."

"Another forgery?"

"Yes, another forgery. It is nine or ten years since you sent a letter to the manager—I saw it—introducing your client, Edmund Gray, gentleman, who was desirous of opening a private account. He paid in a small sum of money, which has been lying to his credit ever since, and has not been touched. In February last he received another letter from you, and again in March and April, forwarding certificates, and requesting him to receive the dividends. With your own hand you placed the papers in the bank. I saw the letters. I would swear to your handwriting."

"These people are as clever as they are audacious."

"At every point a letter from you—a letter which the ablest expert would tell was your handwriting. Your name covers and vouches for everything."

"Did you tell the manager what has happened?"

"Certainly; I told him everything. And this is, in substance, the line he takes. 'Your partner,' he says, 'alleges that those papers have been procured by forgery. He says that the letter of introduction is a forgery. Very good. It may be so. But I have opened this account for a customer who brought me an introduction from the best solicitor in London, whose handwriting I know well and recognize in the letter. Such an allegation would not be enough in itself for me to take action. Until a civil or criminal action is brought—until it is concluded—I could not refuse to treat the customer like all the rest. At the same time, I will take what steps I can to inquire into my customer's antecedents.'"

"Quite right," said Mr. Dering.

"I asked him next what he would do if the customer sent for the papers. He said that if an action were brought he would probably be served with a *subpoena duces tecum*, making him keep and produce these papers as forming part of the documents in the case."

"Certainly, certainly; the manager knows his law."

"'And,' he went on, 'as regards checks, I shall pay them or receive them until restrained.'"

"In other words, he said what we expected. For our own action now."

"We might apply to a judge in chambers for an attachment or a garnisher order. That must be *pendente lite*, an interlocutory proceeding, in the action. As yet, we have not brought an action at all. My partner"—Mr. Dering rubbed his hands cheerfully—"I think we have done very well so far. These are clumsy scoundrels, after all. They thought to divert suspicion by using my name. They thought to cover themselves with my name. But they should have sold and realized without the least delay. Very good! We have now got our hands upon the papers. It would have complicated matters horribly had the stock been sold and transferred. So far we are safe. Because, you see, after what they have heard the bank would certainly not give them up without letting us know. They would warn us; they would put the man off; they would ask him awkward questions about himself. Oh! I think we are safe—quite safe."

Mr. Dering drew a long breath. "I was thinking last night," he continued, "of the trouble we might have if those certificates had changed hands. They might have been bought and sold a dozen times in four months; they might have been sold in separate small lots, and an order of the court necessary for every transaction. We have now nothing but the simple question before us: How did the man Edmund Gray get possession of this property?"

He sat in silence for a few minutes. Then he went on quietly, "To lose this money would be a heavy blow for me—not all my fortune, nor a quarter, but a large sum. I have plenty left; I have no hungry and expectant heirs; my people are all wealthy —but yet a very heavy loss. And then—to be robbed. I have always wondered why we left off hanging robbers. They ought to be hanged, every one. He who invades the sacred right of property should be killed—killed without hope of mercy." He spoke with the earnestness of sincerity. "To lose this property would not be ruin to me, yet it would be terrible. It would take so many years out of my past life. Every year means so much money saved. Forty thousand pounds means ten years of my past—not taken away so that I should be ten years younger, but ten years of work annihilated. Could I forgive the man who would so injure me? Never."

"I understand," said George. "Fortunately, we shall get the papers back. The fact of their possession must connect the possessor with the fraud. Who is he? Can he be warned already? Yet who should tell him? Who knows that we have discovered the business? You, your friend Mr. Ellis, the manager of the bank—no one else. Yes, there is also Checkley—Checkley," he repeated. He could not—yet—express his suspicions as to the old and faithful servant. "Checkley also knows."

At this point Checkley himself opened the door, and brought in a card—that of the bank manager.

"I have called," said the visitor hurriedly, "to tell you of something important that happened this morning. I did not know it when we were talking over this business, Mr. Austin. It happened at ten o'clock, as soon as the doors were open. A letter was brought by hand from Mr. Dering—"

"Another forgery! When will they stop?"

"—asking for those certificates to be given to the bearer—Mr. Edmund Gray's certificates. This was done. They are no longer at the bank."

"Oh! Then they have been warned!" cried George. "Who was the messenger?"

"He was a boy. Looked like an office-boy."

"I will inquire directly if it was one of our boys. Go on."

"That settles the difficulty as to our action in case the papers are wanted by you. We no longer hold them. As to the dividends, we shall continue to receive them to the account of Mr. Edmund Gray until we get an order or an injunction."

"The difficulty," said George, "is to connect the case with Mr. Edmund Gray bodily. At present we have nothing but the letters to go upon. Suppose the real Edmund Gray says that he knows nothing about it. What are we to do? You remember receiving the dividends for him. Has he drawn a check?"

"No; we have never paid any check at all for him."

"Have you seen him?"

"No; I have never seen him."

"It is a most wonderful puzzle. After all, the withdrawal of the papers can only mean a resolution to sell them. He must instruct somebody. He must appear in the matter."

"He may instruct somebody as he instructed me—in the name of Mr. Dering."

"Another forgery?"

"Yes," said George. "We must watch, and find out this mysterious Edmund Gray. After all, it will not help us to say that a forged letter gave certain instructions to do certain things for a certain person—say the queen—unless you can establish the complicity of that person. And that—so far—we certainly have not done. Meantime, what next?"

Obviously, the next thing was to find out if any of the office-boys had taken that letter to the bank. No one had been sent on that errand.

———

CHAPTER XV

CHECKLEY'S CASE

THAT evening Mr. Checkley was not in his customary place at the Salutation, where his presence was greatly desired. He arrived late, when it wanted only a quarter to eleven. The faded barrister was left alone in the room, lingering over the day's pa-

per, with his empty glass beside him. Mr. Checkley entered with
an air of triumph, and something like the elastic spring of a vic-
tor in his aged step. He called Robert, and ordered at his own
expense, for himself, a costly drink—a compound of Jamaica
rum, hot water, sugar, and lemon, although it was an evening in
July, and, for the time of year, almost pleasantly warm. Nor
did he stop here, for, with the manner of a man who just for
once—to mark a joyful occasion—plunges, he rattled his money
in his pocket, and ordered another for the barrister. "For," he
said, "this evening I have done a good work, and I will mark
the day."

When the glasses were brought he lifted his, and cried, "Come,
let us drink to the confusion of all rogues, great and small. Down
with 'em!"

"Your toast, Mr. Checkley," replied the barrister, "would make
my profession useless; if there were no rogues there would be no
law. That, however, would injure me less than many of my
brethren. I drink, therefore, confusion to rogues, great and
small. Down with 'em. This is excellent grog. Down with
'em!" So saying, he finished his glass, and departed to his garret, where, thanks to the grog, he slept nobly, and dreamed that
he was a master in chancery.

The reason of this unaccustomed mirth was as follows: Checkley, by this time, had fully established in his own mind the conclusion that the prime mover in the deed—the act—the thing—
was none other than the new partner, the young upstart, whom
he hated with a hatred inextinguishable. He was as certain about
him as he had been certain about Athelstan Arundel, and for much
the same reasons. Very well. As yet he had not dared to speak;
King Pharaoh's chief scribe would have had the same hesitation
at proffering any theory concerning Joseph. To-night, however—
But you shall hear.

Everybody was out of the office at half-past seven, when he left
it. He walked round the empty rooms, looking into unlocked
drawers—one knows not what he expected to find. He looked
into Mr. Austin's room, and shook his fist and grinned at the
empty chair.

"I'll have you yet," he said. "Oh, fox! fox! I'll have you if
I wait for thirty years!"

It adds an additional pang to old age when one feels that if the end comes prematurely, when one is only eighty or so, there may be a revenge unfinished. I have always envied the dying hero who had no enemies to forgive because he had killed them all.

When he left the place he walked across the inn, and so into Chancery Lane, where he crossed over and entered Gray's Inn by the Holborn archway. He lingered in South Square; he walked all round it twice; he read the names on the door-posts, keeping all the time an eye on No. 22. Presently he was rewarded. A figure which he knew, tall and well-proportioned, head flung back, walked into the inn, and made straight for No. 22. It was none other than Athelstan Arundel. The old man crept into the entrance, where he was partly hidden; he could see across the square, himself unseen. Athelstan walked into the house and up the stairs; the place was quiet; Checkley could hear his steps on the wooden stairs; he heard him knock at a door; he heard the door open, and the voices of men talking.

"Ah!" said Checkley, "now we've got 'em!"

Well, but this was not all. For presently there came into the inn young Austin himself.

"Oh!" said Checkley, finishing his sentence — "on toast. Here's the other; here they are—both."

In fact, George, too, entered the house known as No. 22, and walked up the stairs.

Checkley waited for no more. He ran out of the inn, and he called a cab.

If he had waited a little longer he would have seen the new partner come out of the house and walk away; if he had followed him up the stairs he would have seen him knocking at the closed outer door of Mr. Edmund Gray. If he had knocked at the door opposite he would have found Mr. Athelstan Arundel in the room with his own acquaintance, Mr. Freddy Carstone, the Cambridge scholar and the ornament of their circle at the Salutation. But, being in a hurry, he jumped to a conclusion, and called a cab.

He drove to Palace Gardens, where Sir Samuel had his town-house. Sir Samuel was still at dinner. He sat down in the hall, meekly waiting. After a while the service condescended to ask if he wished a message to be taken in to Sir Samuel.

"From his brother's—from Mr. Dering's office, please tell him. From his brother's office—on most important business—most important—say."

7*

Sir Samuel received him kindly, made him sit down, and gave him a glass of wine. "Now," he said, "tell me what it all means. My brother has had a robbery—papers and certificates and things. Of course they are stopped. He won't lose anything. But it is a great nuisance, this kind of thing."

"He has already lost four months' dividends—four months, sir—on thirty-eight thousand pounds. And do you really think that he will get back his papers?"

"Certainly—or others. They are, after all, only vouchers. How is my brother?"

"Well, Sir Samuel—better than you'd think likely. This morning, to be sure—" He stopped, being loath to tell how his master had lost consciousness. "Well, sir, I've been thinking that the property was gone, and from what I know of them as had to do with the job I thought there was mighty little chance of getting it back. It kept me awake. Oh! it's an awful sum. Close upon forty thousand pounds. He can stand that, and double that—"

"—and double that again," said Sir Samuel, "I should hope so."

"Certainly, sir. But it's a blow. I can feel for him. I'm only a clerk; but I've saved a bit, and put out a bit, Sir Samuel. Cheese-parings, you'd say; but I've enjoyed saving it up—oh! I've enjoyed it. I don't think there is any pleasure in life like saving up—watching it grow and grow and grow—it grows like a pretty flower, doesn't it?—and adding to it. Ah!" he sighed, and drank his glass of wine. "Sir Samuel, if I was to lose my little savings it would break my heart. I'm an old man, and so is he—it would break me up, it would, indeed. Ever since yesterday morning I've been thinking whether anything could happen to make me lose my money. There's death in the thought. Sir Samuel—for an old man and a small man like me there's death in the thought."

"Don't tell anybody where your investments are, and lock up the papers, Checkley. Now, what do you want me to do for you?"

"I want you to listen to me for half an hour, Sir Samuel, and to give me your advice, for the business is too much for me."

"Go on, then. I am listening."

"Very well. Now, sir, I don't know if I shall be able to make my case clear—but I will try. I haven't been about Mr. Dering for fifty years for nothing, I hope. The case is this. Nine years ago, a man, calling himself Edmund Gray, took chambers in South Square, Gray's Inn—forty pounds a year. He is represented as being an elderly man. He has paid his rent regularly, but he visits his chambers at irregular intervals. Eight years ago there was a forgery at your brother's. The check was payable to the order of Edmund Gray — mark that. The money was paid—"

"I remember. Athelstan Arundel was accused, or suspected of the thing."

"He was. And he ran away to avoid being arrested—remember that. And he's never been heard of since. Well, the series of forgeries by which the shares and stocks belonging to Mr. Dering have been stolen are all written in the same handwriting as the first, and are all carried on in the name and for the order of Edmund Gray. That you would acknowledge in a moment if you saw the papers—there are the same lines and curves of the letters—"

"Which proves, I should say, that Athelstan never did it."

"Wait a minute. Don't let's be in a hurry. The forgers by themselves could do nothing. They wanted some one in the office; some one always about the place; some one who could get at the safe; some one who could get from the office what the man outside wanted; some one to intercept the letters—"

"Well?"

"That person, Sir Samuel, I have found."

Sir Samuel sat up. "You have found him?"

"I have. And here's my difficulty. Because, Sir Samuel, he is your brother's new partner; and unless we lodge him in the jug before many days he will be your own brother-in-law."

Sir Samuel changed color, and got up to see that the door behind the screen was shut. "This is a very serious thing to say, Checkley—a very serious thing."

"Oh! I will make it plain. First, as to opportunities; next, as to motives; third, as to facts. For opportunities, then. Latterly, for the last six months, he's been working in the chief's office nearly all day long. There he sat at the little table between the windows, just half turned round to catch the light, with the open safe within easy reach of his hand when the chief wasn't looking; or when—because he doesn't always touch the bell—Mr. Dering would bring papers into my office and leave him alone—ah! alone—with the safe. That's for opportunities. Now for motives. He's been engaged for two years, I understand, to a young lady—"

"To Lady Dering's sister."

"Just so, sir. And, I believe, until the unexpected luck of his partnership, against the wish of Lady Dering's family."

"That is true."

"He had two hundred a year. And he had nothing else—no prospects and no chances. So I think you will acknowledge that there's sufficient motive here for him to try anything."

"Well, if poverty is a motive—no doubt he had one."

"Poverty was the motive. You couldn't have a stronger motive. There isn't in the world a stronger motive—though, I admit, some young men who are poor may keep honest. I did. Mr. Austin, I take it, is one of those that don't keep honest. That's for motive. Now for facts. Mr. Austin had nothing to do with the forgery eight years ago; he was only an articled clerk beginning. But he knew young Arundel, who did the thing, remember. That check was written by young Arundel, who ran away. The letters of this year are written by *the same hand*— by your brother-in-law, Sir Samuel, by Mr. Athelstan Arundel."

"But he is gone; he has disappeared; nobody knows where he is."

Checkley laughed. This was a moment of triumph. "He is back again, Sir Samuel. I have seen him."

"Where? Athelstan back again?"

"I will tell you. All these forgeries use the name of Edmund Gray, of 22 South Square, Gray's Inn. I have told you that before. When the thing is discovered young Austin goes off, and makes himself mighty busy tracking and following up, hunting down, doing detective work, and so on. Oh! who so busy as he? Found out that Edmund Gray was an old man, if you please; and this morning again—so cheerful and lively that it does your heart good—going to settle it all in a day or two. Yah! As if I couldn't see through his cunning! Why! I'm seventy-five years old. I'm up to every kind of dodge; what will happen next, unless you cut in? First, we shall hear that Mr. Edmund Gray has gone abroad, or has vanished, or something. When he's quite out of the way we shall find out that he did the whole thing—him and nobody else. And then, if there's no more money to be made by keeping the papers, they will all come back—from Edmund Gray, penitent—oh! I know."

"But about Athelstan Arundel?"

"To be sure. I'm an old man, Sir Samuel, and I talk too much. Well, I go most nights to a parlor in Holborn—the Salutation it is—where the company is select and the liquor good. There I saw him a week ago. He was brought in by one of the company. I knew him at once, and he wasn't in hiding. Used his own name. But he didn't see me. 'No, no,' thinks I. 'We won't give this away. I hid my face behind a newspaper. He's been staying in Camberwell for the last eight years, I believe, all the time."

"In Camberwell? Why in Camberwell?"

"In bad company—as I was given to understand."

"You don't mean this, Checkley? Is it really true?"

"It is perfectly true, Sir Samuel. I have seen him. He was dressed like a prince—velvet jacket and crimson tie and white waistcoat. And he walked in with just his old insolence—nose up, head back, looking round as if we were not fit to be in the same room with him—just as he used to do."

"By Jove!" said Sir Samuel, thrusting his hands into his pockets. "What will Hilda say—I mean Lady Dering, say—when she hears it?"

"There is more to hear, Sir Samuel—not much more. But it drives the nail home—a nail in their coffin, I hope and trust."

"Go on. Let me hear all."

"You've caught on, have you, to all I said about Edmund Gray, of 22 South Square—him as was mentioned eight years ago—and about the handwriting being the same now as then?"

"Yes."

"So that the same hand which forged the check then has forged the letters now?"

"Quite so."

"I said then—and I say now—that young Arundel forged that check. I say now that he is the forger of these letters, and that Austin stood in with him, and was his confidant. What do you think of this? To-night, after office, I thought I would go and have a look at 22 South Square. So I walked up and down on the other side; my eyes are pretty good still; I thought I

should, perhaps, see something presently over the way. So I
did. Who should come into the square, marching along as if
the old place, benchers and all, belonged to him, but Mr. Athelstan Arundel! He pulled up at No. 22—No. 22, mind—Edmund
Gray's number; he walked upstairs—I heard him—to the second
floor—Edmund Gray's floor."

"Good Lord!" cried Sir Samuel. "This is suspicious with a
vengeance."

"Oh! but I haven't done. I stayed where I was, wondering
if he would come down, and whether I should meet him and ask
him what he was doing with Edmund Gray. And then I was
richly rewarded—oh! rich was the reward—for who should come
into the square but young Austin himself! He, too, went up the
stairs of No. 22. And there I left them both, and came away—
came to put the case into your hands."

"What do you want me to do?"

"I want you to advise me. What shall I do? There is my
case complete—I don't suppose you want a more complete case
—for any court of justice."

"Well—as for that—I'm not a lawyer. As a City man, if a
clerk of mine was in such a suspicious position as young Austin
I should ask him for full explanations. You've got no actual
proof, you see, that he, or Athelstan either, did the thing."

"I beg your pardon, Sir Samuel. I'm only a clerk, and you're
a great City knight, but I don't know what better proof you
want. Don't I see young Austin pretending not to know who
Edmund Gray is, and then going up to his chambers to meet his
pal, Athelstan Arundel? Ain't that proof? Don't I tell you that
the same hand had been at work in both forgeries? Isn't that
hand young Arundel's?"

"Checkley, I see that you are greatly interested in this
matter—"

"I would give—ah!—twenty pounds—yes, twenty hard-earned
pounds—to see those two young gentlemen in the dock—where
they shall be—where they shall be," he repeated. His trembling
voice, cracked with old age, seemed unequally wedded to the malignity of his words and his expression.

"One of these young gentlemen," said Sir Samuel, "is my
brother-in-law. The other, unless this business prevents, will
be my brother-in-law before many days. You will, therefore,

understand that my endeavors will be to keep them both out of the dock."

"The job will be only half complete without; but still—to see young Austin drove out of the place with disgrace—same as the other one was— Why, that should be something—something to think about afterwards."

Checkley went away. Sir Samuel sat thinking what was best to be done. Like everybody else, he quite believed in Athelstan's guilt. Granted that fact, he saw clearly that there was another very black-looking case against him and against George Austin. What should be done? He would consult his wife. He did so.

"What will Elsie say?" she asked. "Yet, sooner or later, she must be told. I suppose that will be my task. But she can wait a little. Do you go to-morrow morning to Mr. Dering, and tell him. The sooner he knows the better."

You now understand why Mr. Checkley was so joyous when he arrived at the Salutation, and why he proposed that toast.

In the morning Sir Samuel saw his brother, and whispered in his ear the whole of the case as prepared and drawn up by Checkley. "What do you say?" he asked, when he had concluded.

"I say nothing." Mr. Dering had heard all the points brought out, one after the other, without the least emotion. "There is nothing to be said."

"But, my dear brother, the evidence!"

"There is no evidence. It is all supposition. If Athelstan committed the first forgery—there is no evidence to show that he did; if he has been living all these years a life of profligacy in England—I have evidence to the contrary in my own possession; if he was tempted by poverty; if young Austin was also tempted by poverty; if the two together—or either separately—could undertake, under temptation, risks so terrible— You see, the whole case is built up on an 'if.'"

"Yet it holds together at every point. It is a perfect case. Who else could do it? Checkley certainly could not. That old man—that old servant."

"I agree with you, Checkley could not do it. Not because he is too old—age has nothing to do with crime—nor because he is an old servant. He could not do it, because he is not clever enough. This kind of thing wants grasp and vision. Checkley hasn't got either. He might be a confederate. He may have stopped the letters. He is miserly—he might be tempted by money. Yet I do not think it possible."

"No; I cannot believe that," said Sir Samuel.

"Yet it is quite as difficult to believe such a thing of young Austin. Oh! I know everything is possible. He belongs to a good family; he has his own people to think of; he is engaged; he has always led a blameless life. Yet—yet—everything is possible."

"I have known cases in the City where the blameless seeming was only a pretence and a cloak—most deplorable cases, I assure you—the cloak to hide a profligate life."

"I think, if that were so, I should not be deceived. Outward signs in such cases are not wanting. I know the face of the profligate, open or concealed. Young Austin presents no sign of anything but a regular and blameless life. For all these reasons, I say, we ought to believe him incapable of any dishonorable action. But I have been in practice for fifty years—fifty years. During this long period I know not how many cases—what are called family cases—have been in my hands. I have had in this room the trembling old profligate of seventy, ready to pay any price rather than let the thing be known to his old wife, who believes in him, and his daughters, who worship him. I have had the middle-aged man of standing in the City imploring me to buy back the paper—at any price—which would stamp him with infamy. I have had the young man on his knees begging me never to let his father know the forgery, the theft, the villainy, the seduction—what not. And I have had women of every age sitting in that chair, confessing their wickedness, which they do, for the most part, with hard faces and cold eyes—not, like the men, with shame and tears. The men fall, being tempted by want of money, which means loss of pride and self-respect and position and comfort. There ought to have been a clause in the Litany, 'From want of money at all ages, and on all occasions, good Lord, deliver us.'"

"True—most true," said Sir Samuel. "'From want of money' —I shall say that the next time I go to church—'from want of money at all ages, and particularly when one is getting on in years, and has a title to keep up, good Lord, deliver us.' Very good, indeed, brother. I shall quote that in the City. To-morrow I have to make a speech at the Helmet Makers' Company. I shall quote that very remarkable saying of yours."

Mr. Dering smiled gravely. "A simple saying, indeed. The greatest temptation of any is the want of money. Why, there is nothing that the average man will not do rather than be without money. He is helpless; he is a slave; he is in contempt—without money. Austin, you tell me, was tempted by want of money. I think not. He was poor; he had enough to keep him; he was frugal; he had simple wants; he had never felt the want of money. No—I do not think that he was tempted by poverty. Everything is possible—this is possible. But, brother, silence. If you speak about this, you may injure the young man, supposing him to be innocent. If he is guilty, you will put him on his guard. And, mind, I shall show no foolish mercy—none—when we find the guilty parties. All the more reason, therefore, for silence."

Sir Samuel promised. But he had parted with the secret—he had given it into the keeping of a woman.

CHAPTER XVI

WHO IS EDMUND GRAY?

ATHELSTAN laughed on the first hearing of the thing—it was on the Tuesday evening, the day after the discovery. George was dining with him. He laughed both loud and long, and with some bitterness. "So the notes were in the safe all along, were they? Who put them there? 'I,' says old Checkley, 'with my pretty fingers—I put them there.'"

"As soon as this other business is over the chief must tell your mother, Athelstan. It ought to come from her. I shall say nothing to Elsie just yet. She shall learn that you are home again, and that your name is clear again, at the same moment."

"I confess that I should be pleased to make them all confess that their suspicions were hasty and unfounded. At the same time, I did wrong to go away—I ought to have stuck to my post.

As for this other business, one thinks with something like satisfaction of the wise old lawyer losing forty thousand pounds. It made him sit up, did it? To sit up indicates the presence of some emotion. Lost forty thousand pounds! And he who holds so strongly to the sanctity of property! Forty thousand pounds!"

"We shall recover the certificates, or get new ones in their place."

"I suppose so. Shares can't be lost or stolen, really. Meantime there may be difficulty, and you must try to find the forger. Has it occurred to you that Checkley is the only man who has had control of the letters and access at all times to the office?"

"It has."

"Checkley is not exactly a fox—he is a jackal; therefore he does somebody's dirty work for him at a wage. That is the way with the jackal, you know. Eight years ago he tried to make a little pile by a little forgery—not the forgery, I am sure—he did jackal; but he forgot that notes are numbered, so he put them back. Now, his friend, the forger, who is, no doubt, a begging-letter writer, has devised an elaborate scheme for getting hold of shares—ignorant that they are of no value."

"Well, he has drawn the dividends for four months."

"That is something, you see; but he hoped to get hold of thirty-eight thousand pounds. It's the same hand, you say, at work. You are quite sure of that?"

"There can be no doubt of it. How could two different hands present exactly the same curious singularities?"

"And all the letters, checks, and transfers for the same person. What is his name?"

"One Edmund Gray, resident at 22 South Square, Gray's Inn."

"No. 22? Oh! that is where Freddy Carstone lives. Do you know anything about the *nommé* Edmund Gray?"

"I have been in search of information about him. He is described by the landlord of the rooms and by his laundress as an elderly gentleman."

"Elderly. Checkley is elderly."

"Yes, I thought of Checkley, of course. But somehow the indications don't fit. My informants speak of a gentleman. Nobody at his kindliest and most benevolent mood could possibly call Checkley a gentleman."

"The word 'gentleman,'" said Athelstan, "is elastic. It stretches with the consumer. It is like the word 'truth' to a politician. It varies from man to man. You cannot lay down any definition of the word 'gentleman.' Do you know nothing more about him?"

"A little. He has held this set of chambers for nine years, and he pays his rent regularly before the day it falls due. Also, I called upon him the other day when his laundress was at work, and wrote a note to him at his table. The room is full of Socialist books and pamphlets. He is, therefore, presumably a Socialist leader."

"I know all these leaders," said Athelstan the journalist. "I've made the acquaintance of most for business purposes. I've had to read up the Socialist literature, and to make the acquaintance of their chiefs. There is no Edmund Gray among them. Stay— there is a Socialist letter in the *Times* of to-day—surely— Waiter"—they were dining at the club where Athelstan was a temporary member—"let me have the *Times* of to-day. Yes, I thought so. Here is a letter from the Socialist point of view, signed by Edmund Gray—and—and—yes—look here, it is most curious—with the same address—22 South Square—a long letter, in small print, and put in the supplement; but it's there. See; signed Edmund Gray. What do you think of that for a forger?"

George read the letter through carefully. It was a whole column long, and it was in advocacy of Socialism pure and simple. One was surprised that the editor had allowed it to appear. Probably he was influenced by the tone of it, which was generous, cheerful, and optimistic. There was not the slightest ring of bitterness about it. "We who look," it said, "for the coming disappearance of property, not by violence and revolution, but by a rapid process of decay and wasting away, regard the present position of the holders of property with the greatest satisfaction. Everywhere there are encouraging signs. Money which formerly obtained five per cent. now yields no more than half that rate. Shares which were formerly paying ten, twelve, and twenty per cent. are now falling steadily. Companies started every day in the despairing hope of the old great gains fail, and are wound up. Land, which the old wars forced up to an extraordinary value, has now sunk so enormously that many landlords have lost three fourths and even more of their income. All these enterprises which require the employment of many hands—as docks, railways, printing-houses, manufactories of all kinds—are rapidly falling into the condition of being able to pay no dividend at all, because the pay of the men and the maintenance of the plant absorb all. When that point is reached the whole capital—the millions embarked in these enterprises—will be lost forever. The stock cannot be sold, because it produces nothing—it has vanished. In other words, sir, what I desire to point out to your readers is that while they are discussing or denouncing Socialism, the one condition which makes Socialism possible and necessary is actually coming upon the world—namely, the destruction of capital. Why have not men in all ages combined to work for themselves? Because capital has prevented them. When there is no capital left to employ them, to bully them, to make laws against their combinations, or to bribe them, they will have to work for themselves or starve. The thing will be forced upon them. Work will be a necessity for everybody; there will be no more a privileged class; all who work will be paid at equal rates for their work; those who refuse to work will be suffered to starve."

The letter went on to give illustrations of the enormous losses in capital during the last fifteen years, when the shrinkage began. It concluded: "For my own part, I confess that the prospect of the future fills me with satisfaction. No more young men idle, middle-aged men pampered, and old men looking back to a wasted life; nobody trying to save, because the future of the old, the widows, the children, the decayed, and the helpless will be a charge upon the strong and the young—that is, upon the *juvenes*, the workers of the state. No more robbery; no more unproductive classes. Do not think that there will be no more men of science and of learning. These, too, will be considered workers. Or no more poets, dramatists, artists, novelists. These, too, will be considered workers. And do not fear the coming of that time. It is stealing upon us as surely, as certainly, as the decay of the powers in old age. Doubt not that when it comes we shall have become well prepared for it. Those of us who are old may lament that we shall not live to see the day when the last shred of property is cast into the common hoard. Those of us who are young have all the more reason to rejoice in their youth, because they may live to see the great day of humanity dawn at last.—EDMUND GRAY, 22 South Square, Gray's Inn."

"You have read this?" asked George.

"Yes; I read it this morning. Letter of a dreamer. He sees what might happen, and thinks that it will happen. Capital is too strong yet."

"Is this the letter of a forger, a conspirator, a thief?"

"It does not strike me in that light. Yet many great thieves are most amiable in their private lives. There is no reason why this dreamer of dreams should not be also a forger and a thief. Still, the case would be remarkable, I admit."

"Can there be two Edmund Grays—father and son?"

"Can there be a clerk to Edmund Gray, impudently using his master's name, and ready to open any letter that may come? Consider—clerk is a friend of old Checkley. Clerk invents the scheme. Checkley does his share. However, we can easily find out something more about the man, because my old friend Freddy Carstone has chambers on the same floor. We will walk over after dinner, and if Freddy happens to be sober—he is always pleasantly, not stupidly, drunk—he will tell us what he knows about his neighbor."

"I ought to see Elsie this evening, but this is more important."

"Much more. Send her a telegram. Waiter, we will take coffee here. So you have got the conduct of the case. What has Checkley got?"

"Nothing. I believe he is jealous of me. I don't know why. But it does not matter what an old man like that thinks."

"Even an old man can strike a match and light a fire. Checkley is a malignant old man. He is quite capable of charging you with the job. I wonder he hasn't done it by this time. Remember my case, old man." Athelstan's face darkened at the recollection. "Dirt sticks sometimes. Look at me. I am smirched all over."

"His manner was very odd this morning — insolent and strange. He began to talk mysteriously of the ingratitude of the forger—"

"Why, he's actually going to do it! Don't you see—he means that *you* are the forger?"

"Oh! does he? Very well, Athelstan "—George finished his

coffee, and got up—"the sooner we find out the mystery of this Edmund Gray the better. Let us seek your tipsy scholar."

They walked from Piccadilly to Holborn, turning the thing over, and making a dozen surmises. Edmund Gray, twins; Edmund Gray, father and son—father wanting to destroy property, a Socialist; son wanting to steal property, an individualist; Edmund Gray, cousins—one the mild philosopher, rejoicing in the decay of wealth, the other a bandit, a robber, and a conspirator; Edmund Gray, father and daughter—the young lady of the advanced type, who has not only thrown over her religion, but her morals also; Edmund Gray, master and clerk; Edmund Gray under domination of a villain; there was in the situation a noble chance for the imagination. George showed a capacity unsuspected; he should have been a novelist. The hypotheses were beautiful and admirable; they wanted one thing—*vraisemblance;* one felt, even while advancing and defending them, that they were impossible.

They turned into the gateway of the inn, and walked down the passage into the square. "Look!" Athelstan caught his companion by the wrist. "Who is that?"

"Checkley himself; he is coming out of No. 22!"

"Yes, out of 22. What is he doing there! Eh? What has he been doing there?"

It was Checkley. The old man, walking feebly, with bent head, came out from the entrance of No. 22, and turned northward into Field Court. They waited, watching him, until he left the square. "What is he doing there?" asked George again. "Come. Edmund Gray must be at home. Let us go up."

They found the outer door shut. They knocked with their sticks; there was no answer.

"What was he doing here?" asked Athelstan.

The scholar's door stood open. The scholar himself was perfectly sober, and welcomed them joyously and boisterously.

"We are here on business, Freddy," said Athelstan.

"You are here to sit and talk and drink whiskey-and-soda till midnight—till two o'clock in the morning. It is not until two in the morning that you can get the full flavor of the inn. It is like a college then—monastic, shut off from the world, peaceful—"

"Business first, then. You know your neighbor, Mr. Edmund Gray?"

"Certainly. We exchange the compliments of the season and the news of the weather when we meet on the stairs. He has been in here, but not often. A man who drinks nothing is your true damper. That, believe me, and no other, was the veritable skeleton at the feast."

"Our business concerns your neighbor, Mr. Edmund Gray. We want you to tell us what you know about him."

"Go on, then. Question, and I will answer if I can."

"Does Mr. Edmund Gray live at these chambers?"

"No. He may sometimes sleep in them, but I should say not often. He calls at irregular intervals. Sometimes in the afternoon, sometimes in the morning, sometimes not for several weeks together. He is most uncertain."

"Do many people call upon him?"

"No one ever calls upon him."

"Does he keep clerks? Does he carry on an extensive correspondence?"

"I have never heard the postman knock at his door."

"Has he a son or a brother, or anything?"

"I don't know. He may have these hindrances, but they are not apparent."

"What is his occupation or trade?"

"Socialist. He is athirst for the destruction of property. Meantime, I believe, he lives on his own. Perhaps his will be spared to the end. He is an old gentleman of pleasant manners and of benevolent aspect. The old women beg of him; the children ask him the time; the people who have lost their way apply to him. He dreams all the time; he lives in a world impossible. Oh! quite impossible. Why, in a world all Socialist I myself should be impossible. They wouldn't have me. My old friend told me the other day that I should not be tolerated. They would kill me. All because I do no work — or next to none."

George looked at Athelstan. "We are farther off than ever," he said.

"Mr. Edmund Gray believes that the kingdom of Heaven is a kind of hive where everybody has got to work with zeal, and where nobody owns anything. Also he thinks that it is close at hand, which makes him a very happy old gentleman."

"This can't be Checkley," said George.

"It would seem not," Athelstan replied. "Did you ever see another old man up here — we saw him coming out just now — one Checkley, a lawyer's clerk?"

"No; not up here. There is an elderly person—a party—of the name who uses the parlor of the Salutation, where I myself sometimes — one must relax; Porson loved a tavern, so did Johnson—I myself, I say, sometimes forget that I used to belong to the combination room, and sit with Checkley and his companions. But I do not think he is a friend of Mr. Gray. As well call the verger the friend of the bishop. Mr. Gray is a gentleman and a scholar. He is a man of generous instincts and culture. He *could* not be a friend of Checkley's."

"Yet Checkley came out of this staircase."

They talked of other things; they talked till midnight. When they came away the scholar was at his best; one more glass — which he took after they left—would have turned the best into the worst.

"We are as far off as before," said George.

"No—we are so much the nearer that we know who Edmund Gray is not. He is not Checkley. He has no clerks. He has no visitors. He comes seldom. George, this looks to me suspicious. We met Checkley stealing out of the door. Why does Edmund Gray keep these chambers? No business done there; no letters brought there; no callers; the man does not live there. The Socialism may be a blind. Why does the man keep on these chambers?"

Meantime at the Salutation the usual company was assembled. "I fear," said the barrister, "that we shall not have our friend the scholar here this evening. As I came down the stairs I saw him opening his door to two gentlemen—young gentlemen. He will display his wonted hospitality upon them this evening instead." He sighed, and called for the glass of old and mild mixed, which was all he could afford. Had the scholar been with them, certainly there would have been a nobler and a costlier glass. He took up the morning paper, and began to read it.

The conversation went on slowly and with jerks. A dull conversation; a conversation of men without ideas; a day-before-yesterday conversation—the slow exchange of short, solid sentences taken from the paper, or overheard and adopted. We sometimes praise the old tavern life, and we regret the tavern talk. We need not; it was dull, gross, ignorant, and flat; it was commonplace and conventional; because it was so dull the men were fain to sing songs and to propose sentiments, and to drink more than was good for them. Why and when do men drink more than is good for them? First, when and because things are desperately dull; there is nothing to interest them; give them animation, thoughts, amusements, and they will not begin to drink. When they have begun, they will go on. When they have arrived at a certain stage, let them drink as fast as they can, and so get out of the way, because they will never mend, and they only cumber the earth. Here is, you see, a complete solution — a short solution—of the whole drink question. It will not be accepted, because people like a long solution—a three-column solution.

The barrister lifted his head. "There is a letter here," he said, interrupting the ex-M.P., who was clearing the way for what he called an argument by an introduction in the usual form. "While on the one hand, gentlemen, I am free to confess—"

"There is a letter here," he repeated, in a louder voice—the barrister was now old, but he could still assume at times the masterful manner of counsel before the court—"which should be read. It is a letter on Socialism."

"Ugh!" said the money-lender. "Socialism? They want to destroy property. Socialism! Don't tell me, sir."

"It is a dream of what might be—a noble—a generous letter." He looked round him. In their dull and fishy eyes there was no gleam or sparkle of response. "I forgot," he said; "you cannot be interested in such a letter. I beg your pardon, sir." He bowed with great courtesy to the ex-M.P. "I interrupted your valuable observations. We shall listen, I am sure, with — the — greatest—" He buried his head in the paper again.

The legislator began again. "As I was a-saying, gentlemen, when I was interrupted, on the subject of education and the rate-payers, being a ratepayer myself, as we all are, and having our taxes to pay, which is the only advantage we ever get from being a ratepayer, while on the one hand I am free to confess—"

"Why!" the barrister interrupted once again, "this letter is from a man on our staircase—No. 22"—Checkley started—"an acquaintance of mine, if I can call him so, and of our friend the scholar. A very able man, now somewhat in years. By name Edmund Gray."

"What?" said Checkley. "Edmund Gray? You know Edmund Gray?"

"Certainly. I have known him this nine years. Ever since he has been in the inn."

"W-w-what sort of a man is he?" Checkley stammered in his eagerness.

"A very good sort of a man. Why do you ask?"

"I want to know for his advantage—oh! yes—yes—for his advantage."

"Yes." The barrister retreated to his paper. "Oh, yes," he added, "quite so."

"For his advantage," Checkley repeated. "Robert, I think the gentleman would take a tumbler, if you will bring it—hot, Robert —strong—with lemon and sugar—a large rummer, Robert."

The barrister's head behind the paper was observed to tremble.

Robert returned with his rummer, the glass spoon tinkling an invitation. Dinner had been but a sorry affair that day—a stop-gap—insufficient in bulk; the tempted man felt a yearning that could not be resisted. He stretched out his hand, and took the glass and tasted it. Then turning to Checkley,

"You have purchased my speech, sir. You were asking me about Mr. Edmund Gray. What do you wish to know!"

"Everything—his business, his private life—anything."

"As for his business, he has none; he is a gentleman living on his means — like myself; but his means are larger than my own; he has a residence elsewhere—I don't know where; he uses his chambers but little; he has a collection of books there, and he keeps them for purposes of study."

"Does he call there every day?"

"No. Only at irregular times. Sometimes not for many weeks together."

"Has he got any friends?"

"I should say that he has no friends at all—at least none that come to the inn. I have never heard or seen any one in his room. A quiet man. No slammer. An excellent man to have on the staircase. No trampler; doesn't tramp up and down like an elephant. Isn't brought home drunk."

"What does he look like?"

"He is a man advanced in years—perhaps seventy; a good-looking man — very cheerful countenance; tall and well set up still; wears a long frock-coat. And that, I believe, is all I know about him."

"That's all you've got to tell me, is it?"

"That is all, Mr. Checkley. Except that he has written a very remarkable letter to the *Times* of this morning."

"Well, sir, it isn't much for your rum-and-water, let me tell you."

The barrister rose, and poured the half-glass that remained into the cinders. "Then let me drink no more than my information was worth," he said; and at the sight of so much magnanimity the broad earth trembled and Mr. Checkley sat aghast.

The ex-statesman cleared his throat and began again. "After the third interruption, gentlemen, I may hope for a hearing. While, therefore, on the one hand—"

CHAPTER XVII

THE VOICE OF DUTY

ELSIE, in her studio, was at work. She was painting a fancy portrait. You have seen how, before her interview with Mr. Dering, she transformed him from a hard and matter-of-fact lawyer into a genial, benevolent old gentleman. She was now elaborating this transformation. It is a delightful process, known to every portrait-painter, whereby a face, faithfully represented, becomes the face of another person, or the face as it might be, so that a hard and keen face, such as Mr. Dering's, may become a face ennobled with spiritual elevation, benevolence, charity, and kindness of heart. Or, on the other hand, without the least change of feature, this hard, keen face may become, by the curve of a line or the addition of a shadow, the face of a cruel and pitiless inquisitor. Or, again, any face, however blurred and marred by the life of its owner, may by the cunning portrait-painter be restored to the face intended by its Maker, that is to say, a sweet and serious face. Great, indeed, is the power, marvellous is the mystery, of the limner's art.

" Now," Elsie murmured, " you look like some great philanthropist—a thoughtful philanthropist, not a foolish person; your
high forehead and your sharp nostril proclaim that you are no
impulsive gusher; your kindly eyes beam with goodness of heart;
your lips are firm, because you hate injustice. Oh! my dear
guardian, how much I have improved you! Something like this
you looked when you told me of my fortune — and like this
when you spoke of your dream and your illusions — something
like this you looked."

She went on working at her fantasy, crooning a simple ditty,
composed of many melodies running into one, as girls use when
they are quite happy. The afternoon was hot. Outside, Elsie's
windows looked upon a nest of little London gardens, where
nasturtiums twisted round strings upon the walls; hollyhocks
and sunflowers, which love the London smoke, lifted their heads;
and Virginia creepers climbed to the house-tops. The little London gardens do sometimes look gay and bright in the yellow
glow of a July afternoon. The window was open, and the room
was almost as hot as the street outside; we get so few hot days
that one here and there cannot be too hot. On the table lay a
photograph of her lover; over the mantel hung her own drawing
in pastel of that swain; on her finger was his ring; round her
neck lay his chain; all day long she was reminded of him if she
should cease for a moment to think of him; but there was no
need of such reminder. It was Friday afternoon, four days after
the great discovery. Elsie had been informed of the event, the
news of which she received after the feminine manner, with an
ejaculation of surprise and an interjection of sympathy. But one
cannot expect a girl on the eve of her marriage to be greatly distressed because her guardian, a rich man, is annoyed by the temporary loss of certain shares. And as to finding the criminal and
getting back those shares—it was man's work. All the troublesome and disagreeable part of the world's work belongs to man.

It was nearly five o'clock. Elsie was beginning to think that
she had done enough, and that, after tea, a walk in the Gardens
might be pleasant. Suddenly, without any noise or warning of
steps outside, her door was opened, and her sister Hilda appeared.
Now, so swift is the feminine perception that Elsie instantly
understood that something had happened — something bad —
something bad to herself. For, first, the door was opened gently,

as in a house of mourning; and, next, Hilda had on a dress—lavender with heliotrope — costly, becoming, sympathetic, and sorrowful—a half-mourning dress—and she stood for a moment at the door with folded hands, her classical head inclined a little downward to the left, and her eyes drooping—an artistic attitude of sadness.   Hilda not only said the right thing and held the proper sentiments, but she liked to assume the right attitude and to personate the right emotion.   Now it is given to woman, and only to her when she is young, tall, and beautiful, to express by attitude all or any of the emotions which transport or torture her fellow-creatures.   Hilda, you see, was an artist.

"Come in, dear," said Elsie.   "I am sure that you have got something disagreeable to tell me."

Hilda kissed her forehead.   "My poor child!" she murmured. "If it could have been told you by anybody else!"

"Well—let us hear it.   Is it anything very disagreeable?"

"It is terrible.   I tremble—I dare not tell you.   Yet I must. You ought to know."

"If you would go on.   It is much more terrible to be kept in suspense."

"It is about George."

"Oh!" said Elsie, flaming.   "I have had so much trouble about George already, that I did think—"

"My dear, all opposition of the former kind is removed, as you know.   This is something very different.   Worse," she added, in a hollow voice — "far worse."

"For Heaven's sake, get along."

"He has told you about the dreadful robbery.   Of course you have talked about nothing else since it happened.   I found my mother full of it."

"Yes; George is in charge of the case.   He says that everything must be recovered, and that Mr. Dering will in the end suffer no more injury than the trouble of it."

"That may be so.   Elsie—I hardly dare to tell you—there is a clue.   Checkley has got that clue, and has told Sir Samuel everything.   He is following up the clue.   I shudder to think of it.   The man is as relentless as a bloodhound."

"Does that clue concern me?"   Her cheek became pale because she guessed—she knew not what.

"Sir Samuel, against his will, is convinced that Checkley has found the clue. He has told me the whole. He has consented to my telling the dreadful story to my mother and to you—and now I am afraid. Yet I must."

Elsie made a gesture of impatience.

"Go back, Elsie, eight years, if you can. Remember the wretched business of our unworthy brother."

"I remember it. Not unworthy, Hilda—our most unfortunate brother. Why, they have found the very notes he was charged with stealing. They were found in the safe on the very day when they made the other discovery. Have they not told you?"

"Checkley told Sir Samuel. He also remembers seeing Athelstan place the packet in the safe."

"Oh! does he dare to say that? Why, Hilda, the robbery was proved to lie between himself and Athelstan. If he saw that, why did he not say so? He keeps silence for eight long years, and then he speaks."

Hilda shook her head sadly. "I fear," she said, "that we cannot accept the innocence of our unfortunate brother. However, Athelstan was accused of forging Mr. Dering's handwriting and signature. In this new forgery the same handwriting is found again—exactly the same. The forger is the same."

"Clearly, therefore, it cannot be Athelstan. That settles it."

"Yes—unfortunately—it does settle it. Because, you see, Athelstan is in London. He is said to have been living in London all the time—in some wretched place called Camberwell, inhabited, I suppose, by runaways and low company of every kind. He has lately been seen in the neighborhood of Gray's Inn, apparently passing under his own name. Checkley has seen him. Another person has seen him."

"Have you come to tell me that Athelstan is charged with this new wickedness?"

"The forger must have had an accomplice in the office—a man able to get at the safe, able to intercept the post, acquainted with Mr. Dering's ways; such a man as—say—Checkley—or—the only other possible—George." Hilda paused.

"Oh! this is too absurd. You are now hinting that George—my George," she said, proudly, "was the confederate of Athelstan—no, of a forger."

"They have been seen together. They have been seen together

at the house from which the forger addresses his letters. Has George told you that he has known all along—for eight years—of Athelstan's residence in London?"

Observe how that simple remark made in the Salutation parlor, that Athelstan must have been living in Camberwell, had by this time grown into a complete record of eight years' hiding, eight years' disgraceful company, on the part of one; and eight years' complicity and guilty knowledge on the part of the other. Hilda had not the least doubt. It was quite enough for her that Checkley said so. Half of our newspapers are conducted on the same confiding principle.

"If George has not told me," Elsie replied, "it must be for some good reason. Perhaps he was pledged to secrecy."

"My dear"—Hilda rose impressively, with fateful face—"the hand that forged the letters is the hand that forged the check—your brother's hand. The hand that took the certificates from the safe"—she laid her own hand upon Elsie's—"the hand of the confederate, my poor sister—is your lover's hand."

"I knew," said the girl, "that you were coming to this. I have felt it from the beginning."

"Remember, the thing was done in the months of February, March, and April. First of all, Athelstan was then, as now, desperately poor; the life that he has led for the last eight years—the life of a—a—Camberwell profligate"—she spoke as if that respectable suburb was the modern Alsatia—"has certainly destroyed whatever was left of honor and of principle. There comes a time, I have read, in the career of every wicked man when he hesitates no longer, whatever means are offered him of making money. Athelstan it was—so they believe—who devised this scheme, which has been as successful as it is disgraceful. My dear Elsie, this is the most terrible disgrace that has ever befallen my family; the most dreadful and the most unexpected calamity for you."

Elsie caught her sister by the wrist. "In the name of God, Hilda, are you telling me what is proved and true, or what is only suspected?"

"I am telling you what is as good as proved—more than suspected."

"As good as proved? Oh!" Elsie drew a long breath. "As good as proved. That is enough. Like Athelstan's guilt eight years ago—" she flared out suddenly, springing up again, and walking about the room. "Oh! it is wonderful!" she cried—"wonderful! What a family we are! We had a brother, and we believed that he was an honorable gentleman, as the son of his father must be. Then there was a charge, a foolish charge, based upon nothing but may-have-been and must-have-been—We believed the charge—"

"Because we had no choice but to believe, Elsie," her sister interrupted. "Do you think we wanted to believe the charge?"

"We should have believed him innocent until the thing was proved. We did not. We cast him out from among us; and now—after eight years—he has come back poor, you say, and sunk so low that he is ashamed to see his people, and we are going to believe another charge based on may-have-been and must-have-been. No, Hilda, I will not believe it—I will not. And then there is George. If I cease to believe in his honor and his truth I cease to believe in everything. I cannot believe in Heaven itself unless I believe in my lover. Why, his heart is light about this business; he is not concerned; he laughs at that old man's ravings. Ravings? If Athelstan is right then his is the hand that has done it all—his, Hilda; Checkley is the man concerned with both crimes."

Hilda shook her head. "No, Elsie, no. The old man is above suspicion."

"Why should he be above suspicion more than George? And you ask me on the first breath of accusation to treat George as you treated Athelstan. Well— Hilda, I will not!"

"I make every allowance for you, Elsie. It is a most dreadful business—a heart-breaking business. You may misrepresent me as much as you please. I will continue to make allowances for you. Meantime, what will you do?"

"Do? What should I do? Nothing, nothing, nothing. I shall go on as if this thing had never happened."

"Sir Samuel ordered me to warn you most seriously. If you consent to see him again—"

"Consent? Consent? Why should I refuse? In a fortnight he will be my husband and my master, whom I must obey. He calls me his mistress now, but I am his servant. Consent to see him—" She sat down, and burst into tears.

"If you see him again," her sister continued, "warn him to

leave the country. The thing is so certain that in a day or two the proofs will be complete, and it will then be too late. Make him leave the country. Be firm, Elsie. Better still, refuse to see him at all, and leave him to his fate. What a fate! What madness!"

"We allowed Athelstan to leave the country. He ought to have stayed. If I advise George at all I shall advise him to stick to his post, and see the business through. If he were to leave the country I would go with him."

"You are infatuated, Elsie. I can only hope that he will fly the country of his own accord. Meantime, there is one other point—"

"What is it? Pray don't spare me, Hilda. After what has gone before it must be a very little point."

"You are bitter, Elsie, and I don't deserve your bitterness. But that is nothing. At such a moment everything must be pardoned and permitted. The point is about your wedding. It is fixed for the 12th of next month, less than three weeks from to-day. You must be prepared to put it off."

"Indeed? Because you say that a thing impossible is as good as proved! Certainly not, Hilda."

"I have come here to-day, Elsie, by Sir Samuel's express wish, in order to soften the blow and to warn you. Whether you will tell that unhappy young man or not is for you to decide. Perhaps, if you do, he may imitate our unworthy brother, and run away. If he does not, the blow will fall to-morrow—to-day—the day after to-morrow—I know not when. He will be arrested; he will be taken before a magistrate; he will be remanded; he will be out on bail. Oh! Elsie, think of marrying a man out on bail! One might as well marry a man in convict dress. Oh! horrible!"

"I would rather marry George in convict dress than any other man in fine raiment. Because, once more, the thing is impossible."

"You carry your faith in your lover beyond bounds, Elsie. Of course, a girl is right to believe in a man's honor. It makes her much more comfortable, and gives her a sense of security. Besides, we always like to believe that we are loved by the best of men. That makes us feel like the best of women. But in this case, when I tell you that Sir Samuel—a man who has always lived among money, so to speak, and knows how money is con-

8*

stantly assailed—is firmly convinced of George's complicity, I do think that you might allow something for human frailty. In the case of Athelstan, what did Mr. Dering say? 'Everything is possible. So I say of George Austin, everything is possible."

"Not everything. Not that."

"Yes, even that. What do you know of his private life? Why has he concealed the fact of Athelstan's residence in London? Why has he never told us of his friendship with that unfortunate outcast?"

"I don't know. He has his reasons."

"It is a most dreadful thing for you," Hilda went on; "and after getting to believe in the man, and—well—becoming attached to him—though such attachments mean little, and are soon forgotten; and after going the length of fixing the day, and ordering the dress and the wedding-cake, and putting up the banns—Oh! it is a wretched business—a horrible misfortune. The only thing to be said is that in such a case, the fact being known to everybody, no one can blame a girl; and perhaps, in the long run, she will suffer no injury from it. Our circle, for instance, is so different from that of this young man's friends that the thing would not even be known among us."

"I believe, Hilda, you will drive me mad."

"My dear, one must look ahead. And remember that I look ahead for you. As for the young man, I dissociate him henceforth from you. What he does and where he goes I do not inquire, or care about any more than I trouble myself about a disgraceful brother. Some acts cut a man off from his mistress—from his sisters—from the world."

"Do not talk any more," said Elsie. "Let the blow, as you call it, fall when it pleases. But, as for me, I shall not warn George that he is to be charged with dishonesty, any more than I will believe him capable of dishonesty."

"Well, my dear, there is one comfort for us. You may resolve on marrying him. But a man charged with a crime—out on bail—cannot marry any girl. And he will be charged, and the evidence is very strong."

"No doubt. As good as proved—as good as proved. Poor George! who never had ten pounds in the world until he was made a partner—"

"True. And there we have the real motive. Seek the motive,

Sir Samuel says, and we shall find the criminal. Here you have the reason of the secret partnership with Athelstan. Poverty is the tempter—Athelstan is the suggester."

Elsie shook her head impatiently.

"Mr. Dering was to give you away. Who will now— Athelstan? How can we—Sir Samuel and I—assist at a wedding where the bridegroom lies under such a charge by one so near to us as Mr. Dering? How can your mother be present? Oh! Elsie—think!"

Elsie shook her head again, with greater impatience.

"Think what a fate you may be dragging upon yourself! Think of possible children with such a brand upon them!"

"I think only of an honorable and an innocent man."

"I have just come from my mother, Elsie. She says positively that if the charge is brought, the wedding must be put off until the man is cleared. And, for the moment, she does not feel strong enough to meet him. You can receive him here, if you please. And she desires that there may be no disputes or arguments about it."

"It is truly wonderful!" Elsie walked to the open window, and gasped as if choking. "Wonderful!" she repeated. "The same fate—in the same manner—threatens George that fell upon Athelstan. And it finds us as ready to believe in the charge and to cast him out. Now, Hilda, go to my mother, and tell her that though the whole world should call George—my George—a villain I will marry him. Tell her that though I should have to take him from the prison-door I will marry him. Because, you see, all things are not possible. This thing is impossible."

"We shall have trouble with Elsie," Lady Dering told her mother. "Call her soft and yielding? My dear, no mule was ever more stubborn. She will marry her convict, she says, even at the prison-door."

CHAPTER XVIII

STUBBORN as a mule. Yes—it is the way with some girls. Man is soft as wax compared with woman—man concedes, compromises, gives way, submits; woman has her own way—when that way is the right way she becomes a pearl above price.

Elsie, when the door was shut and her sister gone, stood silent, immovable. A red spot burned in her cheeks; her eyes were unnaturally bright; her lips parted; she was possessed by a mighty wrath and great determination; she was the tigress who fights for her beloved. Meantime, everything was changed—the sunshine had gone out of the day; the warmth out of the air; her work, that had pleased her so much an hour ago, seemed a poor weak thing not worth thinking about. Everything was a trifle not worth thinking about—the details of her wedding; her presents; her honeymoon; her pretty flat—all became insignificant compared with this threatened charge against her lover. How was it to be met? If it was only a suspicion put into shape by Sir Samuel and old Checkley it would be best to say nothing. If it was really going to be brought against him, would it not be best to warn him beforehand? And about her brother—"

She sat down, and wrote out the facts. To be doing this cleared her brain, and seemed like working for her lover. In March, 1883, a check for seven hundred and twenty pounds, to the order of one Edmund Gray, was cashed in ten-pound notes by a commissionnaire sent from a hotel in Arundel Street, Strand. No one ever found out this Edmund Gray. Athelstan was suspected. The notes themselves were never presented, and were found the other day in Mr. Dering's safe, covered with dust, at the back of some books.

In February, March, and April, by means of forged letters, a great quantity of shares were transferred from the name of Edward Dering to that of Edmund Gray. The writing of the letters was the same as that of the forged check.

These were the only facts. The rest was all inference and presumption. Athelstan had been seen in London; Athelstan had been living all the time in London; Athelstan had been seen going into the house which was given as the residence of Edmund Gray. Well—Athelstan must be seen the very first thing. Further than this point she could not get. She rang the bell, ordered tea to be brought to her own room, and then put on her hat and went out to the Gardens, where she walked about under the trees, disquieted and unhappy. If a charge is going to be brought against you, the most innocent man in the world must be disquieted until he knows the nature of the evidence against him. Once satisfied as to that, he may be happy again. What evidence could they bring against George?

She went home about eight, going without dinner rather than sit down with her mother. It is a miserable thing for a girl to be full of hardness against her mother. Elsie already had had experience, as you have seen. For the present better not to meet at all. Therefore she did not go home for dinner, but took a bun and a cup of coffee—woman's substitute for dinner—at a confectioner's.

When George called, about nine o'clock, he was taken into the studio, where he found Elsie with the traces of tears in her eyes.

"Why, Elsie," he cried, "what is the matter? Why are you crying, my dear? and why are you alone in this room?"

"I choke in this house, George. Take me out of it—take me away. Let us walk about the squares, and talk. I have a good deal to say."

"Now, dear, what is it?"—when they were outside. "What happened? You are trembling—you have been shaken. Tell me, dear."

"I don't think I can tell you just at present—not all."

"Something, then—the rest afterwards. Tell me by instalments."

"You are quite happy, George? Nobody has said anything to make you angry—at the office, or anywhere else?"

"Nobody. We are going on just the same. Mr. Dering thinks and talks about nothing but the robbery. So do I. So does everybody else. I suppose Checkley has told, for every clerk in the place knows about it, and is talking about it. Why do you ask if anybody has made me angry?"

"My dear George, Hilda has been here this afternoon. You know that—sometimes—Hilda does not always say the kindest things about people."

"Not always. I remember when she wrote me a letter asking whether I thought that a lawyer's clerk was a fit aspirant for the hand of her sister. Not always just the kindest things. But I thought we were all on the most affectionate terms, and that everything had been sponged out. She has been saying more kind things about me? What have I done now? Isn't the money difficulty solved?"

"I will tell you some other time—not now—what she said. At the present moment I want to ask you a question. If you have reasons for not answering, say so, and I shall be quite satisfied; but answer me if you can. This is the question. Hilda says that Athelstan is secretly in London, and that you know it, and that you have been seen with him. Is that true?"

"Well, Elsie, the only reason for not telling you that Athelstan is here is that he himself made me promise not to tell you. Athelstan is in London. I see him often. I shall see him this evening after leaving you. He is in London, walking about openly. Why not? I know no reason for any concealment. But he cannot go to see his mother, or enter his mother's house, until this charge against him has been acknowledged to be baseless. As for you, he will be the first person to visit you—and will be your most frequent visitor—when we are married. He is always talking about you. He is longing for the time when he can see you openly. But nothing will persuade him to come here. He is still bitter against his mother and against Hilda."

Elsie sighed. "It is very terrible—and now— But go on."

"I have answered your question, Elsie."

"Oh, no. I have only just begun. You say that Athelstan is in London, but you do not tell me what he is doing and how he fares."

"He fares very well, and he is prosperous."

"Hilda says that he has been living in some wretched quarter of London all these years; that he has been frequenting low company; and that he has been, until the last few weeks, in rags and penniless."

George laughed aloud. "Where on earth did Hilda get this precious information? Athelstan in a low quarter? Athelstan a prodigal? Athelstan in rags? My dearest Elsie, if Lady Dering were not your sister, I should say that she had gone mad with venomous hatred of the brother whom she made so much haste to believe guilty."

"Oh! tell me quick, George. Don't say anything against Hilda, please. I am already— Tell me quick the whole truth."

"Well, dear, the whole truth is this. Athelstan is doing very well. I suppose you might call him prosperous. When he went away he had ten pounds to begin with. People kindly credited him with the nice little sum of seven hundred and twenty pounds obtained by a forgery. We now know that this money has been lying in the safe all the time; how it got there, the Lord knows —perhaps Checkley could tell. He went to America by the cheapest way possible. He had many adventures and many ups and downs, all of which he will tell you before long. Once he had great good-fortune on a silver mine or something; he made thousands of pounds out of it. Then he lost all his money— dropped it down a sink or into an open drain—you know, in America, these traps are plentiful—and started again on his ten pounds. He was a journalist all the time, and he is a jour- nalist still. He is now over here as the London correspondent of a great paper of San Francisco. That, my dear Elsie, is, briefly, the record of your brother since he went away."

"Oh! but are you quite sure, George?—quite—quite sure? Because, if this can be proved—"

"Nothing is more easy to prove. He brought letters to a London bank, introducing him as the correspondent, and empow- ering him to draw certain moneys."

"How long has Athelstan been at home?" She remembered the dates of the recent forgeries, and the alleged fact that all were in the same handwriting.

"You are so persistent, Elsie, that I am certain you have got something serious on your mind—won't you tell me?"

"No, George—not to-night. But how long has Athelstan been in England?"

"I will tell you exactly how and when I met him. Do you re- member three weeks ago, that Sunday evening when we were so happy and so miserable—resolved on braving everything—going to live on love and a crust for the rest of our lives?—you poor, dear, brave girl!" He touched her fingers. "I shall always be thankful for that prospect of poverty, because it revealed my mistress to me in all her loveliness of love and trust and courage."

"Oh! George—you spoil me. But then I know myself better."

"Well—on that evening we went to church together; and after church, as I was not allowed in the house, we walked round and round the square, until the rain came on, and we had to go home. Well, you did not take any notice; but, as you stood on the steps waiting for the door to be opened, a man was standing on the curb under the lamp close by. When the door was shut behind you, I turned and walked away. This man followed me, and clapped me on the shoulder. It was Athelstan."

"And I saw him, and did not know him?"

"He has grown a big beard now, and wore a felt hat. He is a picturesque object to look at. Ought to have been one of Drake's men. I dare say he was in a former existence. He had then been in England about a fortnight, and every day he had prowled about the place in the hope of seeing you—not speaking to you; he trusted that you would not know him again."

"Oh! poor Athelstan! That is nearly three weeks ago. He has been in England five weeks—over a month; and three, four, five months ago—where was he?"

"I told you. In California."

"Oh! then he could not, possibly—not possibly—and it can be proved—and oh! George—George—I am so glad—I am so glad." She showed her joy by a light shower of tears.

"Why, my dear," he said, soothing her—"why are you so troubled and yet so glad?"

"You don't quite understand, George. You don't know the things that are said. All these forgeries are in the same handwriting?"

"Certainly."

"One man has written all these letters and checks and things—both that of eight years ago and those of last March?"

"That is perfectly certain."

"Then don't you see? Athelstan was out of England when these newly discovered forgeries were done. Therefore he had no hand in them. Therefore, again, he could have no hand in the

·earlier one.   Why, you establish his innocence perfectly.   Now you see one of the reasons why I was so glad."

The other reason—that this fact destroyed at one blow the whole of the splendid edifice constructed upon the alleged stay of Athelstan in London—Elsie concealed.   Her heart, it must be acknowledged, was lightened.   You may have the most complete belief in the innocence of a person, but it is well to have the belief strengthened by facts.

"As for me," said George, "I have been so long accustomed to regard him as one of the worst used of men that I never thought of that conclusion.   Of course if the handwriting is the same, and it certainly seems the same—a very good imitation of Mr. Dering's hand—there is nothing now to be said.   Athelstan was in California in the spring.   That settles it.   And the notes were in the safe.   Two clinchers.   But to some minds a suspicion is a charge and a charge is a fact."

"George, you must take me to Athelstan.   Give me his address."

"He is in lodgings in Half Moon Street.   I will ask him if he will meet you."

"No, no; let me go to him.   It is more fitting.   You will see him presently.   Will you tell him that I will call upon him to-morrow morning at eleven?   And tell him, George, that something has happened—something that makes it impossible for me to remain at home even for the short time before our wedding."

"Elsie! this is very serious."

"Yes, it *is* very serious.   Tell him that I shall ask him to receive me until the wedding, or until certain things have happened.   But in any case— Oh! they must happen so—they must—it is too absurd."

"Elsie, my dear, you grow interjectional."

"Yes, yes.   I mean, George, that if things turn out as I hope they may, I will go home again.   If not, we will be married from Athelstan's lodgings."

"And you will not tell me what this terrible business is?"

"Not to-night, George," she repeated.   "It is very serious, and it makes me very unhappy that my mother and sister—"

"It has something to do with me, Elsie, clearly.   Never mind. Tell me when you please.   Whatever you do is sure to be right. I will see him this evening."

"Thank you, George. I think that what I propose is the wisest thing to do. Besides, I want to be with you and Athelstan. Tell him that as he left the house eight years ago I leave it now."

"You? Why, my dear child, what forgeries have you been committing?"

"None. And yet— Well, George, that is enough about me and my troubles. Tell me now about your search into this business. How have you got on?"

"There is nothing new to report. I told you that I left a note on Edmund Gray's table—no answer has come to that. The bank has written to tell him that his letter of introduction was a forgery—no answer. The dividends are accumulating; he draws no checks; he makes no sign. In a word, though this money is lying to his credit, and the shares are transferred to his name, and the letters give his address, there is nothing whatever to convict the man himself. We could not prove his signature, and he has taken none of the money. He might call any day, and say that he knew nothing about it. I wonder he hasn't done it. When he does we shall just have to put everything straight again. As for poor old Checkley I really believe that he is going mad. If I meet him he glares; if he is in his master's room his eyes follow me about under his shaggy eyebrows with a malignity which I have never seen painted. As for being described, words couldn't do it. I suppose he sees that the end is inevitable. Really, Elsie, the man would murder me if he dared."

"The man is dangerous, George, as well as malignant. But I think he will do you no harm in the long run. Have you told Athelstan what is going on?"

"Certainly. He follows the business with the greatest interest. He agrees with me that the thing is done out of the office, with the help of some one in. Now the point is, that the man in the office must have control of the mail. All the letters must pass through his hands. Who is that man? No one but Checkley. Everything turns on that. Now, here is a lucky accident. An old friend of Athelstan's, a man who coaches, has chambers on the same stairs and on the same floor. He knows this Mr. Edmund Gray. We have been to his rooms to question him."

"Is it to see this old friend that Athelstan visits No. 22?"

"Yes. His name is Carstone—commonly called Freddy Carstone—a pleasing man, with a little weakness which seems to endear him to his friends."

"That is the way in which things get distorted in a malignant mind! Well. What did this gentleman tell you about this mysterious Edmund Gray?"

"Nothing definite. That he is some kind of Socialist we knew before; that he has occupied the chambers for ten years or so we knew before. Also that he is an elderly gentleman of benevolent aspect, and that he is irregular in his visits to his chambers. We seem to get no further. We see Checkley coming out of the house. That connects him, to be sure. But that is not much. There is no connection established between Edmund Gray and the forgeries in his name, nor between Checkley and the forgeries. One feels that if one could lay hold of this mysterious elderly gentleman a real step in advance would be taken."

"You talked at first of arresting him on the charge."

"Well, there is no evidence. His name has been used—that is all. On that evidence no magistrate would issue a warrant. Sometimes one's head goes round with the bewilderment of it. I've managed to learn something about Checkley in the course of these inquiries. He is quite a great man, Elsie—a tavern oracle in the evening; a landlord and householder, and collector of his own rents at odd hours; a capitalist and a miser. But he is not, as thought at first, Edmund Gray."

They had by this time got round to the house again. "Go now, George," said Elsie. "See Athelstan this evening. Tell him that I must go to him. I will tell him why to-morrow."

"If he is not at his club I will go to his lodgings. If he is not there I will wait till he comes home. And before I go home I will drop a note for you. Good-night, sweetheart—good-night."

CHAPTER XIX

THE PRODIGAL AT HOME

In the morning Elsie rose at seven, and put together such things as she would want for the three weeks before her marriage, if she were to spend that interval under her brother's care. At eight o'clock she received her letters—including one in a handwriting she did not know. She opened it. "Dear Elsie," it said, "come to me at once. Come early. Come to breakfast at nine. I will wait for you till ten, or any time.—Your affectionate brother, Athelstan."

"Oh!" she murmured. "And I did not know his writing. And to think that I am twenty-one, and he is thirty-one; and that I have never had a letter from him before!"

Her boxes were packed. She put on her jacket and hat, and descended into the breakfast-room, where her mother was already opening her letters and waiting breakfast.

"You are going out, Elsie?" she asked coldly.

"Yes. Hilda told you, I suppose, what she came here for yesterday. In fact, you sent me a message."

"I hope she delivered it correctly."

"She said that you would not sanction my wedding while this charge, or suspicion, was hanging over George's head. And that you would not see him until it was withdrawn or cleared away."

"Certainly. In such a case it would be worse than hypocrisy to receive him with friendliness."

"Then, like Hilda, you accept the conclusion?"

"I am unable to do anything else. The conclusion seems to me inevitable. If not, let him explain. I hope that no time will be lost in bringing the formal charge. It is foolish kindness— real cruelty—to all concerned to keep such a thing hanging over our heads. I say *our* heads, not yours only, Elsie, because you know your brother is implicated—perhaps the real contriver of the dreadful scheme."

"Would you believe me if I were to tell you that Athelstan *could* not be implicated?"

"My dear! believe you? Of course I would believe if I could. Unfortunately, the evidence is too great."

Elsie sighed. "Very well, I will say nothing more. You have driven out my lover as you drove out my brother, for the self-same cause and on the self-same charge. I follow my lover and my brother."

"Elsie"—her mother started. "Do not, I pray you, do anything rash. Remember, a scandal—a whisper even—may be fatal to you hereafter. Sit down and wait. All I ask you to do is to wait."

"No, I will not wait. If those two are under any cloud of suspicion, I, too, will sit under the cloud, and wait until it lifts. I am going to stay with my brother until my wedding. That is to be on the 12th."

"No, no, my poor child! There will be no wedding on the 12th."

"Before that time everything will be cleared up, and I shall be married from this house, so that I have left all my things, my presents—everything."

Her mother shook her head.

"Try not to think so cruelly of George and of Athelstan, mother. You will be sorry afterwards. Try to believe that though a case may look strange, there may be a way out."

"I have told you"—her mother was perfectly cold and unmoved—"that I have come to this conclusion on the evidence. If the young man can explain things, let him do so. There will be no wedding on the 12th, Elsie. You can come home as soon as you are convinced that your brother is an improper person for a young lady to live with, and as soon as you have learned the truth about the other young man. That is to say, I will receive you under those distressing circumstances, provided there has been no scandal connected with your name."

Elsie turned, and left the room. The fifth commandment enjoins that under such circumstances as these the least said the soonest mended.

When a man learns that his sister, his favorite sister, from whom he has been parted for eight years—the only member of his family who stood up for him when he was falsely accused of a disgraceful thing—is about to take breakfast with him, he naturally puts as much poetry into that usually simple meal as circumstances allow. Mostly Athelstan took a cup of coffee and a London egg. This morning he had flowers, raspberries lying in a bed of leaves, a few late strawberries, various kinds of confitures in dainty dishes, toast and cake, with fish and cutlets—quite a little feast. And he had had the room cleared of the bundles of newspapers; the pipes and cigar-cases, and all the circumstances of tobacco were hidden away—all but the smell, which lingered. One thinks a good deal about a sister's visit, under such conditions. At a quarter past nine Elsie arrived. Athelstan hastened to open the door, and to receive her with open arms and kisses strange and sweet. Then, while the people of the house took in her luggage, he led his sister into the room, which was the front room on the ground-floor.

"Elsie!" he said, taking both her hands in his—"eight years since we parted—and you are a tall young lady, whom I left a little girl. To hold your hand—to kiss you, seems strange after so long." He kissed her again on the forehead. She looked up at the tall, handsome man with a kind of terror. It was almost like casting herself upon the care of a strange man.

"I remember your voice, Athelstan, but not your face. You have changed more than I, even."

"And I remember your voice, Elsie—always a soft and winning voice, wasn't it?—to suit soft and winning ways. There never was any child more winning and affectionate than you—never."

"Oh! you are grown very handsome, Athelstan. See what a splendid beard, and the brown velvet jacket and white waistcoat —and the crimson tie. You look like an artist. I wish all men wore colors, as they used to do. I only heard yesterday that you were in London. Hilda told me."

"Was that the reason why you cannot stay at home?"

"Part of the reason. But you shall have breakfast first. You can take me in without any trouble?"

"My dear child, I am more than delighted to have you here. There is a room at the back where you will be quiet; we have only this one room for sitting-room, and I think we shall find it best to go out every day to dinner. That will not hurt us, and George will come every evening. Now, Elsie, you sit here, and I will— No—I quite forgot. You will pour out the tea. Yes

—I see. I thought I was going to wait upon you altogether. There—now you will make a good breakfast, and—and— Don't cry, dear child."

"No, Athelstan." She brushed away the tears. "It is nothing. I shall be very happy with you. But why are you not at home? And why am I here? Oh! it is too cruel—too perverse of them!"

"We had better have it out before breakfast, then. Strawberries don't go well with tears, do they? Nor jam with complainings. Come, Elsie, why need you leave home?"

"Because, in two words, they are treating George as they treated you. I was younger then, or I would have gone away with you."

"Treating George? Oh! I understand. They are pouring suspicion upon him. Well, I saw that that was coming. Old Checkley, I swear, is at the bottom of it."

"Yes; Checkley went to Sir Samuel with the 'case,' as he called it, complete. He proved to their joint satisfaction that nobody could have done the thing except George, assisted by you."

"Oh! assisted by me."

"Yes; while you were in California, I suppose. There is to be a warrant for your arrest—yours and George's—in a few days, they say. Hilda brought the news to my mother. They both believe it, and they want me to break off my engagement. My mother refuses to see George so long as this charge, as she calls it, remains over him. So I came away."

"You did wisely. Well, any one may call up a cloud of suspicion, and it is sometimes difficult to disperse such a cloud. Therefore we must do everything we can to find out who is the real criminal. Now, let us rest quite easy. There can be no arrest—or any charge—or anything but a fuss created by this old villain. It is only troublesome to find one's own people so ready to believe."

"Why did you not tell me that you were home again?"

"Pour out the tea, Elsie, and begin your breakfast. I wanted to reserve the return of the prodigal until you came home after your honeymoon. Then I meant to call mysteriously about sunset, before George was home. I thought I would have a long cloak wrapped about me. I should have begun : 'Madam, you had once a brother.' 'I had'—that is you. 'On his death-bed—'

'My brother dead?'—that's you. '—with this packet.' Oh! we have lost a most beautiful little play. How can I forgive you?"

Then they went on with breakfast, talking and laughing, until, before the meal was finished, they had lost their shyness, and were brother and sister again.

After breakfast Athelstan took a cigarette and an easy-chair. "Now I am going to devote the whole day to you. I have nothing to do for my paper which cannot wait till to-morrow. All this morning we will talk—that is, until we are tired. We will have lunch somewhere, and go to see the pictures. George will come at about seven; we will have dinner and go to the Naval Exhibition. Then we will get home, and have another talk. To-morrow I shall have to leave you to your own devices between ten and six or so. I am very busy some days; on others I can find time for anything. Now that's all cleared up. I am to be your banker and everything."

"Not my banker, Athelstan. Oh! you don't know. I am a great heiress."

"Indeed? How is that?" he asked, a little twinkle in his eye.

"Mr. Dering told me when I was twenty-one, three weeks ago. Somebody has given me an immense sum of money—thirteen thousand pounds."

"That is a very handsome sum. Who gave it to you?"

"That is a secret. Mr. Dering refuses to tell me. I wish I knew."

"I wouldn't wish if I were you. Gratitude is at all times a burden and a worry. Besides, he might be a vulgar person without aspirates or aspirations. Much better not inquire after him. Thirteen thousand pounds at three and a half per cent. means four hundred and fifty pounds a year. A nice little addition to your income. I congratulate you, Elsie; and this evening we will drink the health of the unassuming benefactor—the retiring and nameless recognizer of maidenly worth. Bless him!"

"And now, Athelstan, begin your adventures. Tell me everything—from the day you left us till now. You cannot tell me too much, or talk too long. Before you begin ask any questions about my mother and Hilda that you want to ask. Then we can go on undisturbed."

"I have no questions to ask about either. I have already ascertained from George that both are in good health, and that Hilda has married a man with an immense fortune. That is happiness enough for her, I hope. Now, Elsie, I shall be tedious, I am afraid; but you shall hear everything."

He began. It was such a narrative as thousands of young Englishmen have been able to tell during the last five-and-twenty years. The story of the young man with a few pounds in his pocket, no friends, no recommendations, and no trade. Athelstan landed at New York in this condition. He looked about for employment, and found none. He hastened out of the crowded city; he went West, and got work in the business open to every sharp and clever man—that of journalism. He worked for one paper after another, getting gradually more and more West, until he found himself in San Francisco, where he was taken on by a great paper, which had now sent him over there as its London correspondent. That was all the story; but there were so many episodes in it, so many adventures, so many men whom he remembered, so many anecdotes cropping up—in this eight years' history of a man with an eye, a brain, and a memory—that it was long past luncheon-time when Athelstan stopped and said that he must carry on the next chapter at another time.

"That pile of dollars that you made out of the silver mine, Athelstan—what became of them?"

"What became of them? Well, you see, Elsie, in some parts of the United States money vanishes as fast as it is made. All those dollars dropped into a deep hole of the earth, and were hopelessly lost."

She laughed. "You will tell me some day—when you please —how you lost that fortune. Oh! what a thing it is to be a man, and to have had all those adventures! Now, Athelstan, consider —if it had not been for your bad fortune you would never have had all this good fortune."

"True. Yet the bad fortune came in such an ugly shape. There has been a black side to my history. How was I to tell people why I left my own country? I could make no friends. At the first appearance of friendship I had to become cold, lest they should ask me where I came from and why I left home."

Elsie was silent.

They carried out part of their programme. They went to see the pictures—it was eight years since Athelstan had seen a picture —and after the pictures they walked in the Park. Then they went home and waited for George, who presently appeared. Then they went to one of the Regent Street restaurants and made a little feast. After this, Elsie asked them to come home and spend a quiet evening talking about things.

By common consent they avoided one topic. Edmund Gray was not so much as mentioned, nor was the malignity of Checkley alluded to. They talked of old days, when Athelstan was a big boy and George a little boy and Elsie a child. They talked of the long engagement, and the hopeless time when it seemed as if they were going to marry on two hundred pounds a year; and of that day of miracle and marvel when Mr. Dering gave to one of them a fortune and to the other a partnership. They talked of their honeymoon, and the tour they were going to make, and the beautiful places they would see—Tours and Blois, Chenon-ceaux and Amboise, Angoulême and Poitiers and La Rochelle; and of their return; and the lovely flat, where their friends would be made so welcome. Athelstan was a person of some sympathy. Elsie talked as freely to him as she could to George. They talked till midnight.

Then Elsie got up. "Whatever happens, Athelstan," she said—"mind, whatever happens—you shall give me away on the 12th."

"Now she has left us," said George, "you may tell me why she refused to stay at home."

"Well, I suppose you ought to know. Much for the same reason that I refused to stay at home. They then chose to jump at the conclusion that at one step I had become, from a man of honor, a stupid and clumsy forger. They now choose—I am ashamed to say my mother and sister choose—to believe that you and I together have devised and invented this elaborate scheme of forgery. With this end in view it has been found necessary to contrive certain little fabrications—as that I have been living in London on my wits—that is to say, by the exercise of cheatery—for the last eight years; and that, being in rags and penniless, I persuaded you to join me in this neat little buccaneering job."

"Oh! it is too absurd! But I suspected something. Well, it is perfectly easy to put a stop to that."

"Yes, it is easy. At the same time it will be well to put a stop to it as soon as possible, before the thing assumes serious proportions, and becomes a horrid thing that may stick to you all your life. You have got to do with a malignant man—perhaps a desperate man. He will spread abroad the suspicion as diligently as he can. Let us work, therefore."

"Well, but what can we do that we have not done? How can we fix the thing upon Checkley?"

"I don't know. We must think. We must find out something, somehow. Let us all three work together. Elsie will make the best detective in the world. And let us work in secret. I am very glad—very glad indeed—that Elsie came."

CHAPTER XX

THE WHISPER OF CALUMNY

Whispered words are ever more potent than words proclaimed aloud upon the house-top. If the envious man from the house-top denounces a man of reputation as a thief, a gambler, a patricide, a sororicide, an amicocide, no man regardeth his voice, though he call out with the voice of Stentor; people only stare; these are the words of a madman or a malignant. But whisper these charges in the ear of your neighbor; whisper them with bated breath; say that, as yet, the thing is a profound secret. Then that rumor swiftly flies abroad, until every burgess in the town regards that man askance; and when the time for voting comes, he votes for another man, and will not have him as beadle, sexton, verger, school-master, turncock, policeman, parish doctor, workhouse chaplain, common-councilman, alderman, mayor, or member of Parliament. And all for a whisper.

It was Checkley who set going the whisper which at this moment was running up and down the office, agitating all hearts, occupying all minds, the basis of all conversation.

King Midas's servant, when he was irresistibly impelled to whisper, dug a hole in the ground, and placed his whisper at the bottom of that hole. But the grasses grew up, and sighed the words to the passing breeze, so that the market-women heard them on their way, "The king's ears are the ears of an ass— the ears of an ass—the ears of an ass." The old and trusty servant of Dering & Son buried his secret in the leaves of his copying-book.   Here it was found by the boy who worked the copy-ing-press.   As he turned over the pages he became conscious of a sibilant, malignant, revengeful murmur, "Who stole the bonds? —the new partner.   Who forged the letters?—the new partner. Who robbed the safe?—the new partner."   Here was a pretty thing for a pretty innocent office-boy to hear!   Naturally his very soul became aflame; when the dinner-hour arrived he told another boy, as a profound secret, what he had heard.   That boy told an older boy, who told another still older, who told another, and so up the long official ladder, until everybody in the place knew that the new partner—actually the new partner—the most fortunate of all young men that ever passed his exam.—who had stepped at a bound from two hundred to a thousand at least— this young man, of all young men in the world, had forged his partner's name, robbed his partner's safe, made away with his partner's property.   Who, after this, can trust anybody?

But others there were who refused to believe this thing.   They pointed out that the new partner continued—apparently—on the best of terms with the old partner; they argued that when such things are done friendships are killed and partnerships are dis-solved.   They even went so far, though members of the great profession which believes in no man's goodness, as to declare their belief that the new partner could not possibly, by any temp-tation, do such things.   And there were others who pointed to the fact that the whisper came from the boy of the copying-press ; that he heard it whispered by the fluttering leaves ; and that it was imparted to those leaves by Checkley—old Checkley—whose hatred towards the new partner was notorious to all men—not on account of any personal qualities or private injuries, but out of the jealousy which made him regard the chief as his own property, and because he had been deprived of his power in the office—the power of appointment and disappointment and the raising of screw, which he had previously possessed.   Checkley was de-throned—therefore Checkley spread this rumor.   Others, again, said that if the rumor were really started by Checkley, which could not be proved, seeing that, like all whispers or rumors, the origin was unknown and perhaps supernatural, then Checkley must have very strong grounds for starting such a thing.

Thus divided in opinion, the office looked on expectant.   Ex-pectancy is a thing which gets into the air; it fills every room with whispers; it makes a conspirator or a partisan or a confederate of every one; it divides a peaceful office into camps; it is the cause of inventions, lies, and exaggerations. There were two parties in this office—one which whispered accusations, and the other which whispered denials. Between these hovered the wobblers or mugwumps, who whispered that while on the one hand—on the other hand—and that while they readily admitted—so they were free to confess— Everybody knows the wobbler. He is really, if he knew it, the master of the situation; but, because he is a wobbler, he cannot use his strength. When he is called upon to act he falls into two pieces, each of which begins to wobble and to fall into other two pieces of its own accord. The whole process of a presidential election—except the final voting—was going on in that office of half a dozen rooms, but in whispers, without a single procession, and not one German band. And all unconscious of the tumult that raged about him—a tumult in whispers—a civil war in silence—the object of this was going on his way unconscious and undisturbed.

Now, however, having learned that the old clerk was actually seeking to fix this charge upon him, George perceived the whispering, and understood the charge. When he passed through the first or outer office, in the morning, he perceived that the clerks all looked at him curiously, and that they pretended not to be looking at him, and plied their pens with zeal. On the stairs he met an articled clerk, who blushed a rosy red with consciousness of the thing; on his way to his own room, through his own clerks' room, he felt them looking after him curiously as he passed; and he felt them, when his own door was closed, whispering about him. This made him extremely angry. Yet, for a whisper, one cannot suffer wrath to become visible. That would only please the whisperers. There is only one thing worse than to be suspected rightly—it is to be suspected wrongly, for the latter makes a man mad. What? That he—even he—the man of principle and rule—should be suspected! Does nothing, then—no amount of character, no blamelessness of record—avail? Is the world coming to an end?

George then shut his door, and sat down to his table in a very wrathful and savage frame of mind. And while he was just beginning to nurse and nourish this wrath, coaxing it from a red glow to a roaring flame, a card was brought to him.

"I will see Sir Samuel at once," he said.

It is as well that we do not hear the remarks of the clerks' room and the servants' hall. The service, in fact, is a body of critics whose judgments would, if we only heard them, cause us to reconsider our self-respect. Great philanthropist, great statesman, saintly preacher—if you only knew what they say of you down below!

The clerks—as Sir Samuel Dering, his face composed to the solemnity of a mute, walked into the new partner's room—whispered to each other, "He's going to finish him. There'll be a bolt to-night. He won't dare face it out. He *has* got a nerve!!! The game's up at last. They won't prosecute—you see if they do. If it was one of us, now. Sir Samuel's come to warn him —now you'll see." With other exchanges and surmises.

Sir Samuel, big and important, coldly inclined his head, and took a chair. "A few words," he said—"a few serious words, if you please, sir."

"Pray go on." George sat up and listened. His upper lip stiffened. He knew what was coming. The thing which Sir Samuel proposed to say apparently became difficult. He turned red, and stammered. In fact it is very difficult to inform a highly respectable young man in a highly respectable position that he is going to be charged with a crime of peculiar atrocity.

"I am here," he said, after two or three false starts, "without my brother's knowledge. This is a private and unofficial visit. I come to advise. My visit must be regarded as without prejudice."

"Is it not well to ask, first of all, if your advice is invited?"

"In such a case as this, I venture to obtrude advice," Sir Samuel replied, with dignity. "There are occasions on which a man should speak—he is bound to speak. You will remember that I was to have been your brother-in-law—"

"You *are* to be my brother-in-law. Well, Sir Samuel, go on. I will hear what you have to say."

"You are, as no doubt you suspect and fear, about to be charged, in company with another, with complicity in this long series of forgeries."

"Really. I heard last night, from Elsie, that there was some talk of such a charge. Now, Sir Samuel, a man of your experience must be aware that it is not enough for a foolish old clerk to suggest a charge, but there must be some connection between the accused person and the crime."

"Connection? Good heavens! There is a solid chain of evidence, without a single weak point."

"Is there, indeed? Well, we will not ask for the production of your chain. Let us take it for granted. Go on to the next point."

"I wish, young gentleman, I wish most sincerely, for the credit of yourself and for the happiness of the unfortunate girl who has given you her heart, that my chain was of glass, to fly into a thousand fragments. But it is not. Everything is complete. The motive, the tempter, the conspiracy, the working out, the apparent success—everything complete. The motive—want of money."

"Want of money? Well, I was pretty badly off. That cannot be denied. Go on."

"You wanted money—both of you wanted money. In ninety cases out of a hundred this is the cause—wanted money. So you went and did it. Always the way in the City—they want money—and so they go and do it—go and do it."

"I see. Well, we need not have the tempter and the rest of it. They can wait. Let us go on to the advice."

"Just so. What I came to say is this. You are in a devil of a mess, young gentleman; the whole job is found out; there's no use in trying to brazen it out. Best come down at once."

George nodded, with as much good-humor as he could assume under the circumstances.

"Down at once," Sir Samuel repeated. "It is always best in the long run. In your case, there is every reason why a scandal should be avoided. The thing hasn't got into the papers; we are only yet in the first stage of finding out what has been actually stolen; it has not been a case in which the police could help. Now, my brother is not a vindictive man. I, for my own part, don't want my wife's brother, to say nothing of you, convicted of forgery. Eh? Beastly thing to go down to the City in the morning, and to hear them whispering, 'That's his wife's brother in the papers to-day. Lagged for fifteen years.' Fifteen years for certain, it will be, my fine fellow."

"Fifteen years for certain," George repeated.

"Let me help you out of the mess. Don't make difficulties. Don't stick out your chin. Think of Elsie!"

George nearly lost his self-control—not quite.

"Think of Elsie!" he cried. "Best not mention her name, Sir Samuel, if you please."

"She would be heart-broken if it went so far. If it stops short of that she will soon get over the little disappointment."

"Go on to the next point."

"Well, it is just this. I'll help you both—Athelstan as well as you; yes, I'll help Athelstan. Hang the fellow! Why couldn't he stay at Camberwell? Who cares about him and his bad company, if he keeps himself out of people's way? Now then. Let me have back the money. You haven't drawn anything out of the bank. Give me the papers. Then I'll square it with my brother. I will advance you a hundred or two; you shall go clear out of the country, and never come back again. And then, though it's compounding a felony, we'll just put everything back again, and say nothing more about it."

"Oh! that is very good of you."

"Yes, I know. But I want to make things easy. I don't want a beastly row and a scandal. As for Athelstan, I shouldn't know the fellow if I ever saw him. I hardly remember him. But for you I've always had a liking, until these little events happened."

"Very good, indeed, of you."

"When the thing came out I said to Lady Dering, 'My dear,' I said, 'I'm very sorry for your sister, because it will vex her more than a bit. The engagement, of course, will be broken off; but we must not have a scandal. We cannot afford it. We cannot'"—he smiled—"'we are positively not rich enough. Only the very richest people can afford to have such a scandal. I will try and get things squared,' I said, 'for all our sakes.' That is what I said to Lady Dering. Now be persuaded. Do the right thing. Tell Athelstan what I have told you. The warrant for the arrest of the man Edmund Gray will be issued to-morrow, I suppose, or next day. After that nothing can save you."

"Nothing can save me," George repeated. "Is that all you came to say, Sir Samuel?"

"That is all. A clean breast is all we ask."

"Then, Sir Samuel "—George rose, and took a bundle of papers from the table—"let us find my partner. You shall hear what I have to say."

"Ah! that's right—that's sensible. I know that you would be open to reason. Come. He is sure to be alone at this early hour. Come at once."

They went out together. The clerks noticed their faces full of "business," as we poetically put it—matters of buying and selling being notoriously of the highest importance conceivable. Evidently something very serious, indeed, had passed. But the chief personage still held up his head. "Game, sir; game to the last. But there will be a bolt."

Mr. Dering was in his usual place, before his letters, which were still unopened. He looked ill, worn, and worried.

"Brother," said Sir Samuel, "I bring you a young gentleman who has a communication to make of great importance."

"Is it about this case? Have you—at last—found out something?" The tone, the words, suggested extreme irritability.

"I fear not. You know, I believe, all that we have found out. But now," said Sir Samuel, rubbing his hands—"now comes the long-expected—"

"What I have to say will not take long. I hear from Sir Samuel that he and Checkley between them have got up a case which involves me in these forgeries."

"Quite right," said Sir Samuel—"involves you inextricably."

"And that things have gone so far that I am about to be arrested, tried, and convicted, which he rightly thinks will be a great scandal. So it will—so it certainly will. He, therefore, proposes that I should make a clean breast of the whole business, and give back the stolen bonds. I am sorry that I cannot do this, for a very simple reason—namely, that there is nothing to confess. But there is one thing that I must do. You placed the case in my hands—"

"I did. I asked you to find out. I have brought no charge against you. Have you found out?"

Mr. Dering spoke like a school-master in one of his least amiable moods.

"It is a very improper thing for a person accused of a crime to be engaged in detecting it. So I resign the case—there are the papers. You had better go to some solicitor accustomed to this kind of work."

"Stuff and rubbish!" cried Mr. Dering.

"Sir, you have deceived me." Sir Samuel's face was gradually
9*

resuming its normal length. "You promised to confess, and you have not. You as good as confessed just now. This man is clearly, unmistakably guilty," he added, turning to his brother.

"I have not asked you, my partner," Mr. Dering added, more softly, "to give up the case. I have heard what is said. I have observed that the so-called case is built up entirely on conjecture."

"No, no," said Sir Samuel. "It is a sound structure, complete in every part."

"And there is nothing, as yet, to connect any man with the thing—not even the man Edmund Gray."

"Quite wrong—quite wrong," said Sir Samuel. "In the City, we may not be lawyers, but we understand evidence."

"I cannot choose but give up the case," George replied. "Consider. Already Mrs. Arundel has requested her daughter to break off her engagement; I am forbidden the house; Elsie has left her mother, and gone to her brother. No, sir—take the papers, and give them to some other person."

Mr. Dering mechanically took the papers, and laid his hand upon them.

"Let me remind you," George continued, "how far we have got. We have proved that Edmund Gray is a real person, known to many. We have not proved the connection between him and the robberies committed in his name. He is apparently a most respectable person. The problem before you is still to fix the crime on some one. I shall be glad to hear that it has been successfully solved."

"Glad?" asked Sir Samuel. "*You* will be glad? This is amazing!"

"Eight years ago, Mr. Dering, another man stood here, and was accused of a similar crime. He refused to stay in the house under such a charge. That was foolish. Time has established his innocence. I shall stay. I am your partner. The partnership can only be dissolved by mutual consent. I remain."

Mr. Dering laid his head upon his hand and sighed. "I believe I shall be driven mad before long with this business," he said querulously. He had lost something of his decision of speech. "Well, I will give the case to somebody else. Meantime, look here. Tell me how these things came here."

The "things" were two envelopes containing letters. They

were addressed to Edmund Gray, and had been opened. One of them was George's own note, inviting him to call. The other was the letter from the manager of the bank, asking for other references.

"How did they get here?" asked Mr. Dering again.

"Had you not better ask Checkley?" George rang the bell.

"I found these on the top of my letters, Checkley," said Mr. Dering. "You were the first in the room. You put the letters on the table. I found them on the top of the heap. Nobody had been in the room except you and me. You must have put them there."

Checkley looked at the envelopes, and began to tremble. "I don't know," he said. "I put the letters on the table. They were not among them. Somebody must have put them there."—he looked at the new partner—"some friend of Mr. Edmund Gray—between the time that I left the room and the time when you came."

"I entered the room," Mr. Dering replied, "as you were leaving it."

"Observe," said George, "that in the whole conduct of this business there has been one man engaged who has control of the letters. That man—the only man in the office—is, I believe, the man before us—your clerk, Checkley."

"How came the letters here?" Mr. Dering repeated angrily.

"I don't know," answered Checkley. "He"—indicating George—"must have put them there."

"The devil is in the office, I believe. How do things come here? How do they vanish? Who put the notes in the safe? Who took the certificates out of the safe? All you can do is to stand and accuse each other. What good are you—any of you? Find out—find out! Yesterday there was a handbill about Edmund Gray in the safe. The day before there was a handful of socialist tracts on the letters. Find out, I say."

"Give the thing to detectives," said George.

"Let me take the case in hand, brother." Sir Samuel laid hands on the papers. "I flatter myself that I will very soon have the fellow under lock and key. And then, sir"—he turned to George—"scandal or no scandal, there shall be no pity, no mercy —none."

George laughed. "Well, Sir Samuel, in a fortnight or so I

shall call myself your brother-in-law. Till then, farewell."
He left the office, and returned to his own room, the ripple
of the laughter still upon his lips and in his eyes, so that the
clerks marvelled, and the faith of those who believed in him was
strengthened.

"Before then, young crowing bantam," cried Sir Samuel after
him, "I shall have you under lock and key."

"Ah!" This was Checkley. The little interjection expressed,
far more than any words could do, his satisfaction at the prospect.
Then he left the room, grumbling and muttering.

"I believe that this business will finish me off." Mr. Dering
sighed again, and passed his hand over his forehead. "Night
and day it worries me. It makes my forgetfulness grow upon
me. I am as good as gone. This hour I cannot remember the
last hour. See—I had breakfast at home as usual. I remember
that. I remember setting out. It is ten minutes' walk from
Bedford Row here. I have taken an hour and a half. How? I
do not know. What did I do last night? I do not know, and
I am pursued by this forger—robber—demon. He puts things
in my safe—yesterday a placard that Edmund Gray was going
to give a lecture on something or other; the day before a bundle
of tracts by Edmund Gray. What do these things mean? What
can I do?"

CHAPTER XXI

HE COMES FROM EDMUND GRAY

"NOTHING," said Athelstan, "could possibly happen more fortunately. We have turned whispering conspirators into declared
enemies. Now you are free to investigate in your own way without having to report progress every day."

"About this new business of the letters and the things in
the safe," said Elsie. "It looks to me like *diablerie*. Checkley
couldn't do it. No conjurer in the world could do it. There
must be somebody else in the office to do these things. They
mean defiance. The forger says, 'See—I do what I please with
you. I return your letters addressed to Edmund Gray. I place

placards about Edmund Gray in your safe, for which nobody has a key except yourself. Find me, if you can.'"

"Yes, it's very mysterious."

"A person on two sticks might manage it. Very likely he is concerned in the business. Or a boy under the table would be able to do it. Perhaps there is a boy under the table. There must be. Mr. Dering's table is like the big bed of Ware. I dare say fifty boys might creep under that table, and wait there for a chance. But perhaps there is only one—a comic boy."

"I should like to catch the joker," said George. "I would give him something still more humorous to laugh at."

"If there is no comic boy—and no person with two sticks," Elsie continued, "we are thrown back upon Checkley. He seems to be the only man who receives the letters and goes in and out of the office all day. Well, I don't think it is Checkley. I don't think it can be. George, you once saw Mr. Dering in a very strange condition—unconscious, walking about with open eyes seeing nobody. Don't you think that he may have done this more than once?"

"What do you mean, Elsie?"

"Don't you think that some of these things—things put in the safe, for instance—may have been put there by Mr. Dering himself? You saw him open the safe. Afterwards he knew nothing about it. Could he not do this more than once? might it be a habit?"

"Well—but if he puts the things in the safe—things that belong to Edmund Gray—he must know Edmund Gray. For instance, how did he get my note to Edmund Gray, left by me on his table in Gray's Inn? That must have been given to him by Edmund Gray himself."

"Or by some friend of Edmund Gray. Yes, that is quite certain."

"Come," said Athelstan. "This infernal Edmund Gray is too much with us. Let us leave off talking about him for a while. Let him rest for this evening. Elsie, put on your things. We will go and dine somewhere, and go to the play afterwards."

They did so. They had the quiet little restaurant dinner that girls have learned of late to love so much—the little dinner where everything seems so much brighter and better served than one can get at home. After the dinner they went to a theatre, taking places in the dress circle, where, given good eyes, one sees quite as well as from the stalls at half the money. After the theatre they went home, and there was an exhibition of tobacco and soda water. Those were very pleasant days in the Piccadilly lodgings, even allowing for the troubles which brought them about. Athelstan was the most delightful of brothers, and every evening brought its feast of laughter and of delightful talk. But all through the evening, all through the play, Elsie saw nothing but Mr. Dering, and him engaged in daylight somnambulism. She saw him as George described him, opening the safe, closing it again, and afterwards wholly forgetful of what he had done.

She thought about this all night. Now, when one has a gleam or glimmer of an idea, when one wants to disengage a single thought from the myriads which cross the brain, and to fix it and to make it clear, there is nothing in the world so good as to talk about it. The effort of finding words with which to drag it out makes it clearer. Every story-teller knows that the mere telling of a story turns his characters, who before were mere shadows, and shapeless shadows, into creatures of flesh and blood. Therefore, in the morning she began upon the thought which haunted her.

"Athelstan," she said, "do you know anything about somnambulism?"

"I knew a man once in California who shot a grizzly when he was sleep-walking. At least, he said so. That's the sum of my knowledge on the subject."

"I want to know if people often walk about in the daytime unconscious?"

"They do. It is called 'wool-gathering.'"

"Seriously, Athelstan? Consider. George saw Mr. Dering arrive in a state of unconsciousness. He saw nobody in the room. He opened the safe, and placed some papers there. Then he locked the safe. Then he sat down at the window. Presently he awoke, and became himself again. If he did that once he might do it again."

"Well? And then?"

"You heard yesterday about the letters and the placard and the Socialist tracts. Now, Checkley couldn't do that. He couldn't, and he wouldn't."

"Well?"

"But Mr. Dering could. If he had that attack once he might have it again and again. Why, he constantly complains of forgetting things."

"But the letters yesterday were addressed to Edmund Gray. How do you connect Edmund Gray with Edward Dering?"

"I don't know. But, my dear brother, the more I think of this business the more persuaded I am that Checkley is not the prime mover, or even a confederate."

"The same hand has been at work throughout. If not Checkley's aid to make that hand possible and successful, who is there? And look at the malignity with which he tries to fix it on some one else."

"That may be because he is afraid of its being fixed upon him. Consider that point about the control of the letters. The business could only be done by some one through whose hands passed all the letters."

"Checkley is the only person possible."

"Yes; he understands that. It makes him horribly afraid. He therefore lies with all his might, in order to pass on suspicion to another person. You and George think him guilty—well, I do not. If I were trying to find out the man I should try a different plan altogether."

Her brother had work to do which took him out directly after an early breakfast. When Elsie was left alone she began again to think about Mr. Dering's strange daylight somnambulism; about his continual fits of forgetfulness; about the odd things found on his table and in his safe, all connected with Edmund Gray. Checkley could not have placed those letters on the table; he could not have put those things in the safe.

Elsie looked at the clock. It was only just after nine. She ran to her room, put on her jacket and hat, and called a cab.

She arrived at half-past nine. Checkley was already in his master's room, laying out the table for the day's work as usual. The girl was touched at the sight of this old servant of sixty years' service doing these offices zealously and jealously. She stood in the outer office, watching him through the open door. When he had finished he came out, and saw her.

"Oh!" he grumbled. "It's you, is it? Well—he hasn't come. If you want to see Mr. Dering it's full early. If you want to see the new partner he isn't come. He don't hurry himself. Perhaps you'll sit down a bit, and look at the paper. Here's the *Times*. He'll be here at a quarter to ten."

He sat down at his desk, and took up a pen. But he laid it down again, and began to talk. "We're in trouble, miss. No fault of yours—I don't say it is. We're in trouble. The trouble is going to be worse before it's better. They're not content with robbing the master, but they mock at him and jeer him. They jeer him. They put on his table letters addressed to the man they call Edmund Gray. They open his safe, and put things in it belonging to Edmund Gray. We're not so young as we was, and it tells upon us. We're not so regular as we should be. Sometimes we're late—and sometimes we seem, just for a bit, not to know exactly who we are nor what we are. Oh! it's nothing —nothing but what will pass away when the trouble's over. But think of the black ingratitood, miss—oh! black—black. I'm not blamin' you; but I think you ought to know the trouble we're in—considering who's done it and all."

Elsie made no reply. She had nothing to say. Certainly she could not enter into a discussion with this man as to the part, if any, taken in the business by the new partner. Then Checkley made a show of beginning to write with zeal. The morning was hot; the place was quiet; the old man's hand gradually slackened; the pen stopped; the eyes closed; his head dropped back upon his chair; he was asleep. It is not uncommon for an old man to drop off in this way.

Elsie sat perfectly still. At eleven o'clock she heard a step upon the stairs. It mounted; it stopped; the private door was opened, and Mr. Dering entered. He stood for a moment in the doorway, looking about the room. Now, as the girl looked at him she perceived that he was again in the condition described by George—as a matter of fact, it was in this condition that Mr. Dering generally arrived in the morning. His coat was unbuttoned; his face wore the genial and benevolent look which we do not generally associate with lawyers of fifty years' standing; the eyes were Mr. Dering's eyes, but they were changed—not in color or in form, but in expression. Elsie was reminded of her portrait. That imaginary sketch was no other than the Mr. Dering who now stood before her.

He closed the door behind him, and walked across the room to the window.

Then Elsie, lightly, so as not to awaken the drowsy old clerk, stepped into Mr. Dering's office, and shut the door softly behind her.

The sleep-walker stood at the window, looking out. Elsie crept up, and stood beside him. Then she touched him on the arm. He started, and turned. "Young lady," he said, "what can I do for you?" He showed no recognition at all in his eyes; he did not know her. "Can I do anything for you?" he repeated.

"I am afraid—nothing," she replied.

He looked at her doubtfully. Then, apparently remembering some duty as yet unfulfilled, he left the window, and unlocked the safe. He then drew out of his pocket a manuscript tied up with red tape. Elsie looked into the safe, and read the title— "The New Humanity, by Edmund Gray"—which was written in large letters on the outer page. Then he shut and locked the safe, and dropped the key in his own pocket. This done, he returned to the window, and sat down, taking no manner of notice of his visitor. All this exactly as he had done before in presence of George and his old clerk.

For ten minutes he sat there. Then he shivered, straightened himself, stood up, and looked about the room — Mr. Dering again.

"Elsie!" he cried. "I did not know you were here. How long have you been here?"

"Not very long. A few minutes, perhaps."

"I must have fallen asleep. It is a hot morning. You must forgive the weakness of an old man, child. I had a bad night, too. I was awake a long time, thinking of all these troubles and worries. They can't find out, Elsie, who has robbed me." He spoke querulously and helplessly. "They accuse each other, instead of laying their heads together. Nonsense! Checkley couldn't do it. George couldn't do it. The thing was done by somebody else. My brother came here with a cock-and-bull case, all built up of presumptions and conclusions. If they would only find out!"

"The trouble is mine as much as yours, Mr. Dering. I have had to leave my mother's house, where I had to listen to agreeable prophecies about my lover and my brother. I wish, with you, that they would find out!"

He took off his hat, and hung it on its peg. He buttoned his frock-coat, and took his place at the table, upright and precise. Yet his eyes were anxious.

"They tease me, too. They mock me. Yesterday they laid two letters addressed to this man, Edmund Gray, on my letters. What for? To laugh at me, to defy me to find them out. Checkley swears he didn't put them there. I arrived at the moment when he was leaving the room. Are we haunted? And the day before—and the day before that—there were things put in the safe—"

"In the safe? Oh! but nobody has the key except yourself. How can anything be put in the safe?"

"I don't know. I don't know anything. I don't know what may be taken next. My houses, my mortgages, my lands, my very practice—"

"Nay—they could not. Is there anything this morning?"

He turned over his letters. "Apparently not. Stay! I have not looked in the safe." He got up, and threw open the safe. Then he took up a packet. "Again!" he cried, almost with a scream. "Again! see this!" He tossed on the table the packet which he had himself, only ten minutes before, placed in the safe with his own hands. "See this! thus they laugh at me—thus they torment me!" He hurled the packet to the other side of the room, returned to his chair, and laid his head upon his hands, sighing deeply.

Elsie took up the parcel. It was rather a bulky manuscript. The title you have heard. She untied the tape, and turned over the pages. The work, she saw, contained the views of Edmund Gray. *And it was in the handwriting of Mr. Dering!*

She replaced it in the safe. "Put everything there," she said, "which is sent to you. Everything. Do you know anything at all about this man Edmund Gray?"

"Nothing, my dear child, absolutely nothing. I never saw the man. I never heard of him. Yet he has planted himself upon me. He holds his chambers on a letter of recommendation from me. I was his introducer to the manager of the bank—I—in my own handwriting, as they thought. He drew a check of seven hundred and twenty pounds upon me eight years ago. And he has transferred thirty-eight thousand pounds' worth of shares and stock to his own address."

"Added to which he has been the cause of suspicion and vile

accusation against my lover and my brother, which it will cost a great deal of patience to forgive. Dear Mr. Dering! I am so sorry for you. It is most wonderful and most mysterious. Suppose"—she laid her hand upon his—"suppose that I was to find out for you—"

"You, child? What can you do, when the others have failed?"

"I can but try."

"Try, in Heaven's name! Try, my dear. If you find out you shall be burned for a witch."

"No. If I find out you shall be present at my wedding. You were to have given me away. But now—now—Athelstan shall give me away, and you will be there to see. And it will be a tearful wedding"— the tears came into her own eyes just to illustrate the remark—"because every one will be so ashamed of the wicked things they have said. Sir Samuel will remain on his knees the whole service, and Checkley will be fain to get under the seat. Good-by, Mr. Dering. I am a prophetess. I can foretell. You shall hear in a very few days all about Edmund Gray."

She ran away, without any further explanation. Mr. Dering shook his head, and smiled. He did not believe in contemporary prophecy. That young people should place their own affairs—their love-makings and weddings—before the affairs of their elders was not surprising; but her visit had cheered him. He opened his letters, and went on with the day's work.

As for Elsie, the smile in her eyes died out as she descended the stairs. If she had been herself a lawyer she could not have worn a graver face as she walked across the courts of the venerable inn.

She had established the connection between Mr. Dering and Edmund Gray. It was he, and nobody else, who laid those letters on the table—placed those things in the safe. This being so, it must be he himself, and nobody else, who wrote all the letters, signed the checks, and did all the mischief. He himself! But how? Elsie had read of hypnotism. Wonderful things are done daily by mesmerists and magnetizers under their new name. Mr. Dering was hypnotized by this man Edmund Gray—as he called himself—for his own base ends. Well, she would find out this Edmund Gray. She would beard this villain in his own den.

She walked resolutely to Gray's Inn. She found No. 22—she

mounted the stairs. The outer door was closed. She knocked, but there was no answer. She remembered how George had found his laundress, and visited her at her lodgings—she thought she would do the same. But on the stairs she went down she met an old woman so dirty, so ancient, so feeble, that she seemed to correspond with George's account of her.

"You are Mr. Gray's laundress?" she asked.

"Yes, miss; I am." The woman looked astonished to see such a visitor.

"I want to see him. I want to see him on very important business. Most important to himself. When can I see him?"

"I don't know, miss. He is uncertain. He was here yesterday evening. He said he should not be here this evening. But I don't know."

"Look here." Elsie drew out her purse. "Tell me when you think he will be here, and if I find him I will give you two pounds—two golden sovereigns. If you tell me right I will give you two sovereigns."

She showed them. The old woman looked hungrily at the coins. "Well, miss, he's been here every Saturday afternoon for the last six months. I know it by the litter of papers that he makes. Every Saturday afternoon."

"Very good. You shall have your money if I find him."

In the evening Elsie said nothing about Mr. Dering and her strange discovery. The two young men talked about trying this way and that way, always with the view of implicating Checkley. But she said nothing.

CHAPTER XXII

"I AM EDMUND GRAY"

On Saturday afternoon the policeman on day duty at Gray's Inn was standing near the southern portals of that venerable foundation, in conversation with the boy who dispenses the newspapers from a warehouse constructed in the eastern wall of the archway. It was half-past three by the clock, and a fine day,

which was remarkable for the season—August—and the year.
The sun poured upon the dingy old courts, making them dingier
instead of brighter. Where the paint of the windows and door-
posts is faded and dirty—where the panes are mostly in want of
cleaning—where there are no flowers in the windows—where
there are no trees or leaves in the square—where the bricks want
pointing, and where the soot has gathered in every chink and
blackens every cranny—then the sunshine of summer only makes
a dingy court shabbier. Gray's Inn in July and August, unless
these months are as the August of the year of grace 1891, looks
old, but not venerable. Age should be clean and nicely dressed;
age should wear a front to conceal her baldness; age should
assume false teeth to disguise those gums stripped of their ivory.
It was felt by the policeman. "We want a washin' and a
brightenin' in this old place," he remarked to the journalist.
"We want somethin' younger than them old laundresses," said
the newspaper boy. Great is the goddess Coincidence. Even
while he uttered this aspiration a young lady entered the gate,
and passed into the inn.

"Ha!" breathed the policeman softly.

"Ah!" sighed the journalist.

She was a young lady of adorable face and form, surpassing
the wildest dreams either of policeman or of paper-man—both
of whom possessed the true poetic temperament. She was clothed
in raiment mystic, wonderful, such as seldom indeed gets as far
east as Gray's Inn—something in gray or silver-gray, with an open
front and a kind of jacket. She passed them rapidly, and walked
through the passage into the square.

"No. 22," said the policeman. "Now, who does she want at
No. 22? Who's on the ground-floor of 22?"

"Right hand—architects and surveyors. Left hand—universal translators."

"Perhaps she's a universal translator. They must be all gone
by this time. The first floor is lawyers. They're all gone, too.
I saw the clerks march out at two o'clock. Second floor—
there's Mr. Carstone on the left, and Mr. Edmund Gray on the
right. Perhaps it's Mr. Carstone she's after. I hope it isn't
him. He's a gentleman with fine manners, and they do say a
great scholar; but he's a lushington, and a sweet young thing
like that ought not to marry a man who is brought home every

other night too tipsy to stand. Or there's Mr. Gray—the old gent—perhaps she's his daughter. What's Mr. Edmund Gray by calling, Joe?"

"Nobody knows. He don't often come. An old gentleman —been in the inn a long time—for years. Lives in the country, I suppose, and does no work. Lives on other people's work— my work—honest working-men's work," said the boy, who was a Socialist and advanced.

"Ah! There's something up about Mr. Gray. People are coming to inquire for him. First, it was a young gentleman; very affable he was, and free with his money—most likely other people's money. He wanted to know a good deal about Mr. Gray—more than I could tell him; wanted to know how often he came, and what he was like when he did come—and would I tell him all I knew. He went to the old laundress afterwards. Then it was a little old man—I know him by sight—uses the Salutation parlor of an evening—he wanted to know all about Mr. Gray, too. No half-crown in that quarter, though. He's been spying and watching for him—goes and hides up the pas- sage on the other side of the square. Kind of spider he is. He's watching him for no good, I'll bet. Perhaps the young lady wants to find out about him, too. Joe, there's something up at No. 22. The old gentleman isn't in his chambers, I believe. She'll come out again presently, and it'll be: 'Oh! Mr. Police- man, could you very kindly tell me how I can find Mr. Edmund Gray?' With a shilling perhaps, and perhaps not. I wonder what she wants with Mr. Edmund Gray? Sometimes these old chaps break out in the most surprising manner. Joe, if you ever go into the service, you'll find the work hard and the pay small. But there's compensations in learnin' things. If you want to know human nature, go into the force."

"There's old Mr. Langhorne, up at the top."

"So there is. But no young lady wants to see that poor old chap. He's got no friends, young nor old—no friends and no money. Just now, he's terrible hard up. Took a shillin' off o' me last Sunday to get a bit of dinner with. Fine thing—isn't it, Joe?—to be a gentleman and a barrister all your life, isn't it? —and to end like that? Starvation in a garret—eh? Look out. She will be coming down directly."

But she did not come down. Two hours and more passed, and she did not come down.

The visitor was Elsie Arundel. She walked up the stairs to the second floor. Here she stopped. There was a black door, closed, on the right of her, and another black door, closed, on the left of her. On the lintel of one was the name of Mr. F. W. Carstone. On the lintel of the other was that of Mr. Edmund Gray. Elsie knocked with her parasol at the latter door. There was no reply. "The old laundress," she murmured, "told me that Saturday afternoon was my best chance of finding him. I will wait." She sat down, with hesitation, on the stairs leading to the third floor—they were not too clean—and waited.

She was going to do a very plucky thing—a dangerous thing. She had made a discovery connecting Mr. Dering directly with this Edmund Gray. She had learned that he came to the office in a strange condition—hypnotic—bringing things from Edmund Gray. She now suspected that the only person who carried on the forgeries on Mr. Dering was Mr. Dering himself, acted on and controlled by Edmund Gray—and she wanted to find out who this Edmund Gray was. She would confront him, and tax him with the crime. It was dangerous, but he could not kill her. Besides, he was described as quite an elderly man. He was also described as a benevolent man, a charitable man, a kindly man; and he wrote letters brimful of the most cheerful optimism. Yet he was carrying on a series of complicated forgeries. She resolved to wait for him. She would wait till sundown, if necessary, for him.

The place was very quiet. All the offices were closed, and the clerks gone. Most of the men who lived in the chambers were away, out of town, gone on holiday, gone away from Saturday till Monday. Everything was quite quiet and still; the traffic in Holborn was only heard as a continuous murmur which formed part of the stillness; the policeman, who had now said all he had to say to the newspaper-boy, was walking slowly and with heavy tread round the court. The inn was quite empty and deserted and still. Only, overhead there was the footfall of a man who walked up and down his room steadily, never stopping or ceasing or changing the time, like the beat of a pendulum. Elsie began to wonder, presently, who this man could be, and if he had nothing better to do than to pace his chamber all day long, when the sun was bright, and the leaves on the trees, and the flowers in full bloom?

The clock struck four. Elsie had been waiting half an hour; still Mr. Edmund Gray did not arrive; still the steady beat of the footstep continued overhead.

The clock struck five. Still that steady footfall. Still Elsie sat upon the stairs waiting in patience.

When the clock struck six the footsteps stopped—or changed. Then a door overhead opened and shut, and the steps came down the stairs. Elsie rose, and stood on one side. An old man came down—tall and thin, close-shaven, pale, dressed in a black frock-coat worn to a shiny polish in all those parts which take a polish —a shabby old man, whose hat seemed hardly able to stand upright, and a gentleman—which was perfectly clear from his bearing—a gentleman in the last stage of poverty and decay.

He started, surprised to see a young lady on the stairs.

" You are waiting for Mr. Carstone ?" he asked. " He is out of town. He will not be back till Monday. Nobody ever comes back before Monday. From Saturday to Monday I have the inn to myself. All that time there are no slammers and no strangers. It is an agreeable retreat, if only—" He shook his head, and stopped short.

"I am not waiting for Mr. Carstone. I am waiting for Mr. Edmund Gray."

" He is very uncertain. No one knows when he comes or whither he goeth. I would not wait if I were you. He may come to-day, or to-morrow, or at any time. He comes on Sunday morning, often. I hear him coming upstairs after the chapel-bell stops. He is a quiet neighbor—no slammer or tramper. I would not wait, I say, if I were you."

"I will wait a little longer. I am very anxious to see Mr. Gray."

" He should wait for you," Mr. Langhorne replied politely. " The stairs are not a fit resting-place for you. This old inn is too quiet for such as you. Mirth and joy belong to you—silence and rest to such as me. Even slamming does not, I dare say, greatly displease youth and beauty. Chambers are not for young ladies. Beauty looks for life and love and admiration. They do not exist here. Run away, young lady—leave the inn to the poor old men, like me, who cannot get away if they would."

"Thank you. I must see Mr. Edmund Gray if I can. It will not hurt me to wait a little longer."

"You wish to see Edmund Gray. So do I. So do I. You are a friend of his. Perhaps, therefore, you will do as well. Those who are his friends are like unto him for kindness of heart. Those who wish to be his friends must try to be like unto him. Young lady, I will treat you as the friend of that good man. You can act for him."

"What can I do if I do act for him?" But there was a hungry eagerness in the man's eyes which made her divine what she could do.

"It is Saturday," he replied, without looking at her. He turned away his head. He spoke to the stair-window. "To-morrow is Sunday. I have before this, on one or two occasions, found myself as I do now—without money. I have borrowed of Mr. Carstone and of Mr. Edmund Gray. Sometimes I have paid it back—not always. Lend me—for Mr. Edmund Gray—if you are not rich he will give it back to you—the sum of five shillings—say five shillings. Otherwise I shall have nothing to eat until Monday, when Mr. Carstone returns."

"Nothing to eat? Nothing at all to eat?" Beggars in the street often make the same confession, but somehow their words fail to carry conviction. Mr. Langhorne's, however, did carry conviction.

The old man shook his head. "I had some food yesterday at this time. Since then I have had nothing. There was neither tea nor bread in my rooms for breakfast. When the clock struck six, my dinner-hour, I thought I would walk along the street, and look at the things to eat which are placed in the shop-windows. That relieves a little. But to-morrow will be a bad time—a very bad time. I shall lie in bed. Oh! I have gone through it before. Sometimes "—he dropped his voice—" I have been sore tempted to take something— No, no; don't think I have given way. No, no. Why, I should be disbarred. Not yet—not yet."

Elsie opened her purse. It contained two sovereigns and a shilling or two. "Take all," she said eagerly—"take all the gold, and leave me the silver. Take it instantly." She stamped her foot.

He hesitated. "All?" he asked—"all? Can you spare it? I can never repay—"

"Take it!" she said again, imperiously.

10

He obeyed—he took the gold out of the purse with trembling fingers. Then he raised his rickety old hat—was that a tear that stole into his eyes or the rheum of old age?—and slowly walked down the stairs, holding by the banisters. He was weak, poor wretch! with hunger. But it was his dinner-hour, and he was going to have his dinner.

Elsie sat down again.

It was half-past six—she had been waiting for three hours—when other footsteps entered the house. Elsie sprang to her feet; she turned pale; her heart stood still; for now she realized that if this step was truly that of the man she expected she was about to confront a person certainly of the deepest criminality, and possibly capable of villainy in any other direction. The steps mounted the stairs. I really think that the bravest persons in the world are those who before the event look forward to it with the utmost apprehension. They know, you see, what the dangers are. Elsie was going to face a great danger. She was going to find out, alone and unaided, who this man was, and why and how he worked these deeds of darkness.

The footsteps mounted higher; from the door to the top of the stairs it took but a single minute, yet to Elsie it seemed half an hour, so rapid were her thoughts. Then the man mounted the last flight of steps. Heavens! Elsie was fain to cry out for sheer amazement. She cried out; she caught at the banisters. For before her, taking the key of Mr. Edmund Gray's chambers from his waistcoat pocket, was none other than Mr. Dering himself!

Yes. An elderly man, of truly benevolent aspect, his coat open, flying all abroad; his face soft, gracious, smiling, and full of sunshine; his hat just the least bit pushed back; his left hand in his pocket. Elsie thought again of her portrait at home, in which she had transformed her guardian—and here he was in the flesh transformed according to her portrait!

She stared at him with an amazement that bereft her of speech and of motion. She could only stare. Even if her mother's voice were suddenly to call out to her that it is rude for little girls to stare, she could not choose but stare. For Mr. Dering looked at her with that kind of surprise in his eyes which means, "What have we here to do with beautiful young ladies?" There was not the least sign of any knowledge of her. He looked at her as one suffers the eyes to rest for a moment without interest upon a stranger and a casual passenger in the street.

He opened his outer door, and was about to walk in, when she recovered some presence of mind—not much. She stepped forward. "Can you tell me, please, how I could find Mr. Edmund Gray?"

"Certainly"—he smiled—"nothing easier. I am Edmund Gray."

"You!—you Edmund Gray? Oh! no, no. You cannot be Edmund Gray—you yourself!" All her beautiful theory of hypnotic influence vanished. No mesmerism or magnetic influence at all. "You yourself?" she repeated—"you Edmund Gray?"

"Assuredly. Why not? Why should a man not be himself?"

"Oh! I don't understand. The world is going upside down. I took you—took you for another person."

He laughed gently. "Truly, I am none other than Edmund Gray—always Edmund Gray. My first name I can never change if I wished, because it is my baptismal name. The latter I do not wish to change, because it is our name ancestral."

"I asked because—because—I fancied a resemblance to another person. Were you ever told that you are much like a certain other person?"

"No, I think not. Resemblances, however, are extremely superficial. No two living creatures are alike. We are alone, each living out his life in the great Cosmos, quite alone—unlike any other living creature. However, I am Edmund Gray, young lady. Is isn't often that I receive a visit from a young lady in these chambers. If you have no other doubt upon that point, will you let me ask you, once more, how I can help you? And will you come in, and sit down?"

"Oh! it is wonderful," she cried—"wonderful! most wonderful!" Again she controlled herself. "Are you," she asked again, "the same Mr. Edmund Gray who wrote the letter to the *Times* the other day?"

"Certainly. There is no other person, I believe, of the name in this inn. Have you read that letter?"

"Yes—oh, yes."

"And you have come here to talk to me about that letter?"

"Yes, yes." She caught at the hint. "That is why I came —to talk about that letter. I came in the hope of finding the author of that letter at home."

He threw open the door of his sitting-room.

"Will you step in? We can talk quite quietly here. The inn, at this hour on Saturday, is almost deserted." He closed the outer door, and followed his visitor into the sitting-room. "This," he went on, "is the quietest place in the whole of London. We have not in this square the stately elms of the old garden, but still we have our little advantages—spacious rooms; quiet always in the evening and on Sundays. A few rackety young men, perhaps; but for one who reads and meditates no better place in London. Now, young lady, take the easy-chair, and sit down. We will talk. There are very few people who talk to me about my theories. That is because I am old, so that I have lost my friends, and because my views are in advance of the world. No man is so lonely as the man born before his time. He is the prophet, you know, who must be stoned because he prophesies things unintelligible and therefore uncomfortable—even terrifying. I shall be very glad to talk a little with you. Now, allow me first to open these letters."

Elsie sat down and looked about her. She was in a large, low, wainscoted room, with two windows looking upon the square. The room was quite plainly but quite well furnished. There was a good-sized study-table with drawers; a small table between the windows; a few chairs, a couch, and an easy-chair; and a large bookcase filled with books—books on Socialism, George had told her. A door opened upon a smaller room; there was probably a bedroom at the back. A plain carpet covered the floor. Above the high, old-fashioned mantel were two or three portraits of Socialist leaders. The room, if everything had not been covered with dust, would have been coldly neat, the chairs were all in their places; the window-blinds were half-way down, as the laundress thought was proper—millions of Londoners always keep their blinds half-way down—a subject which must some day be investigated by the Folklore Society; the curtains were neatly looped; it wanted only a Bible on a table at a window to make it the front parlor of a Dalston villa. There were no flowers, no ornaments of any kind.

Mr. Edmund Gray opened half a dozen letters lying on his table, and glanced at them. There were a great many more waiting to be opened.

"All are from people who have read my letter," he said. "They share with me in the new faith of a new humanity. Happy is the man who strikes the note of leading at the right moment. Happy he who lights the lamp just when the darkness is beginning to be felt. Yes, young lady, you are not the only one who has been drawn towards the doctrines of that letter. But I have no time to write to all of them. A letter makes one convert—a paragraph may make a thousand."

Elsie rose from her chair. She had decided on her line. You have heard that her voice was curiously soft and winning; a voice that charms; a voice which would soothe a wild creature, and fill a young man's heart with whatever passion she chose to awaken. She had, besides, those soft eyes which make men surrender their secrets, part with their power and their strength. Did she know that she possessed all this power?—the girl who had no experience save of one man's love, and that the most natural, easy, and unromantic love in the world, when two who are brought up side by side, and see each other every day, presently catch each other by the hand, and walk for the future hand in hand without a word. Yet Delilah herself—the experienced, the crafty, the trained and taught—could not—did not—act more cleverly and craftily than this artless damsel. To be sure, she possessed great advantages over Delilah in the matter of personal charm.

"Oh!" she murmured softly, "it is a shame that you should be expected to waste your valuable time in writing letters to these people. You must not do it. Your time is wanted for the world, not for individuals."

"It is," he replied—"it is. You have said it."

"You are a master—a leader—a prince in Israel—a preacher —a prophet."

"I am—I am. You have said it. I should not myself have dared to say it. But I am."

"No one can doubt it who has read that letter. Be my master, too, as well as the master of—of all these people who write to you."

"Be your master?" He blushed like a boy. "Could I desire anything better?"

"My father and my master," she added, with a little change of color. Girls take fright very easily, and perhaps this old gentleman might interpret the invitation—well, into something other than was meant.

"Yes, yes." He held out his hand. She took it in her own —both her own soft hands—and bowed her head—her comely head—over it.

"I came to-day, thinking only "—oh, Delilah !—" to thank you for your great and generous and noble words, which have put fresh heart into me. And, now that I have thanked you, I am emboldened to ask a favor—"

"Anything, anything."

"You will be my master—you will teach me. Let me, in return, relieve you of this work." She laid her hand on the pile of letters. "Let me answer them for you. Let me be your private secretary. I have nothing to do. Let me work for you." She looked into his face with the sweetest eyes and the most winning smile, and her voice warmed the old man's ear like soft music. Ah, Circe ! "Now that I have seen you—let me be your disciple, your most humble disciple, and "—ah, siren !—" let me be more, Edmund Gray—I cannot say Mr. Gray —let me be more, Edmund Gray." She laid her hand—her soft-gloved, dainty, delicate hand—upon his, and it produced the effect of an electric battery gently handled. "Let me be your secretary."

It was ten o'clock before Elsie reached home that evening, and she refused to tell them—even her own brother and her lover —where she had been or how she had spent her evening.

CHAPTER XXIII

MASTER AND DISCIPLE

IT was Sunday afternoon in Gray's Inn. The new disciple sat at the feet of the master, her Gamaliel ; one does not know exactly the attitude adopted by a young rabbi of old, but in this case the disciple sat in a low chair, her hands folded in her lap, curiously and earnestly watching the master as he walked up and down the room, preaching and teaching.

"Master," she asked, "have you always preached and held these doctrines?"

"Not always. There was a time when I dwelt in darkness like the rest of the world."

"How did you learn these things? By reading books?"

"No. I discovered them. I worked them out for myself by logic, by reason, and by observation. Everything good and true must be discovered by a man for himself."

"What did you believe in that old time? Was it, with the rest of the world, the sacredness of property?"

"Perhaps." He stood in front of her, laying his right forefinger in his left forefinger and inclining his head. "My dear young scholar, one who believes as I believe, not with half a heart, but wholly and without reserve, willingly forgets the time when he was as yet groping blindly in darkness or walking in artificial light. He wishes to forget that time. There is no profit in remembering that time. I have so far drilled and trained myself not to remember that time that I have in fact clean forgotten it. I do not remember what I thought or what I said, or with whom I associated in that time. It is a most blessed forgetfulness. I dare say I could recover the memory of it if I wished, but the effort would be painful. Spare me. The recovery of that part would be humiliating. Spare me, scholar. Yet, if you wish—if you command—"

"Oh! no, no! Forgive me." Elsie touched his hand. He took hers, and held it. Was it with a little joy or a little fear that the girl observed the power she already had over him? "I would not cause you pain. Besides—what does it matter?"

"You know, my child, when the monk assumes the tonsure and the triple cord, he leaves behind him, outside the cell, all the things of the world—ambition, love, luxury, the pride of the eye —all—all. He forgets everything; he casts away everything; he abandons everything — for meditation and prayer. The monk," added the sage, "is a foolish person, because his meditation advances not the world a whit. I am like the monk, save that I think for the world instead of myself. And so, spending days and nights in meditation, I know not what went before— nor do I care. It is a second birth when the new faith takes you and holds you together, so that you care for nothing else. Oh, child! upon you also this shall come—this obsession—this possession—so that your spirit shall know of no time but that spent in the service of the cause. Nay, I go so far that I forget from day to day what passed, except when I was actively engaged for the cause. Yesterday I was here in the afternoon. You came. We talked. You offered yourself as my disciple. I remember every word you said. Could I ever forget a disciple so trustful and so humble? But before you came, where was I? Doubtless here—meditating. But I know not. Then there are things which one must do to live—breakfast, dinner—of these I remember nothing. Why should I? It is a great gift and reward to me that I should not remember unnecessary things—low and common things. Why should I try to do so?"

"No, no," murmured the catechumen, carried away by his earnestness. "Best forget them. Best live altogether in and for the cause." Yet—she wondered—how was she to bring things home to him unless he could be made to remember? He was mad one hour and sane the next. How should she bridge the gulf, and make the madman cross over to *the other side?*

The master took her hand in his and held it paternally. "We needed such a disciple as you," he went on, slightly bending his head over her. "Among my followers there is earnestness without understanding. They believe in the good time, but they are impatient. They want revolution, which is terrific and destroys. I want conviction. There are times when a great idea flies abroad like the flame through the stubble. But men's minds must first be so prepared that they are ready for it. The world is not yet ready for my idea, and I am old, and may die too soon to see the sudden rise of the mighty flood, when that doctrine shall suddenly cease in all mankind. We need disciples. Above all, we need women. Why do women, I wonder, throw themselves away in imitating man, when there are a thousand things that they can do better than any man? I want women — young, beautiful, faithful. I can find work for hundreds of women. Hypatia would be worth to me—to us—far more than he of the golden mouth. Child! your sweet voice, your sweet face, your sweet eyes—I want them. I will take them and use them—expend them—for the great cause. It may be that you will be called upon to become the first martyr of the cause. Hypatia was murdered by a raging mob. You will have against you a mob worse than any of Alexandria. You will have a mob composed of all those who are rich, and all who want to be rich, and all the servile crews at their command. Happy girl! You will be torn to pieces for the cause of humanity. Happy girl! I see the roaring, shrieking mob. I see your slender figure on the steps —what steps? Where? I hear your voice, clear and high. You are preaching to them; they close in round you; you disappear—they have dragged you down; they trample the life out of you. You are dead—dead! and a name forever. And the cause has had its martyr."

It was strange. She who had offered herself as a disciple with deception in her heart, thinking only to watch and wait and spy until she could see her way plain before her, who knew that she was listening to the voice and the dreams of a madman, yet she was carried away—he made her see the mob; she saw herself dragged down and trampled under their heels. She shuddered, yet she was exultant; her eyes glowed with a new light; she murmured, "Yes, yes. Do with me what you please. I am your disciple, and I will be your martyr if you please."

Great and wonderful is the power of enthusiasm. You see, it matters nothing—nothing in the world—what a man has to preach and teach—whether he advocates Obi or telepathy, or rapping, or spirits who hide teacups in coat-pockets—it matters nothing that there is neither common-sense nor evidence nor common reason to back him, if he only possess the magnetic power, he will create a following; he will have disciples who will follow him to the death. What is it—this power? It makes the orator, the poet, the painter, the novelist, the dramatist; it makes the leader of men; it made the first king, the first priest, the first conqueror.

"Come," said Mr. Edmund Gray, "the time passes. I must take you to my place."

They walked out together, master and scholar. The man who was mad walked carelessly and buoyantly; his coat flying open; one hand in his pocket, the other brandishing his walking-stick; his head thrown back; his face full of light, and, though his words were sometimes strong, always full of kindness. Now the sane man, the man of Lincoln's Inn, wore his coat tightly buttoned, walked with a firm, precise step, looked straight before him, and showed the face of one wholly occupied with his own thoughts. There was a man who was mad and a man who was

10*

sane, and certainly the madman was the more interesting of the two.

"This place," said the master, meaning Gray's Inn, "is entirely filled with those who live by and for the defence of property. They absorb and devour a vast portion of it while they defend it. No one, you see, defends it unless he is paid for it. Your country, your family, your honor — you will defend for nothing; but not another man's property—no. For that you must be paid. Every year it becomes more necessary to defend property; every year the hordes of mercenaries increase. Here they are lawyers, and lawyers' clerks—a vast multitude. Outside there are agents, brokers, insurers, financiers—I know not what — all defending property. They produce nothing, these armies; they take their toll; they devour a part of what other people have produced before they hand on the residue to the man who says it is his property."

"Oh!"—but Elsie did not say this aloud—"if these words could only be heard in Lincoln's Inn! If they could be repeated to a certain lawyer." From time to time she looked at him curiously. How if he should suddenly return to his senses? What would he think? How should she explain? "Mr. Dering, you have been off your head. You have been talking the most blasphemous things about property. You would never believe that even in madness you could say such things." No, he never would believe it—never. He could not believe it. What if his brother, Sir Samuel, were to hear those words? Meantime, the apostle walked along unconscious, filled with his great mission. Oh, heavens! that Mr. Dering—Mr. Dering—should believe he had a mission!

The master stopped a passing tram-car. "Let us climb up to the roof," he said. "There we can talk and breathe and look about us, and sometimes we can listen."

On the seat in front of them sat two young men, almost boys, talking together eagerly. Mr. Edmund Gray leaned forward, and listened shamelessly. "They are two young atheists," he said— "they are cursing religion. There is to be a discussion this evening at Battle Arches between a Christian and an Atheist, and they are going to assist. They should be occupied with the question of the day; they cannot, because they, too, are paid defenders of property. They are lawyers' clerks. They are poor, and they are slaves; all their lives they will be slaves, and they will be poor. Instead of fighting against slavery and poverty, which they know and feel, they fight against the unknown and the unintelligible. Pity! Pity!"

They passed two great railway termini, covering an immense area with immense buildings.

"Now," said the sage, "there are millions of property invested in railways. Whenever the railway servants please they can destroy all that property at a stroke. Perhaps you will live to see this done."

"But," said Elsie, timidly, "we must have things carried up and down the country."

"Certainly. We shall go on carrying things up and down the country, but not in the interests of property."

The train ran past the stations and under broad railway arches, called battle arches—where the two young atheists got down, eager for the fray, always renewed every Sunday afternoon with the display of much intellectual skill and much ignorance. It is a duel from which both combatants retire, breathed and flushed, proud of having displayed so much smartness, both claiming the victory, surrounded by admiring followers, and neither of them killed, neither of them hurt, neither of them a bit the worse, and both ready to begin again the following Sunday with exactly the same attack and exactly the same defence. There are some institutions—Christianity, the Church of England, the House of Lords, for instance—which invite and receive perpetual attacks, from which they emerge without the least hurt, so far as one can perceive. If they were all abolished to-morrow what would the spouters do?

The car stopped again, and two girls mounted—two work-girls of the better sort—not, that is to say, the sort which wears an ulster and a large hat with a flaming feather in it—working-girls, dressed quietly and neatly. They ought to have been cheerful, and even gay, for they were both young, both good-looking, both nicely dressed, and it was Sunday afternoon, warm and sunny. Yet they were not cheerful at all. One of them was in a rage royal, and the other, her friend, was in a rage sympathetic—quite a real rage. They were talking loudly on the curb while they waited for the tram; they carried on their conversation as they climbed the stair; they continued it while they chose a seat, and

before they sat down, without the least regard to those who sat
near them—whether they overheard, or wished not to hear, or
anything. They were wholly occupied with themselves and their
rage and their narrative. They neither saw nor heeded any one
else—which is the way that the angry woman has.

"So I told her—I up and told her, I did. 'Yes,' I sez,
'you and your fifteen hours a day and overtime,' I sez; 'and
your fines—so as to rob the poor girls of their money; and your
stinkin' little room, as isn't fit for two, let alone a dozen; and your
flarin' gas,' I sez, 'to choke us and poison us; and your dinners—yah! your dinner,' I sez—'fit for pigs; and your beast
of a husband comin' round with his looks and his leers—'
'You let my husband alone,' she sez. 'His looks and his leers,'
I sez; 'some day the girls'll take him out and drownd him,
head-first, in the gutter,' I sez—'and a good job too!'"

"You didn't say all that, Liz?" asked the other admiringly.
"My! What'd she say to that? Her 'beast of a husband?' And
'his looks and his leers?' Did you really, Liz—and her that jealous?"

"I did. Oh! I let her hear it. For once she did have it.
Then I took my money, and I went off. Never mind what she
called me—that don't matter. She got the truth for once."

"What do you make of this, disciple?" asked the master.

"It seems a quarrel between the girl and her employer."

"These are the makers of property. They are not the soldiers
who defend it. They are those who create it. The girls are employed by the sweater, who stands on the lowest rung of the ladder of property and steals the things as fast as they are made."

"One of them has been turned out. What will she do? Will
she find another place?"

"I don't know. What becomes of the young? It is a difficult
question. No one knows. Some say this, and some say that.
We know what becomes of the old when they are turned out—
they die. But as for the young I know not. You are young,
and you are a woman. Go among the young women who have
been turned out, and find out for yourself—for the world—what
does become of them."

They passed an immense churchyard, with an ancient church
standing in the midst—the churchyard now cleared of its headstones and converted into a beautiful garden after the modern

fashion, in which we have abandoned the pretence of remembering the dead, and plant flowers and turf above their graves for the solace of the living. Why not? Let the nameless dead be remembered by the nameless dead. Their virtues, if they had any, may live after them in their descendants.

"See," said Mr. Edmund Gray, moralizing—"here they lie, those who are soldiers of property and those who are slaves of property. They are mostly the poor of their parish who lie in that garden. No headstones mark their graves. They were born; they toiled for others to enjoy; and they died. Is this the life that men should most desire?"

"Nay," said the disciple. "But there must be strong and weak—clever and dull; there must be inequalities."

"Yes. Inequalities of gifts. One man is stronger, one is sharper, one is cleverer, than another. Formerly, those gifts were used to make their possessor richer and more powerful. The strong man got followers, and made slaves. The clever man cheated the dull man out of his land and his liberty. Henceforth, these gifts will be used for the general good. Patience! You shall understand all in good time."

He stopped the train, and they descended.

Lying east of the Hampstead Road and Camden High Street—and bounded on that side by the canal, the great space occupied by the Midland and Great Northern Goods Depot, by gas-works, wharves, and railway arches—there is a network of streets very little known to any but the parish clergy. No part of London is less interesting than this district. It used to be called Somers Town, but I think that the old name has almost died out. It is about a hundred years old, regarded as a settlement; it possesses three churches at least, two workhouses, one almshouse, and three burial-grounds turned into gardens. It is also cheered by the presence of a coal depot. Many small industries are carried on in this quarter; there are many lodging-houses; the streets are rather grimy, the houses are rather shabby, the people are rather slipshod. They are not criminals; they are, in a way, respectable—that is to say, tolerably respectable. It is not a picturesque suburb; dullness reigns; it is a dull, a dull, a dismally dull quarter. There are children, but they lack mirth; and young girls, but they lack the spring of youth; one would say that there was a low standard in everything, even in the brightness of dress. The place looks better in winter than in summer. To-day the bright sunshine only made the shabbiness of the streets more shabby.

"Is your place here?" asked Elsie.

"Yes, it is here. You wonder why I came here. Because the people here are not all working-people. Some of them are small employers—those of whom I spoke—who stand on the lowest rung of the ladder and steal the things as fast as they are made, and take toll, and hoard them up. The working-man is generous and open to others, compared with these people. I planted my place down in the midst of them. But you shall see—you shall see."

It was like a dream. Elsie walked beside her conductor. Yesterday she made the acquaintance of this man for the first time; she had never seen him before except in his sane condition; he was a madman—a real, dangerous madman—stark, staring mad; he was taking her she knew not where—to some place among strange people; she walked beside him without the least fear—she who would have fled before the most harmless lunatic; and she was going with him as his disciple.

"George," she said afterwards, "I do not know how it happened. I could not choose but go with him. I could not choose but to become his disciple—he compelled me. I lost my will. I even forgot that he was a madman; I gave up my reason and all; I followed him, and I believed all that he told me. How did he get that power? Directly I left him I became myself again. I perceived the mad enthusiast. I saw Mr. Dering caricatured, and proclaiming foolishness. But in his presence I was his servant and his slave."

"Here we are," he said. "This is my place. Let us go in."

CHAPTER XXIV

THE HALL OF THE NEW FAITH

THE place, as Mr. Edmund Gray modestly called it, was a meek and unpretending structure. The word is used advisedly, because no one could call it anything else—not an edifice; not a building; a structure. It turned its gabled front to the street, with a door below and a window above. It was of gray brick, with a slate roof—a very plain and simple structure. It might have been a Primitive Methodist chapel—this connection are fond of such neat and unpretending places; or a room belonging to the Salvation Army; or one of those queer lecture-halls affected by secularists, and generally called the Hall of Science. On the door-post was affixed a small handbill, announcing that every Sunday evening at seven o'clock an address would be pronounced by Edmund Gray, on the subject of "Property." On the same bill, below the line of the principal title, were suggestive sub-titles. Thus,

> "PROPERTY AND ITS ORIGIN."
> "PROPERTY AND ITS EVILS."
> "PROPERTY AND ITS DANGERS."
> "PROPERTY AND LIBERTY."
> "PROPERTY AND PROGRESS."
> "PROPERTY AND ITS DECAY."

The master pointed to the bill. "Read it," he said. "There you have my mission clearly announced. No mistake about it. A bold pronouncement, which cannot be mistaken. I make war against property. I am the enemy irreconcilable—the enemy to the death—of property. I am almost alone against the world, for my followers are a feeble folk and without power. All the interests, all the prejudices, all the powers, all the intellect of the whole world are against me. I stand alone. But I fear nothing, because the future is given over to me and to mine—yea, though I do not live to see the day of victory."

He opened the door, and Elsie entered. She found herself in a room about sixty feet long by twenty broad, and lofty—a fine and goodly room. It was furnished with a long and narrow table running down the middle, and a few benches. Nothing else. The table was laid with a white cloth, and provided with plates of ham and beef, cold sausages, hard-boiled eggs, cakes, toast, muffins, bread and butter, marmalade, jam, shrimps, water-cresses, and tea-cups. In fact, there was spread out a tea of generous proportions.

The room was half filled with thirty or forty people, mostly young, though there were some elderly men. Among them Elsie remarked, without surprise, the decayed barrister of Gray's Inn.

Perhaps he was attracted as much by the loaves as by the sermon. Three quarters of them were young men. Elsie noticed that they were young men of a curious type—their faces keen, their eyes hard, their manner aggressive. They belonged to a church militant. They longed to be fighting. On the appearance of their preacher they flocked about him, shaking hands and inquiring after his health. At least, therefore, he had the affection of his followers.

"My friends," said the prophet, "I bring you a new disciple. She comes to us from the very stronghold of property. Her friends"—yet he had shown no sign of recognition—"are either those who pillage the producer, or those who rob the possessor on pretence of defending him. She is at present only a recruit. She comes to listen and to learn. She will go home to remember and to meditate. She is a recruit now, who will be hereafter a leader."

The people received her with curiosity. They were not of the higher classes, to put it mildly, and they had never had a young lady among them before. Two or three girls who were present— girls from the dress-makers' workrooms—looked at her frock with envy, and at her bonnet and her gloves with a yearning, helpless, heart-sinking admiration. To the young men she seemed a goddess, unapproachable. They stood at a distance. Men of the rank above them would have worshipped—these young men only gaped. Such a girl had nothing to do with their lives.

Apparently they had been waiting for the master, for at the moment a stout woman and a girl appeared, bearing trays with teapots and jugs of hot water, which they placed upon the board. Mr. Edmund Gray took the chair. Elsie began to feel like Alice in Wonderland. She came to see a "place," she expected to hear a sermon or a lecture—and behold, a tea!

"Sit beside me," said the master. "We begin our evening on Sunday with a simple feast, which I provide. It is a sign of brotherhood. Every Sunday we begin with this renewal of fraternity. Those who break bread together are brothers and sisters. In the good time to come every meal shall be in common, and every evening meal shall be a feast. Eat and drink with us, my daughter, so you will understand that you belong to a brotherhood."

"Try some shrimps, miss," said her neighbor on the right, an elderly man, who was a builder's foreman.

History does not concern itself with what Elsie took. She found the meal very much to the purpose after a long afternoon of talk, argument, and emotion. She was young, and she was hungry. The tea was good; the things to eat were good; the cake and toast were admirable. Elsie ate and drank, and wondered what was coming next.

After a little, she began to look round her and to watch the company. There were now, she counted, forty-five of them—forty-five disciples of Mr. Edmund Gray. What had he to teach them? The destruction of property. Out of the four millions of London, forty-five were found who wanted to destroy property—only forty-five. But perhaps all who advocated that step were not present. Her ancient prejudices whispered that this was a reassuring fact, considering that the preacher had preached his doctrines for nine long years. Only forty-five. Next to her the foreman began to talk to her of Fourier and Owen and a dozen half-forgotten leaders in the old experiments. He had been a Chartist in the forties; he was a Socialist in these, the nineties; but he confessed that before any real reform was attempted property must first be destroyed.

"It's the selfishness," he whispered earnestly, "that's got to be torn out by the roots. Take that away, and there's a chance for the world. It never can be taken away till a man finds that he can't work no longer for himself, and that he must work for all, whether he likes it or lumps it. Don't give him the choice nor the chance, I say. Take away property, and there's neither choice nor chance left. You hear Mr. Gray upon that. Oh! he's powerful. What do they say? 'Naked we came into the world; naked we enter into the kingdom of Heaven.' There's a wonderful lot of fine things hangin' to that. You must wait till you hear Mr. Gray upon that theme—kingdom of Heaven! To hear the parsons talk, it's away above the clouds. Not so. It's here—close beside us—on this earth. All we've got to do is to put out our hands and reach it."

"You may put out your hands as much as you like," said one of the younger men; "but you won't reach it, all the same. Property stands between."

"At our place," said a girl sitting opposite—a girl of intelligent face, pale and thin—"we work from eight till eight, and sometimes longer, for twelve shillings a week. I know what things cost, and what they sell for. I could produce enough to keep me—ah! a good deal better than I live now—if I could sell what I made myself—for four hours' work a day. So I work eight hours a day, not counting the dinner-hour, just to keep the boss and to make property for him. My property it is—well, I know, in here we say, *our* property; outside we say, *my* property. Where's your kingdom of Heaven, then, if you reach out your hand ever so far, so long as I've got to work to make somebody else rich? Let's destroy property, and then we shall see."

A desire—a foolish, concealed desire, born of prejudice—seized Elsie to argue, for she perceived in the girl's reasoning certain confusions and intricacies. But she had the courage to suppress the inclination; she refrained. She was a disciple—she must listen.

"I am a slave, like all the rest of us," another young man remarked cheerfully. "My master owns me. He can sell me if he likes, only he calls it by another name. He can't take a whip and lash me, though he'd like to, because if he did I'd break every bone in his body for him; but he can cut down the work and the money. I do editing and reporting for a local paper—thirty shillings a week. The proprietor makes ten pounds a week out of it, and I'm not allowed to tell the truth for fear of advertisers." He added a few words not commonly heard in a place that looked like a chapel on a Sunday evening.

Elsie observed that their faces showed two variations of expression—only two. The majority of the company had the eyes of the dreamer, the theorist, the enthusiast. They are soft eyes, and in repose are heavy, and they look through stone walls into space, far away—space where their dreams are realized, and men and women live according to their theories. In moments of enthusiasm and passion they become flaming fires. These eyes belonged to most of those present. The rest—the minority—were those who are angry and restless and eager for the practical application of the doctrine. These want revolution; they are impatient; they feel for themselves the injustices and oppressions which enthusiasts feel for others. These are always resentful; the others are always hopeful. These want to convert the world at once with bludgeon and with gun; the others are certain that before long the world will be converted by reason. The one despairs of anything but force; the other will have no force. The

one hates his enemy; he would kill him if he could; he has no
words too bad for him. The enthusiast, on the other hand, regards
his enemy with pity, and would at any moment welcome him,
forgive him, and—well—invite him to a fraternal tea, if he would
only desert his ranks and come over. And these are the two divisions in every party, and such is the nature of man that there
must always be these two divisions.

The fraternal tea finished, the company cleared the tables,
everybody lending a hand, perhaps as another sign or pledge of
fraternity. It was then nearly seven o'clock, the hour appointed
for the address. The door was thrown wide open for the admission of the world, but there was no sign that the world took the
least interest in the subject of property. No one came at all.
Elsie learned afterwards that the world outside the hall had long
since grown tired of the subject on which Mr. Gray had been
preaching for nine years. Those who came to the tea were the
inner circle of believers or disciples, a small but faithful company,
to whose members there was rarely any addition.

At seven Mr. Edmund Gray rose to commence his address,
standing at the head of the table, so that it was like an after-
dinner speech. Outside the sun was hot and bright and the air
clear. Within the hall there were the mingled odors and steams
of long-protracted and hearty fraternal tea; the air was heavy,
and the room dark. When the master began to speak a young
man—one of the ardent and wrathful kind—drew out a note-
book and took everything down; all listened with respect, some
with rapt interest. Some nodded; some groaned; some said
"Hear" softly—to encourage the preacher, and to show their
adhesion to principle.

Elsie sat at the right hand of the speaker. His discourses
moved her much less in this public place than in his chambers.
The persuasive voice was there, but it did not persuade her.
Moreover, she could not meet his eyes; their magnetism failed
to touch her. So much the better, because she could listen with
cool judgment and watch the people.

"My friends," he began, "my brothers, and my sisters—we are
all long since agreed that the root of all evil, the first form of
disease, the first fatal step that was leading to so many other mischiefs, was the beginning of property. We have proved that so
often—we are all so entirely agreed upon this vital principle—

that we seldom, and only on rare occasions, find it necessary to do more than assume its truth. That occasion, however, is the present, when we have among us one who comes as a stranger, yet a disciple; one who has a mind open to the influence of reason; one who is anxious to clear herself of the prejudices and absurdities in which she has been from infancy brought up. Let us, therefore, briefly, for her instruction and for the strengthening of our own faith, point out some of the arguments which support this position. It is to us an axiom. To the world it still requires proof. And the world refuses to accept the proof, because it is given over to the chase of the abominable thing."

He proceeded to parade the reasons which made his school regard property as the root of all evil. The line which he pursued was not new; many men have pointed out before Mr. Edmund Gray the selfishness of mankind, as illustrated by the universal game of grab; others, with equal force, have shown that the protection of things causes an immense expenditure and a great shrinkage in things; others have shown that it is the continual efforts of men to get without working the things for which others have worked that fill our jails and keep up an army of police.

"We start with a false principle," the master went on, "which has ruined the world, and still keeps it down. If there are to be rich men, they must become rich at the expense of the rest; they must be few, and the poor must be many. Therefore, the protection of property is the robbery of the poor by law. We all know that; in this place we have agreed, so far, a thousand times; the rich can only become rich by robbing the poor; they rob their land; they rob their work; they rob their whole lives— and they are permitted and encouraged by the law. Shall we, then, change the law? No, it would be a work too vast. Shall we change the minds of men? Not by reason; it is impossible by any argument so long as by law and custom they can still rob the producer of his work. The only way is to destroy all property. When men can no longer by any kind of thought get richer than their neighbors, then they will cease to think for themselves, and think for the whole community. You will say —some one may object—that some are not the same in strength of mind or of body; there will be many, then, who will refuse to work at all, and become burdens on the community. We have thought of that objection. At first, there would be many such, but not for long, because we should kill them. Yes, my friends," he added, with a smile of the sweetest benevolence, "for the good of the community it will be necessary, without any sentimental considerations, to kill all those who refuse to work, all those who shirk their work, all those who persistently do scamped and bad work. They must die. So the commonwealth shall contain none but those who are vigorous, loyal, and true. For the rest death—if it means the death of a million who were once rich—death is the only escape from the difficulty which is so often objected.

"It has been asked again how we differ from the Socialists. In this: We would begin with no theories, no constitution, no code. Only let every man give all his strength, all his heart, all his mind, to the good of the commonwealth; without the least power of enriching himself, saving money—of course, there would be no money; without the chance of getting better food and better clothes than the rest—and we may safely leave the world to take care of itself. Why, my brothers—why, my sisters—should we poor, purblind creatures, unable to comprehend more than a glimpse of that glorious future which awaits the world when property shall be destroyed—why, I say, should we dare to lay down schemes and invent systems for that glorified humanity? Let us leave them to themselves. They will be as far above us, my brothers, as we are already above the holders and the defenders of property."

Elsie looked at the little gathering—five-and-forty—with a little smile. They were then already far above the holders and the defenders of property, and again she thought, " What if these words were heard in Lincoln's Inn ?"

" How, then, can property be destroyed ?"

At this practical question every one sat upright, coughed, and looked interested. Their preacher had often enough declaimed upon the evils of property. He seldom spoke of a practical way. Perhaps the time had come.

"There are, my friends, several ways. They are already beginning to be understood and to be worked. The Irish and the politicians who wanted the Irish vote have shown the world how to destroy property in land. Believe me, that example will be followed. It was an evil day for the holders of property when the government interfered between the landlord and his tenant. That example will bear fruit elsewhere. We shall see everywhere the owners of the land turned out, and their places taken by those who work the land. The next step is from land to houses. Why not with houses as with land? Since a beginning has been made it must be carried on. But there is other property besides lands and houses. There are companies with shares, railways, and so forth. We have only begun to see what united labor can effect—since union of labor is, in fact, not yet begun. When it is fairly started it will pay small respect to shareholders and to dividends. When wages are paid there will be perhaps no dividend left at all. In a single year—nay, a single week—the whole capital invested in all the companies will lose its value; it will be so much waste-paper. My friends, we need not stir hand or foot to bring about this end; it will be done for us by the working-man, and by those who follow the example of Ireland. They will do it for their own selfish ends first, but property once destroyed we shall never again allow it to be created.

"Oh!"—he warmed with his subject; his voice grew more musical; his face glowed—"I see a splendid—a noble sight. I see the great houses in the country fallen to ruin and decay; their contents are stored in museums; the great palaces of the towns are pulled down; the towns themselves are decayed and shrunk; there is no property; there is no one working for himself; the man of science works his laboratory for the community—but he has the honor of his discoveries; the medical man pursues his work with no thought of getting rich; there is plenty to go the round of everything—oh! plenty of the best. We can have what we like, do what we like, dress as we like, teach what we please—provided we work for the State. If we refuse—death! If we give bad work—death! It is the only law. We shall have no lawyers—no power—no magistrates. Oh! great and glorious time—you shall see it, you who are young—yes, you shall see it—while I—I—I—who have dreamed of the time so long—I shall lie low in the grave. What matter—so the time come, and so the world rises free at last to follow out the destiny of a new and glorified humanity?"

He sat down, and laid his head upon his hand as one in prayer. They remained in silence till he raised his head. Then the young man who had called attention to his slavery spoke.

"There is, perhaps, another way," he said, "which might do the job for us. Suppose the chemists were to find out how to produce food—food of any kind—artificially—just as good and as nourishing as if it were butcher-meat or bread. Suppose it could be produced dirt cheap—most chemists' things cost nothing. Then no one would need to work, because he'd have his food found for him. If no one would need to work, no one could get rich any more. And if no one wanted to buy anything, nobody could sell. Then riches wouldn't count, and there you are. Let's get a chemist to take the thing up."

The conversation that followed struck out new ideas. Presently it flagged, and one by one the people stole away.

The master and the disciple returned in the tram as far as Gray's Inn.

The master fell into profound silence a quarter of an hour before the end of the journey. When they got down, Elsie observed, first, that he buttoned his coat; next, that he put on gloves; thirdly, that he pulled his hat forward; and, lastly, that he ignored her presence. He drew himself erect, and walked away, with firm and precise step, in the direction of Bedford Row, which is on the other side of Gray's Inn. He was once more Mr. Edward Dering.

"I wonder," said Elsie, "how much, to-morrow, he will recollect?"

CHAPTER XXV

CAN HE REMEMBER?

It was past ten o'clock that Sunday evening when Elsie arrived home. Athelstan and George were waiting up for her. "Again the mysterious appointment?" asked the former. "Are we to know anything yet?" Elsie shook her head. "Not to-night? Very good. You look tired, Elsie."

"I am tired, thank you. And—and I think I would rather not talk to-night. I will go to my own room. Have patience, both of you, for a day or two longer. Believe me, everything is going well. The only reason why I cannot tell you what I have been doing is that it is so strange—so wonderful—that I have not been able even to shape it into words in my own mind. What is to-day?—the 1st of August?"

"Only eleven days yet—eleven long days," said George, "but also eleven short days."

"I do not forget. Well, you may both of you sit down—go about your business—you need do nothing more. As for me, I think you will have to get on without me every evening this week. But be quite easy. The thing is done." And with that, nodding and laughing, she ran out of the room.

"It is done," repeated George. "The thing is done. Which thing?"

"It is done," repeated Athelstan. "What is done? How was it done? Who did it? When was it done?"

"Since Elsie says it is done, I am bound to accept her assurance. Presumably she has caught old Checkley at South Square, in the very act. Never mind; I am quite sure that Elsie knows what she says."

In her own retreat Elsie sat down to consider.

If you think of it she had a good deal to consider. She had, in fact, a tremendous weapon, an eighty-ton Woolwich, in her possession—a thing which had to be handled so that when it was fired it should not produce a general massacre. All those who had maligned and spoken and thought evil of her brother and her lover should, she thought, be laid prostrate by the mere puff and whiff of the discharge. Checkley should fall backwards, and raise a bump at the back of his head as big as an egg. Sir Samuel and Hilda should be tumbled down in the most ignominious fashion, just as if they had no money at all. And her mother should be forced to cry out that she had been wrong and hasty.

She held in her own hands nothing less than the complete demolition of all this erection of suspicion and malignity—nothing less. She could restore to her brother that which he had never lost, save in the eyes of his own people, who should have been the most jealous to preserve it. No greater service could be rendered to him. And she could clear from her lover's name whatever shreds and mists had been gathered round it by the industrious breath of Checkley—that humble cloud compeller. You see, we all have this much of Zeus in us, even in the compelling of clouds—every man, by the exercise of a little malignity, a little insinuation, and a few falsehoods, can raise quite a considerable mist about the head, or the name, or the figure, or the reputation of any one. Women—some women, that is—are constantly engaged in this occupation; and after they have been at their work it is sometimes hard for the brightest sunshine to melt those mists away.

To be able to clear away clouds is a great thing. Besides this, Elsie had found out what the rest had failed to find out—and by the simplest method. She had learned from the only person who knew at what hour she should be most likely to find the mysterious Edmund Gray, and she had then waited on the stairs until he came. No method more direct, yet nobody thought of it except herself. She had done it. As the result, there was no longer any mystery. The man who forged the first check, the man who wrote those letters and conducted their transfer, was, as they all thought at first, Edmund Gray. No other. And Edmund Gray was Edward Dering—one and the same person—and Edward Dering was a madman, and this discovery it was which so profoundly impressed her. There were no confederates; there was no one wanted to intercept the post; no one had tampered with the safe; the chief himself had received the letters and conducted the correspondence alternately as Edmund Gray himself, or Edmund Gray acting unconsciously for Edward Dering.

Perfectly impossible—perfectly simple—perfectly intelligible. As for the impossibility, a fact may remain when its impossibility is established. Elsie was not a psychologist or a student of the brain. She knew nothing about mental maladies. She only said, after what she had seen and heard, "The man is mad."

Then she thought how she should best act. To establish the identity of Mr. Dering and Edmund Gray must be done. It was the one thing necessary. Very well. That could easily be done, and in a simple way. She had only to march into his office, at the head of a small band of witnesses, and say, "You wanted us to find out Edmund Gray. I have found him! And thou art the man!"

He would deny it. He certainly knew nothing about it. Then she would call upon her witnesses. First, Athelstan's commission-naire, who declared that he should remember, even after eight years or eighty years, the gentleman who sent him to cash that check. "Who is this man, commissionnaire?"

11

"That is Mr. Edmund Gray."

Next, the landlord of his chambers. "Who is this man?"

"That is Mr. Edmund Gray, my tenant for nine years."

Then she would call the eminent barrister, Mr. Langhorne. "Do you know this man?"

"He is my neighbor, Mr. Edmund Gray."

And Freddy Carstone the coach.

"He is my neighbor, Mr. Edmund Gray."

And the laundress, and she would say, "I have done for the gentleman for nine years. He's a very good gentleman, and generous, and his name is Mr. Edmund Gray."

And the people from the hall, and they would make answer, with one consent, "That is Mr. Edmund Gray, our preacher and our teacher."

And she herself would give her testimony, "I have sat with you in your chambers. I have heard you lecture in your hall, surrounded by these good people, and you are Edmund Gray."

The thing was quite easy to do. She could bring forward all this evidence at once, and it would be unanswerable and convincing—even to Sir Samuel.

Except for one thing, which made it difficult.

The discovery would be a most dreadful—a most terrible—revelation to one who believed himself to be the most respectable solicitor in the whole of London; the most trustworthy; the clearest in mind; the keenest in vision; the coolest in judgment. He would learn without the least previous suspicion or preparation, or any softening of the blow, that for many years he had been— What? Is there any other word—any kinder word—any word less terrifying or less humiliating—by which the news could be conveyed to him that he had been mad—mad—mad? Heavens! what a word it is! How terrible to look at with its three little letters which mean so much. All the words that mean much are monosyllables—God; love; joy; hate; fear; glad; sad; mad; bad; hell; home; wife; child; house; song; feast; wine; kiss—everything—they are the oldest words, you see; they have been used from time immemorial by prehistoric man as well as by ourselves.

Mr. Dering had to be told that he was mad. Somehow or other, he must be told that. It seemed at first the only way out of the difficulty. How could this girl communicate the dreadful news to her guardian, who had always been to her considerate, and even affectionate? She shrank from the task. Then she thought she would hand it over to her brother Athelstan. But he was far more concerned about clearing up the hateful business than about softening the blow for Mr. Dering. Or of communicating it to George. What should she do? Mr. Dering was mad. Not mad all the time, but mad now and then—sometimes every day, sometimes with intervals. This kind of madness, I believe, takes many forms—a fact which should make the strongest men tremble. Sometimes it lasts a long time before it is found out. Sometimes, even, it is never found out at all. Solicitors and doctors tell queer stories about it. For instance, that story—quite a common story—of an old gentleman of irreproachable reputation, a speaker and leader in religious circles, a man enormously respected by all classes, concerning whom not his bitterest enemy had a word of scandal—yet, after his death, things deplorable, things incredible, things to be suppressed at any cost, were brought to the knowledge of his lawyers. At certain times he went mad, you see. Then he forgot who he was; he forgot his reputation, his place in the world, and the awful penalties of being found out; he went down; he lived among people of the baser sort, and became an inferior man with another name, and died without ever knowing his own dreadful record. Another of whom I have heard was mad for fifteen years, yet the chief of a great house, who all the time conducted the business with great ability. He was found out at last because he began to buy things. Once he sent home six grand pianos; another time he bought all the cricket-bats that were in stock at a certain shop; and another time he bought all the hats that fitted him at all the hatters' shops within a circle whose centre was Piccadilly Circus and the radius a mile long. After this they gave him a cheerful companion, who took walks abroad with him, and he retired from active business. Some philosophers maintain that we are all gone mad on certain points. In that case, if one does not know it or suspect it, and if our friends neither know nor suspect it, what does it matter? There are also, we all know, points on which some of us are mad, and everybody knows it. There is the man who believes that he is a great poet, and publishes volume after volume, all at his own expense, to prove it; there is the man —but he ought to be taken away and put on a treadmill -who writes letters to the papers on every conceivable subject, with the-day-before-yesterday's wisdom; there is the man who thinks he can paint—we all know plenty of men mad like unto these, and we are, for the most part, willing to tolerate them. Considerations, however, on the universality of the complaint fail to bring consolation to any except those who have it not. In the same way nobody who dies of any disease is comforted with the thought of the rarity or the frequency of that disease; its interesting character has no charm for him. Nor is the man on his way to be hanged consoled by the reminder that thousands have trodden that flowery way before him. To Mr. Dering—proud of his own intellect, self-sufficient and strong—the discovery of these things would certainly bring humiliation intolerable, perhaps even shame unto death itself. How—oh! how could things be managed so as to spare him this pain?

Elsie's difficulties grew greater the more she pondered over them. It was past midnight when she closed the volume of thought and her eyes at the same moment.

In the morning Athelstan kissed her gravely.

"Do you remember what you said last night, Elsie? You said that we could rest at peace, because the thing was done."

"Well, Athelstan, the words could only have one meaning, could they? I mean, if you want me to be more explicit, that the thing is actually done. My dear brother, I know all about it now. I know who signed that first check—who sent the commissionnaire to the bank, who received the notes—who placed them in the safe—who wrote about the transfers—who received the letters, and carried on the whole business. I can place my hand upon him to-day, if necessary."

"Without doubt? With proofs, ample proofs?"

"Without the least doubt—with a cloud of witnesses. My dear brother, do not doubt me. I have done it. Yet—for a reason—to spare one most deeply concerned—for the pity of it—if you knew—give me a few days—a week, perhaps—to find a way if I can. If I cannot then the cruel truth must be told bluntly, whatever happens."

"Remember all the mischief the old villain has done."

"The old villain? Oh! you mean Checkley?"

"Of course; whom should I mean?"

"Nobody—nothing. Brother, if you bid me speak to-day I

will speak. No one has a better right to command. But if this —this person—were to die to-day, my proofs are so ample that there could be no doubt possible. Yes, even my mother—it is dreadful to say it—but she is so hard and so obstinate—even my mother would acknowledge that there is no doubt possible."

Athelstan stooped and kissed her. "Order it exactly as you please, my child. If I have waited eight long years I can wait another week. Another week! Then I shall at last be able to speak of my people at home. I shall go back to California with belongings like other men. I shall be able to make friends; I can even, if it comes in my way, make love, Elsie. Do you think you understand quite what this means to me?"

He left her presently to go about his work.

In the corner of the room stood her easel with the portrait, the fancy portrait, of Mr. Dering the Benevolent—Mr. Dering the Optimist—Mr. Dering as he might be with the same features and the least little change in their habitual setting.

Elsie stood before this picture, looking at it curiously.

"Yes," she murmured, "you are a dear, tender-hearted, kindly, benevolent, simple old thing. You believe in human nature; you think that everybody is longing for the kingdom of Heaven; you think that everybody would be comfortable in it; that everybody longs for honesty. Before I altered you and improved your face, you were justice without mercy; you were law without leniency; you were experience which knows that all men are wicked by choice when they get the chance; you had no soft place anywhere; you held that society exists only for the preservation of property. Oh! you are so much more lovable now—if you would only think so—if you only knew. You believe in men and women—that is a wonderful advance—and you have done well to change your old name to your new name. I think I should like you always to be Edmund Gray. But how am I to tell you? How, in the name of wonder, am I to tell you that you are Edmund Gray? First of all, I must see you; I must break the thing gently; I must force you somehow to recollect as soon as possible. I must make you, somehow, understand what has happened."

She had promised to meet Mr. Edmund Gray at his chambers that evening at five. He showed his confidence in her by giving her a latch-key, so that she might let herself in if he happened not to be in the chambers when she called at five. She would try, then, to bring him back to himself. She pictured his amazement —his shame—at finding himself in strange rooms, under another name, preaching wild doctrines. It would be too much for him. Better go to Mr. Dering, the real Mr. Dering, and try to move him, in his own office, to recollect what had happened. Because, you see, Elsie, unacquainted with these obscure forms of brain-disease, imagined that she might, by artful question and suggestion, clear that clouded memory, and show the lawyer his double figuring as a Socialist.

She waited till the afternoon. She arrived at New Square about three, two hours before her engagement at Gray's Inn.

Mr. Dering received her with his usual kindness. He was austerely benignant.

"I tried to see you last night," she said untruthfully, because the words conveyed the impression that she had called upon him.

"No, no. I was—I suppose I was out. I went out—" His face clouded, and he stopped.

"Yes—you were saying, Mr. Dering, that you went out."

"Last night was Sunday, wasn't it? Yes, I went out. Where did I go?" He drummed the table with his fingers irritably. "Where did I go? Where? What does it matter?"

"Nothing at all. Only it is strange that you should not remember."

"I told you once before, Elsie," he said—"I suffer—I labor—under curious fits of forgetfulness. Now, at this moment, I—it really is absurd—I cannot remember where I was last night. I am an old man. It is the privilege of age to forget yesterday, and to remember fifty years ago."

"I was talking last night to an old gentleman who said much the same. He has chambers, where he goes to write; he has a lecture-hall, where he preaches to the people—"

Mr. Dering looked at her in mild surprise. What did she mean? Elsie colored.

"Of course," she said, "this has nothing to do with you."

"How I spent the evening I know very well," Mr. Dering went on. "Yet I forget. That is the trouble with me. My housekeeper will not give me dinner on Sunday evening, and on that day I go to my club. I get there about five or six. I read the magazines till seven. Sometimes I drop off to sleep—we old fellows will drop off, you know—about seven I have dinner. After dinner I take my coffee, and read—or talk, if there is any one I know. About nine I walk home. That has been my custom for many years. Therefore, that is how I spent the evening of yesterday. But, you see, I cannot remember it. Breakfast I remember, and the church service afterwards. Luncheon I remember; getting home at ten I remember; but the interval between I cannot remember."

"Do you forget other things? Do you remember Saturday afternoon, for instance?"

"Yes—perfectly. I left the office about five. I walked straight home. No, no—that isn't right. It was nearly eight when I got home. I remember. The dinner was spoiled. No, I did not go straight home."

"Perhaps you stayed here till past seven?"

"No — no. I remember looking at the clock as I put on my hat. It was half-past five when I went out—five. What did I do between half-past five o'clock and eight? I forget. You see my trouble, Elsie—I forget. Perhaps I went to the club; perhaps I strolled about; perhaps I came back here. There are three hours to account for—and I have forgotten them all."

━━━━━━━━━

CHAPTER XXVI

WILL HE REMEMBER?

SHOULD she tell him? She could not. The way must, somehow, be prepared. No, she could not tell him just so—in cold blood. How would he look if she were to begin, "I have found out the mystery. You are Edmund Gray. During the hours that you cannot recall you are playing the part of a Socialist teacher and leader; you are actively propagating the doctrines that you hold to be dangerous and misleading?" What would he say? What would he feel when he realized the truth?

On the table lay a copy of the *Times*—a fortnight-old copy—open at the place where there was a certain letter from a certain Edmund Gray. Elsie pointed to it. Mr. Dering sighed. "Again," he said, "they persecute me. Now it is a letter addressed to Edmund Gray lying on my table; now it is the bill of a pernicious lecture by Edmund Gray; to-day it is this paper, with the letter that appeared a week or two ago. Who brought it here? Checkley says he didn't. Who put it on my table?"

Elsie made no reply. It was useless to test her former theory of the boy under the table.

"As for the man who wrote this letter," Mr. Dering went on—"he bears the name of our forger, and writes from the same address. Yet he is not the man—of that I am convinced. This man is a fool, because he believes in the honesty of mankind; he is a generous fool, because he believes that people would rather be good than bad. Nonsense! They would rather be stealing from each other's plates, like the monkeys, than dividing openly. He has what they call a good heart—that is, he is a soft creature—and he is full of pity for the poor. Now, in my young days I was taught—what after-experience has only brought more home to me—that the poor are poor in consequence of their vices. We used to say to them, 'Go away; practise thrift; be sober; work hard. By exercising these virtues we rose out of your ranks. By continuing to exercise them we remain on these levels. Go away. There is no remedy for disease contracted by vice. Go away and suffer.' That's what we said formerly. What they say now is, 'Victims of greed! You are filled with every virtue possible to humanity. You are down-trodden by the capitalist. You are oppressed. Make and produce for others to enjoy. We will change all this. We will put the fruits—the harvest—of your labor in your own hands, and you shall show the world your justice, your noble disinterestedness, your generosity, your love of the common weal.' That's the new gospel, Elsie, but I prefer the old."

Strange that a man should at one time hold, and preach with so much fervor and earnestness, the very creed which, at another time, he denounced as fiercely!

"This man, and such as he," continued Mr. Dering, lifted out of his anxieties by the subject, "would destroy property in order to make the workman rich. Wonderful doctrine! He would advance the world by destroying the only true incentive and stimulant for work, invention, civilization, association, and every good and useful thing. He would destroy property. And then? can he not see what would follow? Why, these people do not know the very alphabet of the thing. By property, they mean the possession by individuals of land or money. But that is only a part of property. Take that away, and the individual remains. And he has got—what you cannot take away—the rest of his property, by which he will speedily repair the temporary loss. Consider, child, if you can, what does a man possess? He has, I say, property—all his own—which cannot be taken from him or shared with another—property in his brain, his trade, his wit, his craft, his art, his skill, his invention, his enterprise, his quickness to grip an opportunity. Again, he has his wife and children—sometimes a very valuable property; he has, besides, his memories, his knowledge, his experience, his thoughts, his hopes, his projects, and his intentions; he has his past and he has his future; he has, or thinks he has, his inheritance in the kingdom of Heaven. Take away all these things bit by bit, what is left? Nothing. Not even the shadow of a man. Not even a naked figure. This, Elsie, is property. These things separate the individual from the mass, and each man from his neighbor. A shallow fanatic, like this Edmund Gray, thinks that wealth is the whole of property. Why, I say, it is only a part of property; it is the external and visible side of certain forms of property. Take all the wealth away to-day—even if you make ten thousand laws, the same qualities—the same forms of property—the same lack of those qualities will produce like results to-morrow. Do you now understand, child, what is meant by property? It is everything which makes humanity. Wealth is only the symbol or proof of society so organized that all these qualities—the whole property of a man —can be exercised freely and without injustice."

"I see," said Elsie, gazing with wonder undisguised. Was this last night's prophet? Could the same brain hold two such diverse views?

"You are surprised, child. That is because you have never taken or understood this larger view of property. It is new to you. Confess, however, that it lends sacredness to things which we are becoming accustomed to have derided. Believe me, it is not without reason that some of us venerate the laws which have been slowly, very slowly, framed; and the forms which have been slowly, very slowly, framed, as experience has taught us wisdom for the protection of man—working man, not loafing, lazy man. It is wise and right of us to maintain all those institutions which

11*

encourage the best among us to work and invent and distribute. By these forms alone is industry protected and enterprise encouraged. Then such as this Edmund Gray"—he laid his hand again upon the letter—"will tell you that property—property—causes certain crimes—*ergo*, property must be destroyed. Everything desirable causes its own peculiar class of crime. Consider the universal passion of love. It daily causes crimes innumerable. Yet no one has yet proposed the abolition of love—eh?"

"I believe not," Elsie replied, smiling. "I hope no one will —yet."

"No. But the desire for property, which is equally universal— which is the most potent factor in the cause of law and order— they desire and propose to destroy. I have shown you that it is impossible. Let the companies pay no dividends; let all go to the working-men; let the lands pay no rent; the houses no rent; let the merchants' capital yield no profit—to-morrow the clever man will be to the front again, using for his own purposes the dull and the stupid and the lazy. That is my opinion. Forgive this sermon, Elsie. You started me on the subject. It is one on which I have felt very strongly for a long time. In fact, the more I think upon it the more I am convinced that the most important thing in any social system is the protection of the individual—personal liberty; freedom of contract; right to enjoy in safety what his ability, his enterprise, and his dexterity may gain for him."

Elsie made no reply for a moment. The conversation had taken an unexpected turn. The vehemence of the upholder of property overwhelmed her as much as the earnestness of its destroyer. Besides, what chance has a girl of one-and-twenty, on a subject of which she knows nothing, with a man who has thought upon it for fifty years? Besides, she was thinking all the time of the other man. And now there was no doubt—none whatever—that Mr. Dering knew nothing of Mr. Edmund Gray—nothing at all. He knew nothing and suspected nothing of the truth. And which should she believe? The man who was filled with pity for the poor, and saw nothing but their sufferings; or the man who was full of sympathy with the rich, and saw in the poor nothing but their vices? Are all men who work oppressed? Or are there no oppressed at all, but only some lazy and stupid and some clever?

"Tell me more another time," she said, with a sigh. "Come back to the case—the robbery. Is anything discovered yet?"

"I have heard nothing. George refuses to go on with the case, out of some scruple because—"

"Oh! I know the cause. Very cruel things have been said about him. Do you not intend to stand by your own partner, Mr. Dering?"

"To stand by him? Why, what can I do?"

"You know what has been said of him—what is said of him—why I have had to leave home—"

"I know what is said—certainly. It matters nothing what is said. The only important thing is to find out—and that they cannot do."

"They want to connect Edmund Gray with the forgeries, and they are trying the wrong way. Checkley is not the connecting link, nor is George."

"You talk in riddles, child."

"Perhaps. Do you think, yourself, that George has had anything whatever to do with the business?"

"If you put it so, I do not. If you ask me what I have a right to think—it is that everything is possible."

"That is what you said about Athelstan. Yet now his innocence is established."

"That is to say, his guilt is not proved. Find me the man who forged that check, and I will acknowledge that he is innocent. Until then he is as guilty as the other man—Checkley—who was also named in connection with the matter. Mind, I say, I do not believe that my partner could do this thing. I will tell him so. I have told him so. If it had to be done over again, I would ask him to become my partner. But all things are possible. My brother is hot upon it. Well—let him search as he pleases. In such a case the solution is always the simplest and the most unexpected. I told him only this morning—he had lunch with me —that he was on a wrong scent, but he is obstinate. Let him go on."

"Yes—let him divide a family—keep up bitterness between mother and son—make a life-long separation between those who ought to love each other most— Oh! it is shameful! It is shameful! And you make no effort—none at all—to stop it."

"What can I do? What can I say, more than I have said? If they would only not accuse each other—but find out something!"

"Mr. Dering—forgive me—what I am going to say "—she began with jerks. "The honor of my brother—of my lover—are at stake."

"Say, child, what you please."

"I think that perhaps"—she did not dare to look at him—"if you could remember sometimes those dropped and forgotten evenings—those hours when you do not know what you have said and done—if you could only remember a little—we might find out more."

He watched her face blushing, and her eyes confused, and her voice stammering, and he saw that there was something behind—something that she hinted, but would not or could not express. He sat upright, suspicious and disquieted.

"Tell me what you mean, child."

"I cannot—if you do not remember anything. You come late in the morning—sometimes two hours late. You think it is only ten o'clock when it is twelve. You do not know where you have been for the last two hours. Try to remember that. You were late on Saturday morning. Perhaps this morning. Where were you?"

His face was quite white. He understood that something was going—soon—to happen.

"I know not, Elsie—indeed—I cannot remember. Where was I?"

"You leave here at five. You have ordered dinner, and your housekeeper tells me that you come home at ten or eleven. Where are you all that time?"

"I am at the club."

"Can you remember? Think—were you at the club last night? George went there to find you, but you were not there—and you were not at home. Where were you?"

He tried to speak, but he could not. He shook his head—he gasped twice.

"You cannot remember? Oh! try, Mr. Dering—try—for the sake of everybody—to put an end to this miserable condition—try."

"I cannot remember," he said again feebly.

"Is it possible—just possible—that while you are away—during these intervals—you yourself may be actually in the company of this Socialist—this Edmund Gray?"

"Elsie! what do you mean?"

"I mean—can you not remember?"

"You mean more, child! Do you know what you mean? If what you suggest is true, then I must be mad—mad. Do you mean it? Do you mean it? Do you understand what you say?"

"Try—try to remember," she replied. "That is all I mean. My dear guardian, is there any one to whom I am more grateful than yourself? You have given me a fortune, and my lover an income. Try—try to remember."

She left him without more words.

He sat looking straight before him—the horror of the most awful thing that can befall a man upon him. Presently he touched his bell, and his old clerk appeared.

"Checkley," he said, "tell me the truth."

"I always do," he replied surlily.

"I have been suffering from fits of forgetfulness. Have you observed any impairing of the faculties? When a man's mental powers are decaying he forgets things; he loses the power of work; his old skill leaves him; he cannot distinguish between good work and bad. He shows his mental decay, I believe, in physical ways—he shuffles as he walks; he stoops and shambles—and in his speech—he wanders and he repeats—and in his food and manner of eating. Have you observed any of these symptoms upon me, Checkley?"

"Not one. You are as upright as a lance; you eat like five-and-twenty; your talk is as good and your work is as good as when you were forty. Don't think such things. To be sure, you do forget a bit. But not your work. You only forget sometimes what you did out of the office—as if that matters. Do you remember the case you tackled yesterday afternoon?"

"Certainly."

"Do you tell me that any man—forty years younger than you—could have tackled that case more neatly? Garn! Go long!"

Checkley went back to his office.

"What did she mean by it, then?" Mr. Dering murmured. "Who put her on to such a suspicion? What did she mean by it? Of course it's nonsense?" So reassuring himself, he yet remained disquieted. For he could not remember.

At half-past five or so Mr. Edmund Gray arrived at his chambers. The outer door was closed, but he found his disciple waiting for him. She had been there an hour or more, she said. She was reading one of the books he had recommended to her. With the words of Mr. Dering in her ears she read as if two voices were speaking to her—talking to each other across her.

She laid down the book, and rose to greet him. "Master," she said, "I have come from Mr. Dering. He is your solicitor, you told me."

"Assuredly. He manages my affairs."

"It is curious—I asked him if he knew you—and he said that he knew nothing about you."

"That is curious, certainly. My solicitor for—for many years. He must have mistaken the name. Or—he grows old—perhaps he forgets people."

"Do you often see him?"

"I saw him this morning. I took him my letter to the *Times*. He is narrow—very narrow—in his views. We argued the thing for a bit. But, really, one might as well argue with a stick as with Dering when property is concerned. So he forgets, does he? Poor old chap! He forgets— Well, we all grow old together." He sighed. "It is his time to-day and mine to-morrow. My scholar, let us talk."

The scholar left her master at seven. On her way out she ran against Checkley, who was prowling round the court. "You!" he cried. "You! Ah! I've caught you, have I? On Saturday afternoon I thought I see you going into No. 22. Now I've caught you coming out, have I?"

"Checkley," she said, "if you are insolent I shall have to speak to Mr. Dering," and walked away.

"There's another of 'em," Checkley murmured, looking after her—"a hardened one, if ever there was. All for her lover and her brother! A pretty nest of 'em. And calls herself a lady!"

CHAPTER XXVII

THE LESSON OF THE STREET

"Child," said the master, "it is time that you should take another lesson."

"I am ready. Let us begin." She crossed her hands in her lap, and looked up obedient.

"Not a lesson this time from books. A practical lesson from men and women, boys and girls, children and infants in arms. Let us go forth, and hear the teaching of the wrecks and the slaves. I will show you creatures who are men and women, mutilated in body and mind—mutilated by the social order. Come. I will show you, not by words, but by sight, why property must be destroyed."

It was seven o'clock, when Mr. Dering ought to have been thinking of his dinner, that Mr. Edmund Gray proposed this expedition. Now, since that other discourse on the sacredness of property, a strange thing had fallen upon Elsie. Whenever her master spoke and taught, she seemed to hear, following him, the other voice speaking and teaching exactly the opposite. Sometimes—this is absurd, but many true things are absurd—she seemed to hear both voices speaking together; yet she heard them distinctly and apart. Looking at Mr. Dering, she knew what he was saying; looking at Mr. Edmund Gray, she heard what he was saying. So that, no sooner had these words been spoken, than, like a response in church, there arose the voice of Mr. Dering. And it said, "Come. You shall see the wretched lives and the sufferings of those who are punished because their fathers or themselves have refused to work and save. Not to be able to get property is the real curse of labor. It is no evil to work, provided one chooses the work and creates for one's self property. The curse is to have to work for starvation wages at what can never create property if the worker should live for a thousand years."

Of the two voices she preferred the one which promised the abolition of poverty and crime. She was young; she was generous; any hope of a return of the Saturnian reign made her heart glow. Of the two old men—the madman and the sane man—she loved the madman. Who would not love such a man? Why, he knew how to make the whole world happy! Ever since the time of Adam we have been looking and calling out and praying for such a man. Every year the world runs after such a man. He promises, but he does not perform. The world tries his patent medicine, and is no better. Then, the year after, the world runs after another man.

Elsie rose and followed the master. It was always with a certain anxiety that she sat or talked with him. Always she dreaded lest, by some unlucky accident, he should awaken and be restored to himself suddenly and without warning—say in his lecture-hall. How would he look? What should she say? "See—in this place, for many years past, you have, in course of madness, preached the very doctrines which in hours of sanity you have most reprobated. These people around you are your disciples. You have taught them, by reason and by illustration, with vehemence and earnestness, to regard the destruction of property as the one thing needful for the salvation of the world. What will you say now? Will you begin to teach the contrary?—they will chase you out of the hall for a madman. Will you go on with your present teaching? —you will despise yourself for a madman." Truly a difficult position. Habit, however, was too strong. There was little chance that Edmund Gray among his own people, and at work upon his own hobby, would become Edward Dering.

They went out together. He led her—whither? It mattered not. North and south and east and west you may find everywhere the streets and houses of the very poor, hidden away behind the streets of the working people and the well-to-do.

The master stopped at the entrance of one of those streets—it seemed to Elsie as if she were standing between two men both alike, with different eyes. At the corner was a public-house with swinging doors. It was filled with men talking, but not loudly. Now and then a woman went in or came out, but they were mostly men. It was a street long and narrow, squalid to the last degree, with small, two-storied houses on either side. The bricks were grimy; the mortar was constantly falling out between them;

the woodwork of doors and windows was insufferably grimy;
many of the panes were broken in the windows. It was full of
children; they swarmed; they ran about in the road, they danced
on the pavement, they ran and jumped and laughed as if their lot
was the happiest in the world and their future the brightest.
Moreover, most of them, though their parents were steeped in
poverty, looked well-fed and even rosy. "All these children,"
said Mr. Edmund Gray, "will grow up without a trade; they will
enter life with nothing but their hands and their legs and their
time. That is the whole of their inheritance. They go to school,
and they like school; but as for the things they learn, they will
forget them, or they will have no use for them. Hewers of wood
and drawers of water shall they be; they are condemned already.
That is the system; we take thousands of children every year, and
we condemn them to servitude—whatever genius may be lying
among them. It is like throwing treasures into the sea, or bury-
ing the fruits of the earth. Waste! Waste! Yet, if the system
is to be bolstered up, what help?"

Said the other voice, "The world must have servants. These
are our servants. If they are good at their work they will rise,
and become upper servants. If they are good upper servants
they may rise higher. Their children can rise higher still, and their
grandchildren may join us. Service is best for them. Good service, hard service, will keep them in health and out of temptation. To lament because they are servants is foolish and sentimental."

Standing in the door-ways, sitting on the door-steps, talking together, were women—about four times as many women as there
were houses. This was because there were as many families as
rooms, and there were four rooms for every house. As they stood
at the end of the street and looked down, Elsie observed that
nearly every woman had a baby in her arms, and that there were
a great many types or kinds of women. That which does not
surprise one in a drawing-room, where every woman is expected
to have her individual points, is noticed in a crowd, where, one
thinks, the people should be like sheep—all alike.

"A splendid place, this street, for such a student as you should
be, my scholar." The master looked up and down; he sniffed
the air, which was stuffy, with peculiar satisfaction; he smiled
upon the grubby houses. "You should come often; you should

make the acquaintance of the people; you will find them so human, so desperately human, that you will presently understand that these women are your sisters. Change dresses with one of them; let your hair fall wild; take off your bonnet—"

"Shall I then be quite like them?" asked Elsie. "Like *them*, master? Oh! not quite like them."

The philosopher obeyed. "Not quite like them," he said. "No, you could never talk like them."

He walked about among the people, who evidently knew him, because they made way for him, nodded to him, and pretended, such was their politeness, to pay no attention to the young lady who accompanied him.

"Every one of them is a study," he continued. "I could preach to you on every one as a text. Here is my young friend, Alice Parden, for instance"—he stopped before a pale girl of seventeen or so, tall and slender, but of drooping figure, who carried a baby in her arms. "Look at her. Consider. Alice is foolish, like all the Alices of this street. Alice must needs marry her chap a year ago, when she was sixteen and he was eighteen. Alice should be still at her club in the evening and her work in the daytime. But she must marry, and she is a child-mother. Is he out of work still?" Alice nodded, and hugged her baby closer. Mr. Edmund Gray shook his head in admonition, but gave her a coin, and went on. "Now, look at this good woman" —he stopped before a door where an Amazon was leaning—a woman five feet eight in height, with brawny arms and broad shoulders and a fiery furnace for a face—a most terrible and fearful woman. "How are you this evening, Mrs. Moss? And how is your husband?"

Long is the arm of coincidence. Mrs. Moss was just beginning to repose after a row royal; she was slowly simmering and slowly calming. There had been a row royal—a dispute, an argument, a quarrel, and a fight—with her husband. All four were only just concluded. All four had been conducted on the pavement, for the sake of coolness and air and space. The residents stood around; the controversy was sharp and animated; the lady bore signs of its vehemence in a bruise, rapidly blackening, over one eye, and abrasions on her knuckles. The husband had been conducted by his friends from the spot to the public-house at the corner, where he was at present pulling himself together, and forgetting the weight of his consort's fists, and solacing his spirit with strong drink.

"How is my husband?" the lady repeated. "Oh! I'll tell you—I'll tell you, Mr. Gray, how my husband is. Oh! how is he? Go look for him in the public-house. You shall see how he is, and what he looks like." She descended two steps, still retaining the advantage of the lowest. Then, describing a semicircle with her right arm, she began an impassioned harangue. The residents fled, right and left, not knowing whether in her wrath she might not mistake the whole of them, collectively, for her husband. The men in the public-house, hearing her voice, trembled, and looked apprehensively at the door. But Mr. Gray stood before her without fear. He knew her better than to run away. The lady respected his courage, and rejoiced in a sympathetic listener. Presently she ran down; she paused; she gasped; she caught at her heart; she choked; she wept. She sat down on the door-step—this great strong woman, with the brawny arms and the fiery face—and she wept. The residents crept timidly back again, and gathered round her, murmuring sympathy; the men in the public-house trembled again. Mr. Gray grasped her by the hand, and murmured a few words of consolation; for indeed there were great wrongs, such as few wives, even in this street, expect, and undeniable provocations. Then he led his scholar away.

At the next house he entered, taking Elsie with him to a room at the back, where a woman sat, making garments. She was a middle-aged woman, and, though very poorly dressed, not in rags; the room was neat, except for the garments lying about. She looked up cheerfully—her eyes were bright, her face was fine— and smiled. "You here, Mr. Gray?" she said. "Well, I was thinking only yesterday how long it is since you came to see me last. I mustn't stop working, but you can talk."

"This is a very special friend of mine," said the master. "I have known her for ten years, ever since I began to visit the street. She is always cheerful, though she has to live on sweating work and sweating pay; she never complains; she lives like the sparrows, and eats about as much as a sparrow; she is always respectable; she goes to church on Sundays; she is always neat in her dress. Yet she must be always hungry."

"Ah!" said the woman, "you'd wonder, miss, if you knew how little a woman can live upon."

"Oh! but," said Elsie—"to have always to live on that little!"

"She is the daughter of a man once thought well-to-do."—"He was most respectable," said the woman—"He died, and left nothing but debts. The family were soon scattered, and—You see this street contains some of those who have fallen low down as well as those who are born low down. It is Misfortune Lane as well as Poverty Lane. To the third and fourth generation, misfortune, when it begins—the reason of its beginning is the wickedness of one man—still persecutes and follows the family."

"Thank you, miss," said the woman—"and if you will come again sometimes— Oh! you needn't be afraid. No one would hurt a friend of Mr. Gray." So they went out.

On the next door-step, and the next, and the next, there sat women old and young, but all of these had the same look and almost the same features—they were heavy-faced, dull-eyed, thick-lipped, unwashed, and unbrushed. "These," said the master, "are the women who know of nothing better than the life they lead here. They have no hope of rising; they would be unhappy out of this street. They bear children, they bring them up, and they die. It is womanhood at its lowest. They want warmth, food, and drink, and that is nearly all. They are the children and grandchildren of women like themselves, and they are the mothers of women like themselves. Savage lands have no such savagery as this, for the worst savages have some knowledge, and these women have none. They are mutilated by our system. We have deprived them of their souls. They are the products of our system. In a better order these people could not exist; they would not be allowed parents or birth. The boy would still be learning his trade, and the girl would be working at hers. That little woman who meets her troubles with so brave a heart has been sweated all her life—ever since her misfortunes began; she takes it as part of the thing they call life; she believes that it will be made up to her somehow in another world. I hope it will."

"All these people," said the other voice, "are what they are because of the follies and the vices of themselves and their fathers. The boy-husband has no trade. Whose fault is that? The rickety boy and the rickety girl bring into the world a rickety baby. Whose fault is that? Let them grow worse instead of better, until they learn by sharper suffering that vice and folly bring their punishment."

"You see the children," continued the master, "and the mothers. You do not see any old men, because this sort mostly die before they reach the age of sixty. Those who are past work and yet continue to live go into the house. The girls you do not see, because those who are not forced to work all the evening as well as all the day are out walking with their sweethearts. Nor the men, because they are mostly in the public-house. They are all hand-to-mouth working-men—they live by the job when they can get any. When they are out of work they live upon each other. We hide this kind of thing away in back-streets like this, and we think it isn't dangerous. But it is. Formerly, the wreckage huddled together bred plagues and pestilences, which carried off rich and poor with equal hand, and so revenged itself. In other ways the wreckage revenges itself still."

"This kind of people," said the other voice, "may be dangerous. We have a police on purpose to meet the danger. They would be quite as dangerous if you were to give them free dinners and house them without rent. The class represents the untamable element. They are always a danger. To cry over them is silly and useless."

They walked down the street. Everybody knew Mr. Edmund Gray. He had a word for all. It was evident that he had been a visitor in the street for a long time; he had the air of a proprietor; he entered the houses and opened doors and sat down and talked, his disciple standing beside him and looking on. He asked questions and gave advice—not of a subversive Socialistic kind, but sound advice, recognizing the order that is, not the order that should be.

All the rooms in this street were tenanted, mostly a family to each. In many of them work was going on still, though it was already eight o'clock. Sometimes it would be a woman sitting alone in her room like a prisoner in a cell, stitching for dear life; sometimes three or four women or girls, sitting all together, stitching for dear life; sometimes a whole family, little children and all, making matches, making canvas bags, making paper bags, making card-boxes, all making—making—making for dear life. And the fingers did not stop, and the eyes were not lifted, though the visitors opened the door and came in and asked questions, to which one replied in the name of all the rest.

It is an old, old story—everybody knows the slum ; people go to gaze upon it ; it is one of the chief sights of Victorian London, just as a hundred and fifty years ago it was one of the sights to see the women flogged at Bridewell. Not such a very great advance in civilization, perhaps, after all.

"It is a hive—the place is swarming with life," said the girl, who had never before seen such a street.

" Life means humanity. All these people are so like you, my scholar, that you would be surprised. You would not be like them if you were dressed in these things, but they are like you. They want the same things as you—they have the same desires—they suffer the same pains. What makes your happiness? Food, warmth, sufficiency, not too much work. These are the elements for you as well as for them. In my system they will have all these—and then perhaps they will build up, as you have done, an edifice of knowledge, art, and sweet thoughts. But they are all like you. And most in one thing. For all women of all classes, there is one thing needful. These girls, like you, want love. They all want love. Oh, child ! they are so like you—so very like you—these poor women of the lowest class. So very like their proud sisters." He paused for a moment. Elsie made no reply. " You see," he continued, " they are so hard at work that they cannot even lift their eyes to look at you—not even at you, though they so seldom see a girl among them so lovely and so well dressed. One would have thought—but there is the whip that drives—that dreadful whip—it hangs over them and drives them all day long without rest or pause. Their work pays their rent, and keeps them alive. It just keeps them alive, and that is all. No more. It must be hard to work all day long for another person, if you come to think of it. Happily, they do not think. And all this grinding poverty, this terrible work, that one family may be able to live in a great house and to do nothing."

" They are working," said the other voice, " because one man has had the wit to create a market for their work. His thrift, his enterprise, his clearness of sight, have made it possible for these girls to find the work that keeps them. If they would have the sense not to marry recklessly there would be fewer working girls, and wages would go up. If their employer raised their wages only a penny a day he would benefit them but little, and would ruin himself. They must learn—if they can—the lesson of forethought by their own sufferings. No one can help them."

As Mr. Edmund Gray walked into the houses and out again Elsie went with him, or she waited outside while he went in. Sometimes she heard the chink of coin; sometimes she heard words of thanks. The Socialist, whatever he taught, practised the elementary form of charity possible only for those who have money. Elsie remarked this little point, but said nothing.

" What you see here," said the master, " is the lowest class of all—if one ever gets to the lowest level. For my own part, I have seen men and women so wretched that you would have called them *miserrimi*—of all created beings the most wretched. Yet have I afterwards found others more wretched still. In this street are those who make the lowest things; those who can make nothing, and have no trade, and live on odd jobs; and those who can neither make nor work, but thieve and lie about."

" I see all that; but, dear master, what will your new order do for such people? Will it make those who will not work industrious?"

" It will give every producer the fruits of his own labor; it will teach a trade to every man, and find men work. And those who cannot work, it will lock up until they die. They shall have no children. Perhaps it will kill them all. It might be better. We will have no human failures in our midst. That street is full of lessons, all calling aloud for the destruction of property."

Then the other voice spoke: " The presence of the human failure is a lesson always before us—a warning and a lesson to rich and poor alike. As he is, so all may be. None are so rich but they may be brought to poverty; none so poor but they may be poorer. So far from hiding away the wreckage, it is always in our sight. It prowls about the streets; we can never escape it. And it fills all hearts with terror; it spurs all men to industry and invention and perseverance. The human failure inspires a never-ending hymn in praise of property."

CHAPTER XXVIII

THE LESSON OF THE STREET—(*Continued*)

ELSIE's guide stopped to greet a woman whom he knew. She had the usual baby on her arm. She was a sad-faced woman, with some refinement in her looks; she was wretchedly dressed, thin, pale, and dejected.

"The same story?"

"Yes, sir. It's always the same," she sighed hopelessly. "But he would work if he could get anything to do. Nobody will employ a man who's had a misfortune. It's hard—because such a thing may happen to anybody. It's like measles, my husband says. He can't get drunk, because there's no money. That's my only comfort."

He gave her some money, and she passed on her way.

"Her husband was a clerk," Mr. Gray explained, "who took to drink and robbed his employer. His father was a barrister, who died young. His grandfather was a well-known—almost a great lawyer. I know the whole family history. I learned it"—he stopped for a moment, as if his memory suddenly failed him—"somehow—a long time ago. It is a story which shows how our sins and follies fall upon our own children. This family sprang from the gutter. First, the working-man; then his son, the shopkeeper; then his grandson, who became a great lawyer; then his great-grandson, not so great a lawyer. He, you see, is the first of the family who begins life as a gentleman and is brought up among gentlemen; he inherited money; he had a practice; he married in the class called gentle, and had children. But he lost all his money, and in despair he killed himself. Cousinly affection is a cold thing at best. It helped the widow to a pittance, and sent her boys to a cheap school. At fifteen they had to take whatever employment they could get. Observe that this branch of the family was now going downhill very fast. The future of a boy who has been taught no trade and has cu-

tered no profession is black indeed. One of the boys went out to
New Zealand, which has little to give a friendless boy. Another
enlisted, served three years, and has never got any work since. I
believe he carries boards about the street. Another became a
tenth-rate actor, and now starves on fifteen shillings a week, paid
irregularly. Another—the youngest—was put into a merchant's
office. He rose to a hundred and twenty pounds a year; he married a girl of the clerkly class—that woman you saw; he took to
drink; he embezzled his master's money; he went to prison; he
is now hopelessly ruined. He cannot get any lower in the social
scale. What will his children do? They have no friends. They
will grow up like the children around them; they will join the
hopeless casuals; they will be hewers of wood. Property, my
child—property has done this. He stole. In our society nobody will be tempted to steal. He drank—with us he would be
kept judiciously under control until he could be trusted again.
That would be the care of the State. He is another victim of
property. When his grandfather was framing Acts of Parliament
for the protection of property, he did not dream that he was making another engine for the oppression of his grandchildren."

Said the other voice: " We rise by our virtues. We sink by our
vices. Let these people suffer. Their sufferings should make the
rest of us wiser. Teach the children to rise again as their great-
grandfather rose. Do not contend against the great law which
metes out suffering in return for vice."

"Those," continued the Socialist professor, " who do most to
make a few men rich are the real enemies of what they suppose
themselves to be defending. Given a thousand women sweated
for one man, and there presently arises indignation either among
the women or among the bystanders. From indignation we get
revolution, because the employer never gives way. He cannot.
He would lose, if he did, his wealth, which is his heaven. If you
divide the thousand women into companies of ten, each company
under its own sweater, and all the sweaters under other sweaters,
you make a hierarchy of sweaters, culminating in one at the top.
That was the old state of things. The man at the top was a
chief, a patriarch; he knew his people; he sweated them, but
kindly; he tossed them crumbs; he looked after the sick and the
old. Now all this is changing. The old family tie—such as it
was—is dissolved. The man at the top has disappeared; a board

12

of directors has taken his place; there is nothing left but the board and its employees. The men who work are no longer interested in the business of the firm, except so far as their pay is concerned. Their pay will go up, and the dividends will go down. And with every increase of wages so much property is destroyed. Let everything—everything—be turned into companies to help the destruction of property."

Said the other voice: "Property is strengthened by being diffused. Companies organize labor; they give capital its proper power; they are not easily intimidated; they interest all who can save anything. Let us turn into companies every industrial and distributive business in the country."

"All times of change," the master went on, "are times of interest. We are living at a time when great changes are impending—the greatest changes possible. Before great changes there is always a period of unconscious preparation. The minds of people are being trained. Without any perception of the fact, old ideas are dying out and new ones are coming into existence. When the revolution actually arrives everybody is ready for it, and nobody is surprised. It was so with the Reformation. For a hundred years and more the idea of the Great Revolt had been slowly growing in men's minds. When it came at last there was no surprise, and there were few regrets. For a hundred years and more the ideas of the French Revolution had been talked about by philosophers; these ideas sank down among the people. Nobody was surprised, not even the nobles themselves, when the end came. So with our revolution. It is coming—it is coming—its ideas are no longer timidly advanced—here and there—by a fanatic here or a philosopher there; they are lying in the hearts of the people, ready to spur them into action; they are helping on the cause by successive steps, every one of which means nothing less than the abolition of property. These things are new to you, child. You were only born yesterday or the day before. I was born a hundred years ago or thereabouts. Consider again "—he leaned against a lamp-post for greater ease, and discoursed as one addressing an audience—" consider, I say, this great question of companies and their results. Formerly, one man made things which he took to market—sold or exchanged, and went home again. He, by himself, did everything. Then one man made, and another man sold. The next improvement was for twenty men to work, for one to receive and to collect their work, and for another to sell it. In this way the twenty remained poor, and the two became rich. So they went on, and trade flourished, and the twenty producers more and more fell into the power of the two, who were now very rich and strong. Now the merchants are forming themselves into companies, and the companies are amalgamating with each other, and the small people may contemplate ruin. For these—now merchants, shopkeepers, manufacturers, workmen—there will be nothing but service in the companies; no possibility of acquiring property, nothing but service all their lives. Now do you see how that helps the cause? They will become accustomed to work, but not for themselves; they will grow accustomed to work for a bare living, and no more; they won't like either, but they will ask why the second should go with the first; the two great obstacles to Socialism will be removed. Then, either the step I spoke of just now—the abolition of the dividends—or, which is just as likely, a revolution, when the servants of the companies shall make the State take over all and work them for the good of all. Some there are who think that the workman will have hope and power for union crushed out of him. I think not; but if so—woe to the rich! The Jacquerie and the French Revolution will be spoken of as mild ebullitions of popular feeling compared with what will happen then. But I think not. I do not believe that the working-man will sink again. He has got up so far. But he needs must climb higher.

"You think it would be impossible"—by this time a small crowd had got round them, but the speaker still addressed his disciple as if no one else at all was listening—"for the State to take over the great producing and distributing companies. But it has been done already. The State has the post and the telegraph services. They will deal with railways, steamers, coaches, cabs, omnibuses, trains, canals, water, gas, electric light, breweries, bakeries, factories, shops, just as they have dealt with these two. The State can take it all. The State will take the management of all. But, you say, the shares of the company will become funds. They will, and the funds will pay interest—but the interest will become rapidly lower and lower, so that what was once five per cent. is now but two and a half, and before long shall be two—one and a half—one—and nothing at all. There will be no cry of spoliation, because the holders of stock will be forced gradually into looking more and more to their own efforts, and because widows and sick people and old people, to whom the stocks were once so useful, will be all provided for by the State as a matter of right, and without any of the old humiliation of pauperdom. Pauper? Oh! heavenly word! Child, in the world of the future—the world which you will help to mould—we shall all be paupers—every one."

He spoke with fine enthusiasm, his face lit up, his eyes bright. The girl was almost carried away, until the other voice began, coldly and judicially,

"Nothing is so good for man as to be ruled and kept in discipline, service, and subjection. It is a foolish and a mischievous dream which supposes all men eager for advance. The mass of mankind asks for no advancement. It loves nothing and desires nothing but the gratification of the animal. Give it plenty of animalism and it is satisfied. That condition of society which keeps the mass down and provides for the rise of the ambitious few is the only condition which is reasonable and stable. Base your social order on the inertness of the mass. Make the workman do a good day's work; pay him enough, so that he shall have some of the comforts he desires; educate the clever boy, and make him foreman, head-man, manager, or artist, journalist, dramatist, novelist. Give him the taste for wealth. Let him have some. Then he, too, will be ready to fight, if necessary, in the army of order."

While the other voice was speaking, there came slouching around the corner, into the street where he held the fifth—perl..ps the tenth—part of a room—a really excellent specimen of the common or London thief—the habitual criminal. He was a young man—the habitual criminal is generally young, because in middle and elderly life he is doing long sentences; he had a furtive look, such as that with which the jackal sallies forth on nocturnal adventures; he had a short, slight figure, a stooping and slouching gait, and narrow shoulders. His eyes were bright, but too close together; his mouth was too large, and his jowl too heavy; his face was pale; his hair was still short, though growing rapidly; his hands were pendulous; his round hat was too big for his little head; he wore a long, loose overcoat. His face, his figure, his look, proclaimed aloud what he was.

He stopped at the corner, and looked at the little crowd. Everybody, for different reasons, is attracted by a crowd. Professionals sometimes find in crowds golden opportunities. This crowd, however, was already dispersing. The speaker had stopped. Perhaps they had heard other and more fervid orators on the Socialist side. Perhaps they were not in the least interested in the subject. You see, it is very difficult to get the hand-to-mouth class interested in anything except those two organs.

"This street," said the master, observing him with professional interest, "is full—really full—of wealth for the observer. Here is a case now—an instructive though a common case." The fellow was turning away, disappointed, perhaps, at the melting of the crowd and any little hope he might have based upon their pockets. "My friend"—he heard himself called, and looked round suspiciously—"you would like, perhaps, to earn a shilling honestly, for once."

He turned slowly; at the sight of the coin held up before him his sharp eyes darted right and left to see what chance there might be of a grab and a bolt. Apparently, he decided against this method of earning the shilling.

"What for?" he asked.

"By answering a few questions. Where were you born."

"I dunno."

"Where were you brought up? Here? in this street? Very well. You went to school with the other children; you were taught certain subjects up to a certain standard. What trade were you taught?"

"I wasn't taught no trade."

"Your father was, I believe, a thief?" The lad nodded. "And your mother, too?" He nodded again, and grinned. "And you yourself and your brothers and sisters are all in the same line, I suppose?" He nodded and grinned again. "Here is your shilling." The fellow took it, and shambled away.

"Father, mother, the whole family, live by stealing. Where there is no property there can be no theft. In our world such a creature would be impossible. He could not be born; such parents as his could not exist with us; he could not be developed; there would be no surroundings that would make such a development possible. He would be what, I believe, men of science call a sport; he would be a deformity. We should put him in a hospital, and keep him there until he died."

"In that world," said the other voice, "there would be deformities of even a worse kind than this—the deformities of hypocrisy and shams. By a thousand shifts and lies and dishonesties the work of the world would be shifted on the shoulders of the weak. The strong man has always used his strength to make the weak man work for him, and he always will. The destruction of property would be followed by the birth of property on the very self-same day. There is the power of creation—of invention—which is also a kind of property. Laws cannot destroy that power. Laws cannot make men industrious. Laws cannot make the strong man work for the weak. Laws cannot prevent the clever man from taking advantage of the stupid man. When all the failures, all the deformities, have been killed off, the able man will still prey upon the dull-witted. Better let the poor wretch live out his miserable life, driven from prison to prison, an example for all the world to see."

It was at this point that Elsie discovered the loss of her purse. Her pocket had been picked by one of the intelligent listeners in the crowd. She cried out on finding what had happened, in the unphilosophic surprise and indignation with which this quite common accident is always received.

"Child," said the master, "when there is no longer any property money will vanish; there will be no purses; even the pocket will disappear, because there will no longer be any use for a pocket. Did the purse contain much? Suppose you had nothing to lose and nothing to gain. Think of the lightness of heart, the sunshine on all faces, which would follow. I fear you are rich, child. I have observed little signs about you which denote riches. Your gloves are neat and good; your dress seems costly. Better far if you had nothing."

"Master, if I were like that girl on the other side would you like me better? Could I be more useful to the cause if I dressed like her?"

The girl was of the common type—they really do seem, at first, all alike—who had on an ulster, and a hat with a feather, and broken boots.

"If I were like her," Elsie went on, "I should be ignorant—and obliged to give the whole day to work, so that I should be useless to you—and my manners would be rough and my language coarse. It is because I am not poor that I am what I am. The day for poverty is not come yet, dear master."

"In the future, dear child, there shall be no poverty and no riches. To have nothing will be the common lot. To have all will be the common inheritance. Oh! there will be differences; men shall be as unlike then as now; we shall not all desire the same things. You and such as you will desire art of every kind. You shall have what you desire. In our world, as in this, like will to like. You shall have the use for yourselves of pictures, of musical instruments, of everything that you want. The rest of the world will not want these things. If they do, more can be made. You shall have dainty food—the rest of the world will always like coarse and common fare. Think not that we shall level up or level down. All will be left to rise or to sink. Only they shall not starve, they shall not thieve, they shall not be sweated. Oh! I know they paint our society as attempts to make all equal. And they think that we expect men no longer to desire the good things in the world. They will desire them—they will hunger after them—but there will be enough for all. The man who is contented with a dinner of herbs may go to a Carthusian convent, which is his place, for we shall have no place for him in a world which recognizes all good gifts and assigns to every man his share."

Then spoke the other voice, but sadly, "Dreams! Dreams! There are not enough of the good things to go round—good things would become less instead of more. Without the spur there is no work. Without the desire of creating property all that is worth anything in life will perish—all but the things that are the lowest and the meanest and the commonest. Men will not work unless they must. By necessity alone can the finest work be ordered and executed. As men have been so will men always be. The thing that hath been, that shall be again."

"You have learned some of the lessons of Poverty Lane, scholar," said the master. "Let us now go home."

CHAPTER XXIX

"I KNOW THE MAN"

"ANOTHER evening of mystery, Elsie?" said Athelstan.

"Yes, another, and perhaps another. But we are getting to an end. I shall be able to tell you all to-day or to-morrow. The thing is becoming too great for me alone."

"You shall tell us when you please. Meantime, nothing new has been found out, I believe. Checkley still glares, George tells me. But the opinion of the clerks seems, on the whole, more favorable, he believes, than it was. Of that, however, he is not, perhaps, a good judge."

"They shall all be turned out," cried Elsie. "How dare they so much as to discuss—"

"My sister, it is a very remarkable thing, and a thing little understood, but it is a true thing. People, people—clerks and *le service* generally—are distinctly a branch of the great human tribe. They are anthropoid. Therefore, they are curious and prying and suspicious. They have our own faults, my dear."

All day Elsie felt drawn as with ropes to Mr. Dering's office. Was it possible that after that long evening among the lessons of Poverty Lane he should remember nothing? How was she to get at him? How was she to make him understand or believe what he had done? Could she make the sane man remember the actions and words of the insane man? Could she make the insane man do something which would absolutely identify him with the sane man? She could always array her witnesses, but she wanted more—she wanted to bring Mr. Dering himself to understand that he was Mr. Edmund Gray.

She made an excuse for calling upon him. It was in the afternoon, about four, that she called. She found him looking aged, his face lined, his cheek pale, his eyes anxious.

"This business worries me," he said. "Day and night it is with me. I am persecuted and haunted with this Edmund Gray.

His tracts are put into my pockets; his papers into my safe; he laughs at me; he defies me to find him. And they do nothing. They only accuse each other. They find nothing."

"Patience," said Elsie softly. "Only a few days—a day or two—then—with your help—we will unravel all this trouble. You shall lose nothing."

"Shall I escape this mocking devil—this Edmund Gray?"

"I cannot promise. Perhaps. Now, my dear guardian, I am to be married next Wednesday. I want you to be present at my wedding."

"Why not?"

"Because things have been said about George; and because your presence will effectually prove that you do not believe them."

"Oh! believe them? I believe nothing. It is, however, my experience that there is no act, however base, that any man may not be tempted to do."

"Happily, it is my experience," said the girl of twenty-one, "that there is no act of baseness, however small, that certain men could possibly commit. You will come to my wedding, then. Athelstan will give me away."

"Athelstan? Yes, I remember. We found those notes, didn't we? I wonder who put them into the safe? Athelstan! Yes. He has been living in low company, I heard—Camberwell —rags and tatters."

"Oh!" Elsie stamped impatiently. "You will believe anything—anything, and you a lawyer! Athelstan is in the service of a great American journal. Rags and tatters!"

"American? Oh! yes." Mr. Dering sat up and looked interested. "Why, of course. How could I forget it. Had it been yesterday evening I should have forgot. But it is four years ago. He wrote to me from somewhere in America. Where was it? I've got the letter. It is in the safe. Bring me the bottom right-hand drawer. It is there, I know." He took the drawer which Elsie brought him, and turned over the papers. "Here it is among the papers of that forgery. Here is the letter." He gave it to Elsie. "Read it. He writes from America, you see. He was in the States four years ago—and— and— What is it?"

"Oh!" cried Elsie, suddenly springing from her chair—"oh!
12*

do you know what you have given me? Oh! do you know what you have told me? It is the secret—the secret of my fortune. Oh! Athelstan gave it to me—Athelstan—my brother!"

Mr. Dering took the letter from her, and glanced at the contents. "I ought not to have shown you the letter," he said. "I have violated confidence. I forgot. I was thinking of the trouble—I forgot. I forget everything now—the things of yesterday as well as the things of to-day. Yes; it is true, child—your little fortune came to you from your brother. But it was a secret that he alone had the right to reveal."

"And now I know it—I know it. Oh! what shall I say to him?" The tears came to her eyes. "He gave me all he had —all he had—because—oh! for such a simple thing—because I would not believe him to be a villain. Oh! my brother—my poor brother! He went back into poverty again. He gave me all—because—oh! for such a little thing— Mr. Dering!"—she turned almost fiercely upon him—"after such a letter, *could* you believe that man to be a villain? Could you? Tell me! After such a deed and such a letter!"

"I believe nothing. My experience, however, tells me that any man, whoever he is, may be led to commit—"

"*No!* I won't have it said again— Now, listen, Mr. Dering. These suspicions must cease. There must be an end. Athelstan returned six weeks ago—or thereabouts. That can be proved. Before that time he was working in San Francisco on the journal. That can be proved. While these forgeries, with which he is now so freely charged, were carried on here, he was abroad. I don't ask you to believe or to disbelieve or to bring up your experience—oh! such experience—one would think you had been a police magistrate all your life."

"No, Elsie." Mr. Dering smiled grimly. "There was no need to sit upon the bench; the police magistrate does not hear so much as the family solicitor. My dear, prove your brother's innocence by finding out who did the thing. That is, after all, the only thing. It matters nothing what I believe—he is not proved innocent—all the world may be suspected of it—until the criminal is found. Remove the suspicions which have gathered about your lover by finding the criminal. There is no other way."

"Very well, then. I will find the criminal, since no one else can."

Mr. Dering went on, without heeding her words.

"They want to get out a warrant against Edmund Gray. I think, for my own part, that the man Edmund Gray has nothing to do with the business. He is said to be an elderly man and a respectable man—a gentleman—who has held his chambers for ten years."

"They need not worry about a warrant," Elsie replied. "Tell your brother, Mr. Dering, that it will be perfectly useless. Meantime—I doubt if it is any good asking you—but—if we want your help, will you give me all the help you can?"

"Assuredly. All the help I can. Why not? I am the principal person concerned."

"You are, indeed," said Elsie gravely, "the principal person concerned. Very well, Mr. Dering—now I will tell you more. I know the—the criminal. I can put my hand upon him at any moment. It is one man who has done the whole, beginning with the check for which Athelstan was suspected—one man alone."

"Why, child, what can you know about it? What can you do?"

"You were never in love, Mr. Dering, else you would understand that a girl will do a great deal—oh! a great deal more than you would think—for her lover—it is not much to think for him and to watch for him—and for her brother—the brother who has stripped himself of everything to give his sister—" She was fain to pause, for the tears which rose again and choked her voice.

"But, Elsie, what does this mean? How can you know what no one else has been able to find out?"

"That is my affair, Mr. Dering. Perhaps I dreamed it."

"Do you mean that you will get back all the papers—all the transfers—the dividends that have been diverted—everything?"

"Everything is safe. Everything shall be restored. My dear guardian, it is a long and a sad story. I cannot tell you now. Presently, perhaps—or to-morrow. I do not know how I shall be able to tell you. But for your property, rest easy. Everything will come back to you—everything—except that which cannot be stored in the vaults of the bank."

The last words he heard not, or understood not.

"I shall get back everything!" The eyes of the individualist lit up, and his pale cheek glowed—old age has still some pleasures. "It is not until one loses property that one finds out how precious it has become.   Elsie, you remember what I told you a day or two ago—ah! I don't forget quite everything—a man is not the shivering naked soul only, but the complete figure, equipped and clothed, armed and decorated, bearing with him his skill, his wit, his ingenuity, his learning, his past and his present, his memories and his rejoicings, his sorrows and his trials, his successes and his failures, and his property—yes, his property. Take away from him any of these things, and he is mutilated ; he is not the perfect soul.   Why, you tell me that my property is coming back—I awake again ; I feel stronger already ; the shadows are flying before me ; even the terror of that strange forgetfulness recedes, and the haunting of Edmund Gray.   I can bear all, if I get my property back again.   As for this forger—this miscreant—this criminal—you will hale him before the judge—"

"Yes, yes.   We will see about the miscreant afterwards. The first thing is to find the man, and recover your property, and to dispel the suspicions resting on innocent persons.   If I do the former you must aid me in the latter."

"Assuredly.   I shall not shrink from that duty."

"Very well.   Now tell me about yourself.   Sometimes it does good to talk about our own troubles.   Tell me more about these forgetful fits.   Do they trouble you still?"   Her eyes and her voice were soft and winning.   One must be of granite to resist such a voice and such eyes.

"My dear"—Mr. Dering softened—"you are good to interest yourself in an old man's ailments.   It is Anno Domini that is the matter with me.   The forgetful fits are only symptoms—and the disease is incurable.   Ask the oak why the leaves are yellow. It is the hand of winter.   That is my complaint.   First the hand of winter, then the hand of death.   Meantime, the voice of the grasshopper sings loud and shrill."   In presence of the simple things of age and death even a hard old lawyer grows poetic.

"Tell me the symptoms, then.   Do you still forget things?"

"Constantly.   More and more.   I forget everything."

"Where were you yesterday evening, for instance?"

"I don't know.   I cannot remember.   I have left off even trying to remember.   At one time I racked my brains for hours to find out, and failed.   Now I remember nothing.   I never know when this forgetfulness may fall upon me.   At any hour.   For instance—you ask me about yesterday evening.   I ordered dinner at home. My housekeeper this morning reminded me that I did not get home last night till eleven. Where was I? Where did I spend the evening?"

"At the club?"

"No—I took a cab this morning, and drove there under pretence of asking for letters. I asked if I was there last night. The hall-porter stared. But I was not there. I thought that I might have fallen asleep here. I have done so before. Checkley tells me that I went away before him. Where was I?—child!"—he leaned forward, and whispered, with white cheeks—"I have read of men going about with disordered brains doing what they afterwards forgot. Am I one of those unfortunates? Do I go about with my wits wandering? Oh! horrible! I picture to myself an old man—such as myself—of unblemished reputation and blameless life—wandering about the streets demented—without conscience—without dignity—without self-respect—committing follies—things disgraceful—even things which bring men before the law—" He shuddered. He turned pale.

"No, no," murmured Elsie. "You could not. You could never—"

"Such things are on record. They have happened. They may happen again. I have read of such cases. There was a man once—he was, like myself, a solicitor—who would go out and buy things, not knowing what he did. He bought new hats—every day twenty new hats; cricket-bats, though he was long past the game of cricket; once he bought six grand pianos—six—though he knew not the use of any instrument. Then they gave him a companion, and he found out what he had done. The shame and the shock of it killed him. I have thought of that man of late. Good heavens! Think, if you can, of any worse disaster. Let me die—let me die, I say, rather than suffer such a fate—such an affliction. I see myself brought before the magistrate—me—myself—at my age, charged with this and with that. What defence? None, save that I did not remember."

"That could never be," said Elsie confidently, because she knew the facts. "If such a thing were to befall, your character would never be changed. You might talk and think differently, but you could never be otherwise than a good man. You to haunt low company? Oh! you could not even in a waking dream. People who dream, I am sure, always remain themselves, however strangely they may act. How could you—you—after such a life as yours, become a haunter of low company? One might, perhaps, suppose that Athelstan had been living among profligates because he is young and untried—but you?—you? Oh! no. If you had these waking dreams—perhaps you have them—you would become—you would become—I really think you would become "—she watched his face—" such—such a man as—as—Mr. Edmund Gray, who is so like yourself, and yet so different."

He started. "Edmund Gray again? Good heavens! It is always Edmund Gray!"

"He is now a friend of mine. I have only known him for a week or two. He does not think quite as you do. But he is a good man. Since, in dreams, we do strange things, you might act and speak and think as Edmund Gray."

"*I* speak and think as— But—am I dreaming? Am I forgetting again? Am I awake? Edmund Gray is the man whom we want to find."

"I have found him," said Elsie quietly.

"The forger—if he is the forger—"

"No, no. Do not make more mistakes. You shall have the truth in a day or two. Would you like to see Edmund Gray? Will you come with me to his chambers? Whenever you call you—you, I say—will find him at home."

"No, no. I know his doctrines—futile doctrines—mischievous doctrines. I do not wish to meet him. What do you mean by mistake? There are the letters—there are the forgeries. Are there two Edmund Grays?"

"No—only one. He is the man they cannot find. I will show you, if you like, what manner of man he is."

"No. I do not want to see a Socialist. I should insult him. You are mysterious, Elsie. You know this man—this mischievous doctrinaire—this leveller—this spoliator. You tell me that he is a good man—you want me to see him. What, I ask, do these things mean?"

"They mean many things, my dear guardian. Chiefly they mean that you shall get back your property, and that suspicion shall be removed from innocent persons—and all this, I hope, before next Wednesday, when I am to be married. We must all be happy on my wedding-day."

"Will—will Mr. Edmund Gray be there as well?"

"He has promised. And now, my dear guardian, if you will come round to Gray's Inn with me, I will show you the chambers of Mr. Edmund Gray."

"No, no. Thank you, Elsie—I do not wish to make the personal acquaintance of a Socialist."

"He has chambers on the second floor. The principal room is large and well furnished. It is a wainscoted room, with two windows looking on the square. It is not a very pretty square, because they have not made a garden or laid down grass in the middle—and the houses are rather dingy. He sits there in the evening. He writes and meditates. Sometimes he teaches me, but that is a new thing. In the morning he is sometimes there between nine o'clock and twelve. He has an old laundress, who pretends to keep his rooms clean."

She murmured these words softly, thinking to turn his memory back and make him understand what had happened.

"They are pleasant rooms, are they not?" He made no reply —his eyes betrayed trouble. She thought it was the trouble of struggling memory. "He sits here alone, and works. He thinks he is working for the advancement of the world. There is no one so good, I think, as Edmund Gray."

He suddenly pushed back the chair, and sprang to his feet.

"My scholar! You speak of me?"

It was so sudden that Elsie cried out, and fell backwards in her chair. She had brought on the thing by her own words, by conjuring up a vision of the chambers. But—the trouble was not the struggle of the memory getting hold of evasive facts.

"Why, child," he remonstrated, "you look pale. Is it the heat? Come, it is cooler outside. Let us go to the chambers in Gray's Inn. This old fellow—this Dering—here he sits all day long. It is Tom Tiddler's ground. It is paved with gold, which he picks up. The place—let us whisper, because he must be in the outer office—it reeks of property—reeks of property."

He took his hat and gloves. "My scholar, let us go." With the force of habit he shut and locked the safe, and dropped the bunch of keys into his pocket.

CHAPTER XXX

ATHELSTAN'S DISCOVERY

ON the evening of that same day the same discovery was made by another of the persons chiefly concerned.

You have seen that Athelstan on his return made haste to find out the commissionnaire who had presented the forged check. Happily, the man remembered not only the circumstance itself, but also his employer on that occasion. A generosity far above what is commonly found among those who employ the services of that corps endeared and preserved the memory of the day. He had received, in fact, half a sovereign for an eighteenpenny job; and the commissionnaire is not like the cabby, to whom such windfalls are common. Not at all. With the former we observe the letter of the law.

After eight years this man's memory was rewarded. This thrice-blessed job produced yet more golden fruit. Heard one ever of a more prolific job?

After breakfast, Athelstan was informed that a commission-naire desired to speak with him. It was his one-armed friend.

"Beg your pardon, sir," he said, saluting after the military manner—"you said I was to come and tell you, first thing, if I found your man for you."

"Certainly. I told you also that I would give you a five-pound reward for finding my man, as you call him. Well—I will be as good as my word if you have found him."

"I saw him yesterday. The very same old gentleman that sent me to the bank that day. He's older, and he doesn't look so jolly, and he walks slower; but I knew him at once."

"Oh! are you quite sure? Because a resemblance, you know—"

"Well, sir, I can swear to him. I remember him as well as I remember anybody. He sat in the chair, and he laughed, and he said, 'You've been quick over the job, my man. There's something extra, because you might have dropped the money down a grating, or run away with it, or something,' he says. 'Here's half a sovereign for you, my man,' says he; 'and I dare say you can do with it.' 'I can so, sir,' I says, 'and with as many more like them as I can pick up.' Then he laughed, and I laughed, and we both laughed. And that's the same man that I saw yesterday evening."

"Oh! this is very curious. Are you quite sure?"

"I'd swear to him anywhere. A man can't say fairer."

"No—as you say—a man can hardly say fairer, can he? Now, then, when did you see him?"

"It was between six and seven. I'd been doing a message for a gentleman in the Strand—a gentleman in the dining-room line to a gentleman in Holborn in the sausage-and-tripe line—and I was going back with a letter, and going through Lincoln's Inn for a short cut. Just as I was getting near the gate to the Fields, I saw coming out of the door at No. 12 the very man you want to find. I wasn't thinking about him, not a bit—I was thinking of nothing at all, when he come out of the door and walked down the steps. Then I knew him. Lord! I knew him at once. 'You're the man,' I says to myself, 'as give me the half-sov. instead of eighteenpence.' Well, I stood at the corner, and waited to see if he would remember me. Not a bit of it. He stared at me hard, but he never recollected me a bit—I could see that. Why should he? Nobody remembers the servant any more than they remember the private in the ranks. The very same old gentleman; but he's grown older, and he didn't look jolly any more. P'r'aps he's lost his money."

"Came out of No. 12, did he? Why, Dering & Son's office is there. What does this mean?"

"I thought I'd like to find out something more about him; and I thought that a five-pound note was better worth looking after than eighteenpence—so I let the letter from the tripe-and-sausage man lay a bit, and I followed my old gentleman at a good distance."

"Oh! you followed him. Very good. Did you find out where he lived? I can tell you that. He went to No. 22 South Square, Gray's Inn."

"No, he didn't, sir. But you are not very far wrong. He went through Great Turnstile; then he crossed Holborn and turned into Featherstone Buildings, which is all lodging-houses.

But he doesn't live there. He walked through the Buildings, and so into Bedford Row, and he stopped at a house there—"

"What! in Bedford Row?"

"Yes, in Bedford Row—and he pulls out a latch-key, and lets himself in. That's where he lives. No. 49 Bedford Row, on the west side, very near the bottom. He lives in Bedford Row. Well, sir, I like to do things proper, and so, to make the job complete, I went to the Salutation, Holborn, where they keep a directory, and I looked out his name. The gentleman that lives at No. 49 Bedford Row is named Edward Dering—and among the names of No. 12 New Square, Lincoln's Inn, is the name of Dering & Son. So, sir, I don't think it is too much to say that your man is Mr. Dering, who belongs both to Bedford Row and Lincoln's Inn. He's the man who sent me to the bank eight years ago."

Athelstan stared at him. "*He* the man?" he cried. "You are talking impossibilities. He can't be the man."

"Nobody else, sir. If that was Mr. Dering that I saw yesterday walking home from New Square to Bedford Row—he's the man who sent me for the money."

To this statement the man stuck firm. Nor could he be moved by any assertion that his position was impossible. "For, my friend," said Athelstan, "the man who sent you with the check was the man who robbed Mr. Dering."

"Can't help that, sir. If the gentleman I saw yesterday walking from Lincoln's Inn to Bedford Row was Mr. Dering—then he robbed hisself."

"That's foolishness. Oh! there must be some explanation. Look here! Mr. Edward Dering leaves his office every evening between six and seven. I will be in New Square on the west side this evening at six. You be there, as well. Try not to seem as if you were watching for anybody. Stand about at your ease."

"I'll make it sentry-go, sir," said the old soldier. "I'll walk up and down in front of the door same as some of our chaps got to do in front of shops. You trust me, sir, and I won't take no notice of you."

This little plot, in fact, was faithfully carried out. At six o'clock Athelstan began to walk up and down outside the gate which opens upon Lincoln's Inn Fields—the commissionnaire at the same time was doing sentry-go in front of No. 12, in New Square.

When the clock struck six there was a rush and a tramp of hurrying feet; these were the clerks set free for the day. There are not many solicitors' offices in New Square, and these once gone the place becomes perfectly quiet. At half-past six there was the footfall as of one man on the stairs, and he descended slowly. He came out of the door presently, an old bent figure with white hair and shrivelled face. Paying no heed to the sentry, he walked away with feeble step in the direction of Chancery Lane. Checkley this was, on his way to look after his tenants and his property.

Athelstan looked after him, through the gate. Then he called his old soldier. "See that man?" he asked. "That's the man who sent you to the bank."

"No, he isn't." The man was stout on that point. "Not a bit like him. That old man's a servant, not a gentleman. See the way he holds his hands. Never a gentleman yet carried his hands that way. You can always tell 'em by their hands. The other day I met an old pal—seemed to forget me, he did. Wanted to make out that he'd never been in the army at all. So I lay by for a bit. Then I gets up—and he gets up too. ' 'Tention!' says I, and he stood to 'tention like a good old Tommy Atkins. You watch their hands, whatever they say. Always tell 'em by their hands. That old man he's a servant. He isn't a gentleman. He can't sit among the swells and order about the waiters. He hasn't learned that way. He'd get up himself, if you asked him, and put the napkin under his arm, and bring you a glass of sherry wine. He's not my man. You wait a bit."

At a quarter to seven another footstep was heard echoing up and down the empty building. Then an old man—erect, thin, tightly buttoned, wearing neat gloves and carrying an umbrella—came out of the door. His face was hard, even austere. His walk was firm. The sentry, as this person walked out of the gate, followed at a distance. When he was beside Athelstan, he whispered, "That's the man. I'd swear to him anywhere. That's the man that sent me to the bank."

Athelstan heard in unbounded astonishment. That the man? Why, it was Mr. Dering himself!

"Let us follow him," he whispered. "Not together. On opposite sides of the road. Good heavens! this is most wonderful. Do not lose sight of him."

To follow him was perfectly easy, because Mr. Dering turned

neither to the right nor to the left, but marched straight on through Great Turnstile, across Holborn, through Featherstone Buildings, and into Bedford Row. At No. 49, his own house. Where else should he stop?

Athelstan took out his purse and gave the man the five pounds. "I don't know what it means," he said. "I can't understand a word. But I suppose you have told me the truth. I don't know why you should make up a lie—"

"It's Gauspel truth," said the man.

"And therefore, again, I don't understand it. Well—I've got your name and your number. If I want you again I will send for you."

The man saluted and walked away. Half a sovereign for an eighteenpenny job, and eight years afterwards five pounds on account of the same job. Robbery, was it? Robbery—and the old man pretending to be robbed and robbing himself. Now what did that mean? Laying it on to some poor, harmless, innocent cove, the soldier guessed; laying it on to some one as he had a spite against—the old villain!—very likely this young governor—most likely. Donations on account of that same job, very likely—the old villain!

As for Athelstan, he returned to Lincoln's Inn Fields, where, the evening being fine and the sun warm and the place quiet except for the children at play, he walked up and down the east or sunny side for half an hour, turning the thing over in his mind:

For, you see, if Mr. Dering went through the form of robbing himself and finding out the robbery and coldly suffering the blame to fall upon him—then Mr. Dering must be one of the most phenomenally wicked of living men. Or, if Mr. Dering robbed himself and did not know it—then Mr. Dering must be mad.

Again, if such a thing could be done on a small scale, it might be done on a larger scale with the same result—namely, suspicion to fall upon a blameless person; obloquy to gather round his name—for in some cases simply to be charged is almost as fatal as to be convicted; and perfect impunity for himself. "This is not my own writing, but a forgery," said the man who had been robbed. Then, who is the forger? You—you. None but you. The bare suspicion becomes a certainty in the minds of those who were once that man's friends. And his life is cankered at the outset. He thought of his own life—the bitterness of alienation and exile.

Never any time for eight years when he could explain the reasons of his exile. Debt, the cultivation of wild oats, failure to pass examinations—anything would do for such a reason except suspicion of forgery. Athelstan was a cheerful young man. He seldom allowed himself to be cast down by the blows of fate. Nevertheless, during his whole time of exile, the drop of bitterness that poisoned his cup was that he could not tell the whole story because the world would believe no more than half—that half, namely, which contained the accusation. When one walks about thinking, there comes a time when it seems no good to think any longer. The mind can only get a certain amount out of a case at one sitting. That amount absorbed, the best thing is to go on to something else. Athelstan went on to dinner. He left his sister to the care of her young man, and dined by himself. He took a steak at a Holborn restaurant, with an evening paper, which he considered professionally. After dinner he returned to his subject. Perhaps he should get a step further. No—perhaps on account of the sweet influence of dinner he got no further at all. Here was an astonishing fact. How to account for it? You have seen. By one of two ways—malignity unspeakable or madness—madness of a very curious kind—the madness of a man whose calm, cool judgment had made him appear to his friends as one with an intellect far above any ordinary weaknesses of humanity. Mr. Dering mad? Then the chancellor of the exchequer, the speaker of the House of Commons, the president of the Royal Society, the president of the Institute of Civil Engineers, the Cambridge professors of mathematics—all these men might be mad as well. And nobody to know it or to suspect it. Mr. Dering mad?—and yet, if not, what was he?

There was one way. He had tried it already once. He left the restaurant, and turned eastward. He was going to try South Square, Gray's Inn, again. Perhaps Mr. Edmund Gray would be in his rooms.

He was not. The door was shut. But the opposite door stood open, that of Freddy Carstone. Athelstan knocked, and was admitted with eloquence almost tumultuous.

"Just in time," said the coach. "I've got a new brand of whiskey, straight from Glasgow. You shall sample it. Have you had dinner yet? So have I. Sit down. Let us talk, and smoke tobacco, and drink whiskey-and-soda."

"I will do the talking and the tobacco, at any rate."

"I love Virtue," said Freddy. "She is a lovely goddess—for if Virtue feeble were, Heaven itself would stoop to her. She has only one fault. There is reproach in her voice, reproach in her eye, and reproach in her attitude. She is an uncomfortable goddess. Fortunately, she dwells not in this venerable foundation. Do not imitate Virtue, old boy. Let me— That's right. We shall then start fair upon the primrose path—the broad and flowery way—though I may get farther down than you. Athelstan the Wanderer—Melmoth the Wanderer—Childe Harold the Pilgrim — drink, and be human." He set the example. "Good whiskey—very good whiskey. Athelstan, there's a poor devil upstairs, starving for the most part—let's have him down. It's a charity." He ran upstairs, and immediately returned with the decayed advocate, who looked less hungry than usual, and a shade less shabby—you have seen how he borrowed of Mr. Edmund Gray through Elsie.

"Now," said the host, "I call this comfortable—a warm August evening; the window open; a suspicion of fresh air from the gardens; soda-and-whiskey; and two men for talk. Most evenings one has to sit alone. Then there's a temptation to—to close the evening too quickly."

"Freddy, I want to hear more about your neighbor. You told me something, if you remember, a week or two ago."

"Very odd thing. Old Checkley at the Salutation is always pestering about Mr. Edmund Gray. What has he to do with Mr. Edmund Gray? Wanted me to answer his questions."

"And me," said Mr. Langhorne—"I did answer them."

"Well—Mr. Edmund Gray is— What is he? An old gentleman, of cheerful aspect, who is apparently a Socialist. We must all be allowed our little weaknesses. All I ask for is—" He reached his hand for the whiskey. "This old gentleman carries his hobbies so far as to believe in them seriously. I've talked to him about them."

"I have heard him lecture at Camden Town," said the barrister. "I go there sometimes on Sunday evening. They have a tea-feast, with ham and cake and toast. It is a pleasant gathering. It reminds one of the early Church."

"Well, Athelstan, what else can I tell you? Hark!" There was a step heard ascending the stairs. "I believe that is the old man himself. If it is, you shall see him. I will bring him in."

He went out to meet the unknown footstep on the landing. He greeted the owner of that footstep; he stopped him; he persuaded him to step into the opposite room. "You must be lonely, Mr. Gray, sitting by yourself. Come in, and have an hour's talk. Come in. This way. The room is rather dark. Here is Mr. Langhorne, your overhead neighbor, whom you know; and here is Mr. Athelstan Arundel, whom you don't know. Those who do know him like him, except for his virtue, which is ostentatious in one so young."

It was now nearly nine o'clock. The lamp was not lit, and the room lay in twilight. It is the favorite shade for ghosts. A ghost stood before Athelstan, and shook hands with him—the ghost of Mr. Dering.

"I am happy," the ghost held out his hand, "to make your acquaintance, Mr. Arundel. An old man, like myself, makes acquaintances, but not friends. His time for new friendships is gone. Still, the world may be full of pleasant acquaintances."

He sat down, taking a chair in the window; the shade of the curtain fell upon his face, so that nothing could be seen but a white circle.

"Let us have candles, Freddy," said Athelstan.

"By all means." Freddy lit a lamp on the table and two candles on the mantelshelf. By their light the lineaments and figure of the ghost came out more distinctly. Athelstan gazed on it with bewilderment; his head went round; he closed his eyes; he tried to pull himself together.

He sat up; he drank half a glass of whiskey-and-soda; he stared steadily at the figure he had not seen for eight years, since— Good heavens! and this man had done it himself! And he was as mad as a hatter.

Mr. Edmund Gray looked serenely cheerful. He lay back in the long chair, his feet extended and crossed; his elbows on the arms of the chair, his finger-tips touching; his face was wreathed with smiles; he looked as if he had always found the world the best of all possible worlds.

Athelstan heard nothing of what was said. His old friend Freddy Carstone was talking in his light and airy way, as if nothing at all mattered. He was not expected to say anything.

Freddy liked to do all the talking for himself—therefore he sat watching a man under an illusion so extraordinary that it made him another man. Nothing was changed in him—neither features nor voice nor dress—yet he was another man. "Why," asked Athelstan—"why did he write that check for seven hundred and twenty pounds?"

Presently Freddy stopped talking, and Mr. Edmund Gray took up the conversation. What he said—the doctrines which he advanced—we know already. "And these things," said Athelstan to himself, "from those lips! Is it possible?"

At ten o'clock Mr. Edmund Gray rose. He had to write a letter; he prayed to be excused. He offered his hand again to Athelstan. "Good-night, sir," he said. "To the pleasure of seeing you again."

"Have we never met before, Mr. Gray?" Athelstan asked.

"I think not. I should remember you, Mr. Arundel, I am sure," Mr. Gray replied politely. "Besides, I never forget a face. And yours is new to me. Good-night, sir."

CHAPTER XXXI

CHECKLEY SEES A GHOST

To Checkley, watching every evening, though not always at the same time, sooner or later the same discovery was certain to come. It happened, in fact, on Friday evening, the day after Athelstan shook hands with Mr. Edmund Gray. On that night he left the office between six and seven, walked to his lodgings in Clerkenwell, made himself a cup of tea, and hurried back to Gray's Inn. Here he planted himself, as usual, close to the passage in the northeast corner of South Square, so that he could slip in on occasion and be effaced. Like many of the detective tribe, or like the ostrich, fount of many fables, he imagined himself, by reason of this retreat, entirely hidden from the observation of all. Of course, the exact contrary was the result. The policeman regarded him with the liveliest curiosity; the laundresses watched him daily; the newspaper vendor came every evening from the gateway to see what this ancient spy was doing, and why he lurked stealthily in the passage and looked out furtively. He was one of the little incidents or episodes which vary the daily routine of life in the inn. Many of these occur every year; the people who come to their offices at ten and go away at five know nothing about them; the residents who leave at ten and return at six or seven or twelve know nothing about them. But the service know, and they talk and conjecture. Here was an elderly man—nay, an old, old man, apparently eighty years of age. What did he want, coming night after night to hide himself in a passage and peer out into the square? What, indeed? The policeman, who had done duty in Hyde Park, could tell instructive stories from his own experience about frisky age; the laundresses remembered gentlemen for whom they had "done," and pranks with which those gentlemen amused themselves; but no one knew a case parallel to this. Why should an old man stand in the corner, and secretly look out into the square? He generally arrived at half-past seven, and he left his post at nine, when it was too dark to see across the square. Then he went to the Salutation, and enjoyed society, conversation, and a cheerful glass, as you have seen.

The time he chose was unfortunate, because Mr. Edmund Gray, when he called at his chambers, generally did so at half-past six or seven, on his way to the Hall of Science, Kentish Town. Therefore, Checkley might have gone on watching for a long time—say an æon—watching and waiting in vain. But an accident happened which rewarded him richly for all his trouble. It was on Friday Elsie, provided by this time with a latch-key to the chambers, arrived at Gray's Inn at six. She was going to spend the evening with the master. She walked in, ascended the staircase—Mr. Gray had not yet arrived—opened the door, shut it behind her, and entered the room.

The hand of woman was now visible in the general improvement of the room. The windows were clean and bright; the wainscoted walls had been cleaned; the ceiling whitewashed; the carpet had been swept and the furniture dusted; there were flowers on the table; there was an easel, on which stood Elsie's fancy portrait of Mr. Dering, so wonderfully like Mr. Gray—a speaking likeness; books lay about the table—they were all books on the labor question, on the social question, on the problems of the day; all the books on all

13

the questions with which men now torture themselves, and think thereby to advance the coming of the kingdom of Heaven. There were new curtains—dainty curtains of lace—hanging before the windows; and the window-blinds themselves were clean and new. Elsie looked about her with a certain satisfaction; it was her own doing, the work of her own hand, because the old laundress was satisfied to sit down and look on. "At the least," she said, "the poor, dear man has a clean room." Then she remembered that in a day or two she would leave him to his old solitude, and she sighed, thinking how he clung to her, and leaned upon her, and already looked upon her as his successor—"a clean room," she said, "when I have left him. Perhaps he will leave the room, too, and be all day long what he used to be. Sane or mad? I love him best when he is mad."

The table was covered with manuscripts. These were part of the great work which he was about to give to the world.

Elsie had never seen the room behind this. A guilty curiosity seized her. She felt like the youngest of Bluebeard's wives. She felt the impulse; she resisted; she gave way; she opened the door, and looked in.

She found a room nearly as large as the sitting-room. The windows were black with dust and soot. She opened one, and looked out upon a small green area outside, littered with paper and bottles and all kinds of jetsam. The floor of the room was deep with dust; the chairs and the dressing-table were covered with it. The bed was laid, but the blankets were devoured by moths; there was not a square inch left whole. It looked as if it had been brought in new, and covered with sheets and blankets, and so left, the room unopened, the bed untouched, for the ten years of Mr. Edmund Gray's tenancy.

Between the bedroom and the sitting-room was a small dark room, containing a bath, a table for washing up, knives and forks in a basket, teacups and saucers.

"The pantry," said Elsie, "and the scullery, and the house-maid's closet, all together. Oh! beautiful! And to think that men live in such dens—and sleep there contentedly night after night in this lonely, ghostly old place. Horrible!" A rattling behind the wainscoting warned her that ghosts can show themselves even in the daytime. She shuddered, and retreated to the sitting-room. Here she took a book, and sat by the open window, heedless of the fact that she could be seen by any one from the square.

It was seven o'clock before Mr. Edmund Gray arrived. "Ah! child," he cried tenderly, "you are here before me. I was delayed—some business. What was it? Pshaw! I forget everything. Never mind—I am here; and before we take a cab I want you once more to go through with me the points of my new catechism. Now, if you are ready."

"Quite ready, master."

At half-past seven Checkley arrived at his corner and took a preliminary survey of the square. "There he is," said the policeman. "There he is again," said two laundresses, conversing on a door-step. "There he is as usual," said the newspaper boy. "Now," asked all in chorus, "what's he want there?"

Mr. Checkley looked out from his corner, saw no one in the square, and retreated into his passage. Then he looked out again, and retreated again. If any one passed through the passage, Checkley was always walking off with great resolution in the opposite direction.

Presently, in one of his stealthy peerings, he happened to look up. Then he started; he shaded his eyes; he looked his hardest. Yes; at the open window, freely displayed, without the least attempt at concealment, he saw the head and face of Miss Elsie Arundel. There! There! What more was necessary? Edmund Gray was Athelstan Arundel, or George Austin, or both— and Elsie Arundel was an accomplice after the act. There! There! He retreated to the seclusion of the passage, and rubbed his hands. This would please Sir Samuel. He should hear it that very night. This ought to please him very much, because it made things so clear at last. There she was—upstairs; in the chambers of Mr. Edmund Gray; in the very room! There! There! There!

Perhaps he was mistaken. But his sight was very good—for distant things. In reading a newspaper he might make mistakes, because he was one of those elderly persons who enjoy their newspaper most when they can nail it upon the wall, and sit down to read it from the other side of a large room. He looked up again. The setting sun shining on the window of the side where he stood—the eastern side was reflected upon the windows of No. 22—Elsie's shapely head—she had taken off her hat—was bathed in the reflected sunshine. No doubt about her at all. There she was. There! There! There! The old man was fain to take a walk up Verulam Buildings and back again to disguise his delight at this discovery. He walked chuckling and cracking his fingers, so that those who saw him—but there are not many in Raymond's Buildings on an August evening—thought that he must be either a little mad or a little drunk or a little foolish. But nobody much regards the actions of an ancient man. It is only the respect of his grandchildren or the thought of his possessions that gives him importance. Only the strong are regarded, and an old man who looks poor gets no credit even for foolishness and silly chuckles. Then Checkley went back to his corner. Oh! what was that? He rubbed his eyes again; he turned pale; he staggered; he caught at the door-posts. What was that? He shaded his eyes, and looked again—bent and trembling and shaking all over. Said the policeman, "Looks as if he's going to get 'em again." Said the laundresses, "He looks as if he'd seen a ghost." The newspaper boy stepped half-way across the square. "He's looking at Mr. Edmund Gray and the young lady. Jealous—p'r'aps—knows the young lady—wouldn't have believed it, prob'ly."

Yes, Checkley was looking at that window. No doubt of that at all. He was not able to disguise his astonishment; he no longer pretended to hide himself. For he saw, sitting in the window, the young lady whom he believed to be an accomplice in the crime; and standing over her, with an expression of fatherly affection, was none other than Mr. Dering himself.

Yes, Mr. Dering. Most wonderful! What did it mean? Had Mr. Dering resolved to clear up the mystery of Edmund Gray? Had he penetrated the chambers, and found there—not Edmund Gray, but Elsie Arundel?

"My friend," said the policeman, standing before him so that the view of the window was intercepted, "you seem interested over the way."

"I am. I am. Oh! yes. Much interested."

"Well, don't you think you've looked at that old gentleman long enough? Perhaps he wouldn't like so much looking at. There's a young lady, too. It isn't manners to be staring at a young lady like a stuck pig."

"No, no, policeman—I've seen enough, thank you."

"And, still talkin' in a friendly way, do you think Mr. Edmund Gray over there would like it if he knew there was a detective or a spy watching every evening on the other side of the square? What's the little game, guv'nor? Anything in our line? Not with that most respectable old gentleman, I do hope—though sometimes— Well, what is it? Because we can't have you goin' on as you have been goin' on, you know."

"Policeman"—Checkley pulled him aside and pointed to the little group at the window—"you see that old gentleman there —do you know him?"

"Certainly. Known him ever since I came to the inn—two years ago. The people of the inn have known him for ten years, I believe. That's Mr. Edmund Gray. He's not one of the regular residents, and he hasn't got an office. Comes here now and then when he fancies the place—Mr. Edmund Gray, that is. I wish all the gentlemen in the inn were half as liberal as he is."

"Oh! it's impossible! Say it again, policeman. Perhaps I'm a little deaf—I'm very old, you know—a little deaf, perhaps. Say it again."

"What's the matter with the man?" For he was shaking violently, and his eyes stared. "Of course that is Mr. Edmund Gray."

"What does the girl do with him? Why are they both there together?"

"How should I know why she calls upon him? She's a young lady, and a sweet young thing, too. He's her grandfather, likely."

Checkley groaned.

"I must go somewhere and think this out," he said. "Excuse me, policeman. I am an old man, and—and—I've had a bit of a shock, and— Good-evening, policeman." He shaded his eyes again and looked up. Yes, there they were, talking. Then Elsie rose, and he saw her putting on her hat. Then she retreated up the room. But still he stood watching.

"Not had enough yet, guv'nor?" asked the policeman.

"Only a minute. I want to see her go out. Yes, there they are —going out together. It is, after all— Oh! there is no mistake."

"There is no mistake, guv'nor," said the policeman. "There goes Mr. Edmund Gray, and there goes that sweet young thing along of him. Ah! there's many advantages about being a gentleman. No mistake, I say, about them two. Now, old man,

you look as if you'd had a surprise.   Hadn't you better go home
and take a drop of something."

It was earlier than Checkley generally went to the Salutation.
But he delayed no longer.   He tottered across the square, showing very much of extreme feebleness, looking neither to the right
nor to the left, his cheek white, his eyes rolling. The people
looked after him, expecting that he would fall.   But he did not.
He turned into the tavern, hobbled along the passage, and sank
into an arm-chair in the parlor.

"Good gracious! Mr. Checkley," cried the barmaid as he passed,
" whatever is the matter?"

Some of the usual company were already assembled, although
it was as yet hardly eight.   The money-lender was there, sitting
in his corner, taking his tobacco and his grog in silence.   The
decayed barrister was there, his glass of old and mild before him,
reading the morning newspaper.   The ex-M.P. was there.   When
Checkley tumbled into the room, they looked up in surprise.
When he gazed about him wildly and gasped, they were astonished, for he seemed like unto one about to have a fit.

"Give me something, Robert—give me something," he cried.
"Quick—something strong.   I'll have it short.   Quick—quick!"

Robert brought him a small glass of brandy, which he swal-
lowed hastily.

"Oh!" he groaned, sitting up, " I've seen—I've seen—"

"You look as if you'd seen a ghost," said the barmaid, who had
come along with a glass of water.   "Shall I bathe your forehead?"

"No, no.   I am better now—I am all right again.   Gentlemen"—he looked round the room solemnly—"I've seen this
evening a good man—an old man—a great man—a rich man,
gentlemen, wrecked and cast away and destroyed and ruined
with a little devil of a woman to laugh at him!"

"They don't generally laugh at the men when they are ruined,"
said Mr. Langhorne.   "They laugh while they are ruining them.
It's fun to them.   So it is to the men.   Great fun it is while it
lasts.   I dare say the little woman won't really laugh at him.   In
my case—"

His case was left untold, because he stopped and buried his
head in his newspaper.

Then Shylock spoke.   He removed his pipe from his lips and
spoke, moved, after his kind, by the mention of the words wreck

and ruin, just as the vulture pricks up its feathers at the word death:

"To see a rich man wrecked and ruined, Mr. Checkley, is a thing which a man may see every day. The thing is, not to lose by their wreck—to make money out of it. Rich men are always being wrecked and ruined. What else can you expect if men refuse to pay their interest and to meet their bills? The melancholy thing—ah! the real sadness—is the ruin of a man who has trusted his fellow-creatures and got taken in for his pains. Only this morning I find that I've been let in by a swindler—a common swindler, gentlemen—who comes round and says he can't pay up—can't pay up—and I'm welcome to the sticks. Which kind of man might your friend be, Mr. Checkley, the man who's trusted his neighbor and got left, or the neighbor who's ramped the man that trusted him?"

"It isn't money at all," Checkley replied.

"Then, sir, if it isn't money," said the money-lender, "I don't know why you come in frightening this honorable company out of their wits. If it isn't money, how the devil can the gentleman be wrecked and ruined?"

For two hours Mr. Checkley sat in silence, evidently not listening to what was said. Then he turned to Mr. Langhorne, the barrister: "You've known Mr. Edmund Gray a long time, I believe?"

"Nine years—ten years—since he came to the inn."

"Always the same man, I suppose?" said Checkley. "Never another man?—not sometimes a young man?—or two young men? —one rather a tall young man, looks as if the world was all his? —supercilious beast!"

"Never more than one man at once," replied the barrister, with a show of forensic keenness. "He might have been two young men rolled into one, but not to my knowledge; always the same man to look at, so far as I know—and the same man to talk with."

"Oh! yes, yes. There's no hope left—none. He's ruined and lost, and cast away and done for."

He rose and walked out. The company looked after him and shook their heads. Then they drew their chairs a little closer, and the gap made by his departure vanished.

CHAPTER XXXII

THE DAY AFTER THE GHOST

WHEN Mr. Dering arrived at his office next morning he observed that his table had not been arranged for him. Imagine the surprise of the housewife, should she come down to breakfast and find the ham and the toast and the tea placed upon the table without the decent cloth! With such eyes did Mr. Dering gaze upon the pile of yesterday's letters lying upon his blotting-pad, the pens in disorder, the papers heaped about anyhow, the dust of yesterday everywhere. Such a thing had never happened before in his whole experience of fifty-five years. He touched his bell sharply.

"Why," he asked, hanging up his coat without turning round —"why is not my table put in order?" He turned, and saw his clerk standing at the open door. "Good heavens! Checkley, what is the matter?"

For the ancient servitor stood with drooping head and melancholy face and bent shoulders. His hands hung down in the attitude of one who waits to serve. But he did not serve. He stood still, and made no reply.

He understood now. Since the apparition of South Square he had had time to reflect. He now understood the whole business from the beginning to the end. One hand there was, and only one, concerned with the case. Now he understood the meaning of the frequent fits of abstraction, the long silences, this strange forgetfulness which made his master mix up days and hours, and caused him to wonder what he had done and where he had been on this and that evening. And somebody else knew. The girl knew. She had told her lover. She had told her brother. That was why the new partner laughed and defied them. It was on his charge that young Arundel had been forced to leave the country. It was he who declared that he had seen him place the stolen notes in the safe. It was he who had charged young Austin, and whispered suspicions into the mind of Sir Samuel. Now the truth would come out, and they would all turn upon him, and his master would have to be told. Who would tell him? How could they tell him? Yet he *must* be told. And what would be done to the jealous servant? And how could the old lawyer, with such a knowledge about himself, continue to work at his office? All was finished. He would be sent about his business. His master would go home, and stay there—with an attendant. How could he continue to live without his work to do? What would he do all day? With whom would he talk? Everything finished and done with. Everything—

He stood, therefore, stricken dumb, humble, waiting for reproof.

"Are you ill, Checkley?" asked Mr. Dering. "You look ill. What is the matter?"

"I am not ill," he replied, in a hollow voice, with a dismal shake of the head. "I am not exactly ill. Yes, I am ill. I tried to put your table in order for you this morning, but I couldn't, I really couldn't. I feel as if I couldn't never do anything for you—never again. After sixty years' service, it's hard to feel like that."

He moved to the table, and began mechanically laying the papers straight.

"No one has touched your table but me for sixty years. It's hard to think that another hand will do this for you—and do it quite as well you'll think. That's what we get for faithful service." He put the papers all wrong, because his old eyes were dimmed with unaccustomed moisture. Checkley had long since ceased to weep over the sorrows of others, even in the most moving situations, when, for instance, he himself carried off the sticks instead of the rent. But no man is so old that he cannot weep over his own misfortunes. Checkley's eye was therefore dimmed with the tear of compassion, which is the sister of charity.

"I do not understand you this morning, Checkley. Have you had any unpleasantness with Mr. Austin—with any of the people?"

"No, no. Only that I had better go before I am turned out. That's all. That's all"—he repeated the words in despair. "Nothing but that."

13*

"Who is going to turn you out? What do you mean, Checkley? What the devil do you mean by going on like this? Am I not master here? Who can turn you out?"

"You can, sir, and you will—and I'd rather, if you'll excuse the liberty, go out of my own accord. I'm a small man—only a very small man—but, thank God! I've got enough to give me a crust of bread and cheese to live upon."

"I tell you what, Checkley—you had better go home, and lie down, and rest a little. You are upset. Now, at our age we can't afford to be upset. Go home, and be easy. Old friends don't part quite so easily as you think." Mr. Dering spoke kindly and gently. One must be patient with so old a servant.

Checkley sobbed and choked. Like a child he sobbed. Like a child of four Checkley choked and sniffed. "You don't understand," he said. "Oh, no—you can't understand. It's what I saw last night."

"This is very wonderful. What did you see? A ghost?"

"Worse than a ghost. Who cares for a ghost? Ghosts can't turn a man out of his place and bring him to be a laughing-stock. No, no. It was a man that I saw, not a ghost."

"If you can find it possible to talk reasonably"—Mr. Dering took his chair, and tore open an envelope—"when you can find it possible to talk reasonably, I will listen. Meantime, I really think that you had better go home and lie down for an hour or two. Your nerves are shaken; you hardly know what you are saying."

"I was in Gray's Inn yesterday evening—by accident—at eight." He spoke in gasps, watching his master curiously. "By accident—not spying. No—by accident. On my way to my club—at the Salutation. Walking through South Square. Not thinking of anything. Looking about me—careless-like."

"South Square, Gray's Inn? That is the place where the man Edmund Gray lives; the man we want to find and cannot find."

"Oh! Lord! Lord!" exclaimed the clerk. "Is it possible?" He lifted his hand, and raised his eyes to heaven, and groaned. Then he resumed his narrative.

"Coming through the passage, I looked up to the windows of No. 22—Mr. Edmund Gray's chambers, you know."

"I believe so." Mr. Dering's face betrayed no emotion at all. "Go on—I am told so."

"In the window I saw Mr. Edmund Gray himself—himself."

"Curious. You have seen him—but why not?"

"The man we've all been so anxious to find. The man who endorsed the check, and wrote the letters, and got the papers—there he was!"

"Question of identity. How did you know him, since you had never seen him before?"

This question Checkley shirked.

"He came down-stairs five minutes afterwards, while I was still looking up at the windows. Came down-stairs, and walked out of the square—made as if he was going out by way of Raymond's Buildings—much as if he might be going to Bedford Row."

"These details are unimportant. Again—how did you know him?"

"I asked the policeman who the gentleman was. He said it was Mr. Edmund Gray. I asked the newspaper boy at the Holborn entrance. He said it was Mr. Edmund Gray, and that everybody knew him."

"So everybody knows him. Well, Checkley, I see nothing so very remarkable about your seeing a man so well known in the inn. It adds nothing to our knowledge. That he exists we know already. What share, if any, he has had in this case of ours remains still a mystery. Unless, that is, you have found out something else."

Checkley gazed upon his master with a kind of stupor. "No, no," he murmured. "I can't."

"What did you do, when you found out that it was the man?"

"Nothing."

"You did nothing. Well, under the circumstances, I don't know what you could have done."

"And he walked away."

"Oh! he walked away. Very important, indeed. But, Checkley, this story does not in the least account for your strange agitation this morning. Have you anything more to tell me? I see that you have, but you seem to experience more than usual difficulty in getting it out."

The clerk hesitated. "Do you," he asked at last—"do you —happen—to know Gray's Inn?"

"I dare say I have been there—years ago.   Why?"

"Oh! you haven't been there lately, have you?"

"Not lately—not for forty years, or some such inconsiderable period.   Why?"

"I thought you might yourself have met Mr. Edmund Gray—been to his chambers, perhaps."

Mr. Dering sat upright, and laid his hand upon his letters. "Checkley," he said, "I am always willing to make allowance for people in mental distress, but I think I have made allowance enough.   Come to the point.   Have you lost any money?"

"No, no; not so bad as that—but bad enough.   No, I couldn't afford to lose money.   I haven't got enough to spare any.   But I got a shock—kind of stroke—partly because of the man I met, and partly because of the person with him."

"Oh! who was that?   Are we arriving at something?"

"I hadn't told you that.   The person who was sitting at the open window with him, who came down-stairs with him, and walked out of the square with him, was no other than your own ward—Miss Elsie Arundel herself!"

"Oh! why not?" asked Mr. Dering carelessly.   "She told me —yesterday, was it?—that she knows him."

"If it had been any one else she was with," he replied, mixing up his grammar—"if it had been any one else who was with her —I wouldn't have been surprised.   But to see the two together. That gave me a turn that I can't get over."

"Still—why not? Miss Elsie Arundel has already told me that she is acquainted with Mr. Edmund Gray."

"What?   She has told you—she has actually told you?   Oh! what has she told you?   Oh! Lord! Lord!   What is a man to say or to do?   She told you—   What is best to do?"   He wrung his hands in his distress and his perplexity.

"I cannot understand, Checkley," said Mr. Dering, with emphasis, "the reason for this display of excitement.   Why should she not tell me, or anybody else?   Do you suppose that my ward is doing anything clandestine?   She has told me that she is acquainted with this man.   She asserts further that we have made a great mistake about him.   What she means, I cannot understand.   She says, in fact, that this gentleman is a perfectly honorable person.   It is possible that he has deceived her.   It is also possible that the name of Edmund Gray had been wrongfully used in the papers which belong to the case. Certainly it was an Edmund Gray who endorsed the first check; and an Edmund Gray having an address at 22 South Square whose name is connected with the later business. Well, we shall see presently. When do you take out the warrant for the arrest of this man? By the way, Elsie Arundel implores me not to allow that step. When are you going to do it?

"This morning, I was going to do it. Everything is ready—but—"

"But what?"

"I can't do it now."

"The man is clean gone off his head."

"Leave it till to-morrow—only to-morrow—or Monday. Before then, something is certain to turn up. Oh! certain sure it is. Something must turn up."

"There is certainly something that you are keeping behind, Checkley. Well—wait till Monday. To-day is Saturday. He can't do very much mischief between this and Monday. That's enough about Edmund Gray. Now, here is another point, to which I want a direct answer from you. My brother asserts, I believe on your authority, that Athelstan Arundel has been living in a low and profligate manner in some London suburb, and that he was in rags and poverty early this year. What is your authority for this?"

"Why, I heard him confess—or not deny—that he'd been living in Camberwell in bad company. It was at the Salutation I heard it. He didn't see me. I'd got my head behind a paper. He never denied it."

"Humph! And about the rags?"

"I don't know anything about the rags."

"Very likely there is as much foundation for the one charge as for the other. Three or four years ago he was in America, to my knowledge. He wrote to me from America. I now learn, on the authority of his sister, that he only came back a month ago, and that he has been and is still in the service of an American paper. What have you got to say to that?"

"Nothing. I don't feel as if I could say anything. It's all turned upsy-down. That won't do, I suppose, no more than the rest."

"But, my friend, if that is true, your theory of conspiracy and confederacy, which you took so much pains to build up, falls to the ground as far as Athelstan is concerned."

"Yes. Oh! I haven't nothing to say." It was a mark of the trouble which possessed him that his language reverted to that of his young days, before he had learned the art of correct speech from the copying of legal documents. He preserved the same attitude with bent head and hanging hands, a sad and pitiful object.

"Since Athelstan was not in London during the months of March and April, he could have had no hand in the later forgeries. And it is acknowledged that the same hand was concerned both in the earlier and the later business."

"Yes, yes—the same hand. Oh! yes—the same hand," he repeated with pathos unintelligible to his master. "The same hand—the same hand; yes, yes—the same hand—that's the devil of it—same hand done it all."

"Then what becomes of your charge against my young partner? You were extremely fierce about it. So was my brother. You had no proofs—nor had he. If the same hand was in both forgeries, it could not have been the hand of George Austin. What do you say to that?"

"Nothing. I'm never going"—still standing, hands hanging —"to say anything again as long as I live."

"But you were very fierce about it, Checkley. You must either find more proofs or withdraw your accusation."

"Oh! if that's all, I withdraw—I withdraw everything."

"Why did you bring that charge then, Checkley? You've been making yourself very busy over the character of my partner. You have permitted yourself to say things in the office before the clerks about him. If it turns out that he has had nothing to do with the business you will be in a very serious position."

"I withdraw—I withdraw everything," the old clerk replied, but not meekly. He was prepared to withdraw, but only because he was forced.

"Remember, too, that it was you who brought the charge against young Arundel."

"I withdraw—I withdraw everything."

"You went so far as to remember—the other day—having seen him replace the notes in the safe. What do you say to that?"

" I withdraw."

" But it was a direct statement—the testimony of an eye-witness. Was it true or not?—I don't know you this morning, Checkley. First, you appear shaking and trembling; then you tell me things which seem in no way to warrant so much agitation. Next, you withdraw an accusation which ought never to have been made except with the strongest proof. And now you wish to withdraw an alleged fact."

Checkley shook his head helplessly.

" I acknowledge that the business remains as mysterious as before. Nothing has been found out. But there remains an evident and savage animosity on your part towards two young gentlemen in succession. Why? What have they done to you?"

Checkley made reply in bold words, but still standing with hanging hands, " I withdraw the animosity. I withdraw everything. As for young Arundel, he was a supercilious beast. We were dirt beneath his feet. The whole earth belonged to him. He used to imitate my ways of speaking, and he used to make the clerks laugh at me. I hated him then. I hate him still. It was fun to him that an old man, nigh seventy, with no education, shouldn't speak like a young gentleman of Oxford and Cambridge College. He used to stick his hat on the back of his head as if it was a crown, and he'd slam the door after him as if he was a partner. I hated him. I was never so glad as when he ran away in a rage. He was coming between you and me, too—oh! I saw it. Cunning he was. Laying his lines for to come between you and me."

" Why—you were jealous, Checkley."

" I was glad when he ran away. And I always thought he'd done it, too. As for seeing him put the notes back in the safe, I perceive now that I never did see him do it. Yet I seemed to think at the time that I'd remembered seeing him do a kind of a sort of a something like it. I now perceive that I was wrong. He never done it. He hadn't the wits to contrive it. That sort is never half sharp. Too fine-gentleman for such a trick. Oh! I know what you are going to say next. ' How about the second young fellow?' I hate him, too. I hate him because he's the same supercilious beast as the other, and because he's been able to get round you. He's carneyed you—no fool like an old fool—and flattered you—till you've made him a partner. I've worked for you, heart and soul, for sixty years and more, and this boy comes in and cuts me out in a twelvemonth."

"Well! but, Checkley—hang it!—I wouldn't make *you* a partner."

"You didn't want no partners. You could do your work, and I could do mine and yours too, even if you did want to go asleep of an afternoon."

"This is grave, however. You hated Mr. Austin, and therefore you bring against him this foul charge. This is very grave, Checkley."

"No, I thought he was guilty. I did, indeed. Everything pointed that way. And I don't understand about young Arundel, because he came into the Salutation with the Cambridge gentleman who gets drunk there every night, and he said that he'd lived at Camberwell for eight years with bad company as I wouldn't name to you, sir. I thought he was guilty. I did, indeed."

"And now?"

"Oh! now it is all over. Everything's upsy-down. Nobody's guilty. I know now that he hasn't had anything to do with it. He's a young man of very slow intelligence and inferior parts. He couldn't have had anything to do with it. We ought to have known that."

"Well, but who has done it, after all?"

"That's it." Checkley was so troubled that he dropped into a chair in the presence of his master. "That's it. Who's done it? Don't you know who done it? No, I see you don't so much as suspect. No more don't I. Else—what to do—what to say— Lord only knows!" He turned and ran; he scuttled out of the room, banging the door behind him.

"He's mad," said Mr. Dering. "Poor man! Age makes men forgetful, but it has driven Checkley mad."

CHAPTER XXXIII

THE THREE ACCOMPLICES

On that same evening the three accomplices—probably on the proceeds of their iniquities—were dining together at the Savoy. After dinner they sat on the veranda overlooking the river and the Embankment. 'Tis sweet, what time the evening shades prevail, while one is still in the stage of physical comfort and mental peace attendant upon an artistic little banquet, to view from the serene heights of a balcony at that hotel the unquiet figures of those who flit backwards and forwards below. They —alas!—have not dined so well, or they could not walk so fast, or drag their limbs so hopelessly, or lean over the wall so sadly.

Elsie leaned her head upon her hands, looking down upon this scene, though not quite with these thoughts. Young ladies who are quite happy, and are going to be married next week, do not make these comparisons. Happiness is selfish. When one is quite happy, everybody else seems quite happy too—even Lazarus and the leper. We must never be happy if we do not wish to be selfish.

Coffee was on the table. Athelstan had a cigar. They were all three silent. During dinner they had talked gayly, because everybody knows that you cannot talk with strange people listening. After dinner they sat in silence, because it is only when the waiters are gone that one is free to talk.

"Elsie," said George presently, "you have something to tell us—something you have discovered. For my own part, since I handed the case over to anybody else, I feel as if I were not interested in it. But still, one would like to know—just for curiosity's sake—when Checkley is to be 'run in.'"

"Yes," said Elsie, "I must tell you. Perhaps I ought to have told you before. Yet there was a reason. Now—you will be greatly astonished, George."

"Before you begin, Elsie"—Athelstan removed his cigar—"I

must tell you that yesterday evening I, too, made a discovery—
what the Americans call a pivotal discovery—a discovery that dis-
covers everything. I should have told you last night, but you
announced your communications for this evening, and I thought
we would expose our discoveries at the same time."

"You have found out, too!" Elsie cried. "I see by your face
that you have. Well, Athelstan, so much the better. Now, tell
your discovery first, and I will follow."

"It is this. I have discovered Edmund Gray. I have sat
with him, and discoursed with him, in Freddy Carstone's chambers. He came in, sat beside me, and conversed for more than
an hour."

"Oh!" said Elsie. "Then you know all—as much as I know."

"Observe," George interposed, "that *I* know nothing as yet."

"Wait a moment, George. Learn that I have myself known
Mr. Edmund Gray for a fortnight. You will think, perhaps, that
I ought to have told you before. Well—but there is a reason—
besides, the way, to begin with, did not lie quite clear before me.
Now the time has come when you should advise as to the best
course to follow."

"You have certainly been more mysterious than any oracle,
Elsie. Yet you will bear witness, if it comes to bearing witness,
that I accepted your utterances and believed in them."

"You certainly did, George. And now, Athelstan, tell him
the whole."

"In one word, then—Edmund Gray, the man we have been
looking after so long, is none other than Edward Dering, of 12
New Square, Lincoln's Inn, solicitor."

"I don't understand," said George, bewildered. "Say it all
again."

Athelstan repeated his words.

"That is my discovery, too," said Elsie. "Now you know all,
as you understand."

"But I don't understand. How can one man be another
man?"

"I sat beside one man," Athelstan added, "for an hour and
more; and lo! all the time he was another man."

"And still I am fogged. What does it mean?"

"It means, George, what you would never suspect. The one
man received me as a stranger. He knew nothing about me; he

had never heard my name, even. Yet the other man knows me so well. It was very odd at first. I felt as if I was talking to a sleep-walker."

"Oh!" cried George, "I know now. You have seen Mr. Dering in a kind of sleep-walking state—I, too, have seen him thus. But he said nothing."

"You may call it sleep-walking if you like. But, George, there is another and a more scientific name for it. The old man is mad. He has fits of madness, during which he plays another part, under another name. Now, do you understand?"

"Yes; but—is it possible?"

"It is more than possible; it is an actual certainty. Wait. Let Elsie tell her story."

Then Elsie began, with a little air of triumph, because it is not given to every young lady to find out what all the men have failed to find.

"Well—you see—I was always thinking over this business, and wondering why nothing was found out about it, and watching you look this way and that, and it occurred to me that the first thing of all was to find out this Mr. Edmund Gray, and lay hands upon him. At first I thought I would just go and stand outside his door all day long and every day until he came. But that seemed a waste of time. So I remembered how you found his door open, and went in, and spoke to the laundress. I thought that I would do the same thing, and sit down there, and wait until he should come. But I was afraid to sit in the rooms of a strange man all alone—no, I could not do it. So I just found out the old woman—the laundress—as you did, George, and I gave her money, and she told me that Mr. Gray was at his chambers almost every Saturday afternoon. Very well; if anybody chose to wait for him all Saturday afternoon, he would certainly be found. So on Saturday afternoon I took a cab and drove to Holborn, and got to the place before his arrival. But again, as it was not quite nice to stand at an open doorway in a public square, I thought I would wait on the stairs. So I mounted—the doors were all closed—nobody was left in the place at all—I thought I should be perfectly safe and undisturbed, when I heard the noise of footsteps overhead—a tramp, tramp, tramp up and down, with every now and then a groan—like a hungry creature in a cage. This kept on for a long time, and frightened me horribly. I was still more frightened when a door overhead opened and shut, and the footsteps came down-stairs. They belonged to a man—an elderly man—who seemed as much frightened at seeing me as I was at seeing him. He asked me whether I wanted any one; and when I said I wanted Mr. Edmund Gray, he said that he was a friend of Mr. Gray's, and that, since I was a friend too, I might act for Edmund Gray, and lend him some money. He looked desperately poor and horribly hungry, and thin and shabby, the poor old man!"

"So you acted for Edmund Gray. That was old Langhorne. He is a barrister, who lives in the garret, and is horribly down on his luck. Go on."

"Poor Elsie!" said George. "Think of her, all alone on the staircase!"

"When he was gone, there was no sound at all. The place was perfectly quiet. The time passed so slowly—oh! so slowly. At last, however, I heard a step. It came up the stairs. Oh! my heart began to beat. Suppose it should be Mr. Edmund Gray? Suppose it was some other person? Suppose it was some horror of a man? But I had not long to wait, because Mr. Edmund Gray himself stood on the landing. He stared at me, rather surprised to find a young lady on the stairs, but he showed no sign of recognition whatever. I was a complete stranger to him."

"And was the man Mr. Dering?"

"He was—Mr. Dering. There was just the least little change in him. He wore his coat open instead of buttoned. He had no gloves, his hat was not pulled over his eyes, and his face was somehow lighter and brighter than usual."

"That is so," said Athelstan. "Exactly with these little changes he presented himself to me."

"Perhaps there is another man in the world exactly like him."

"Futile remark! Go on, Elsie."

"Then I guessed in a moment what it meant. I stepped forward, and asked him if he was Mr. Edmund Gray. And then I followed him into his rooms. George, there is no manner of doubt whatever. Mr. Dering has periods—whether regular or not I cannot tell—when he loses himself, and becomes in imagination another man. He is mad, if you like, but there is method in his madness. The other man is just himself turned inside out. Mr. Dering believes in the possible wickedness of everybody; the other man believes in the actual goodness of every man. Mr. Dering considers property the only stable foundation of society; the other man considers property the root of all evil. Mr. Dering is hard and jealous; the other man is full of geniality and benevolence. Mr. Dering is Justice; the other man is Mercy."

"Very neatly put, Elsie. There is quite an eighteenth-century balance about your sentences and sentiments. So far"—Athelstan contributed his confirmation—"so far as I could judge, nothing could be more true. I found my man the exact opposite of himself."

"Can such a thing be possible? If I were to speak to him, would he not know me?"

"You forget, George. You have seen him in that condition, and he did not know you."

"Nothing is more common"—Athelstan, the journalist, began to draw upon the encyclopædic memory which belongs to his profession—"than such a forgetfulness of self. Have you ever been into a lunatic asylum? I have—for professional purposes. I have discoursed with the patients, and been instructed by the physicians. Half the time many of the patients are perfectly rational; during the other half they seem to assume another mind with other memories. It is not real possession, as the ancients called it, because they never show knowledge other than what they have learned before. Thus, a sane man who cannot draw would never in insanity become an artist. So Mr. Dering, when he is mad, brings the same logical power and skill to bear upon a different set of maxims and opinions. Said a physician to me at this asylum of which I speak, 'There are thousands of men and women, but especially men, who are mad every now and then, and don't know it. Most of the crimes are, I believe, committed in moments of madness. A young fellow steals money—it is because at the moment he is so mad that he even persuades himself that borrowing is not stealing; that he is only borrowing; that he can get it back, and put it back, before it is found out. What is uncontrollable rage but sudden madness? There are the men who know that they are mad on some point or other, and cunningly hide it, and are never found out. And there are the men who are mad, and don't know it. In their mad times they commit all kinds of extravagances and follies, yet somehow they escape detection.' So he talked; and he told me of a man who was a lawyer in one town with a wife and family, and also a lawyer in another with a different wife and family. But one lawyer never found out the other; and the thing was only discovered when the man got a paralytic stroke and died in a kind of bewilderment, because, when the time came for him to be the other man, he found himself lying in a strange bedroom with a strange family round him. I had long forgotten the asylum. I did the place for my paper three or four years ago, and scored by the description. Since last night I have been recalling my experience, and applying it. You see, there can never be any physical change. This is no Hyde and Jekyll business. Whatever happens must be conducted with the same body and the same mind. The same processes of mind in which the man is trained remain, but his madness requires a new setting."

"One cannot understand," said Elsie.

"No. But then one cannot understand everything. That's the real beauty of this world; we are planted in the midst of things; we can give names to them—Adam began that way, didn't he?—but we can't understand any of them; and most people think that when we have given a name we have succeeded in understanding. Well, Elsie—we don't understand. But we may find out something. I take it that the other man grew up by degrees in his brain, so that there is no solution of the continuity of thought and recollection. The Edmund Gray developed himself. He has been developed for nearly ten years, since he has occupied the same chambers all the time."

"But about the forgeries?" George sprang to his feet. "I declare," he cried, "I had quite forgotten the real bearing on our case."

"Edmund Gray," said Elsie, "says that his own lawyer who manages his affairs is Edward Dering. If he were to write letters while Edmund Gray, he would not impose upon Edward Dering."

"He cannot write to two men," said Athelstan. "There must be a border-land between the waking and the dreaming, when the two spirits of Edmund Gray and Edward Dering contend for the mastery, or when they command each other—when Edmund Gray endorses checks and Edward Dering writes letters and conducts transfers for his client—his double—himself."

"I have seen him in such a state," said George. "At the time I never suspected anything but a passing trouble of mind, which caused him to be so wrapped up in his thoughts as not to be able to distinguish anything. He was then, I doubt not now, carrying out the instructions of Edmund Gray, or he was Edmund Gray acting for himself. Checkley whispered not to disturb him. He said that he had often seen him so."

"I have never tried to understand," said Elsie; "but I saw that Edmund Gray was Mr. Dering gone mad, and that he himself, and nobody else, was the perpetrator of all these forgeries; and I have been trying to discover the best way—the kindest way to him—the surest way for us—of getting the truth known. George, this is the secret of my mysterious movements. This is why I have not given you a single evening for a whole fortnight. Every evening—both Sundays—I have spent with this dear old man. He is the most delightful—the most gentle—the most generous—old man that you ever saw. He is full of ideas—oh! quite full—and they carry you out of yourself, until you awake next morning to find that they are a dream. I have fallen in love with him. I have had the most charming fortnight—only one was always rather afraid that he might come to himself, which would be awkward."

"Well, Elsie, have you found a way?"

"I think I have. First, I have discovered that when he is surrounded with things that remind him of Edmund Gray, he remains Edmund Gray. Next, I have found out that I can, by talking to him even at his office, when he has his papers before him, turn him into Edmund Gray."

"You are a witch, Elsie."

"She is," said George, looking at her in the foolish lover's way. "You see what she has turned me into—a long time ago—and she has never turned me back again."

"I have been thinking too," said Athelstan. "For our purposes, it would be enough to prove the identity of Edmund Gray and Edward Dering. That explains the resemblance of the handwriting and of the endorsement. My commissionnaire's recollection of the man also identifies the check as drawn by himself for himself under another name. It explains the presence of the notes in the safe. It also shows that the long series of letters which passed between him and the broker were written by himself for himself. Here, however, is a difficulty. I can understand Edward Dering believing himself to be Edmund Gray, because I have seen it. But I cannot understand Edward Dering believing himself to be the solicitor to Edmund Gray and writing at his command."

"But I have seen him in that condition," said Elsie. "It was while he was changing from one to the other. He sat like one who listens. I think that Edmund Gray was at his elbow speaking to him. I think I could make him write a letter by instruction from Edmund Gray. That he should believe himself acting for a client in writing to the broker is no more wonderful than that he should believe himself another man altogether."

"Show me, if you can, the old man acting for an imaginary client. Meantime, I mentioned the point as a difficulty. Prove, however, to Mr. Dering and to the others concerned that he is Edmund Gray, and all is proved. And this we can do by a host of witnesses."

"I want more than this, Athelstan," said Elsie. "It would still be open to the enemy to declare that George, or you, or I, had made use of his madness for our own purposes. I want a history of the whole case written out by Edmund Gray himself—a thing that we can show to Mr. Dering and to everybody else. But I dread his discovery. Already he is suspicious and anxious. I sometimes think that he is half conscious of his condition. We must break it to him as gently as we can. But the shock may kill him. Yet there is no escape. If the forgeries were known only to ourselves, we might keep the discovery a secret; and only, if necessary—but it would not be necessary—keep some sort of watch over him and warn the bank. But Checkley has told the clerks and the people at the bank, and there are ourselves to think of, and my mother and Hilda. No; we must let them all know."

"And, if one may mention one's self," said Athelstan, "my own little difficulty presses. Because, you see, I don't know how long I may be kept here. Perhaps to-morrow I might go on to St. Petersburg or to Pekin. Before I go, Elsie, I confess that I should like my mother to understand that—that she was a little hasty—that is all."

"You are not going to St. Petersburg, brother." Elsie took

his hand. "You are not going to leave us any more. You are going to stay. I have made another discovery."

"Pray, if one may ask—"

"Oh! you may ask. I have seen a letter—Mr. Dering showed it to me. It was written from the States three or four years ago. It showed where you were at that time—and showed me more, Athelstan—it showed me how you lost the pile of money that you made over that silver mine—you remember, Athelstan?"

He made no reply.

"Oh! do you think that I am going to accept this sacrifice? George, you do not know. The donor of that great sum of money which Mr. Dering held for me—we have often wondered who it was—I have only found out to-day—it was Athelstan. He gave me all he had—for such a trifling thing—only because I would not believe that he was a villain—all he had in the world —and went out again into the cold. He said he dropped his money down a gully or a grating on the prairie—some nonsense. And he sent it all to me, George. What shall we do?"

"Is this really true, Athelstan? Did you really give up all this money to Elsie?"

"She says so."

"It is quite true, George. I saw the letter—Mr. Dering showed it to me—in which he sent that money home, and begged Mr. Dering to take care of it, and to give it to me on the day when I should be one-and-twenty. He cannot deny it. Look at him. He blushes—he is ashamed—he hangs his head—he blows tobacco-smoke about in clouds, hoping to hide his red cheeks. And he talks of going on to St. Petersburg, when we know this secret and have got the money! What do you call this conduct, George?"

"Athelstan—there is no word for it. But you must have it back. You must and shall. There can be no discussion about it. And there is not another man in the world, I believe, who would have done it."

"Nonsense. I should only have lost it if I had kept it," Athelstan replied, after the Irish fashion.

"You hear, Athelstan. It is yours. There can be no discussion. That's what I like a man for. While we women are all talking and disputing the man puts down his foot, and says, 'There can be no discussion.' Then we all stop, and the right

14

thing is done. It is yours, brother; and you shall have it, and you shall stay at home with us always and always." She laid her hand upon his shoulder, and her arm round his neck, caressing him with hand and voice.

The man who had wandered alone for eight years was not accustomed to sisterly caresses. They moved him. The thing itself moved him.

"All this belongs to another chapter," he said huskily. "We will talk of it afterwards, when the business in hand is despatched."

"Well, then—that is agreed. You are to have your money back; my mother is to take her suspicions back; Mr. Dering is to have his certificates back and his dividends; Checkley is to take his lies back; Sir Samuel is to have his charges back; George and I are going to have our peace of mind back. And we are all going to live happy ever afterwards."

"As for Wednesday, now," said George—"it is not an unimportant day for us, you know."

"Everything is ready. On Sunday morning my mother is always at home before church. I will see her then, and acquaint her with the news that the wedding will take place, as originally proposed, at her house. This will astonish her very much, and she will become angry and polite and sarcastic. Then I shall tell her to prepare not only for a wedding-feast but also for a great, a very great surprise. And I shall also inform her that I shall be given away by my brother. And then—then—if I know my mother aright—she will become silent. I shall do that to-morrow morning. In the evening, George, you will get your best man, and I will get your sisters, my bridesmaids, and we will come here, or go to Richmond or somewhere—and have dinner and a cheerful evening. Am I arranging things properly?"

"Quite properly. Pray go on."

"Sunday afternoon I have promised to spend with my master—Edmund Gray. He is going to read me a new paper he has just finished, in which he shows that property can be destroyed by a painless process—Athelstan, put all your money into your pocket, and keep it there—in less than a twelvemonth, and with it all crime, all sweating, all injustice. No, Athelstan, he is not mad. When he argues on this theme he is persuasive and eloquent. He convinces everybody. I shall hear him out, and then I shall try to make him write down all that has happened. If we can only get such a confession, it would be better than anything else. But it may be difficult. He does not like being questioned about . himself. If I do succeed—I don't know quite what I ought to do next. He must be told. Some time or other he must have the truth. I thought of asking all the people mentioned to meet at his office on Monday at noon, when Mr. Dering is always himself. On Sunday I would not. He has to address his people on Sunday evening. Let him do so undisturbed. I will leave him in happiness that one night longer. But you two—you will be anxious. Come on Sunday evening—between eight and nine— to the Hall of Science. Then you will hear him and see me. And I will let you know how I have prospered."

"Sunday evening," said George. "Monday comes next, then Tuesday; and before Wednesday, my Elsie, the character of these two convicts has to be completely whitewashed, even to the satisfaction of Hilda herself. Are we not running it pretty close?"

"Unbeliever! Doubter! I tell you that you shall be married with all your friends round you, and that Athelstan shall give me away. And you shall go away on your holiday with a quiet heart and nothing to trouble you. What a foolish boy not to be able to trust his bride even for such a simple thing as getting a confession out of a madman!"

"Do you sport a crest, old man?" asked Athelstan.

"I believe there is some kind of a sort of a thing somewhere around. But crests are foolishness."

"Not always. Take a new one, George—a real one. Stamp it on your spoons and forks, and in your books, and on your carriage. Let it be simply the words, 'Dux Foemina Facti.'"

CHAPTER XXXIV

ELSIE AND HER MOTHER

"Can you spare me a few minutes, mother?"

Mrs. Arundel looked up from the desk where she was writing a letter, and saw her daughter standing before her. She started and changed color, but quickly recovered, and replied coldly, "I did not hear you come in, Elsie. What do you want with me?"

Outside, the bells were ringing for church; it was a quarter to eleven; Mrs. Arundel was already dressed for church. She was one of those who do not see any incongruity between church and a heart full of animosities. She was bitter against her daughter and hard towards her son, and she hated her son-in-law elect with all the powers of her passionate nature. But, my brothers, what an array of bare benches should we see in every place of worship were those only admitted who came with hearts of charity and love!

"Do you wish to keep me long, Elsie? If so, we will sit down. If not, I am ready for church, and I do not like to arrive late. People in our position should show a good example."

"I do not think that I shall keep you very long. But if you sit down, you will be so much more comfortable."

"Comfort, Elsie, you have driven out of this house."

"I will bring it back with me, then. On Monday evening, mother, I am coming back."

"Oh! What do you mean, child? Has the blow really fallen? I heard that it was impending. Is the young man—is he—a prisoner?"

"No, mother. You are quite mistaken. You have been mistaken all along. Yet I shall come back on Monday."

"Alone, then?"

"I shall leave it to you whether I come back alone, or with the two men whom I most regard of all the world—my lover and my brother."

"You know my opinions, Elsie. There has been no change in them. There can be none."

"Wednesday is my wedding-day."

"I am not interested in that event, Elsie. After your wedding with such a man, against the opinions, the wishes, the commands of all whom you are bound to respect, I can only say that you are no longer my daughter."

"Oh! how can you be so fixed in such a belief? Mother, let me make one more appeal to your better feelings. Throw off these suspicions. Believe me, they are baseless. There is not the shadow of a foundation for this ridiculous structure they have raised. Consider. It is now—how long?—three weeks since they brought this charge, and they have proved nothing—absolutely nothing. If you would only be brought to see on what false assumptions the whole thing rests."

"On solid foundations—hard facts—I want no more."

"If I could prove to you that Athelstan was in America until a month ago?"

"Unhappy girl! He is deceiving you. He has been living for eight years in profligacy near London. Elsie, do not waste my time. It should be enough for me that my son-in-law, Sir Samuel Dering, a man of the clearest head and widest experience, is convinced that it is impossible to draw any other conclusions."

"It is enough for me," Elsie rejoined quickly, "that my heart tells me that my brother and my lover cannot be such creatures."

"You have something more to say, I suppose." Mrs. Arundel buttoned her gloves. The clock was now at five minutes before eleven.

"Yes. If it is no use at all trying to appeal to—"

"No use at all," Mrs. Arundel snapped. "I am not disposed for sentimental nonsense."

"I am sorry, because you will be sorry afterwards. Well, then, I have come to tell you that I have made all the preparations, with George's assistance, for Wednesday."

"Oh!"

"Yes. The wedding-cake will be sent in on Tuesday. My own dress—white satin, of course, very beautiful—is finished, and tried on. It will be sent in on Monday evening. The two bridesmaids' dresses will also come on Monday. George has arranged at the church. He has ordered the carriages and the bouquets, and has got the ring. The presents you have already in the house. We shall be married at three. There will be a little gathering of the cousins after the wedding, and you will give them a little simple dinner in the evening, which will, I dare say, end with a little dance. George has also seen to the red cloth for the steps, and all that. Oh! and on Thursday evening you will give a big dinner-party to everybody."

"Are you gone quite mad, Elsie?"

"Not mad at all, my dear mother. It is Sir Samuel who is mad, and has driven you and Hilda mad. Oh! everything will come off exactly as I tell you. Perhaps you don't believe it?"

"You are mad, Elsie.   You are certainly mad."

"No, my dear mother, I am not mad.   Oh! it is so absurd, if it were not so serious.   But we are determined, George and I, not to make this absurdity the cause of lasting bitterness.   Therefore, my dear mother, I do not want to be married from my brother's lodgings, but from your house.   You will come to my wedding, I prophesy, full of love—full of love "—her eyes filled with tears —"for me and for George and for Athelstan—full of love and of sorrow and of self-reproach.   I am to be given away by my brother—you will come, I say, with a heart full of love and of pity for him."

Mrs. Arundel gazed at her stonily.

"Everybody will be there, and you will receive all your friends after the wedding.   I have taken care of the invitations.   Hilda will be there too, horribly ashamed of herself.   It will be a lovely wedding, and we shall go away with such good wishes from yourself as you would not in your present state of mind believe possible.   Go now to church, my dear mother, prepared for a happy and a joyful day."

"I sometimes believe, Elsie," said Mrs. Arundel, more coldly still, "that you have been deprived of your senses.   So far from this, I shall not be present at your wedding.   I will not interfere with your holding your marriage here if you like; you may fill the house with your friends if you please.   I shall myself take shelter with my more dutiful daughter.   I refuse to meet my unhappy son.   I will not be a consenting party to the tie which will entail a lifelong misery—"

"My dear mother—you will do everything exactly as I have prophesied.   Now, do not say any more, because it will only make our reconciliation a little more difficult.   I ought to go to church on the Sunday before my wedding, if any day in the week. If you would only recover your trust in my lover's honor, I could go to church with you and kneel beside you.   But without that trust— Oh! go, my dear mother.   You will find my prophecy come true, word for word—believe me or not."

Mrs. Arundel went to church.   During the service she felt strange prickings of foreboding and of compunction and of fear, anxiety, and hope, with a little sadness, caused by the communication and the assurances of her daughter.   Even in such a case as this the thinker of evil is sometimes depressed by the arrival of the prophet of good. When Mrs. Arundel came away from church, she became aware that she had not heard one single word of the sermon. Not that she wanted very much to hear the sermon, any more than the first or second lesson—all three being parts of the whole which every person of respectability must hear once a week. Only, it was disquieting to come away after half an hour's discourse with the feeling that she did not remember a single syllable of it. She took her early dinner with the other daughter, to whom she communicated Elsie's remarkable conduct, and her prediction and her invitation. It was decided between them that her brain was affected—no doubt, only for a time—and that it was not expedient for them to interfere; that it was deplorable, but a part of what might have been expected; and that time would show. Meanwhile, Sir Samuel reported that it had been resolved to get a warrant for the arrest of the man Edmund Gray, who hitherto had eluded all attempts to find him.

"He appears to be a real person," the knight concluded—"an elderly man, whose character, so far as we can learn, is good. It is, however, significant that nothing has been discovered concerning his profession or calling. That is mysterious. For my own part, I like to know how a man earns his daily bread. I have even consulted a person connected with the police. Nothing is known or suspected about him. But we shall see as soon as he is before the magistrate."

"And Wednesday is so close! Oh! my dear Sir Samuel, hurry them up. Even at the last moment—even at the risk of a terrible scandal—if Elsie could be saved!"

"Well," said Sir Samuel, "it is curious—I don't understand it —we had arranged for the application for a warrant for Friday morning. Would you believe it? that old donkey Checkley won't go for it—wants it put off—says he thinks it will be of no use. What with this young man Austin at first, and this old man Checkley next, we seem in a conspiracy to defeat the ends of justice. But to-morrow I shall go myself to my brother. It is time this business was finished."

"Yes, yes," said Mrs. Arundel. "And, my dear Sir Samuel, before Wednesday—let it be before Wednesday, I implore you, for all our sakes!"

"My dear madam, it shall be to-morrow."

At noon, Elsie returned to Half Moon Street, where George was waiting for her.

"I have made one more attempt," she said, with tears, "but it was useless. Her head is as hard about you as ever it was about Athelstan. It is wonderful that she should have so little faith. I suppose it comes of going into the City and trying to make money. Edmund Gray would say so. I would have told her all, but for the old man's sake. He knows nothing; he suspects nothing; and I want to make the case so complete that there shall be no doubt—none whatever—possible in the minds of the most suspicious. Even Checkley must be satisfied. I shall finish the work, I hope, this afternoon. Oh! George—is it possible? Is our wedding-day next Wednesday—actually next Wednesday? And the hateful cloud shall be blown away, and—and —and—"

For the rest of this chapter look into the Book of Holy Kisses, where you will very likely find it.

CHAPTER XXXV

PLENARY CONFESSION

EARLY on Sunday afternoon Elsie started upon her mission. She was anxious, because she was entering upon a most important business, and one requiring the greatest delicacy in the handling. It was enough—more than enough—that her witnesses should be able, one after the other, to identify Mr. Dering with Mr. Edmund Gray; but how much more would her hands be strengthened if she could produce a full and complete narrative of the whole affair, written by the hand which had done it all? To get that narrative was her business with the master that afternoon. But she was hopeful, partly because she knew her power over the philosopher; and partly because, like every woman who respects herself, she had always been accustomed to get exactly what she wanted, either by asking, coaxing, flattering, or taking.

The master was waiting for her—one should never keep a

master waiting—and she was a little late. He was impatient; he had so much to talk about and to teach—one point suggested another in his mind—so much to say; he grudged the least delay; he walked about the room, chafing because the hour appointed was already five minutes in the past; he would scold her; she must really learn to be punctual; they had only about five short hours before them for all he had to say. Was this the zeal of a student? But at that point she opened the door, and ran in, breathless, smiling, eager, holding out both her hands, a dainty, delicate maiden all his own—his disciple—his daughter—the daughter of the New Humanity—and he forgot his irritation, and took her hands in his, and kissed her forehead. "Child," he sighed, "you are late. But never mind. You are here. Why, you have grown so precious to me that I cannot bear you to be a minute late. It is such a happiness—such a joy in the present— such a promise for the future—that I have such a disciple! Now sit down—take off your bonnet. I have put a chair for you at the window—and a table for you to write. Here is your note-book. Now—you have thought over what I taught you last? That is well. Let us resume at the point where we left off—the rise of the co-operative spirit, which is the rise of the New Humanity."

He talked for two hours—two long, eloquent hours; he walked about the room; or he stopped before his disciple, emphasizing with the forefinger of admonition—repeating—illustrating by anecdote and memory—he had a prodigious memory. The scholar listened intelligently. Sometimes she asked a question; sometimes she made notes. You must not think that she was a sham scholar; her interest in the master's system was not simulated. Above all things she loved to hear this enthusiast talk —who would not love to hear of the New Jerusalem? Always he made her heart to glow with the vision that he conjured up before her eyes of a world where there should be no more sorrow nor crying, nor any more pain, nor any of the former things. He made her actually see—what others only read of—the Foursquare City itself, with its gates open night and day, its jasper walls, and its twelve foundations of precious stones. "Why," he said, "the gates are open night and day because there is no property to defend; and the walls are of jasper because it is the most beautiful of minerals, and because it can be polished like a mirror, so that

14*

the country around is reflected on its surface, which shows that it all belongs to the city; and the precious stones are the twelve cardinal virtues of Humanity, on which the Order of the Future shall rest—namely, Faith, Brotherly Love, Obedience, Patience, Loyalty, Constancy, Chastity, Courage, Hope, Simplicity, Tenderness, and Industry. It is an allegory—the whole book is an allegory—of Humanity." And she saw, beside the city, the river of life with the tree of life for the healing of all nations.

Then she clean forgot the purpose for which she had come; she was carried away; her heart beat—her cheek glowed. Oh! lovely vision! Oh! great and glorious prophet! He made a heaven, and placed it on this earth. Now the mind of man can conceive of no other happiness but that which humanity can make out of the actual materials found upon this earthly ball. The heaven, even of the most spiritual, is a glorified world; the hell, even of the most gentle, is a world of fleshly pain; no other heaven attracts; no other hell terrifies; there is no promise or hope or prospect or inheritance that man desires or poet can feign or visionary can preach but an earthly heaven; it must be a heaven containing sunshine and shower, kindly fruits in due season, love and joy and music and art, and men and women who love each other and labor for each other. Such a world—such a New Jerusalem—the master drew every day; he loved it and lingered over it; he painted over and over again this splendid vision. He was never tired of painting it, or his hearers of gazing upon it. But to-day he spoke with greater fulness, more clearly, more brilliantly, more joyously than ever. Was the prophet really a man of seventy years and more? For his mind was young—the enthusiast, like the poet, never grows old. His voice might have been the voice of a boy—a marvellous boy—a Shelley—preaching the glories of the world when property should be no more.

He ceased, and the vision which he had raised quickly faded away. They were back again in the dingy old inn; they were among the solicitors and the money-lenders and the young fellows who have their chambers in the place. The inn is about as far from the New Jerusalem as any place under the sun; it is made over bodily and belongs—every stair—every chamber—to the interests of property.

He ceased his prophecy, and began to argue, to reason, to chop logic, which was not by any means so interesting. At last he stopped this as well. "You have now, dear child," he said, "heard quite as much as you can profitably absorb. I have noticed for the last two or three minutes your eyes wandering and your attention wearied. Let us stop—only remember what I have just said about the diseases of the body politic. They are akin to those that affect the human body. By comparing the two we may learn not only cause, but also effect. We have our rheumatisms, gouts, asthmas, neuralgias, colds and coughs, fevers, and other ills. So has the body politic. Whence come our diseases? From the ignorance, the follies, the vices, the greed and gluttony of our forefathers. So those of the body politic. Take away property, and you destroy greed. With that, half the diseases vanish."

Elsie heard, and inclined her head. It did occur to her that perhaps property in the body politic might be represented by food in the body human, but she forbore. The master was one who did not invite argument. Nearly all the great teachers of the world, if you think of it, have conveyed their wisdom in maxims and aphorisms.

He took out his watch. "It is nearly four," he said. "Shall we go on to the hall?"

"Not yet. There is no need for us to be there before six. We have two good hours before us. Let us use them more pleasantly than in sitting alone in the hall—you must own that it is stuffy. We will talk about other things—about ourselves—not about me, because I am quite an insignificant person, but about you, dear master." She was now about to enter upon her plan of duplicity. She felt horribly ashamed, but it had to be done. She strengthened herself; she resolved; she suppressed the voice of conscience.

"About me?" asked the master. "But what is there to talk about?"

"Oh! there is ever so much." She took his right hand in her own and held it, knowing that this little caress pleased and moved him. "Master—what a wonderful chance it was that brought me here! I can never sufficiently wonder at it. I have told George—George Austin—my lover, you know; and Athelstan—he is my brother." She looked at him sharply, but there was no sign of recognition of those two names. Edmund Gray had no remembrance of either. "I have told them about you, and of your great work, and how you are teaching me, and everything. But when they ask me who you are, where you have lived, and all about you, I can tell them nothing. Oh! I know it matters nothing about me and my own friends; but, my dear master, we have to think of the future. When the cause has spread, and spread, and spread, till it covers the whole world, people will want to know all about the man who first preached its principles. Who will be able to tell them? No one. You are alone; you have no wife or children. Your name will remain forever attached to the cause itself. But you—you—the man—what will you be? Nothing. Nothing but a name. You ought to write an autobiography."

"I have sometimes thought I would do so"—his face became troubled; "but—but—"

"But you are always occupied with working for the world. You have no time, of course. I quite understand that; and it worries you—does it not?—to be called upon to turn your thoughts from the present back to the past."

"Yes, yes; it does—it does. Elsie, you exactly express the difficulty."

"And yet—you must own—you must confess—it is natural for the world to want to know all about you. Who was the great Edmund Gray? Why, they will want to know every particular—every single particular: where you were born—where you were educated—who were your masters—what led you to the study of humanity and its problems—where you lived—if you were married, and to whom—what you read—who were your friends. Oh! there is no end to the curiosity of the world about their great men."

"Perhaps." He rose, and looked out of the window. When men are greatly pleased they must always be moving. "I confess that I have never thought of these things at all. Yet, to be sure—you are right." He murmured and purred.

"No, but I have thought of them, ever since I had the happiness of being received by you. Master, will you trust me? Shall I become your biographer? You cannot find one more loving. You have only to give me the materials. Now—let me ask you a few questions, just for a beginning—just to show you the kind of thing I shall want to know."

He laughed, and sat down again. "Why, my life has not got

in it one single solitary incident or episode or adventure. There are no misfortunes in it. There is not such a thing as a disease in it. I have always been perfectly well. There is not even a love episode or a flirtation in it. There are not even any religious difficulties in it. Without love, ill-health, misfortune, religious doubts—where is the interest in the life, and what is there to tell ?"

" Well, a life that has no incident in it must be the life of a student. It is only a student who never falls in love."

" Or," said the philosopher, " a money-getter."

" Happily, there are not many students, or we women should be disconsolate indeed. Do you know, master, that you can only be excused such a dreadful omission in your history by that one plea ? Sit down again, master," for again he was walking about restlessly, partly disturbed by her questions, and partly flattered and pleased by her reasons. She opened her note-book, and began to ask questions about himself—very simple questions, such as would not introduce any disturbing points. He answered readily, and she observed with interest that he gave correctly the facts of his own—Edward Dering's—history.

He was born, he said, in that class which upholds property— the better class—meaning the richer. His father was a wealthy solicitor, who lived in Bedford Row. He was born in the year 1815—Waterloo year. He was the eldest of a family of five— three daughters and two sons. He was educated at Westminster. On leaving school, his father offered him the advantage of a university course, but he refused, being anxious to begin as early as possible his life's work—as he thought—in the defence of property. He was therefore articled to his father, and at the age of twenty-two he passed his examination and was admitted.

" And then you were young—you were not yet a student— you went into society. You saw girls, and danced with them. Yet you never fell in love, and were never married. How strange! I thought everybody wanted love. A man's real life only begins, I have always been taught, with love and marriage. Love means everything."

" To you, my child, no doubt it does. Such as you are born for love," he added gallantly. " Venus herself smiles in your eyes and sits upon your lips. But as for me, I was always studious more or less, though I did not for long find out my true

line. I worked hard—I went out very little. I was cold by
nature, perhaps. I had no time to think about such things.
Now, when it is too late, I regret the loss of the experience.
Doubtless if I had that experience I should have gained greatly
in the power of persuasion. I should have a much more potent
influence over the women among my hearers. If I were a married man I should be much more in sympathy with them."

"No—n—no—" Elsie hesitated a little. "Perhaps women—
especially the younger kind—get on better with unmarried men.
However, you were not married."

"At first, then, I was a solicitor with my father. Then—presently—" His face put on the troubled look again.

"You continued," Elsie interrupted quickly, "to work at your
profession, though you took up other studies?"

"No, no—not quite that."

"You began to take up social problems, and gradually abandoned your profession?"

"No, no—not that either—quite."

"You found you could not reconcile your conscience any longer
to defending property?"

"No—I forget exactly. It is strange that one should forget a
thing so simple. I am growing old, I suppose. Well—it matters not. I left the profession. That is the only important thing
to remember. That I did so, these chambers prove. I came out
of it. Yes, that was it. Just at the moment, my head being full of
other things, I cannot remember the exact time or the manner of
my leaving the profession. I forget the circumstances, probably
because I attached so little importance to it. The real point is
that I came out of it and gave myself up to these studies."

She noted this important point carefully, and looked up for more.

"There, my dear child, is my whole life for you—without an
incident or an episode. I was born; I went to school; I became
a solicitor; I gave up my profession; I studied social economy;
I made my great discovery; I preached it. Then—did I say my
life was without an episode and without love? No, no—I was
wrong. My daughter—I have at last found love and a child—
and a disciple. What more have I to ask?"

"My master!" No daughter could be more in sympathy with
him than this girl.

"It is all most valuable and interesting," she said, "though the facts are so few. Books will be written, in the future, on these facts, which will be filled out with conjecture and inference. Even the things that you think of so little importance will be made the subject of comment and criticism. Well—but my biography of you will be the first and best and most important. I shall first make a skeleton life out of the facts, and then fill in the flesh and blood, and put on the clothes, and present you, dear master, just as you are."

"Ask me what you will, but not too often. It worries me to remember the past. My dear, I am like a man who has made himself—who has risen from the gutter. He cannot deny the fact, but he doesn't like to be talking about it; and he is insulted if any one charges him with the fact, or alludes to it in any way in his presence. That is my case exactly. I have made myself. I have raised myself from the gutter—the gutter of property. I actually worked in defence of property till I was sixty years old and more. Now I am rather ashamed of that fact. I do not deny it—you must put it into your biography—but I do not like talking about it."

"You were once a solicitor, and you are now a prophet. What a leap! What a wonderful leap! I quite understand. Yet sometimes, now and then, for the sake of the curious, impertinent world, look back and tell me what you see."

" I suppose it is because I am so absorbed in my work that it is difficult for me to remember things. Why, Elsie, day after day, from morning to evening, I sit here at work. And in the evening I remember nothing of the flight of time. The hours strike, but I hear them not. Only the books on the table show what has been my occupation. And you want me to go back, not to yesterday, but ten, twenty, thirty years ago. My dear child, I cannot. Some of the past is clear to me—a day here and there I remember clearly. All my evenings at the Hall of Science; my lessons with you—those I remember. But to recall days passed in meditation and absorbing study is not possible. No, no—I cannot even try."

He spoke with a little distress, as if the very thought of the necessary effort troubled him.

"Believe me, my dear master," said Elsie, "I would not vex you. Only for some of the things which you do remember. For instance, the world always wants to know about the private fortunes of its great men. Your own affairs, you told me once, are in the hands of a—Mr.—Mr.—what is his name?"

"Dering—Dering. A very well-known solicitor. His office is in New Square, Lincoln's Inn—he manages my money matters. I am, I believe, what the world calls wealthy."

"That gives you independence and the power of working for humanity, does it not?"

"It does," said the scourge and destroyer of property, unconscious of the incongruity. "Dering, my solicitor, is, I believe, a very honest man. Narrow in his views—wedded to the old school —quite unable to see the advance of the tide. But trustworthy. He belongs to a tribe which is indispensable so long as property is suffered to exist."

"Yes—only so long. Property and lawyers will go out hand in hand."

"And magistrates," he added, with enthusiasm. "And courts of justice and prisons. And criminals, because the chief incentive to crime will be destroyed. What a glorious world without a law, or a lawyer, or a policeman!"

"Mr. Dering, is it? Why, my dear master, I know something about Mr. Dering. My brother Athelstan was articled to him. He became a managing clerk for him. Then there was trouble about a check. Something was wrong about it. He was unjustly blamed or suspected, and he left the house. I wonder, now, whether you could throw any light upon that business of the check?"

"I, my dear child? A single solitary check at a lawyer's office? How should I possibly know anything about it?"

"Oh! but you might remember this check, because, now I think of it, your own name was connected with it. Yes—it was. I am certain it was. The check was drawn in March, in the year 1883—a check for seven hundred and twenty pounds, payable to your order—the order of Edmund Gray."

"A check for seven hundred and twenty pounds? In March, 1883? That must have been— Yes, yes—that was about the time. Now, this is really most remarkable, child, most remarkable that you should actually hit upon a check—one of thousands issued from that office—which I should remember perfectly. Life is full of coincidences—one is always hearing odd things said, meeting faces which one knows. Well, it is most remarkable, because I received a check for that very amount at that very time from Dering. Oh! I remember perfectly. It was when I had a scheme. I thought it then—being younger than I am now—a very good scheme indeed. It was intended for the gradual destruction of property. I did not understand at that time so fully as I do now the rising of the tide and the direction of the current which is steadily advancing to overwhelm property without any feeble efforts on my part. Yet my scheme was good so far as it went, and it might have been started with good effect, but for the apathy of the workers. You see, they were not educated up to it. I had already begun upon my scheme by advancing to certain working-men sums which should make them independent of their employers until they should have produced enough to sell directly, without the aid of an employer, at their own co-operative stores. Unfortunately, most of them drank the money; the few who used it properly, instead of backing up their fellow-workmen, became themselves employers, and are now wealthy. Well, I thought I would extend this method. I thought that if I got together a chosen band—say, of seventy or so—and if, after teaching them and educating them a bit, I gave them, say, ten pounds apiece, to tide them over the first few weeks, that I might next open a distributive and co-operative store for them, and so take the first step to abolishing the middle-man—the man of trade."

"I see; and so you drew the money for that purpose."

"Yes. But, as I told you, I was obliged to abandon my scheme. The men were not sufficiently advanced. They listened; they professed great willingness to receive the money; but they gave me no encouragement to hope that they would carry out my plan. So it fell through. And the men remain to this day with their employers. And so—you see—I never used the money. I remember that I had the check cashed in ten-pound notes for the purpose."

"What became of the notes?"

"I don't know. They are in the bank, I suppose—wandering about the world. I gave them back to Dering."

"Oh! my dear master"—Elsie sprang to her feet, and laid a sheet of paper on the table—"this is most providential. I cannot tell you what a dreadful cause of trouble this check has been to us. It has half ruined my brother's life. For Heaven's sake, write it all down for me. Quick! quick! before you forget it all."

CHAPTER XXXVI

PLENARY CONFESSION—(*Continued*)

"I shall not forget it.   Nevertheless, Elsie, if a statement of the facts can be of any use to you"—he changed his seat and took up the pen—"certainly I will write it for you."

"I am requested," he wrote, "by Miss Elsie Arundel, my scholar, to state what I know of a certain transaction which took place in March, 1883.   The facts are as follows: I had need of a sum of seven hundred and twenty pounds.   For certain purposes I wanted it in ten-pound notes.   I asked my agent, Mr. Dering, to give me a check; and as I thought that I should want the money immediately, perhaps in an hour or so, I asked him to make it payable to my order, and not to cross the check. He drew the check, and gave it to me in his office.   I then went to the hotel where I was stopping—a place in Norfolk Street, Strand, and sent a commissionnaire to the bank for the money.   He brought it, as I had requested, in ten-pound notes. In a few days I discovered that my plan could not be even commenced without the greatest danger of defeating its own object. I therefore took the notes to Mr. Dering's office, and placed them in his safe.   I suppose that he has long since returned them to the bank."

"There, child," he said, reading the statement aloud.   "That is what I recollect about the matter."

"Sign it."   Elsie gave him the pen again.   "Sign it, dear master!   Oh! thanks—thanks a thousand times!   You don't know—oh! you will never know or understand—I hope—how precious this document will be for me"—she folded the paper in an envelope, and placed it in her hand-bag—"and for my people —my brother and all.   Oh! my dear master!"   She stooped and kissed his hand, to hide the tears in her eyes.   Athelstan's name was safe now, whatever happened. He would be completely cleared at last.

"Why, my dear scholar—my dear daughter." Mr. Edmund Gray was moved himself almost to tears at this unexpected burst of feeling. "As if there was anything I would not do for you if I could. I, who have never loved any woman before, love one now. She is my daughter—my grandchild. So your brother will be helped by this little reminiscence—will he? Actually, your brother! I wonder if there is anything more that I could remember for you in this uneventful life of mine."

"Oh no!—that would be too much to hope. Yet there is a chance—just a chance. I wonder if I may tell you. There is still time before us. If we are at the hall by six we shall do very well. It is no more than half-past four. Shall I tell you the trouble! Oh! But it is a shame. And you with this great work laid upon you! No, no—I must not." Oh! Delilah! oh! Circe! for she looked as if, in spite of her unwilling words, she wanted to tell it very badly indeed.

"Nay, my dear. You must, and you shall. What? You are in trouble, and you will not tell me what it is? You—my scholar —my clear-eyed disciple, who can see what these dull creatures of clay around us can never understand—you are in trouble, and you hesitate to tell me? Fie! fie! Speak now. Tell me all."

"I have told you that I have a lover, and that I am engaged to be married."

"Yes, yes. His name, too, you have told me. It is George —George Austin. There were Austins once—I seem to remember —but that does not matter."

"We are to be married on Wednesday."

"So soon? But you have promised that I shall not lose my pupil?"

"No, dear master. As soon as we come back from our holiday I will come and see you again and learn of you. Do not doubt that. I can never again let you go out of my life. I shall bring my—my husband with me."

"If I thought your marriage would take you away from me, I should be the most unhappy of men. But I will spare you for a month—two months—as long as you please. Now, tell me what is on your mind."

"George was one of Mr. Dering's managing clerks—your Mr. Dering, you know." Mr. Edmund Gray nodded gravely. "He had no money when we were engaged, and we thought that we were going to be quite a poor and humble pair. But a great piece of good fortune happened to him, for Mr. Dering made him a partner."

"Did he? Very lucky for your friend. But I always thought that Dering ought to have a partner. At his age it was only prudent—necessary, even."

"So we were made very happy, and I thought we were the luckiest couple in the world. But just then there was a discovery made at the office—a very singular discovery—I hardly know how to describe it, because it is not quite clear to me even yet. It was concerned with the buying or selling or transfer of certain stocks and shares and coupons, and that kind of thing. Mr. Dering seems not to remember having signed the papers concerned. There is a fear that they are in wrong hands. There is suspicion of forgery, even. I am ashamed even to mention such a thing to you, but my lover's name has been connected with the business; and Mr. Dering's clerk, Checkley—you know Checkley?—"

"Certainly—Dering's old servant."

"Has openly charged George—on no evidence, to be sure—of having forged the letters, or of having assisted in the forgery."

"This is very serious."

"It is very serious, but we do not intend to let the thing interfere with our wedding. Only, unless I can remove the last ray of suspicion before Wednesday, we shall spend our honeymoon at home, in order to watch the case from day to day."

"Buying or selling stocks? Dering would be constantly doing that."

"It appears that these transactions were the only things of the kind that he has done this year. That is to say, he denies having done these."

"Well—as for these having been the only transactions of the kind, he managed a good bit of such business for me this last spring."

"Did he? Do you remember the details of that business?"

"Clearly. It was only yesterday, so to speak."

"Was it the purchase or transfer of stock or shares?"

"Certainly. To a very large amount. I have told you about my industrial village, have I not? The village where all are to be equal—all are to work for a certain time every day, and no longer—all are to be paid in rations and clothes and houses, and there is to be no private property—my ideal village."

"I know. A lovely village."

"It was early in the spring that I finished my designs for it. Then it occurred to me that it would be well if, instead of always going to my lawyer for money, I had a large sum at my command lying at my bank. So I instructed Dering to transfer to my name a great quantity of stocks lying in his name. He was a trustee or a—well—it is rather unusual, but I like having all my business affairs managed for me, and— But this will not interest you"—this with the look of irritation or bewilderment which sometimes passed over his face. "The important thing is that it was done, and that my bank received those transfers, and has instructions to receive the dividends."

"Oh! And has all the papers, I suppose?"

"It had them. But I thought that perhaps my old friend might think it looked like want of confidence if I left them there, so I sent for them, and took them to his office. They are now in the safe. I put them there myself with my own hand, or he did with his own hand—I forget. Sometimes—it is very odd—when I think of things done at that office I seem to have done it myself, and sometimes I think that he did it. Not that it matters."

"Not at all. The papers are actually in the safe again?"

"Certainly. I—that is—he—he or I—put them there."

"Oh! my dear master"—Elsie clapped her hands—"this is even more important than the other. You do not know—you cannot guess—what mischiefs you are able to stop. If I had only been able to talk to you about these things before! The paper you have already written is for my brother. Now sit down, my master, and write another that will do for me."

"I will do anything you ask me—and everything. But as for this, why not ask Dering? His memory never fails. His mind is like a box which holds everything and can never be filled. Perhaps he would not like these private affairs—as between solicitor and client—to be talked about."

"We cannot go to Mr. Dering. There are certain reasons which would not interest you. All we want is a clear, straightforward statement, an exact statement, of what happened. Sit down now and write me a full account of each transaction."

"Certainly ; if it will be of the least use to you."

"Early in the present year," he began, "I found that my plan of an industrial village, if it was to be carried into effect, would want all the money I could command. It occurred to me that it would be well to transfer a certain sum from the hands of my agent, and to place it in my own bank ready to hand. I began then, in March, with a sum of six thousand pounds, which Dering, by my instructions, handed over to my bank in the form of shares and stocks. I believe they were transfers of certain stocks held by him in his own name, but forming part of my fortune—my large private fortune. The bank was instructed to receive the dividends in that sum. A month or so later I obtained from Dering other stock to the value of twelve thousand pounds, the papers of which were also given to my bank. And after that I took out papers representing twenty thousand pounds ; so that I had in my hands, ready to be sold out and used at a moment's notice, no less than thirty-eight thousand pounds. All this money I intended to devote to my industrial village. The scheme is still one in which I put my whole confidence. But it has not yet been carried into effect, in consequence of the difficulty of finding working-men equal to the situation. They understand working for the man who has the money ; they do not understand working for the man who has none—that is, for each other and for themselves. For my own part, I could only find working-men of that stamp. Perhaps I am too much in the study. I do not go about enough among working-men. There must be some advanced to my stage of development. Well, for want of men, I could not start my village, and I have not used the money. As for the papers, I have taken them out of the bank and placed them in Dering's safe."

Elsie looked over his shoulder, reading every word. "The letters which Mr. Dering wrote to the stock-broker in accordance with your instructions. They were written for him—perhaps—by you. It is unusual, but—"

"I told you," he replied sharply. "What is the use of saying things twice? There are some things which confuse a man. I wrote them—he wrote them—he acted for me—or I acted for myself. What matter? The end is as I have written down for you. Now, will this paper be of any use to you?"

"Of the greatest use. Please sign it, dear master."

He obeyed, and signed "Edmund Gray."

"There is one thing more." Elsie saw in his face signs of disquiet, and hastened on. "You have got your bank-book here?"

"Yes. The manager sent it here with an impertinent note about references, which I have sent on to Dering. What do you want with the bank-book? It is in one of those drawers. See—here it is—check-book too."

"If I were you, master, I would have no more trouble about the money. You have given Mr. Dering the transfers and papers—why not give him back the money as well? Do not be bothered with money-matters. It is of all things important to you to be free from all kinds of business and money-matters. Who ever heard of a prophet drawing a check? You sit here, and work and meditate. You go to the Hall of Science, and teach. It is the business of your friends to see that all your necessities are properly supplied. Now, if you will in these minor matters suffer your friends to advise—"

"Surely. I ask for nothing else."

"Then, dear master, here is your check-book, and here your bank-book. Draw a check, payable to the order of Edward Dering, for all the money that is lying here—I see it is seven hundred and twenty-three pounds five shillings and threepence. I will take care of the check—so. Oh! you have signed Edward Dering—careless master! Draw another—now sign it Edmund Gray. That will do. And you had better at the same time write a letter to the bank, asking the manager in future to receive the dividends for the account of Mr. Dering. I will write the letter, and you shall sign it. Now—no, no—not Edward Dering—Edmund Gray. Your thoughts are wandering. There! Now, dear master, you are free from everything that might trouble you."

The master pushed back the blotting-pad with impatience, and rose from the chair. Elsie took possession of the signed checks, the check-book, the bank-book, and the letter. She had all—the statement in Edmund Gray's own handwriting—all—all—that was wanted to clear up the business from the beginning to the end. She put everything together in her hand-bag. She glanced at her companion; she perceived that his face was troubled. "I wish," he said fretfully, "that you had not worried me with those questions about the past. They disturb me. The current of my thoughts is checked. I am full of Dering and his office and his safe—his safe—and all—"

Elsie trembled. His face was changing—in a minute he would have returned to Mr. Dering, and she would have had to explain. "Master," she cried, laying her hand upon his arm, "think. We are going to the Hall of Science—your Hall of Science—yours. The people are waiting for their prophet. You are to address them. To-night you must surpass yourself, because there are strangers coming. Tell us—once again—all over again—of that world where there is no crime, no suffering, no iniquity, no sin, no sorrow—where there are no poor creatures deprived by a cruel social order of liberty, of leisure, of comfort, of virtue, of every-thing—poor wretches born only to toil and to endure. Think of them. Speak for them. Plan for them. Make our hearts burn within us for shame and rage. Oh! master "—for his face was troubled still and doubtful, as if he were hovering on the border-land between himself and his other self—" no one can speak to them like you; no one has your power of speech ; make them feel that new world—make them see it—actually see it with their earthly eyes—make them feel it in their hearts."

"Child "—he sighed; his face fell back into repose—" you comfort me. I was falling—before you came to me I used often to fall—into a fit of gloom—I don't know why. Something irritates me ; something jars ; something awakens a feeling as if I ought to remember—remember—what? I do not know. I am better now. Your voice, my dear, at such a moment is to me like the sound of David's harp to Saul. It chases away the shadows. Oh! I am better already. I am well. If you want to ask any other questions, do so. As for those transactions—they are perfectly correct in form and everything. I cannot for the life of me understand why Dering, who is a practical man—"

"Never mind Dering, my dear master—or those transactions. Think only of the world of the New Humanity. Leave the transactions and the papers to me. I hope that you will never find out why they were wanted, or how they were to be used. Now let us start. We shall be in excellent time."

The Hall of Science was half full of people—the usual gather-ing—those who came every Sunday evening and took the simple feast of fraternity. The table was spread with the white cloth, on which were laid out the toast and muffins, the ham and shrimps, and bread and butter and watercresses; and on the appearance of the chief the tea was brought up, and they all sat down. Now, it had been observed by all that since the adhesion of this young lady the leader's discourses had been much more confident, his manner had been clearer, his points more forcibly put. This was because, for the first time, he had had an opportunity of discussing his own doctrines with a mind able to follow him. Nothing so valuable to a teacher of new things as a sympathetic woman for listener and disciple. Witness the leading example of the Prophet Mohammed. Also, their leader had never before been so cheerful—so hopeful—so full of life and youth and spring. He was young again; he talked like a young man, though his hair was gray. This was because he loved a woman, for the first time in his life; he called it paternal affection; whatever kind of love it was, it worked in him the same miracle that love always works in man—young or old—it gave him back the fire of youth.

This evening he sat at the head of the table, dispensing his simple hospitality with a geniality and a heartiness unknown before the arrival of this young lady. He talked, meantime, in the lofty vein, above the style and manner common to his hearers, but not above their comprehension; he spoke of a higher life attainable by man at his best, when the victory over nature should be complete, and every force should be subdued and made slave to man, and all diseases should be swept away, and the perfect man should stand upon the earth at last, lord and master of all—Adamus Redivivus. When that time should come there would be no property, of course; everything was to be in common; but the new life would be full of love and joy; there would be long-continued youth, so that none should be made to rise from the feast unsatisfied; nay, it seemed to this dreamer that every one should continue at the feast as long as he pleased, till he was satiated and desired a change. Long-continued youth; all were to be young and to keep young; the girls were to be beautiful and the men strong; he pronounced—he—the hermit —the anchorite—the celibate who knew not love—a eulogy on the beauty of women; and he mourned over those men who miss their share of love.

The hearts of those who heard were uplifted, for this man had
15

the mesmeric faculty of compelling those who heard him to feel what he wanted them to feel. Most of them had been accustomed to regard their leader as a man of benevolent manners but austere principles. Now he was tender and human, full of sympathy even with those weak vessels who fall in love, and for the sake of love are content to be all their lives slaves—yea, even slaves to property.

After tea, the tables being cleared, the chief pronounced his weekly address or sermon. It was generally a discourse on the principles, which all professed, of equality and the abolition of property. To-night, he carried on the theme on which he had spoken at tea-time, and discoursed on the part which should be played by love in the New Humanity. Never before had he spoken so convincingly. Never had orator an audience more in sympathy with him.

Shortly after the beginning of the address, there arrived two gentlemen, young and well dressed, who sat down modestly, just within the door, and listened. The people turned, and looked at them with interest. They were not quite the kind of young man peculiar to the street or to the quarter.

When the lecture was over, and the audience crowded together to talk before they separated, Elsie slipped across to the new-comers, and led them to the lecturer. "Master," she said, "this is my brother Athelstan."

Mr. Edmund Gray shook hands with him. "Why, Elsie," he said, "your brother and I have met already in Gray's Inn."

"And this is my friend George Austin, partner of Mr. Dering."

"Mr. Austin," said Mr. Edmund Gray, "I am glad to meet the man who is about to enter into the most sacred of all bonds with one whom I venture to love, sir, as much as you yourself can do, though I love her as my daughter, and you love her as your bride. You will be the happiest of men. Take care, sir, that you deserve your happiness."

"This day," said Elsie, "you have rendered us all such a service as can never be acknowledged or repaid or forgotten. Yet we hope and pray that somehow you will never understand how great it is."

CHAPTER XXXVII

LE CONSEIL DE FAMILLE

"Checkley," said Mr. Dering on Monday morning, "here is a note from Miss Elsie Arundel. She makes an appointment with me at four o'clock this afternoon. Keep me free for that hour. Her brother Athelstan is coming with her. What's the matter, man?"

"It's coming, then. I knew it would come." Checkley groaned. "It's all over at last."

"What is all over?"

"Everything. But don't you believe it. Tell 'em it's a lie made up to screen themselves. They can't prove it. Nobody can prove it. I'll back you up. Only don't you believe it. Mind—it is a lie—a made-up lie."

"I don't know what has been the matter with you for the last day or two, Checkley. What am I not to believe? What is a lie? Who is making up a lie which cannot be proved?"

"Oh! I can't say the word—I can't. It's all over at last—at last." He ran out of the room, and slammed the door behind him.

"My dear mother"—Hilda drove to Pembridge Square directly after breakfast—"I have had a most curious letter from Elsie. What does it mean? She orders—she does not invite—she positively orders—Sir Samuel—actually orders Sir Samuel!—and myself to attend at Mr. Dering's office at four. We are ordered to assist, she says, at the demolition of the structure we have so carefully erected. What structure? What does she mean? Here is the letter."

"I too, dear, have had a letter from her. She says that at four o'clock this afternoon all the wrongful and injurious suspicions will be cleared away, and that if I value the affection of my son and herself—the affection of herself—I must be present. Hilda,

what does this mean?   I am very much troubled about the letter.
On Saturday, she came here and informed me that the wedding
would be held on Wednesday just as if nothing had happened;
and she foretold that we should all be present, and that Athelstan
would give her away—Athelstan.   It is a very disquieting letter,
because, my dear, do you think we could all of us—could we possibly be wrong, have been wrong from the very beginning, in
Athelstan's case?   Could Sir Samuel be wrong in George's
case?"

"My dear mother, it is impossible.   The case, unhappily, is too
clear to admit of any doubt.   Sir Samuel, with his long experience,
could not be wrong."

"Then, Hilda dear, what can Elsie mean?"

"We have been talking about it all through breakfast.   The
only conclusion we can come to is that there is going to be a
smothering up of the whole business.   Mr. Dering, who has been
terribly put out with the case, must have consented to smother
up the matter.   We think that the papers have been returned
with the money received on dividends and coupons, and that Mr.
Dering has agreed to take no further proceedings.   Now, if he
would do that, Athelstan, of course, would come under the Act of
Indemnity; and as the notes were never used by him, but were
returned to their owner, it becomes as easy to recognize his innocence as that of the other man.   Do you see?"

"Yes.   But that will not make them innocent."

"Certainly not.   But it makes all the difference in the world.
Oh! there are families everywhere who have had to smother up
things in order to escape a scandal.   Well, I hope you will agree
with us, and accept the invitation."

"I suppose I must.   But how about removing all the suspicions?"

"Oh! that is only Elsie's enthusiastic way.   She will go on, if
she likes, believing that George had nothing to do with it.   He
will have every inducement to live honestly for the future.   We
can easily pretend to believe that Athelstan was always innocent,
and we can persuade him—at least I hope we can persuade him—
to go abroad.   Sir Samuel kindly says that he will advance a hundred pounds in order to get rid of him.   Then there will be no
scandal, and everybody will be satisfied.   As for our relations
with Elsie and her husband, we can arrange them afterwards.

Perhaps they will agree to live in a distant suburb—say Redhill, or Chislehurst, or Walthamstow—so that there may be a good excuse for never having them to the house. Because—smothering or no smothering—I can no longer have the same feelings towards Elsie as before. Her obstinate infatuation for that man exasperates me only to think of it. Nor have I the least intention of being on intimate relations with a forger who has only just escaped being a convict. Sir Samuel entirely agrees with me."

The mother sighed. "I could have wished that we were mistaken. Perhaps, after all, there may be something that Elsie has found out, some unexpected—"

"Say a miracle at once, my dear mother. It is just as likely to happen."

The first to arrive at the office in the afternoon was Elsie herself, carrying a hand-bag.

"You were going to bring your brother, Elsie," said Mr. Dering. "Where is he? And what is your important business with me? I suppose it is something about this wretched forgery, which really seems destined to finish me off. I have heard of nothing else—I think of nothing else—ever since it happened."

"First, has anything new been discovered?"

"I hardly know," Mr. Dering replied wearily. "They seem to have found the man Edmund Gray; but Checkley has suddenly cooled. Formerly, he clamored perpetually that we must lose no time in getting a warrant for his arrest; he now wants to put it off and put it off. He was going on very strangely this morning. My dear, I sometimes think that my old clerk is off his head."

"And you yourself—have you had any return of your forgetfulness?"

"Worse—worse. Every day, worse. I now know when to look for a return of these fits. Every morning I ask myself what I did the day before. Always there are the same hours of forgetfulness—the morning and the evening. Last night, where was I? Perhaps somebody will find out for me—for I cannot remember."

"Shall I find out for you, Mr. Dering? If I were to tell you where you spent the evening yesterday, would you—would you?—"

"What? How can you find out?"

Elsie bent her head. The moment had almost arrived, and she was afraid. She had come with the intention of clearing her brother and her lover at the cost of letting her guardian know that he was insane. A dreadful price to pay for their honor. But it had to be paid. And it must be done in the sight of all, so that there should be no possible margin left for malignity or suspicion.

"This business," she said, "concerns the honor of the two men who are dearer to me than all the world beside. Remember that —nothing short of that would make me do what I have been doing—what I am now doing. Their honor—oh! their honor. Think what it means to them. Self-respect, dignity, everything; the happiness of their homes; the pride of their children. Compared with one man's honor, what matters another man's humiliation? What matters the loss of that man's self-respect? What matters his loss of dignity? Their honor, Mr. Dering, think of that—their honor!"

He bowed his head gravely, wondering what was to follow.

"A man's honor, as you say, Elsie, is the greatest thing in the world to him. Compared with that, another man's self-respect need not, I should say, as a general principle, be considered at all. Self-respect may be regained unless honor is lost."

"Remember that, then, Mr. Dering, when you hear what I have to say. Promise me to remember that. Oh! if there were a thousand reasons, formerly, why I would not pain you by a single word, there are ten thousand now—although you understand them not."

"Why, Elsie, you are troubling your little head about trifles. You will not offend me, whatever you say."

"It is so important a thing," she went on, "that I have asked my mother and sister and Sir Samuel to meet us here at four o'clock, in order that they, too, may hear as well as you. Athelstan is with George. They have one or two persons to introduce to you."

"All this seems to promise a meeting of some interest, and, so far as one may judge from the preamble, of more than common importance. Well, Elsie, I am quite in your hands. If you and your brother between you will kindly produce the forger and give me back my property, I shall be truly grateful."

"You shall see, Mr. Dering. But as for the gratitude— Oh! here is Sir Samuel."

The City knight appeared, large and important. He shook hands with Elsie and his brother, and took up his position on the hearth-rug, behind his brother's chair. "Well, Elsie," he said, "we are to hear something very important indeed, if one may judge by the tone of your letter, which was imperative."

"Very important indeed, Sir Samuel."

The next to arrive were Mrs. Arundel and Hilda. They wore thick veils, and Hilda was dressed in a kind of half-mourning. They took chairs at the open window, between the historic safe and the equally historic small table. Lastly, George and Athelstan walked in. They received no greetings.

Mr. Dering rose. "Athelstan," he said, "it is eight years since you left us." He held out his hand.

"Presently, Mr. Dering," said Athelstan. He looked round the room. His mother trembled, dropped her head, and put her handkerchief to her eyes, but said nothing. His sister looked out of the window. Sir Samuel took no notice of him at all. Athelstan took a chair—the clients' chair—and placed it so as to have his mother and sister at the side. He wasn't therefore compelled to look at them across the table. He sat down, and remained in silence and motionless.

The court was now complete. Mr. Dering sat in his chair before his table, expectant, judicial. Sir Samuel stood behind him. Mrs. Arundel and Hilda, the two ladies, sat at the open window. Elsie stood opposite to Mr. Dering, on the other side of the table, her hand-bag before her. She looked like counsel about to open the case for plaintiff. Athelstan—or plaintiff—naturally occupied the clients' chair on Mr. Dering's left; and George, as naturally —the other plaintiff—stood behind him.

"Now, Elsie, if you please," Mr. Dering began.

"I shall want your clerk, Checkley, to be present, if you please."

Mr. Dering touched his bell. The clerk appeared. He stood before them like a criminal, pale and trembling. He looked at his master appealingly. His hands hung beside him. Yet not a word of accusation had been brought against him.

"Lord! man alive!" cried Sir Samuel, "what on earth has come over you?"

Checkley shook his head sadly, but made no reply.

"I want to ask you a question or two, Checkley," said Elsie

quietly. "You have told Mr. Dering—you have told Sir Samuel —that you saw my brother furtively put a parcel—presumably the stolen notes—into the safe at the very moment when you were charging him with forgery. Now, consider. That was a very serious thing to say. It was a direct statement of fact. Before, the charge rested on suspicion alone; but this is fact. Consider carefully. You may have been mistaken. Any of us may make a mistake."

"It was true—Gospel truth—I see him place a parcel—edging along sideways—in the safe. The parcel we found afterwards in the safe containing all the notes." The words were confident, but the manner was halting.

"Very well. Next, you told Sir Samuel that my brother had been living in some low suburb of London with profligate companions, and that he had been even going about in rags and tatters."

"Yes, I did. I told Sir Samuel what I heard. Mr. Carstone told me. You'd better ask him. I only told what I heard."

George went out, and returned, bringing with him Mr. Freddy Carstone. He looked round the room, and stared with surprise at Mr. Dering, but said nothing. He had been warned to say nothing, except in answer to questions.

"Now, Mr. Carstone," Elsie asked him, "how long is it since you met my brother after his return to England?"

"About three weeks ago I met him. It was in Holborn. I invited him into the Salutation Tavern."

"Did you tell Mr. Checkley here anything about his way of living?"

"I remember saying, foolishly, that he looked too respectable to have come from America; and I said in joke that I believed he had been in Camberwell all the time."

"Nothing about profligacy?"

"Nothing at all."

"Nothing about rags and tatters?"

"Certainly not. In fact, I knew nothing at all about Athelstan's life during the eight years that he has been away."

"Have you anything to say, Checkley? You still stick to the parcel story, do you? Very well; and to the Camberwell and profligacy story?"

Checkley made no answer.

"Now, then.   There is another question.   You made a great point about certain imitations of Mr. Dering's writing found in a drawer of Athelstan's table?"

"Well, they were there, in your brother's hand."

"George, you have something to say on this point."

"Only this.   I was not long articled at that time.   The table was taken from the room in which I sat, and placed here for some special work.   Now, the imitations of Mr. Dering's handwriting were made by myself and another clerk in joke.   I remember them perfectly.   They were written at the back of a letter addressed to me."

Mr. Dering went to the safe, and produced the bundle containing all the papers in the case.   He unrolled the bundle, and placed the contents on the table.

Everybody was now serious.   Lady Dering looked out of the window no longer.   Mrs. Arundel had drawn her chair to the table.

Elsie picked out the paper containing the imitations.   "Tell me," she said, "if you remember—mind, everybody, this bundle of papers has never been shown to George—tell me the name of your correspondent."

"It was Leonard Henryson."

She gave the paper to Mr. Dering.   "You see," she said.

The lawyer gave it to his brother, who passed it on to his wife, who gave it to her mother.   Mrs. Arundel laid it on the table, and raised her veil.

"The next point," said Elsie, "is about Athelstan's whereabouts during the last eight years.   One letter was received by you, Mr. Dering, four years ago.   You have already shown it to me.   Will you let me read this letter aloud for all to hear?"   It was in the bundle with the stopped notes.   He bowed assent, and she read it.

"Twelve thousand pounds!" cried Sir Samuel—"twelve thousand pounds!   All he had!   Good heavens!"

"All he had in the world," said Elsie.   "And all for a child who refused to believe that her brother could be a villain!   All he had in the world!"   Her eyes filled with tears—but she dashed them aside, and went on.   "He was in the States four years ago.   That, I suppose, will no longer be denied.   The next question is —when did he return to this country?"

15*

George left the room again, and returned with a young gentle-man.

"This gentleman," Elsie continued, "comes from Messrs. Chenery & Sons, bankers, of New York and London. He has brought a letter with him. Will you kindly let me see it, sir? It is," she explained, "a letter of credit brought over by my brother from California. You see the date—June 20th of this year."

Mr. Dering read it, and gave it to his brother, who gave it to his wife as before.

"It says that Mr. Athelstan Arundel, one of the staff of a cer-tain Californian paper, will leave New York on June the 21st by the *Shannon*, and that he is authorized to draw on Messrs. Chenery & Sons for so much. Thank you." The young gentle-man retired.

"Now, Mr. Dering, are you satisfied that Athelstan was in America four years ago; that he left America two months ago, and that he was then on the staff of a Californian paper?"

"There seems no reason to doubt these facts. But"—he put his forefinger on the check payable to the order of Edmund Gray—"are we any nearer to the forger of this check?"

"I am coming to that presently. I am going to show you all, so that there shall be no doubt whatever, who is the forger—the one hand—in the business. Wait a little."

Strangely enough, every eye fell upon Checkley, who now trembled and shook with every sign of terror.

"Sit down, Checkley," said his master. "Elsie, do we want this gentleman any longer? His name I have not the pleasure of knowing."

"Oh! come," said Mr. Carstone, who was nearest. "You know my name, surely."

George warned him with a look, and he subsided into si-lence.

"I think I shall want you, Mr. Carstone," Elsie replied, "if you will kindly take a chair and wait. Now, Sir Samuel, I think I am right in saying that your belief in the guilt of George rested entirely on the supposed complicity of Athelstan. That gone, what becomes of your charge? Also, there is no doubt, I believe, that one hand, and one hand alone, has committed the whole long list of letters and forgeries. If, therefore, Athelstan could not execute the second business, how could he do the first? But I have more than arguments for you."

Sir Samuel coughed. Mrs. Arundel sighed.

"As regards the charge against George, apart from his supposed intimacy with an imaginary criminal, the only suspicious thing is that he may have had access to the open safe. Well, Checkley also may have had access. Don't be afraid, Checkley— we are not going to charge you with the thing at all. You are not the forger. In fact, there was a third person who had access to the safe."

She opened her hand-bag and took out a packet of papers.

Then she sat down, with these in her hand, and, leaning over the table, she looked straight and full into Mr. Dering's eyes, and began to talk slowly in a low and murmuring voice. And now, indeed, everybody understood that something very serious indeed was going to be said and done. At the last moment a way had occurred to Elsie. She would let them all see for themselves what had happened, and she would spare her guardian the bitter shame and pain of being exposed in the presence of all this company.

"Mr. Dering," she began, "you have strangely forgotten that you know Mr. Edmund Gray. How could you come to forget that? Why, it is ten years at least since you made his acquaintance. He knows you very well. He does not pretend to have forgotten you. You are his solicitor. You have the management of his property—his large, private fortune—in your hands. You are his most intimate friend. It is not well to forget old friends, is it? You must not say that you forget Edmund Gray."

Mr. Dering changed color. His eyes expressed bewilderment. He made no reply.

"You know that Edmund Gray leaves this room every evening on his way to Gray's Inn; you remember that. And that he comes here every morning, but not till eleven or twelve—two hours after the time that you yourself used to come. His head is always so full of his thoughts and his teaching that he forgets the time between twelve and four, just as you forget the evening and the morning. You are both so much absorbed that you cannot remember each other."

Mr. Dering sat upright, the tips of his fingers touching. He listened at first gravely—though anxiously. Presently a remarkable change passed over his face; he became full of anxiety. He listened as if he were trying to remember—as if he were trying to understand.

"Edmund Gray," he said, speaking slowly. "Yes, I remember my client Edmund Gray. I have a letter to write for him. What is it? Excuse me a moment; I must write that note for him." He took pen and paper, and hastily wrote a note, which Elsie took from him, read, and gave to Sir Samuel.

"You want to tell the banker that Mr. Edmund Gray has returned you the transfers. Yes—thank you. I thought you could not forget that client, of all others."

He leaned back smiling—his expression no longer anxious, but pleased and happy. The change transformed him. He was not Mr. Dering, but another.

"Go on, child."

"The rooms of Gray's Inn are quiet all day long. It is a peaceful place for study, is it not? You sit there, your books before you, the world forgotten."

"Quite forgotten," said Mr. Dering.

"No, no," cried Checkley, springing to his feet. "I won't have it done. I—"

"Sit down." George pushed him back into his chair. "Another word, and you leave the room."

CHAPTER XXXVIII

LE CONSEIL DE FAMILLE—(Continued)

"It is a peaceful day," Elsie continued, "that you pass—for the most part alone—you with your books. Sometimes you come here to call upon your old friend and solicitor, Mr. Dering."

"Sometimes," he replied. "We are very old friends. Though his views are narrow. Where is he?" He looked about the room. "You are all waiting to see him? He will be here directly. He is always here about this time."

"Yes, directly. You remember what I said to you on Sunday

concerning certain transactions? I told you how important it was to have the exact truth about them."

"Certainly. I remember. I wrote an account of them for you."

"You did. Are these papers what you wrote?"

He looked at them for a moment. "These are my papers," he said. "They are what I wrote at your request. They contain a perfectly true account of what happened."

"Now, before I go on, you will not mind—these people here do not know Mr. Edmund Gray—you will not mind my asking a few persons to testify that you are really Mr. Edmund Gray?"

"My dear child, ask all the world if you wish; though I do not understand why my identity should be doubted."

"Not quite all the world. Mr. Carstone, will you tell us the name of this gentleman?"

"He is Mr. Edmund Gray, my neighbor at No. 22 South Square, Gray's Inn."

Mr. Edmund Gray inclined his head, and smiled.

George went outside, and returned, followed by a small company, who, in answer to Elsie, stepped forward, one after the other, and made answer.

Said one: "I am the landlord of the rooms, at 22 South Square, tenanted by Mr. Edmund Gray. He has held the rooms for ten years. This gentleman is Mr. Edmund Gray, my tenant."

Said another: "I am a barrister, and the tenant of the rooms above those held by Mr. Edmund Gray. I have known him—more or less—for ten years. This gentleman is Mr. Edmund Gray."

Said a third: "I am a commissionnaire. I remember this gentleman very well, though it is eight years since he employed me, and only for one job then. I went from a hotel in Norfolk Street, Strand, to a bank with a check which I was to cash for him in ten-pound notes. He gave me half a sovereign."

"Quite so," said Mr. Edmund Gray. "I remember you, too. It was a check for seven hundred and twenty pounds, the particulars of which you have in my statement, Elsie. I well remember this one-armed commissionnaire."

And a fourth: "I am the laundress who does for Mr. Edmund Gray. I have done for him for ten years. This gentleman is Mr. Edmund Gray."

And a fifth: "I am a news-agent, and I have a shop at the entrance of Gray's Inn. This gentleman is Mr. Edmund Gray, of 22 South Square. I have known him in the inn for ten years."

To each in turn Mr. Dering nodded, with a kindly smile.

"Athelstan," said Elsie, "will you tell us when and where you have met Mr. Edmund Gray?"

"I met him last week in Carstone's rooms on the same landing. He sat with us for an hour or more."

"It is quite true," said Mr. Dering, "I had the pleasure of meeting Mr. Arundel on that occasion."

"I also saw him," Athelstan continued, "at a small lecture-hall at Kentish Town on Sunday evening—yesterday."

"To complete the evidence," said Elsie, "I have myself spent many hours almost daily with Mr. Edmund Gray during the last fortnight or so. Is not that true, dear master?"

"Quite true, my scholar."

"Brother—brother"—Sir Samuel touched his arm—"I implore you—rouse yourself. Shake off this fancy."

"Let him alone, Sir Samuel," said George—"let him alone. We have not done with him yet."

"Yes," cried Mrs. Arundel, who had now left her seat and was leaning over the table, following what was said with breathless interest—"let us finish out this comedy or tragedy—as the case may be. Let no one interrupt."

"I have also met you, sir"—Mr. Dering addressed Checkley, who only groaned and shook. "It was outside a tavern. You took me in, and offered me a drink."

Checkley shook his head, either in sadness or in denial, but replied not—and at the thought of offering Mr. Dering a drink everybody laughed, which was a relief.

"Dear master," Elsie went on, in her soft voice, "I am so glad that you remember all these things. It makes one's task so much easier. Why, your memory is as strong as ever, in spite of all your work. Now, I am going to read the two statements you wrote down yesterday afternoon. Then you may recall anything else you might like to add. Remember that as regards this first affair, the check for seven hundred and twenty pounds, my brother was charged, on suspicion only, with having forged it. Now listen." She read the brief statement which you have already seen, concerning the business of the first check. "That is your history of the affair?"

"Quite so. Dering drew the check at my request. I cashed it. I found that I had no need of the notes, and I returned them. That is very simple."

"It is all so simple that nobody ever guessed it before. Now we come to the transfers made in the spring of the present year. You wrote a second statement regarding them. I will read that as well. Please listen very carefully."

She read the other statement, which you have also seen already. She read it very slowly, so that there should be no mistake possible. During the reading of these documents Sir Samuel's face expressed every possible shade of surprise. Mrs. Arundel, leaning over the table, followed every line. Hilda wept—her head gracefully inclined over her pocket-handkerchief, as if it were an urn.

"This is your account of the business?"

"Certainly. There is nothing more to be added. It is a plain statement of the facts. I do not understand how they could be in any way doubted or misrepresented."

"Would you, Sir Samuel, like to ask Mr. Edmund Gray any question?"

"I don't understand. He says that Mr. Dering wrote a letter for him."

Elsie showed him the letter they had seen Mr. Dering write, while he was passing from one to the other.

"Where are the transfers?" Sir Samuel went on. "He says they were placed by himself in the safe."

Mr. Edmund Gray rose and walked to the safe. He laid his hands upon a packet and took it out. "These are the papers," he said.

Sir Samuel opened the roll and looked them over. "They seem all right," he said. "This is very wonderful."

"Wonderful — and sad — most lamentable," whispered Lady Dering.

"Wonderful indeed!" Mrs. Arundel echoed. "Most wonderful! most unexpected!"

"A moment more, and I have done." Elsie again took up the tale. "Here is a check to the order of Mr. Dering, signed by Mr. Edmund Gray for the whole of the money lying in his name at the bank. You agree, master, that it is best for the future that all your affairs should be in the hands of your solicitor?"

"I quite agree."

"Here is a letter to the manager of the bank, requesting him to pay over Edmund Gray's dividends to the account of Mr. Dering. And now I think I have proved my case. Here in the safe were the ten-pound notes received by Mr. Edmund Gray, and placed there by him. Here were the transfers and certificates placed there by him. You have heard half a dozen people testify to the fact that you have Edmund Gray before you. His statement of the business has been read to you. It shows, what no other theory of the case could show, how the thing was really done. Lastly, it shows the absolute and complete innocence of my brother and of George. Have you anything more to say, Sir Samuel?"

"Nothing—except that I was misled by a statement concerning a profligate life among low companions, without which no suspicion could have fallen upon either of you gentlemen. It was"—he pointed to the unhappy Checkley—"a vile and malignant falsehood. Do you hear, sir? Vile and malignant. It only remains for us all to make such reparation as we may—nothing would suffice, I know, but such reparation as we can—by the expression of the shame and regret that we all feel."

"Athelstan," said his mother, "what can I say? Oh! what can I say?"

Athelstan rose—during the long business he had sat motionless in the clients' chair, his head in his hand. Now he rose and stepped over to his mother. "Hush!" he said. "Not a word. It is all forgotten—all forgiven."

But Hilda sank upon her knees and caught his hands.

"George," said Sir Samuel, "forgive me. The case looked black against you at one time. It did indeed. Forgive me." He held out his hand.

Then there was great hand-shaking, embracing, and many tears. As for Checkley, he crept out and vanished in the retreat of his own room. "It is all over," he murmured—"all over. I've lost four hundred pounds a year. That's gone. All over—all over!"

Mr. Edmund Gray looked on this happy scene of family reconciliation with benevolence and smiles.

Family reconciliations must not be prolonged; you cannot sit over a family reconciliation as over a bottle of port. It must be quickly despatched. Sir Samuel whispered to Hilda that they had better go.

"Come," said Lady Dering. "We will all meet again this evening at Pembridge Square—and to-morrow evening—and on Wednesday afternoon. Elsie, you are a witch and a sorceress and a wise woman. You said that Athelstan should give you away, and he will. Brother, come with us. Leave Elsie to George. Oh! how handsome you are looking, my poor, ill-used brother. Try to forgive us if you can."

She turned to Mr. Edmund Gray. "Sir," she said, "we ought to be very grateful to you—indeed, we are—for enabling us to clear away the odious cloud of suspicion which had rolled over our heads. It was very good of you to draw out those statements for my sister. But I do think that if Mr. Dering had told his old friends about you—about Mr. Edmund Gray—we should have been spared a great deal of trouble and unnecessary shame. Good-day, sir."

Sir Samuel lingered a moment. He looked as if he would appeal to Mr. Edmund Gray as to a brother. "Don't speak to him," Elsie whispered. "Let him alone. He will become himself again presently. Let him alone."

So he went out, and the door was shut, and Edmund Gray was left alone with George and the scholar.

"My master"—Elsie sat down beside him—"I fear you have been interrupted. But indeed it was necessary. Don't ask why. Things get into a muddle sometimes, don't they? You have gathered something of the trouble, too. Now that is all over—past and gone."

"I am glad for your sake, child."

"Master—dear master—I have a confession to make. When I found out who you were—I mean what manner of man you were —my only thought at first was to coax you and wheedle you and flatter you till you gave me exactly the information that I wanted. I confess it. That was my only purpose. Nay—more— for the sake of my lover and my brother I would do it again. Well—I found that the only way to win your confidence was to pretend to be your scholar and to believe all you taught. So I pretended. So I won your confidence. So I obtained all I wanted.

So I have made it impossible for even the most malignant creature in the world to pretend that these two men had anything to do with what they called a forgery. But—believe me, dear master—while I pretended, I was punished, because my pretence is turned to certainty."

"Child, I knew it. You could not pretend—no woman could pretend so as to deceive me on a point so simple."

"Dear master, you do not know the possibilities of feminine craft. But I pretend no more. Oh! I care not how you make your attempt, whether you destroy property or not. Mr. Dering says that property is civilization—but I don't care. To me it is enough to dream—to know—that there is an earthly paradise possible, if only men will think so and will keep it before their eyes, though it be as far off as the blue hills. It is beautiful only to think of it; the soul is lifted up only to think that there is such a place. Keep the eyes of your people on this glorious place, dear master; make it impossible for them to forget it or to let it go out of their sight. Then, half unconsciously, they will be running, dragging each other, forcing each other—exhorting each other to hurry along the dusty road which leads to that earthly paradise with its four-square city of the jasper wall. Preach about it, master. Write about it. Make all men talk about it and think about it."

She threw her arms round his neck, and kissed him.

"Master, we shall be away for a month or two. Then we shall come back, and I shall sit at your feet again. You shall come and stay with us. We will give you love, and you shall give us hope. I have made my confession. Forgive me."

They left him sitting alone. Presently he arose, put all the papers back in the safe, and walked slowly away—to Gray's Inn.

Next morning when he opened his letters he found one marked "Private." It was from Sir Samuel.

"DEAR EDWARD," it said—"We are all very glad to tell you that the business of the shares and certificates is now completely cleared up. Checkley is not in any way concerned in it—nor is George Austin. And I am happy to say there is a complete solution of the former mystery, which entirely clears Hilda's brother. Under these circumstances, we are agreed that it is best for you not to trouble yourself about any further investigations. You will find in the safe the transfers, a check to yourself of all the money received by Edmund Gray, and an order in the bank concerning the dividends. You have been the victim of a very remarkable hallucination. I

need not explain further. Mr. Edmund Gray, however, is undoubtedly insane.
I hear, and have myself observed, that you have been greatly disturbed and
distressed by these mysterious events. Now that they are settled finally—I
may say that only a happy chance set us on the right track—we all hope
that you will be satisfied with our assurance, and that you will not trouble
yourself any more in the matter.

" Your affectionate brother,

"SAMUEL DERING."

Mr. Dering, after reading this letter, got up and looked in the
safe, where he found the papers referred to. He rang the bell.
" Checkley, who has been at my safe ?"

"Nobody but you."

"Don't tell lies. Who put those papers in the safe?"

"They must have been put there yesterday—you were in the
room."

" Yesterday—what happened yesterday ?"

Checkley was silent.

"Who was here yesterday? Go on, Checkley. Don't be
afraid."

"Sir Samuel was here—and Lady Dering—and Mrs. Arundel
—and Miss Elsie—and your partner—and Mr. Athelstan. Two
or three more came in and went away."

"That will do. You need tell me no more. I don't want to
know the particulars. Checkley, my day's work is done. I have
thought so for some time past. Now I am certain, I shall retire."

"No, no!" cried Checkley, the tears running down his face.
"Not to retire—after all these years—not to retire."

"I know now the meaning of my fits of forgetfulness. I have
feared and suspected it for a long time. While I am lost to myself, I am going about the world, doing I know not what. And
I will not ask. I may be this Edmund Gray, who preaches Socialism and gives me his precious tracts. I may be some one else.
I say, Checkley, that I know now what has happened to me.
Deny it if you can—if you can, I say."

Checkley did not offer any denial. He hung his head. "This
is the meaning of Elsie's strange hints and queer protestations.
Half my time I am a madman—a madman. Checkley, ask Mr.
Austin to come to me at once. My day is done." He closed
his open blotting-pad and placed the unopened letters beside it.

Then he rose and pushed back his chair—the chair in which he had sat for fifty years and more. "My day is done—my day is done."

CHAPTER XXXIX

THE LAST

MR. DERING left his office, went back to Gray's Inn, and sat down again before the Ivory Gate. Those who have once sat for an hour or two in this place return to it again and again, and never leave it. It is, to begin with, the most beautiful gate ever erected. The brain and wit and fancy of man could never conceive such a gate, could never execute such a conception. It is all of pure ivory, carved with flowers such as never grew; curving and flowing lines leading nowhere; figures of maidens lovely beyond all dreams; philosophers whose wisdom reaches unto the heavens; statesmen who discern the gathering forces and control the destinies of a nation; inventors who conquer nature; physicians who prolong life; ecclesiastics who convert the Carthusian cell into a bower of delight; poets who here find their fantasies divine; men and women in work-a-day dress who wear the faces of the heavenly host.

All the dreamers lie here, not asleep, but dreaming. Their eyes are open, but they do not see each other; they see these dreams. Those of the young who are also generous come here and dream until they grow older and are chained to their work and can dream no more. Men of all conditions come here—even the little shop-boy—even the maiden who cleans the knives and polishes the boots—all are here. The young prince is here; the little charity boy is here; the lad whose loftiest ambition is that he may one day stand in the pulpit of the little Baptist village-chapel is here; here is the undergraduate who was captain of Eton and will be senior classic and Member of Parliament and minister—even prime-minister—and will belong to history. The poet is here, and the painter, and sometimes hither comes the novelist, and, but more rarely, the dramatist. Hither comes the musician to lift up his soul with thoughts that only music can give; and the singer, so that he sings more than is apparent from the words; and the actor, so that he puts things into the play never dreamed by him who wrote it. Great is the power, great the gifts, of this noble Gate of Ivory.

Sitting before that gate, such a dreamer as Edmund Gray receives strange visions. He sees clearly and near at hand the things which might be, yet are not, and never can be until man lays down his garb of selfishness and puts on the white robes of Charity. To that dreamer the Kingdom of Heaven, which seems to some so far off and to others impossible, so that they deride the name of it, is actually close at hand—with us—easy to enter if we only choose. He exhorts his fellows to enter with him. And they would follow, but they cannot, because they are held back by custom and necessity. They must obey the laws of the multitude, and so they stay where they are. And when the dreamer passes away his memory is quickly lost, and the brightness quickly leaves those dimly lighted lives. Yet other dreamers come—every day there arises an Edmund Gray.

Now when Edmund Gray takes the place of Edward Dering, in which guise does the soul, in the end, leave the earth? Are the dreams of Edmund Gray perhaps the logical development of the doctrines held by Edward Dering? Is the present stage of individual property—where every man works for himself and his household—one through which the world must pass before it can reach the higher level of working each for all? First men and women hunt, separate; they live apart in hollow trees and caves. Then they live together, and the man hunts for his wife and children. Next, they live in communities, which grow into towns and tribes and nations. Then men rely upon the protection of the law, and work for themselves again. That is our present stage; it has lasted long—very long. Perhaps it will break up some day; perhaps sooner than we think. Who knows? All things are possible—even the crash and wreck of a civilization which has taken thousands of years to build up. And upon it may come— one knows not—that other stage which now belongs to the dreamer before the Ivory Gate.

The wedding was held then, as Elsie said it should be, shorn of none of its splendors, and relieved of the cloud which had hung over them so long and threatened them so gloomily. Athelstan the Exile—Athelstan the Ne'er-do-well—Athelstan the Profligate—Athelstan the Resident of Camberwell—Athelstan the Smirched and Soiled—stood beside the altar, tall and gallant, and gave away the bride for all the world to see—nobody in the least ashamed of him. There was not any breath of scandal left. Here he was, returned from his travels, a tall and proper man, dressed in broadcloth, perhaps with money in purse, prosperous and successful in the sight of all. His mother gazed upon him when she should have been looking at the bride or into her Prayer Book. Her eyes were red, but then a mother is allowed a tear or two when her daughter leaves the nest. And as to those who had whispered words about family jars, quarrels, and estrangements, or had spoken against the fair fame of the groom, they were now as mute as mice.

All the richer members of the House of Arundel—the City Arundels—were present. One of them—chief partner in a leading firm of accountants—afterwards computed, for the greater increase of the family glory, how many hundreds of thousands of pounds were gathered together at one moment beneath that sacred roof. He counted the members, and made that little addition, during the performance of the ceremony. Those of the Austins who were not disgracefully poor—there are some branches of the family, I believe, pretty low down—were also present. And the company went to Pembridge Square after the service, gazed admiringly at the wedding-presents, and drank the health of the bride and bridegroom, and gathered with cousinly curiosity round the returned prodigal. But they knew nothing—mind you—of his connection with Camberwell. And nothing about his supposed complicity in the Edmund Gray business. There had been, happily, no scandal.

Among the company in the church was Mr. Dering. He stood tall and erect, his coat buttoned, his face keen and hard, the family lawyer stamped by nature and long custom.

Presently, when the service was about half-way through, a change came over him. His face relaxed; the lines curved just a little laterally, the austerity vanished, his eyes brightened. He took off his gloves furtively, and opened his coat. He was Edmund Gray. In that capacity he afterwards drank to the bride, and wished her happiness. And he walked all the way from Pembridge Square to South Square, Gray's Inn.

I see in the future an old man growing feeble; he leans upon the arm of a girl whom he calls his scholar, his disciple, and his child. His face is serene; he is perfectly happy; the advent of that kingdom whose glories he preaches is very nigh at hand. He lives in the house of his disciple; he has forgotten the very existence of his lawyer; he goes no more to Lincoln's Inn: always he is lying, night and day, before that miracle of carven work in ivory. There he watches—it is his vision—the long procession of those who work, and sing at their work, and are happy, work they ever so hard, because they work each for all and all for each. And there is no more sorrow or crying and no more pain. What hath the Gate of Horn—through which is allowed nothing but what is true—bitterly true—absolutely true—nakedly, coldly, shiveringly true—to show in comparison with this? A crowd trampling upon each other; men who enslave and rob each other; men and women and children lying in misery; men and women and children starving. Let us fly, my brothers—let us swiftly fly—let us hasten—to the Gate of Ivory.

THE END

WALTER BESANT'S WORKS.

We give, without hesitation, the foremost place to Mr. Besant, whose work, always so admirable and spirited, acquires double importance from the enthusiasm with which it is inspired.—*Blackwood's Magazine*, Edinburgh.

Mr. Besant wields the wand of a wizard, let him wave it in whatever direction he will. . . . The spell that dwells in this wand is formed by intense earnestness and vivid imagination.—*Spectator*, London.

There is a bluff, honest, hearty, and homely method about Mr. Besant's stories which makes them acceptable, and because he is so easily understood is another reason why he is so particularly relished by the English public.—*N. Y. Times*.

ALL IN A GARDEN FAIR. 4to, Paper, 20 cents.

ALL SORTS AND CONDITIONS OF MEN. Illustrated. 12mo, Cloth, $1 25; 8vo, Paper, 50 cents.

ARMOREL OF LYONESSE. Illustrated. 12mo, Cloth, $1 25; 8vo, Paper, 50 cents.

CHILDREN OF GIBEON. 12mo, Cloth, $1 25; 8vo, Paper, 50 cents.

DOROTHY FORSTER. 4to, Paper, 20 cents.

FIFTY YEARS AGO. Illustrated. 8vo, Cloth, $2 50.

FOR FAITH AND FREEDOM. Illustrated. 12mo, Cloth, $1 25; 8vo, Paper, 50 cents.

HERR PAULUS. 8vo, Paper, 35 cents.

KATHERINE REGINA. 4to, Paper, 15 cents.

LIFE OF COLIGNY. 32mo, Cloth, 40 cents; Paper, 25 cents.

LONDON. Illustrated. 8vo, Cloth, Ornamental, Uncut Edges and Gilt Top, $3 00.

SELF OR BEARER. 4to, Paper, 15 cents.

ST. KATHERINE'S BY THE TOWER. Illustrated. 12mo, Cloth, $1 25. Paper, 50 cents.

THE BELL OF ST. PAUL'S. 8vo, Paper, 35 cents.

THE HOLY ROSE. 4to, Paper, 20 cents.

THE INNER HOUSE. 8vo, Paper, 30 cents.

THE WORLD WENT VERY WELL THEN. Illustrated. 12mo, Cloth, $1 25; 4to, Paper, 25 cents.

TO CALL HER MINE. Illustrated. 4to, Paper, 20 cents.

UNCLE JACK AND OTHER STORIES. 12mo, Paper, 25 cents.

BY CONSTANCE F. WOOLSON.

JUPITER LIGHTS. A Novel. 16mo, Cloth, $1 25.

EAST ANGELS. A Novel. 16mo, Cloth, $1 25.

ANNE. A Novel. Illustrated. 16mo, Cloth, $1 25.

FOR THE MAJOR. A Novelette. 16mo, Cloth, $1 00

CASTLE NOWHERE. Lake-Country Sketches. 16mo, Cloth, $1 00.

RODMAN THE KEEPER. Southern Sketches. 16mo, Cloth, $1 00.

Delightful touches justify those who see many points of analogy between Miss Woolson and George Eliot.—*N. Y. Times.*

For tenderness and purity of thought, for exquisitely delicate sketching of characters, Miss Woolson is unexcelled among writers of fiction —*New Orleans Picayune.*

Characterization is Miss Woolson's forte. Her men and women are not mere puppets, but original, breathing, and finely contrasted creations.—*Chicago Tribune.*

Miss Woolson is one of the few novelists of the day who know how to make conversation, how to individualize the speakers, how to exclude rabid realism without falling into literary formality.—*N. Y. Tribune.*

Constance Fenimore Woolson may easily become the novelist laureate —*Boston Globe.*

Miss Woolson has a graceful fancy, a ready wit, a polished style, and conspicuous dramatic power; while her skill in the development of a story is very remarkable.—*London Life.*

Miss Woolson never once follows the beaten track of the orthodox novelist, but strikes a new and richly loaded vein which, so far, is all her own ; and thus we feel, on reading one of her works, a fresh sensation, and we put down the book with a sigh to think our pleasant task of reading it is finished. The author's lines must have fallen to her in very pleasant places ; or she has, perhaps, within herself the wealth of womanly love and tenderness she pours so freely into all she writes. Such books as hers do much to elevate the moral tone of the day—a quality sadly wanting in novels of the time.—*Whitehall Review,* London.

R. D. BLACKMORE'S NOVELS.

His descriptions are wonderfully vivid and natural. His pages are brightened everywhere with great humor ; the quaint, dry turns of thought remind you occasionally of Fielding.—*London Times.*

Mr. Blackmore always writes like a scholar and a gentleman—*Athenæum,* London.

His tales, all of them, are pre-eminently meritorious. They are remarkable for their careful elaboration, the conscientious finish of their workmanship, their affluence of striking dramatic and narrative incident, their close observation and general interpretation of nature, their profusion of picturesque description, and their quiet and sustained humor. Besides, they are pervaded by a bright and elastic atmosphere which diffuses a cheery feeling of healthful and robust vigor. While they charm us by their sprightly vivacity and their naturalness, they never in the slightest degree transcend the limits of delicacy or good taste. While radiating warmth and brightness, they are as pure as the new-fallen snow. . . . Their literary execution is admirable, and their dramatic power is as exceptional as their moral purity.—*Christian Intelligencer,* N. Y.

LORNA DOONE. Illustrated. 12mo, Cloth, $1 00 ; 8vo, Paper, 40 cents.

KIT AND KITTY. 12mo, Cloth, $1 25 ; Paper, 35 cents.

SPRINGHAVEN. Illustrated. 12mo, Cloth, $1 50 ; 4to, Paper, 25 cents.

CHRISTOWELL. 4to, Paper, 20 cents.

CRADOCK NOWELL. 8vo, Paper, 60 cents.

EREMA ; OR, MY FATHER'S SIN. 8vo, Paper, 50 cents.

MARY ANERLEY. 16mo, Cloth, $1 00 ; 4to, Paper, 15 cents.

TOMMY UPMORE. 16mo, Cloth, 50 cents ; Paper, 35 cents ; 4to, Paper, 20 cents.

THE ODD NUMBER SERIES.

DAME CARE. By Hermann Sudermann. Translated by Bertha Overbeck. With Portrait. 16mo, Cloth, Ornamental, $1 00.

TALES OF TWO COUNTRIES. By Alexander Kielland. Translated by William Archer. An Introduction by H. H. Boyesen. With Portrait. 16mo, Cloth, Ornamental, $1 00.

TEN TALES BY FRANÇOIS COPPÉE. Translated by Walter Learned. With Fifty Pen-and-ink Drawings by Albert E. Sterner, and an Introduction by Brander Matthews. 16mo, Cloth, Ornamental, $1 25.

MODERN GHOSTS. Selected and Translated from the Works of Guy de Maupassant, Pedro Antonio de Alarcón, Alexander Kielland, Leopold Kompert, Gustavo A. Becquer, and G. Magherini Graziani. An Introduction by George William Curtis. 16mo, Cloth, Ornamental, $1 00.

THE HOUSE BY THE MEDLAR-TREE. By Giovanni Verga. Translated from the Italian by Mary A. Craig. An Introduction by W. D. Howells. 16mo, Cloth, Ornamental, $1 00.

PASTELS IN PROSE. (From the French.) Translated by Stuart Merrill. With 150 Illustrations (including Frontispiece in Color) by H. W. McVickar. An Introduction by W. D. Howells. 16mo, Cloth, Ornamental, $1 25.

MARÍA: A South American Romance. By Jorge Isaacs. Translated by Rollo Ogden. An Introduction by Thomas A. Janvier. 16mo, Cloth, Ornamental, $1 00.

THE ODD NUMBER: Thirteen Tales by Guy de Maupassant. The Translation by Jonathan Sturges. An Introduction by Henry James. 16mo, Cloth, Ornamental, $1 00.

OTHER VOLUMES IN PREPARATION.